P9-DTC-030

# THE FANTASIES OF ROBERT A. HEINLEIN

# THE FANTASIES OF ROBERT A. HEINLEIN

Robert A. Heinlein

A Tom Doherty Associates Book
New York

This is a work of fiction. All the characters and events portrayed in this book are either fictitious or are used fictitiously.

THE FANTASIES OF ROBERT A. HEINLEIN



This book is printed on acid-free paper.

Edited by David G. Hartwell

Book Design by Jane Adele Regina

A Tor Book
Published by Tom Doherty Associates, LLC
175 Fifth Avenue
New York, NY 10010

www.tor.com



Library of Congress Cataloging-in-Publication Data
Heinlein, Robert A. (Robert Anson)
[Short stories. Selections]
The fantasies of Robert A. Heinlein / Robert A. Heinlein.—1st ed.
p. cm.
"A Tom Doherty Associates book."
Contents: Magic, Inc.—"And he built a crooked house"—"They—"—Waldo—the unpleasant profession of Jonathan Hoag—Our fair city—The man who traveled in elephants—"—All You Zombies,—."
ISBN 0-312-87245-3 (alk. paper)
1. Fantasy fiction, American. I. Title.
PS3515.E288A6 1999
813'.54—dc21 99-38362
CIP

First Edition: November 1999

Printed in the United States of America

0 9 8 7 6 5 4 3 2 1

# CONTENTS

# THE FANTASIES OF ROBERT A. HEINLEIN

# Magic, Inc.

"*Whose spells are you using,* Buddy?"

That was the first thing this bird said after coming into my place of business. He had hung around maybe twenty minutes, until I was alone, looking at samples of waterproof pigment, fiddling with plumbing catalogues, and monkeying with the hardware display.

I didn't like his manner. I don't mind a legitimate business inquiry from a customer, but I resent gratuitous snooping.

"Various of the local licensed practitioners of thaumaturgy," I told him in a tone that was chilly but polite. "Why do you ask?"

"You didn't answer my question," he pointed out. "Come on—speak up. I ain't got all day."

I restrained myself. I require my clerks to be polite, and, while I was pretty sure this chap would never be a customer, I didn't want to break my own rules. "If you are thinking of buying anything," I said, "I will be happy to tell you what magic, if any, is used in producing it, and who the magician is."

"Now you're not being co-operative," he complained. "We like for people to be co-operative. You never can tell what bad luck you may run into not co-operating."

"Who d'you mean by 'we,'" I snapped, dropping all pretense of politeness, "and what do you mean by 'bad luck'?"

"Now we're getting somewhere," he said with a nasty grin, and settled himself on the edge of the counter so that he breathed into my face. He was short and swarthy—Sicilian, I judged—and dressed in a suit that was overtailored. His clothes and haberdashery matched perfectly in a color scheme that I didn't like. "I'll tell you what I mean by 'we'; I'm a field representative for an organization that protects people from bad luck—if they're smart, and co-operative. That's why I asked you whose charms you're usin'. Some of the magicians around here aren't co-operative; it spoils their luck, and that bad luck follows their products."

"Go on," I said. I wanted him to commit himself as far as he would.

"I knew you were smart," he answered. "F'r instance—how would you like for a salamander to get loose in your shop, setting fire to your goods and maybe scaring your customers? Or you sell the materials to build a house, and it turns out there's a poltergeist living in it, breaking the dishes and souring the milk and kicking the furniture around. That's what can come of dealing with the wrong magicians. A little of that and your business is ruined. We wouldn't want that to happen, *would we?*" He favored me with another leer.

I said nothing, he went on, "Now, we maintain a staff of the finest demonologists in the business, expert magicians themselves, who can report on how a magician conducts himself in the Half World, and whether or not he's likely to bring his clients bad luck. Then we advise our clients whom to deal with, and keep them from having bad luck. See?"

I saw all right. I wasn't born yesterday. The magicians I dealt with were local men that I had known for years, men with established reputations both here and in the Half World. They didn't do anything to stir up the elementals against them, and they did not have bad luck.

What this slimy item meant was that I should deal only with the magicians they selected at whatever fees they chose to set, and they would take a cut on the fees and also on the profits of my business. If I didn't choose to "co-operate," I'd be persecuted by elementals they had an arrangement with—renegades, probably, with human vices—my stock in trade spoiled and my customers frightened away. If I still held out, I could expect some really dangerous black magic that would injure or kill me. All this under the pretense of selling me protection from men I knew and liked.

A neat racket!

I HAD HEARD OF SOMETHING of the sort back East, but had not expected it in a city as small as ours.

He sat there, smirking at me, waiting for my reply, and twisting his neck in his collar, which was too tight. That caused me to notice something. In spite of his foppish clothes a thread showed on his neck just above the collar in back. It seemed likely that it was there to support something next to his skin—an amulet. If so, he was superstitious, even in this day and age.

"There's something you've omitted," I told him. "I'm a seventh son, born under a caul, and I've got second sight. My luck's all right, but I can see bad luck hovering over you like cypress over a grave!" I reached out and snatched at the thread. It snapped and came loose in my hand. There was an amulet on it, right enough, an unsavory little wad of nothing in particular and about as appetizing as the bottom of a bird cage. I dropped it on the floor and ground it into the dirt.

He had jumped off the counter and stood facing me, breathing hard. A knife showed up in his right hand; with his left hand he was warding off the evil eye, the first and little fingers pointed at me, making the horns of Asmodeus. I knew I had him for the time being.

"Here's some magic you may not have heard of," I rapped out, and reached into a drawer behind the counter. I hauled out a pistol and pointed it at his face. "Cold iron! Now go back to your owner and tell him there's cold iron waiting for him, too—both ways!"

He backed away, never taking his eyes off my face. If looks could kill, and so forth. At the door he paused and spat on the doorsill, then got out of sight very quickly.

I put the gun away and went about my work, waiting on two customers who came in just as Mr. Nasty Business left. But I will admit that I was worried. A man's reputation is his most valuable asset. I've built up a name, while still a young man, for dependable products. It was certain that this bird and his pals would do all they could to destroy that name—which might be plenty if they were hooked in with black magicians!

Of course the building-materials game does not involve as much magic as other lines dealing in less durable goods. People like to know, when they are building a home, that the bed won't fall into the basement some night, or the roof disappear and leave them out in the rain.

Besides, building involves quite a lot of iron, and there are very few commercial sorcerers who can cope with cold iron. The few that can are so expensive it isn't economical to use them in building. Of course if one of the café-society crowd, or somebody like that, wants to boast that they have a summerhouse or a swimming pool built entirely by magic, I'll accept the contract, charging accordingly, and sublet it to one of the expensive, first-line magicians. But by and large my business uses magic only in the side issues—perishable items and doodads which people like to buy cheap and change from time to time.

So I was not worried about magic *in* my business, but about what magic could *do* to my business—if someone set out deliberately to do me mischief. I had the subject of magic on my mind anyhow, because of an earlier call from a chap named Ditworth—not a matter of vicious threats, just a business proposition that I was undecided about. But it worried me, just the same. . . .

I closed up a few minutes early and went over to see Jedson—a friend of mine in the cloak-and-suit business. He is considerably older than I am, and quite a student, without holding a degree, in all forms of witchcraft, white and black magic, necrology, demonology, spells, charms, and the more practical forms of divination. Besides that, Jedson is a shrewd, capable man in every way, with a long head on him. I set a lot of store by his advice.

I expected to find him in his office, and more or less free, at that hour, but he wasn't. His office boy directed me up to a room he used for sales conferences. I knocked and then pushed the door.

"Hello, Archie," he called out as soon as he saw who it was. "Come on in. I've got something." And he turned away.

I came in and looked around. Besides Joe Jedson there was a handsome, husky woman about thirty years old in a nurse's uniform, and a fellow named August Welker, Jedson's foreman. He was a handy all-around man with a magician's license, third class. Then I noticed a fat little guy, Zadkiel Feldstein, who was agent for a good many of the second-rate magicians along the street, and some few of the first-raters. Naturally, his religion prevented him from practicing magic himself, but, as I understand it, there was no theological objection to his turning an honest commission. I had had dealings with him; he was all right.

This ten-percenter was clutching a cigar that had gone out, and watching intently Jedson and another party, who was slumped in a chair.

This other party was a girl, not over twenty-five, maybe not that old. She was blond, and thin to the point that you felt that light would shine through her. She had big, sensitive hands with long fingers, and a big, tragic mouth: Her hair was silver-white, but she was not an albino. She lay back in the chair, awake but apparently done in. The nurse was chafing her wrists.

"What's up?" I asked. "The kid faint?"

"Oh no," Jedson assured me, turning around. "She's a white witch—works in a trance. She's a little tired now, that's all."

"What's her specialty?" I inquired.

"Whole garments."

"Huh?" I had a right to be surprised. It's one thing to create yard goods; another thing entirely to turn out a dress, or a suit, all finished and ready to wear. Jedson produced and merchandised a full line of garments in which magic was used throughout. They were mostly sportswear, novelty goods, ladies' fashions, and the like, in which style, rather than wearing qualities, was the determining factor. Usually they were marked "One Season Only," but they were perfectly satisfactory for that one season, being backed up by the consumers' groups.

But they were not turned out in one process. The yard goods involved were made first, usually by Welker. Dyes and designs were added separately. Jedson had some very good connections among the Little People, and could obtain shades and patterns from the Half World that were exclusive with him. He used both the old methods and magic in assembling garments, and employed some of the most talented artists in the business. Several of his dress designers freelanced their magic in Hollywood under an arrangement with him. All he asked for was screen credit.

But to get back to the blond girl——

"That's what I said," Jedson answered, "whole garments, with good wearing qualities too. There's no doubt that she is the real McCoy; she was under contract to a textile factory in Jersey City. But I'd give a thousand dollars to see her do that whole-garment stunt of hers just once. We haven't had any luck, though I've tried everything but red-hot pincers."

The kid looked alarmed at this, and the nurse looked indignant. Feldstein started to expostulate, but Jedson cut him short. "That was just a figure of speech; you know I don't hold with black magic. Look, darling," he went on, turning back to the girl, "do you feel like trying again?" She nodded and he added, "All right—sleepy time now!"

And she tried again, going into her act with a minimum of groaning and spitting. The ectoplasm came out freely and sure enough, it formed into a complete dress instead of yard goods. It was a neat little dinner frock, about a size sixteen, sky blue in a watered silk. It had class in a refined way, and I knew that any jobber who saw it would be good for a sizable order.

Jedson grabbed it, cut off a swatch of cloth and applied his usual tests, finishing by taking the swatch out of the microscope and touching a match to it.

He swore. "Damn it," he said, "there's no doubt about it. It's not a new integration at all; she's just reanimated an old rag!"

"Come again," I said. "What of it?"

"Huh? Archie, you really ought to study up a bit. What she just did isn't really creative magic at all. This dress"—he picked it up and shook it—"had a real existence someplace at some time. She's gotten hold of a piece of it, a scrap or maybe just a button, and applied the laws of homeopathy and contiguity to produce a simulacrum of it."

I understood him, for I had used it in my own business. I had once had a section of bleachers, suitable for parades and athletic events, built on my own grounds by old methods, using skilled master mechanics and the best materials—no iron, of course. Then I cut it to pieces. Under the law of contiguity, each piece remained part of the structure it had once been in. Under the law of homeopathy, each piece was potentially the entire structure. I would contract to handle a Fourth of July crowd, or the spectators for a circus parade, and send out a couple of magicians armed with as many fragments of the original stands as we needed sections of bleachers. They would bind a spell to last twenty-four hours around each piece. That way the stands cleared themselves away automatically.

I had had only one mishap with it; an apprentice magician, who had the chore of being on hand as each section vanished and salvaging the animated fragment for further use, happened one day to pick up the wrong piece of wood from where one section had stood. The next time we used it, for the Shrine convention, we found we had thrown up a brand-new four-room bungalow at the corner of Fourteenth and Vine instead of a section of bleachers. It could have been embarrassing, but I stuck a sign on it.

MODEL HOME NOW ON DISPLAY

and ran up another section on the end.

An out-of-town concern tried to chisel me out of the business one season, but one of their units fell, either through faulty workmanship on the pattern or because of unskilled magic, and injured several people. Since then I've had the field pretty much to myself.

I could not understand Joe Jedson's objection to reanimation. "What difference does it make?" I persisted. "It's a dress, isn't it?"

"Sure it's a dress, but it's not a new one. That style is registered somewhere and doesn't belong to me. And even if it were one of my numbers she had used, reanimation isn't what I'm after. I can make better merchandise cheaper without it; otherwise I'd be using it now."

The blond girl came to, saw the dress, and said, "Oh, Mr. Jedson, did I do it?"

He explained what had happened. Her face fell, and the dress melted away at once. "Don't you feel bad about it, kid," he added, patting her on the shoulder, "you were tired. We'll try again tomorrow. I know you can do it when you're not nervous and overwrought."

She thanked him and left with the nurse. Feldstein was full of explanations, but Jedson told him to forget it, and to have them all back there at the same time tomorrow. When we were alone I told him what had happened to me.

He listened in silence, his face serious, except when I told him how I had kidded my visitor into thinking I had second sight. That seemed to amuse him.

"You may wish that you really had it—second sight, I mean," he said at last, becoming solemn again. "This is an unpleasant prospect. Have you notified the Better Business Bureau?"

I told him I hadn't.

"Very well then. I'll give them a ring and the Chamber of Commerce too. They probably can't help much, but they are entitled to notification, so they can be on the lookout for it."

I asked him if he thought I ought to notify the police. He shook his head. "Not just yet. Nothing illegal has been done, and, anyhow, all the chief could think of to cope with the situation would be to haul in all the licensed magicians in town and sweat them. That wouldn't do any good, and would just cause hard feelings to be directed against you by the legitimate members of the profession. There isn't a chance in ten that the sorcerers connected with this outfit are licensed to perform magic; they are almost sure to be clandestine. If the police knew about them, it's because they are protected. If they don't know about them, then they probably can't help you."

"What do you think I ought to do?"

"Nothing just yet. Go home and sleep on it. This Charlie may be playing a lone hand, making small-time shake-downs purely on bluff. I don't really think so; his type sounds like a mobster. But we need more data; we can't do anything until they expose their hand a little more."

We did not have long to wait. When I got down to my place of business the next morning I found a surprise waiting for me—several of them, all unpleasant.

It was as if it had been ransacked by burglars, set fire to, then gutted by a flood. I called up Jedson at once. He came right over. He didn't have anything to say at first, but went poking through the ruins, examining a number of things. He stopped at the point where the hardware storeroom had stood, reached down and gathered up a handful of the wet ashes and muck. "Notice anything?" he asked, working his fingers so that the debris sloughed off and left in the hand some small metal objects—nails, screws, and the like.

"Nothing in particular. This is where the hardware bins were located; that's some of the stuff that didn't burn."

"Yes, I know," he said impatiently, "but don't you see anything else? Didn't you stock a lot of brass fittings?"

"Yes."

"Well, find one!"

I poked around with my toe in a spot where there should have been a lot of brass hinges and drawer pulls mixed in with the ashes. I did not find anything but the nails that had held the bins together. I oriented myself by such landmarks as I could find and tried again. There were plenty of nuts and bolts, casement hooks, and similar junk, but no brass.

Jedson watched me with a sardonic grin on his face.

"Well?" I said, somewhat annoyed at his manner.

"Don't you see?" he answered. "It's magic, all right. In this entire yard there is not one scrap of metal left, *except cold iron!*"

It was plain enough. I should have seen it myself.

He messed around awhile longer. Presently we came across an odd thing. It was a slimy, wet track that meandered through my property, and disappeared down one of the drains. It looked as if a giant slug, about the size of a Crosley car, had wandered through the place.

"Undine," Jedson announced, and wrinkled his nose at the smell. I once saw a movie, a Megapix superproduction called the *Water King's Daughter.* According to it undines were luscious enough to have interested Earl Carroll, but if they left trails like that I wanted none of them.

He took out his handkerchief and spread it for a clean place to sit down on what had been sacks of cement—a fancy, quick-setting variety, with a trade name of Hydrolith, I had been getting eighty cents a sack for the stuff, now it was just so many big boulders.

He ticked the situation off on his fingers. "Archie, you've been kicked in the teeth by at least three of the four different types of elements—earth, fire, and water. Maybe there was a sylph of the air in on it, too, but I can't prove it. First the gnomes came and cleaned out everything you had that came out of the ground, except cold iron. A salamander followed them and set fire to the place, burning everything that was burnable, and scorching and smoke-damaging the rest. Then the undine turned the place into a damned swamp, ruining anything that wouldn't burn, like cement and lime. You're insured?"

"Naturally." But then I started to think. I carried the usual fire, theft, and flood insurance, but business-risk insurance comes pretty high: I was not covered against the business I would lose in the meantime, nor did I have any way to complete current contracts. It was going to cost me quite a lot to cover those contracts; if I let them slide it would ruin the good will of my business, and lay me open to suits for damage.

The situation was worse than I had thought, and looked worse still the more I thought about it. Naturally I could not accept any new business until the mess was cleaned up, the place rebuilt, and new stock put in. Luckily most of my papers were in a fireproof steel safe; but not all, by any means. There would be accounts receivable that I would never collect because I had nothing to show for them. I work on a slim margin of profit, with all of my capital at work. It began to look as if the firm of Archibald Fraser, Merchant and Contractor, would go into involuntary bankruptcy.

I explained the situation to Jedson.

"Don't get your wind up too fast," he reassured me. "What magic can do, magic can undo. What we need is the best wizard in town."

"Who's going to pay the fee?" I objected. "Those boys don't work for nickels, and I'm cleaned out."

"Take it easy, son," he advised, "the insurance outfit that carries your risks is due to take a bigger loss than you are. If we can show them a way to save money on this, we can do business. Who represents them here?"

I told him—a firm of lawyers downtown in the Professional Building.

I got hold of my office girl and told her to telephone such of our customers as were due for deliveries that day. She was to stall where possible and pass on the business that could not wait to a firm that I had exchanged favors with in the past. I sent the rest of my help home—they had been standing around since eight o'clock, making useless remarks and getting in the way—and told them not to come back until I sent for them. Luckily it was Saturday; we had the best part of forty-eight hours to figure out some answer.

We flagged a magic carpet that was cruising past and headed for the Professional Building. I settled back and determined to enjoy the ride and forget my troubles. I like taxicabs—they give me a feeling of luxury—and I've liked them even better since they took the wheels off them. This happened to be one of the new Cadillacs with the teardrop shape and air cushions. We went scooting down the boulevard, silent as thought, not six inches off the ground.

Perhaps I should explain that we have a local city ordinance against apportation unless it conforms to traffic regulations—ground traffic, I mean, not air. That may surprise you, but it came about as a result of a mishap to a man in my own line of business. He had an order for eleven-odd tons of glass brick to be delivered to a restaurant being remodeled on the other side of town from his yard. He employed a magician with a common carrier's license to deliver for him. I don't know whether he was careless or just plain stupid, but he dropped those eleven tons of brick through the roof of the Prospect Boulevard Baptist Church. Anybody knows that magic won't work over consecrated ground; if he had consulted a map he would have seen that the straight-line route took his load over the church. Anyhow, the janitor was killed, and it might just as well have been the whole congregation. It caused such a commotion that apportation was limited to the streets, near the ground.

It's people like that who make it inconvenient for everybody else.

OUR MAN WAS IN—Mr. Wiggin, of the firm Wiggin, Snead, McClatchey & Wiggin. He had already heard about my "fire," but when Jedson explained his conviction that magic was at the bottom of it he balked. It was, he said, most irregular. Jedson was remarkably patient.

"Are you an expert in magic, Mr. Wiggin?" he asked.

"I have not specialized in the thaumaturgic jurisprudence, if that is what you mean, sir."

"Well, I don't hold a license myself, but it has been my hobby for a good many years. I'm sure of what I say in this case; you can call in the independent experts you wish—they'll confirm my opinion. Now suppose we stipulate, for the sake of argument, that this damage was caused by magic. If that is true, there is a possibility that we may be able to save much of the loss. You have authority to settle claims, do you not?"

"Well, I think I may say yes to that—bearing in mind the legal restrictions and the terms of the contract." I don't believe he would have conceded that he had five fingers on his right hand without an auditor to back him up.

"Then it is your business to hold your company's losses down to a minimum. If I find a wizard who can undo a part, or all, of the damage, will you guarantee the fee, on behalf of your company, up to a reasonable amount, say 25 percent of the indemnity?"

He hemmed and hawed some more, and said he did not see how he could possibly do it, and that if the fire had been magic, then to restore by magic might be compounding a felony, as we could not be sure what the connections of the magicians involved might be in the Half

World. Besides that, my claim had not been allowed as yet; I had failed to notify the company of my visitor of the day before, which possibly might prejudice my claim. In any case, it was a very serious precedent to set; he must consult the home office.

Jedson stood up. "I can see that we are simply wasting each other's time, Mr. Wiggin. Your contention about Mr. Fraser's possible responsibility is ridiculous, and you know it. There is no reason under the contract to notify you, and even if there were, he is within the twenty-four hours allowed for any notification. I think it best that we consult the home office ourselves." He reached for his hat.

Wiggin put up his hand. "Gentlemen, gentlemen, please! Let's not be hasty. Will Mr. Fraser agree to pay half of the fee?"

"No. Why should he? It's your loss, not his. *You* insured *him*."

Wiggin tapped his teeth with his spectacles, then said, "We must make the fee contingent on results."

"Did you ever hear of anyone in his right mind dealing with a wizard on any other basis?"

Twenty minutes later we walked out with a document which enabled us to hire any witch or wizard to salvage my place of business on a contingent fee not to exceed 25 percent of the value reclaimed. "I thought you were going to throw up the whole matter," I told Jedson with a sigh of relief.

He grinned. "Not in the wide world, old son. He was simply trying to horse you into paying the cost of saving them some money. I just let him know that I knew."

It took some time to decide whom to consult. Jedson admitted frankly that he did not know of a man nearer than New York who could, with certainty, be trusted to do the job, and that was out of the question for the fee involved. We stopped in a bar, and he did some telephoning while I had a beer. Presently he came back and said, "I think I've got the man. I've never done business with him before, but he has the reputation and the training, and everybody I talked to seemed to think that he was the one to see."

"Who is it?" I wanted to know.

"Dr. Fortescue Biddle. He's just down the street—the Railway Exchange Building. Come on, we'll walk it."

I gulped down the rest of my beer and followed him.

Dr. Biddle's place was impressive. He had a corner suite on the fourteenth floor, and he had not spared expense in furnishing and decorating it. The style was modern; it had the austere elegance of a society physician's layout. There was a frieze around the wall of the signs of the zodiac done in intaglio glass, backed up by aluminum. That was the only decoration of any sort, the rest of the furnishing being very plain, but rich, with lots of plate glass and chromium.

We had to wait about thirty minutes in the outer office; I spent the time trying to estimate what I could have done the suite for, subletting what I had to and allowing 10 percent. Then a really beautiful girl with a hushed voice ushered us in. We found ourselves in another smaller room, alone, and had to wait about ten minutes more. It was much like the waiting room, but had some glass bookcases and an old print of Aristotle. I looked at the bookcases with Jedson to kill time. They were filled with a lot of rare old classics on magic. Jedson had just pointed out the *Red Grimoire* when we heard a voice behind us.

"Amusing, aren't they? The ancients knew a surprising amount. Not scientific, of course, but remarkably clever——" The voice trailed off. We turned around; he introduced himself as Dr. Biddle.

He was a nice enough looking chap, really handsome in a spare, dignified fashion. He was about ten years older than I am—fortyish; maybe—with iron-gray hair at the temples and a small, stiff, British major's mustache. His clothes could have been out of the style pages of *Esquire*. There was no reason for me not to like him; his manners were pleasant enough. Maybe it was the supercilious twist to his expression.

He led us into this private office, sat us down, and offered us cigarettes before business was mentioned. He opened up with, "You're Jedson, of course. I suppose Mr. Ditworth sent you?"

I cocked an ear at him; the name was familiar. But Jedson simply answered, "Why, no. Why would you think that he had?"

Biddle hesitated for a moment, then said half to himself, "That's strange. I was certain that I had heard him mention your name. Does either one of you," he added, "know Mr. Ditworth?"

We both nodded at once and surprised each other. Biddle seemed relieved and said, "No doubt that accounts for it. Still—I need some more information. Will you gentlemen excuse me while I call him?"

With that he vanished. I had never seen it done before. Jedson says there are two ways to do it, one is hallucination, the other is an actual exit through the Half World. Whichever way it's done, I think it's bad manners.

"About this chap Ditworth," I started to say to Jedson. "I had intended to ask you——"

"Let it wait," he cut me off, "there's not time now."

At this Biddle reappeared. "It's all right," he announced, speaking directly to me. "I can take your case. I suppose you've come about the trouble you had last night with your establishment?"

"Yes," I agreed. "How did you know?"

"Methods," he replied, with a deprecatory little smile. "My profession has its means. Now, about your problem. What is it you desire?"

I looked at Jedson; he explained what he thought had taken place and why he thought so. "Now I don't know whether you specialize in demonology or not," he concluded, "but it seems to me that it should be possible to evoke the powers responsible and force them to repair the damage. If you can do it, we are prepared to pay any reasonable fee."

Biddle smiled at this and glanced rather self-consciously at the assortment of diplomas hanging on the walls of his office. "I feel that there should be reason to reassure you," he purred. "Permit me to look over the ground——" And he was gone again.

I was beginning to be annoyed. It's all very well for a man to be good at his job, but there is no reason to make a side show out of it. But I didn't have time to grouse about it before he was back.

"Examination seems to confirm Mr. Jedson's opinion; there should be no unusual difficulties," he said. "Now as to the . . . ah . . . business arrangements——" He coughed politely and gave a little smile, as if he regretted having to deal with such vulgar matters.

Why do some people act as if making money offended their delicate minds? I am out for a legitimate profit, and not ashamed of it; the fact that people will pay money for my goods and services shows that my work is useful.

However, we made a deal without much trouble, then Biddle told us to meet him at my place in about fifteen minutes. Jedson and I left the building and flagged another cab. Once inside I asked him about Ditworth.

"Where'd you run across him?" I said.

"Came to me with a proposition."

"Hm-m-m——" This interested me; Ditworth had made me a proposition, too, and it had worried me. "What kind of a proposition?"

Jedson screwed up his forehead. "Well, that's hard to say—there was so much impressive sales talk along with it. Briefly, he said he was the local executive secretary of a nonprofit association which had as its purpose the improvement of standards of practicing magicians."

I nodded. It was the same story I had heard. "Go ahead."

"He dwelt on the inadequacy of the present licensing laws and pointed out that anyone could pass the examination and hang out his shingle after a couple of weeks' study of a *grimoire* or black book without any fundamental knowledge of the arcane laws at all. His organization would be a sort of bureau of standards to improve that, like the American Medical Association, or the National Conference of Universities and Colleges, or the Bar Association. If I signed an agreement to patronize only those wizards who complied with their requirements, I could display their certificate of quality and put their seal of approval on my goods."

"Joe, I've heard the same story," I cut in, "and I didn't know quite what to make of it. It sounds all right, but I wouldn't want to stop doing business with men who have given me good value in the past, and I've no way of knowing that the association would approve them."

"What answer did you give him?"

"I stalled him a bit—told him that I couldn't sign anything as binding as that without discussing it with my attorney."

"Good boy! What did he say to that?"

"Well, he was really quite decent about it, and honestly seemed to want to be helpful. Said he thought I was wise and left me some stuff to look over. Do you know anything about him? Is he a wizard himself?"

"No, he's not. But I did find out some things about him. I knew vaguely that he was something in the Chamber of Commerce; what I didn't know is that he is on the board of a dozen or more blue-ribbon corporations. He's a lawyer, but not in practice. Seems to spend all his time on his business interests."

"He sounds like a responsible man."

"I would say so. He seems to have had considerably less publicity than you would expect of a man of his business importance—probably a retiring sort. I ran across something that seemed to confirm that."

"What was it?" I asked.

"I looked up the incorporation papers for his association on file with the Secretary of State. There were just three names, his own and two others. I found that both of the others were employed in his office—his secretary and his receptionist."

"Dummy setup?"

"Undoubtedly. But there is nothing unusual about that. What interested me was this: I recognized one of the names."

"Huh?"

"You know, I'm on the auditing committee for the state committee of my party. I looked up the name of his secretary where I thought I had seen it. It was there all right. His secretary, a chap by the name of Mathias, was down for a whopping big contribution to the governor's personal campaign fund."

We did not have any more time to talk just then, as the cab had pulled up at my place. Dr. Biddle was there before us and had already started his preparations. He had set up a little crystal pavilion, about ten feet square, to work in. The entire lot was blocked off from spectators on the front by an impalpable screen. Jedson warned me not to touch it.

I must say he worked without any of the usual hocus-pocus. He simply greeted us and entered the pavilion, where he sat down on a chair and took a loose-leaf notebook from a pocket and commenced to read. Jedson says he used several pieces of paraphernalia too. If so, I didn't see them. He worked with his clothes on.

Nothing happened for a few minutes. Gradually the walls of the shed became cloudy, so that everything inside was indistinct. It was about then that I became aware that there was something else in the pavilion besides Biddle. I could not see clearly what it was, and, to tell the truth, I didn't want to.

We could not hear anything that was said on the inside, but there was an argument going on—that was evident. Biddle stood up and began sawing the air with his hands. The thing threw back its head and laughed. At that Biddle threw a worried look in our direction and made a quick gesture with his right hand. The walls of the pavilion became opaque at once and we didn't see any more.

About five minutes later Biddle walked out of his workroom, which promptly disappeared behind him. He was a sight—his hair all mussed, sweat dripping from his face, and his collar wrinkled and limp. Worse than that, his aplomb was shaken.

"Well?" said Jedson.

"There is nothing to be done about it, Mr. Jedson—nothing at all."

"Nothing you can do about it, eh?"

He stiffened a bit at this. "Nothing *anyone* can do about it, gentlemen. Give it up. Forget about it. That is my advice."

Jedson said nothing, just looked at him speculatively. I kept quiet. Biddle was beginning to regain his self-possession. He straightened his hat, adjusted his necktie, and added, "I must return to my office. The survey fee will be five hundred dollars."

I was stonkered speechless at the barefaced gall of the man, but Jedson acted as if he hadn't understood him. "No doubt it would be," he observed. "Too bad you didn't earn it. I'm sorry."

Biddle turned red, but preserved his urbanity. "Apparently you misunderstood me, sir. Under the agreement I have signed with Mr. Ditworth, thaumaturgists approved by the association are not permitted to offer free consultation. It lowers the standards of the profession.

The fee I mentioned is the minimum fee for a magician of my classification, irrespective of services rendered."

"I see," Jedson answered calmly, "that's what it costs to step inside your office. But you didn't tell us that, so it doesn't apply. As for Mr. Ditworth, an agreement you sign with him does not bind us in any way. I advise you to return to your office and reread our contract. We owe you nothing."

I thought this time that Biddle would lose his temper, but all he answered was, "I shan't bandy words with you. You will hear from me later." He vanished then without so much as a by-your-leave.

I heard a snicker behind me and whirled around, ready to bite somebody's head off. I had had an upsetting day and didn't like to be laughed at behind my back. There was a young chap there, about my own age. "Who are you, and what are you laughing at?" I snapped. "This is private property."

"Sorry, bud," he apologized with a disarming grin. "I wasn't laughing at you; I was laughing at the stuffed shirt. Your friend ticked him off properly."

"What are you doing here?" asked Jedson.

"Me? I guess I owe you an explanation. You see, I'm in the business myself——"

"Building?"

"No—magic. Here's my card." He handed it to Jedson, who glanced at it and passed it on to me. It read:

JACK BODIE
LICENSED MAGICIAN, 1ST CLASS
TELEPHONE CREST 3840

"You see, I heard a rumor in the Half World that one of the big shots was going to do a hard one here today. I just stopped in to see the fun. But how did you happen to pick a false alarm like Biddle? He's not up to this sort of thing."

Jedson reached over and took the card back. "Where did you take your training, Mr. Bodie?"

"Huh? I took my bachelor's degree at Harvard and finished up postgraduate at Chicago. But that's not important; my old man taught me everything I know, but he insisted on my going to college because he said a magician can't get a decent job these days without a degree. He was right."

"Do you think you could handle this job?" I asked.

"Probably not, but I wouldn't have made the fool of myself that

Biddle did. Look here—you want to find somebody who *can* do this job?"

"Naturally," I said. "What do you think we're here for?"

"Well, you've gone about it the wrong way. Biddle's got a reputation simply because he's studied at Heidelberg and Vienna. That doesn't mean a thing. I'll bet it never occurred to you to look up an old-style witch for the job."

Jedson answered this one. "That's not quite true. I inquired around among my friends in the business, but didn't find anyone who was willing to take it on. But I'm willing to learn; whom do you suggest?"

"Do you know Mrs. Amanda Todd Jennings? Lives over in the old part of town, beyond the Congregational cemetery."

"Jennings . . . Jennings. Hm-m-m—no, can't say that I do. Wait a minute! Is she the old girl they call Granny Jennings? Wears Queen Mary hats and does her own marketing?"

"That's the one."

"But she's not a witch; she's a fortuneteller."

"That's what you think. She's not in regular commercial practice, it's true, being ninety years older than Santy Claus, and feeble to boot. But she's got more magic in her little finger than you'll find in Solomon's Book."

Jedson looked at me. I nodded, and he said:

"Do you think you could get her to attempt this case?"

"Well, I think she might do it, if she liked you."

"What arrangement do you want?" I asked. "Is 10 per cent satisfactory?"

He seemed rather put out at this. "Hell," he said, "I couldn't take a cut; she's been good to me all my life."

"If the tip is good, it's worth paying for," I insisted.

"Oh, forget it. Maybe you boys will have some work in my line someday. That's enough."

Pretty soon we were off again, without Bodie. He was tied up elsewhere, but promised to let Mrs. Jennings know that we were coming.

The place wasn't too hard to find. It was an old street, arched over with elms, and the house was a one-story cottage, set well back. The veranda had a lot of that old scroll-saw gingerbread. The yard was not very well taken care of, but there was a lovely old climbing rose arched over the steps.

Jedson gave a twist to the hand bell set in the door, and we waited for several minutes. I studied the colored-glass triangles set in the door's side panels and wondered if there was anyone left who could do that sort of work.

Then she let us in. She really was something incredible. She was so tiny that I found myself staring down at the crown of her head, and noting that the clean pink scalp showed plainly through the scant, neat threads of hair. She couldn't have weighed seventy pounds dressed for the street, but stood proudly erect in lavender alpaca and white collar, and sized us up with lively black eyes that would have fitted Catherine the Great or Calamity Jane.

"Good morning to you," she said. "Come in."

She led us through a little hall, between beaded portieres, said, "Scat, Seraphin!" to a cat on a chair, and sat us down in her parlor. The cat jumped down, walked away with an unhurried dignity, then sat down, tucked his tail neatly around his carefully placed feet, and stared at us with the same calm appraisal as his mistress.

"My boy Jack told me that you were coming," she began. "You are Mr. Fraser and you are Mr. Jedson," getting us sorted out correctly. It was not a question; it was a statement. "You want your futures read, I suppose. What method do you prefer—your palms, the stars, the sticks?"

I was about to correct her misapprehension when Jedson cut in ahead of me. "I think we'd best leave the method up to you, Mrs. Jennings."

"All right, we'll make it tea leaves then. I'll put the kettle on; 'twon't take a minute." She bustled out. We could hear her in the kitchen, her light footsteps clicking on the linoleum, utensils scraping and clattering in a busy, pleasant disharmony.

When she returned I said, "I hope we aren't putting you out, Mrs. Jennings."

"Not a bit of it," she assured me. "I like a cup of tea in the morning; it does a body comfort. I just had to set a love philter off the fire—that's what took me so long."

"I'm sorry——"

"'Twon't hurt it to wait."

"The Zekerboni formula?" Jedson inquired.

"My goodness gracious, no!" She was plainly upset by the suggestion. "I wouldn't kill all those harmless little creatures. Hares and swallows and doves—the very idea! I don't know what Pierre Mora was thinking about when he set that recipe down. I'd like to box his ears!

"No, I use Emula campana, orange, and ambergris. It's just as effective."

Jedson then asked if she had ever tried the juice of vervain. She looked closely into his face before replying. "You have the sight yourself, son. Am I not right?"

"A little, mother," he answered soberly, "a little, perhaps."

"It will grow. Mind how you use it. As for vervain, it is efficacious, as you know."

"Wouldn't it be simpler?"

"Of course it would. But if that easy a method became generally known, anyone and everyone would be making it and using it promiscuously—a bad thing. And witches would starve for want of clients—perhaps a good thing!" She flicked up one white eyebrow. "But if it is simplicity you want, there is no need to bother even with vervain. Here——" she reached out and touched me on the hand. "*'Bestarberto corrumpit viscera ejus virilis'.*" That is as near as I can reproduce her words. I may have misquoted it.

But I had no time to think about the formula she had pronounced. I was fully occupied with the startling thing that had come over me. I was in love, ecstatically, deliciously in love—with Granny Jennings! I don't mean that she suddenly looked like a beautiful young girl—she didn't. I still saw her as a little, old, shriveled-up woman with the face of a shrewd monkey, and ancient enough to be my great-grandmother. It didn't matter. She was she—the Helen that all men desire, the object of romantic adoration.

She smiled into my face with a smile that was warm and full of affectionate understanding. Everything was all right, and I was perfectly happy. Then she said, "I would not mock you, boy," in a gentle voice, and touched my hand a second time while whispering something else.

At once it was all gone. She was just any nice woman, the sort that would bake a cake for a grandson or sit up with a sick neighbor. Nothing was changed, and the cat had not even blinked. The romantic fascination was an emotionless memory. But I was poorer for the difference.

The kettle was boiling. She trotted out to attend to it, and returned shortly with a tray of tea things, a plate of seed cake, and thin slices of homemade bread spread with sweet butter.

When we had drunk a cup apiece with proper ceremony, she took Jedson's cup from him and examined the dregs. "Not much money there," she announced, "but you shan't need much; it's a fine full life." She touched the little pool of tea with the tip of her spoon and sent tiny ripples across it. "Yes, you have the sight, and the need for understanding that should go with it, but I find you in business instead of pursuing the great art, or even the lesser arts. Why is that?"

Jedson shrugged his shoulders and answered half apologetically, "There is work at hand that needs to be done. I do it."

She nodded. "That is well. There is understanding to be gained in any job, and you will gain it. There is no hurry; time is long. When your own work comes you will know it and be ready for it. Let me see your cup," she finished, turning to me.

I handed it to her. She studied it for a moment and said, "Well, you have not the clear sight such as your friend has, but you have the insight you need for your proper work. And more would make you dissatisfied, for I see money here. You will make much money, Archie Fraser."

"Do you see any immediate setback in my business?" I said quickly.

"No. See for yourself." She motioned toward the cup. I leaned forward and stared at it. For a matter of seconds it seemed as if I looked through the surface of the dregs into a living scene beyond. I recognized it readily enough. It was my own place of business, even to the scars on the driveway gateposts where clumsy truck drivers had clipped the corner too closely.

But there was a new annex wing on the east side of the lot, and there were two beautiful new five-ton dump trucks drawn up in the yard with my name painted on them!

While I watched I saw myself step out of the office door and go walking down the street. I was wearing a new hat, but the suit was the one I was wearing in Mrs. Jennings's parlor, and so was the necktie—a plaid one from the tartan of my clan. I reached up and touched the original.

Mrs. Jennings said, "That will do for now," and I found myself staring at the bottom of the teacup. "You have seen," she went on, "your business need not worry you. As for love and marriage and children, sickness and health and death—let us look." She touched the surface of the dregs with a finger tip; the tea leaves moved gently. She regarded them closely for a moment. Her brow puckered; she started to speak, apparently thought better of it, and looked again. Finally she said, "I do not fully understand this. It is not clear; my own shadow falls across it."

"Perhaps I can see," offered Jedson.

"Keep your peace!" She surprised me by speaking tartly, and placed her hand over the cup. She turned back to me with compassion in her eyes. "It is not clear. You have two possible futures. Let your head rule your heart, and do not fret your soul with that which cannot be. Then you will marry, have children, and be content." With that she dismissed the matter, for she said at once to both of us, "You did not come here for divination; you came here for help of another sort." Again it was a statement, not a question.

"What sort of help, mother?" Jedson inquired.

"For this." She shoved my cup under his nose.

He looked at it and answered, "Yes, that is true. Is there help?" I looked into the cup, too, but saw nothing but tea leaves.

She answered, "I think so. You should not have employed Biddle, but the mistake was natural. Let us be going." Without further parley she fetched her gloves and purse and coat, perched a ridiculous old hat on the top of her head, and bustled us out of the house. There was no discussion of terms; it didn't seem necessary.

WHEN WE GOT BACK TO the lot her workroom was already up. It was not anything fancy like Biddle's, but simply an old, square tent, like a gypsy's pitch, with a peaked top and made in several gaudy colors. She pushed aside the shawl that closed the door and invited us inside.

It was gloomy, but she took a big candle, lighted it and stuck it in the middle of the floor. By its light she inscribed five circles on the ground—first a large one, then a somewhat smaller one in front of it. Then she drew two others, one on each side of the first and biggest circle. These were each big enough for a man to stand in, and she told us to do so. Finally she made one more circle off to one side and not more than a foot across.

I've never paid much attention to the methods of magicians, feeling about them the way Thomas Edison said he felt about mathematicians—when he wanted one he could hire one. But Mrs. Jennings was different. I wish I could understand the things she did—and why.

I know she drew a lot of cabalistic signs in the dirt within the circles. There were pentacles of various shapes, and some writing in what I judged to be Hebraic script, though Jedson says not. In particular there was, I remember, a sign like a long flat Z, with a loop in it, woven in and out of a Maltese cross. Two more candles were lighted and placed on each side of this.

Then she jammed the dagger—athame, Jedson called it—with which she had scribed the figures into the ground at the top of the big circle so hard that it quivered. It continued to vibrate the whole time.

She placed a little folding stool in the center of the biggest circle, sat down on it, drew out a small book, and commenced to read aloud in a voiceless whisper. I could not catch the words, and presume I was not meant to. This went on for some time. I glanced around and saw that the little circle off to one side was now occupied—by Seraphin, her cat. We had left him shut up in her house. He sat quietly, watching everything that took place with dignified interest.

Presently she shut the book and threw a pinch of powder into the flame of the largest candle. It flared up and threw out a great puff of smoke. I am not quite sure what happened next, as the smoke smarted my eyes and made me blink, besides which, Jedson says I don't understand the purpose of fumigations at all. But I prefer to believe my eyes. Either that cloud of smoke solidified into a body or it covered up an entrance, one or the other.

Standing in the middle of the circle in front of Mrs. Jennings was a short, powerful man about four feet high or less. His shoulders were inches broader than mine, and his upper arms were thick as my thighs, knotted and bowed with muscle. He was dressed in a breechcloth, buskins, and a little hooded cap. His skin was hairless, but rough and earthy in texture. It was dull, lusterless. Everything about him was the same dull monotone, except his eyes, which shone green with repressed fury.

"Well!" said Mrs. Jennings crisply, "you've been long enough getting here! What have you to say for yourself?"

He answered sullenly, like an incorrigible boy caught but not repentant, in a language filled with rasping gutturals and sibilants. She listened awhile, then cut him off.

"I don't care who told you to; you'll account to me! I require this harm repaired—in less time than it takes to tell it!"

He answered back angrily, and she dropped into his language, so that I could no longer follow the meaning. But it was clear that I was concerned in it; he threw me several dirty looks, and finally glared and spat in my direction.

Mrs. Jennings reached out and cracked him across the mouth with the back of her hand. He looked at her, killing in his eyes, and said something.

"So?" she answered, put out a hand and grabbed him by the nape of the neck and swung him across her lap, face down. She snatched off a shoe and whacked him soundly with it. He let out one yelp, then kept silent, but jerked every time she struck him.

When she was through she stood up, spilling him to the ground. He picked himself up and hurriedly scrambled back into his own circle, where he stood, rubbing himself. Mrs. Jennings's eyes snapped and her voice crackled; there was nothing feeble about her now. "You gnomes are getting above yourselves," she scolded. "I never heard of such a thing! One more slip on your part and I'll fetch your people to see you spanked! Get along with you. Fetch your people for your task, and summon your brother and your brother's brother. By the great Tetragrammaton, get hence to the place appointed for you!"

He was gone.

Our next visitant came almost at once. It appeared first as a tiny spark hanging in the air. It grew into a living flame, a fireball, six inches or more across. It floated above the center of the second circle at the height of Mrs. Jennings's eyes. It danced and whirled and flamed, feeding on nothing. Although I had never seen one, I knew it to be a salamander. It couldn't be anything else.

Mrs. Jennings watched it for a little time before speaking. I could see that she was enjoying its dance, as I was. It was a perfect and beautiful thing, with no fault in it. There was life in it, a singing joy, with no concern for—with no *relation* to—matters of right and wrong, or anything human. Its harmonies of color and curve were their own reason for being.

I suppose I'm pretty matter-of-fact. At least I've always lived by the principle of doing my job and letting other things take care of themselves. But here was something that was worthwhile in itself, no matter what harm it did by my standards. Even the cat was purring.

Mrs. Jennings spoke to it in a clear, singing soprano that had no words to it. It answered back in pure liquid notes while the colors of its nucleus varied to suit the pitch. She turned to me and said, "It admits readily enough that it burned your place, but it was invited to do so and is not capable of appreciating your point of view. I dislike to compel it against its own nature. Is there any boon you can offer it?"

I thought for a moment. "Tell it that it makes me happy to watch it dance." She sang again to it. It spun and leaped, its flame tendrils whirling and floating in intricate, delightful patterns.

"That was good, but not sufficient. Can you think of anything else?"

I thought hard. "Tell it that if it likes, I will build a fireplace in my house where it will be welcome to live whenever it wishes."

She nodded approvingly and spoke to it again. I could almost understand its answer, but Mrs. Jennings translated. "It likes you. Will you let it approach you?"

"Can it hurt me?"

"Not here."

"All right then."

She drew a T between our two circles. It followed closely behind the athame, like a cat at an opening door. Then it swirled about me and touched me lightly on my hands and face. Its touch did not burn, but tingled, rather, as if I felt its vibrations directly instead of sensing them as heat. It flowed over my face. I was plunged into a world of light, like the heart of the aurora borealis. I was afraid to breathe at first, finally had to. No harm came to me, though the tingling was increased.

It's an odd thing, but I have not had a single cold since the salamander touched me. I used to sniffle all winter.

"Enough, enough," I heard Mrs. Jennings saying. The cloud of flame withdrew from me and returned to its circle. The musical discussion resumed, and they reached an agreement almost at once, for Mrs. Jennings nodded with satisfaction and said:

"Away with you then, fire child, and return when you are needed. Get hence——" She repeated the formula she had used on the gnome king.

The undine did not show up at once. Mrs. Jennings took out her book again and read from it in a monotonous whisper. I was beginning to be a bit sleepy—the tent was stuffy—when the cat commenced to spit. It was glaring at the center circle, claws out, back arched, and tail made big.

There was a shapeless something in that circle, a thing that dripped and spread its slimy moisture to the limit of the magic ring. It stank of fish and kelp and iodine, and shone with a wet phosphorescence.

"You're late," said Mrs. Jennings. "You got my message; why did you wait until I compelled you?"

It heaved with a sticky, sucking sound, but made no answer.

"Very well," she said firmly, "I shan't argue with you. You know what I want. You will do it!" She stood up and grasped the big center candle. Its flame flared up into a torch a yard high, and hot. She thrust it past her circle at the undine.

There was a hiss, as when water strikes hot iron, and a burbling scream. She jabbed at it again and again. At last she stopped and stared down at it, where it lay, quivering and drawing into itself. "That will do," she said. "Next time you will heed your mistress. Get hence!" It seemed to sink into the ground, leaving the dust dry behind it.

When it was gone she motioned for us to enter her circle, breaking our own with the dagger to permit us. Seraphin jumped lightly from his little circle to the big one and rubbed against her ankles, buzzing loudly. She repeated a meaningless series of syllables and clapped her hands smartly together.

There was a rushing and roaring. The sides of the tent billowed and cracked. I heard the chuckle of water and the crackle of flames, and, through that, the bustle of hurrying footsteps. She looked from side to side, and wherever her gaze fell the wall of the tent became transparent. I got hurried glimpses of unintelligible confusion.

Then it all ceased with a suddenness that was startling. The silence rang in our ears. The tent was gone; we stood in the loading yard outside my main warehouse.

It was there! It was back—back unharmed, without a trace of damage by fire or water. I broke away and ran out the main gate to where my business office had faced on the street. It was there, just as it used to be, the show windows shining in the sun, the Rotary Club emblem in one corner, and up on the roof my big two-way sign:

ARCHIBALD FRASER
BUILDING MATERIALS & GENERAL CONTRACTING

Jedson strolled out presently and touched me on the arm. "What are you bawling about, Archie?"

I stared at him. I wasn't aware that I had been.

WE WERE DOING BUSINESS AS usual on Monday morning. I thought everything was back to normal and that my troubles were over. I was too hasty in my optimism.

It was nothing you could put your finger on at first—just the ordinary vicissitudes of business, the little troubles that turn up in any line of work and slow up production. You expect them and charge them off to overhead. No one of them would be worth mentioning alone, except for one thing: they were happening too frequently.

You see, in any business run under a consistent management policy the losses due to unforeseen events should average out in the course of a year to about the same percentage of total cost. You allow for that in your estimates. But I started having so many small accidents and little difficulties that my margin of profit was eaten up.

One morning two of my trucks would not start. We could not find the trouble; I had to put them in the shop and rent a truck for the day to supplement my one remaining truck. We got our deliveries made, but I was out the truck rent, the repair bill, and four hours' overtime for drivers at time and a half. I had a net loss for the day.

The very next day I was just closing a deal with a man I had been trying to land for a couple of years. The deal was not important, but it would lead to a lot more business in the future, for he owned quite a bit of income property—some courts and an apartment house or two, several commercial corners, and held title or options on well-located lots all over town. He always had repair jobs to place and very frequently new building jobs. If I satisfied him, he would be a steady customer with prompt payment, the kind you can afford to deal with on a small margin of profit.

We were standing in the showroom just outside my office and talking, having about reached an agreement. There was a display of Sunprufe paint about three feet from us, the cans stacked in a neat pyramid. I swear that neither one of us touched it, but it came crashing to the floor, making a din that would sour milk.

That was nuisance enough, but not the pay-off. The cover flew off one can, and my prospect was drenched with red paint. He let out a yelp; I thought he was going to faint. I managed to get him back into my office, where I dabbed futilely at his suit with my handkerchief, while trying to calm him down.

He was in a state, both mentally and physically. "Fraser," he raged, "You've got to fire the clerk that knocked over those cans! Look at me! Eighty-five dollars worth of suit ruined!"

"Let's not be hasty," I said soothingly, while holding my own temper in. I won't discharge a man to suit a customer, and don't like to be told to do so. "There wasn't anyone near those cans but ourselves."

"I suppose you think I did it?"

"Not at all. I know you didn't." I straightened up, wiped my hands, and went over to my desk and got out my checkbook.

"Then you must have done it!"

"I don't think so," I answered patiently. "How much did you say your suit was worth?"

"Why?"

"I want to write you a check for the amount." I was quite willing to; I did not feel to blame, but it had happened through no fault of his in my shop.

"You can't get out of it as easily as that!" he answered unreasonably. "It isn't the cost of the suit I mind—" He jammed his hat on his head and stumped out. I knew his reputation; I'd seen the last of him.

This is the sort of thing I mean. Of course it could have been an accident caused by clumsy stacking of the cans. But it might have been a poltergeist. Accidents don't make themselves.

DITWORTH CAME TO SEE ME a day or so later about Biddle's phony bill. I had been subjected night and morning to this continuous stream of petty annoyances, and my temper was wearing thin. Just that day a gang of colored bricklayers had quit one of my jobs because some moron had scrawled some chalk marks on some of the bricks. "Voodoo marks," they said they were, and would not touch a brick. I was in no mood to be held up by Mr. Ditworth; I guess I was pretty short with him.

"Good day to you, Mr. Fraser," he said quite pleasantly, "can you spare me a few minutes?"

"Ten minutes, perhaps," I conceded, glancing at my wrist watch.

He settled his brief case against the legs of his chair and took out some papers. "I'll come to the point at once then. It's about Dr. Biddle's claim against you. You and I are both fair men; I feel sure that we can come to some equitable agreement."

"Biddle has no claim against me."

He nodded. "I know just how you feel. Certainly there is nothing in the written contract obligating you to pay him. But there can be implied contracts just as binding as written contracts."

"I don't follow you. All my business is done in writing."

"Certainly," he agreed; "that's because you are a businessman. In the professions the situation is somewhat different. If you go to a dental surgeon and ask him to pull an aching tooth, and he does, you are obligated to pay his fee, even though a fee has never been mentioned—"

"That's true," I interrupted, "but there is no parallel. Biddle didn't 'pull the tooth.'"

"In a way he did," Ditworth persisted. "The claim against you is for the survey, which was a service rendered you before this contract was written."

"But no mention was made of a service fee."

"That is where the implied obligation comes in, Mr. Fraser; you told Dr. Biddle that you had talked with me. He assumed quite correctly that I had previously explained to you the standard system of fees under the association—"

"But I did not join the association!"

"I know, I know. And I explained that to the other directors, but they insist that some sort of an adjustment must be made. I don't feel myself that you are fully to blame, but you will understand our position, I am sure. We are unable to accept you for membership in the association until this matter is adjusted—in fairness to Dr. Biddle."

"What makes you think I intend to join the association?"

He looked hurt. "I had not expected you to take that attitude, Mr. Fraser. The association needs men of your caliber. But in your own interest, you will necessarily join, for presently it will be very difficult to get efficient thaumaturgy except from members of the association. We want to help you. Please don't make it difficult for us."

I stood up. "I am afraid you had better sue me and let a court decide the matter, Mr. Ditworth. That seems to be the only satisfactory solution."

"I am sorry," he said, shaking his head. "It will prejudice your position when you come up for membership."

"Then it will just have to do so," I said shortly, and showed him out.

After he had gone I crabbed at my office girl for doing something I had told her to do the day before, and then had to apologize. I walked up and down a bit, stewing, although there was plenty of work I should have been doing. I was nervous; things had begun to get my goat—a dozen things that I haven't mentioned—and this last unreasonable demand from Ditworth seemed to be the last touch needed to upset me completely. Not that he could collect by suing me—that was preposterous—but it was an annoyance just the same. They say the Chinese have a torture that consists in letting one drop of water fall on the victim every few minutes. That's the way I felt.

Finally I called up Jedson and asked him to go to lunch with me.

I felt better after lunch. Jedson soothed me down, as he always does, and I was able to forget and put in the past most of the things that had been annoying me simply by telling him about them. By the time I had had a second cup of coffee and smoked a cigarette I was almost fit for polite society.

We strolled back toward my shop, discussing his problems for a change. It seems the blond girl, the white witch from Jersey City, had finally managed to make her synthesis stunt work on footgear. But there was still a hitch; she had turned out over eight hundred left shoes—and no right ones.

We were just speculating as to the probable causes of such a contretemps when Jedson said, "Look, Archie. The candid-camera fans are beginning to take an interest in you."

I looked. There was a chap standing at the curb directly across from my place of business and focusing a camera on the shop.

Then I looked again. "Joe," I snapped, "that's the bird I told you about, the one that came into my shop and started the trouble!"

"Are you sure?" he asked, lowering his voice.

"Positive." There was no doubt about it; he was only a short distance away on the same side of the street that we were. It was the same racketeer who had tried to blackmail me into buying "protection," the same Mediterranean look to him, the same flashy clothes.

"We've got to grab him," whispered Jedson.

But I had already thought of that. I rushed at him and had grabbed him by his coat collar and the slack of his pants before he knew what was happening, and pushed him across the street ahead of me. We were nearly run down, but I was so mad I didn't care. Jedson came pounding after us.

The yard door of my office was open. I gave the mug a final heave that lifted him over the threshold and sent him sprawling on the floor. Jedson was right behind; I bolted the door as soon as we were both inside.

Jedson strode over to my desk, snatched open the middle drawer, and rummaged hurriedly through the stuff that accumulates in such places. He found what he wanted, a carpenter's blue pencil, and was back alongside our gangster before he had collected himself sufficiently to scramble to his feet. Jedson drew a circle around him on the floor, almost tripping over his own feet in his haste, and closed the circle with an intricate flourish.

Our unwilling guest screeched when he saw what Joe was doing, and tried to throw himself out of the circle before it could be finished. But Jedson had been too fast for him—the circle was closed and sealed; he bounced back from the boundary as if he had struck a glass wall, and stumbled again to his knees. He remained so for the time, and cursed steadily in a language that I judged to be Italian, although I think there were bad words in it from several other languages—certainly some English ones.

He was quite fluent.

Jedson pulled out a cigarette, lighted it, and handed me one. "Let's sit down, Archie," he said, "and rest ourselves until our boy friend composes himself enough to talk business."

I did so, and we smoked for several minutes while the flood of invective continued. Presently Jedson cocked one eyebrow at the chap and said, "Aren't you beginning to repeat yourself?"

That checked him. He just sat and glared. "Well," Jedson continued, "haven't you anything to say for yourself?"

He growled under his breath and said, "I want to call my lawyer."

Jedson looked amused. "You don't understand the situation," he told him. "You're not under arrest, and we don't give a damn about your legal rights. We might just conjure up a hole and drop you in it, then let it relax." The guy paled a little under his swarthy skin. "Oh yes," Jedson went on, "we are quite capable of doing that—or worse. You see, we don't like you."

"Of course," he added meditatively, "we might just turn you over to the police. I get a soft streak now and then." The chap looked sour. "You don't like that either? Your fingerprints, maybe?" Jedson jumped to his feet and in two quick strides was standing over him, just outside the circle. "All right then," he rapped, "answer up and make 'em good! Why were you taking photographs?"

The chap muttered something, his eyes lowered. Jedson brushed it aside. "Don't give me that stuff—we aren't children! Who told you to do it?"

He looked utterly panic-stricken at that and shut up completely.

"Very well," said Jedson and turned to me. "Have you some wax, or modeling clay, or anything of the sort?"

"How would putty do?" I suggested.

"Just the thing." I slid out to the shed where we stow glaziers' supplies and came back with a five-pound can. Jedson pried it open and dug out a good big handful, then sat at my desk and worked the linseed oil into it until it was soft and workable. Our prisoner watched him with silent apprehension.

"There! That's about right," Jedson announced at and slapped the soft lump down on my blotter pad. He commenced to fashion it with his fingers, and it took shape slowly as a little doll about ten inches high. It did not look like much of anything or anybody. Jedson is no artist—but Jedson kept glancing from the figurine to the man in the circle and back again, like a sculptor making a clay sketch directly from a model. You could see the chap's nervous terror increase by the minute.

"Now!" said Jedson, looking once more from the putty figure to his model. "It's just as ugly as you are. Why did you take that picture?"

He did not answer, but slunk farther back in the circle, his face nastier than ever.

"Talk!" snorted Jedson, and twisted a foot of the doll between a thumb and forefinger. The corresponding foot of our prisoner jerked out from under him and twisted violently. He fell heavily to the floor with a yelp of pain.

"You were going to cast a spell on this place, weren't you?"

He made his first coherent answer. "No, no, mister! Not me!"

"Not you? I see. You were just the errand boy. Who was to do the magic?"

"I don't know—Ow! Oh, God!" He grabbed at his left calf and nursed it. Jedson had jabbed a pen point into the leg of the dolly. "I really *don't* know. Please, please!"

"Maybe you don't," Jedson grudged, "but at least you know who gives you your orders, and who some of the other members of your gang are. Start talking."

He rocked back and forth and covered his face with his hands. "I don't dare, mister," he groaned. "Please don't try to make me——"

Jedson jabbed the doll with the pen again; he jumped and flinched, but this time he bore it silently with a look of gray determination.

"O.K.," said Jedson, "if you insist——" He took another drag from his cigarette, then brought the lighted end slowly toward the face of the doll. The man in the circle tried to shrink away from it, his hands up to protect his face, but his efforts were futile. I could actually see the skin turn red and angry and the blisters blossom under his hide. It made me sick to watch it, and, while I didn't feel any real sympathy for the rat, I turned to Jedson and was about to ask him to stop when he took the cigarette away from the doll's face.

"Ready to talk?" he asked. The man nodded feebly, tears pouring down his scorched cheeks. He seemed about to collapse. "Here—don't faint," Jedson added, and slapped the face of the doll with a finger tip. I could hear the smack land, and the chap's head rocked to the blow, but he seemed to take a brace from it.

"All right, Archie, you take it down." He turned back. "And you, my friend, talk—and talk lots. Tell us everything you know. If you find your memory failing you, stop to think how you would like my cigarette poked into dolly's eyes!"

And he did talk—babbled, in fact. His spirit seemed to be completely broken, and he even seemed anxious to talk, stopping only occasionally to sniffle, or wipe at his eyes. Jedson questioned him to bring out points that were not clear.

There were five others in the gang that he knew about, and the setup was roughly as we had guessed. It was their object to levy tribute on everyone connected with magic in this end of town, magicians and their customers alike. No, they did not have any real protection to offer except from their own mischief. Who was his boss? He told us. Was his boss the top man in the racket? No, but he did not know who the top man was. He was quite sure that his boss worked for someone else, but he did not know who. Even if we burned him again he could not tell us. But it was a big organization—he was sure of that. He himself had been brought from a city in the East to help organize here.

Was he a magician? So help him, no! Was his section boss one? No—he was sure; all that sort of thing was handled from higher up. That was all he knew, and could he go now? Jedson pressed him to remember other things; he added a number of details, most of them insignificant, but I took them all down. The last thing he said was that he thought both of us had been marked down for special attention because we had been successful in overcoming our first "lesson."

Finally, Jedson let up on him. "I'm going to let you go now," he told him. "You'd better get out of town. Don't let me see you hanging around again. But don't go too far; I may want you again. See this?" He held up the doll and squeezed it gently around the middle. The poor devil immediately commenced to gasp for breath as if he were being compressed in a strait jacket. "Don't forget that I've got you anytime I want you." He let up on the pressure, and his victim panted his relief. "I'm going to put your alter ego—doll to you! —where it will be safe, behind cold iron. When I want you, you'll feel a pain like that"—he nipped the doll's left shoulder with his fingernails; the man yelped—"then you telephone me, no matter where you are."

Jedson pulled a penknife from his vest pocket and cut the circle three times, then joined the cuts. "Now get out!"

I thought he would bolt as soon as he was released, but he did not. He stepped hesitantly over the pencil mark, stood still for a moment, and shivered. Then he stumbled toward the door. He turned just before he went through it and looked back at us, his eyes wide with fear. There was a look of appeal in them, too, and he seemed about to speak. Evidently he thought better of it, for he turned and went on out.

When he was gone I looked back at Jedson. He had picked up my notes and was glancing through them. "I don't know," he mused, "whether it would be better to turn his stuff at once over to the Better Business Bureau and let them handle it, or whether to have a go at it ourselves. It's a temptation."

I was not interested just then. "Joe," I said, "I wish you hadn't burned him!"

"Eh? How's that?" He seemed surprised and stopped scratching his chin. "I didn't burn him."

"Don't quibble," I said, somewhat provoked. "You burned him through the doll, I mean with magic."

"But I didn't, Archie. Really I didn't. He did that to himself—and it wasn't magic. I didn't do a thing!"

"What the hell do you mean?"

"Sympathetic magic isn't really magic at all, Archie. It's just an application of neuropsychology and colloidal chemistry. He did all that to himself, because he believed in it. I simply correctly judged his mentality."

The discussion was cut short; we heard an agony-loaded scream from somewhere outside the building. It broke off sharply, right at the top. "What was that?" I said, and gulped.

"I don't know," Jedson answered, and stepped to the door. He looked up and down before continuing. "It must be some distance away. I didn't see anything." He came back into the room. "As I was saying, it would be a lot of fun to——"

This time it was a police siren. We heard it from far away, but it came rapidly nearer, turned a corner, and yowled down our street. We looked at each other. "Maybe we'd better go see," we both said, right together, then laughed nervously.

It was our gangster acquaintance. We found him half a block down the street, in the middle of a little group of curious passers-by who were being crowded back by cops from the squad car at the curb.

He was quite dead.

He lay on his back, but there was no repose in the position. He had been raked from forehead to waist, laid open to the bone in three roughly parallel scratches, as if slashed by the talons of a hawk or an eagle. But the bird that made those wounds must have been the size of a five-ton truck.

There was nothing to tell from his expression. His face and throat were covered by, and his mouth choked with, a yellowish substance shot with purple. It was about the consistency of thin cottage cheese, but it had the most sickening smell I have ever run up against.

I turned to Jedson, who was not looking any too happy himself, and said, "Let's get back to the office."

We did.

WE DECIDED AT LAST TO do a little investigating on our own before taking up what we had learned with the Better Business Bureau or with the police. It was just as well that we did; none of the gang whose names we had obtained was any longer to be found in the haunts which we had listed. There was plenty of evidence that such persons had existed and that they had lived at the addresses which Jedson had sweated out of their pal. But all of them, without exception, had done a bunk for parts unknown the same afternoon that their accomplice had been killed.

We did not go to the police, for we had no wish to be associated with an especially unsavory sudden death. Instead, Jedson made a cautious verbal report to a friend of his at the Better Business Bureau, who passed it on secondhand to the head of the racket squad and elsewhere, as his judgment indicated.

I did not have any more trouble with my business for some time thereafter, and I was working very hard, trying to show a profit for the quarter in spite of setbacks. I had put the whole matter fairly well out of my mind, except that I dropped over to call on Mrs. Jennings occasionally and that I had used her young friend Jack Bodie once or twice in my business, when I needed commercial magic. He was a good workman—no monkey business and value received.

I was beginning to think I had the world on a leash when I ran into another series of accidents. This time they did not threaten my business; they threatened *me*—and I'm just as fond of my neck as the next man.

In the house where I live the water heater is installed in the kitchen. It is a storage type, with a pilot light and a thermostatically controlled main flame. Right alongside it is a range with a pilot light.

I woke up in the middle of the night and decided that I wanted a drink of water. When I stepped into the kitchen—don't ask me why I did not look for a drink in the bathroom, because I don't know—I was almost gagged by the smell of gas. I ran over and threw the window wide open, then ducked back out the door and ran into the living room, where I opened a big window to create a cross draft.

At that point there was a dull *whoosh* and a *boom,* and I found myself sitting on the living-room rug.

I was not hurt, and there was no damage in the kitchen except for a few broken dishes. Opening the windows had released the explosion, cushioned the effect. Natural gas is not an explosive unless it is confined. What had happened was clear enough when I looked over the scene. The pilot light on the heater had gone out; when the water in the tank cooled, the thermostat turned on the main gas jet, which continued immediately to pour gas into the room. When an explosive mixture was reached, the pilot light of the stove was waiting, ready to set it off.

Apparently I wandered in at the zero hour.

I fussed at my landlord about it, and finally we made a dicker whereby he installed one of the electrical water heaters which I supplied at cost and for which I donated the labor.

No magic about the whole incident, eh? That is what I thought. Now I am not so sure.

THE NEXT THING THAT THREW a scare into me occurred the same week with no apparent connection. I keep dry mix—sand, rock, gravel—in the usual big bins set up high on concrete stanchions so that the trucks can drive under the hoppers for loading. One evening after closing time I was walking past the bins when I noticed that someone had left a scoop shovel in the driveway pit under the hoppers.

I have had trouble with my men leaving tools out at night; I decided to put this one in my car and confront someone with it in the morning. I was about to jump down into the pit when I heard my name called.

"Archibald!" it said—and it sounded remarkably like Mrs. Jennings's voice. Naturally I looked around. There was no one there. I turned back to the pit in time to hear a cracking sound and to see that scoop covered with twenty tons of medium gravel.

A man can live through being buried alive, but not when he has to wait overnight for someone to miss him and dig him out. A crystallized steel forging was the prima-facie cause of the mishap. I suppose that will do.

There was never anything to point to but natural causes, yet for about two weeks I stepped on banana peels both figuratively and literally. I saved my skin with a spot of fast footwork at least a dozen times. I finally broke down and told Mrs. Jennings about it.

"Don't worry too much about it, Archie," she reassured me. "It is not too easy to kill a man with magic unless he himself is involved with magic and sensitive to it."

"Might as well kill a man as scare him to death!" I protested.

She smiled that incredible smile of hers and said, "I don't think you have been really frightened, lad. At least you have not shown it."

I caught an implication in that remark and taxed her with it. "You've been watching me and pulling me out of jams, haven't you?"

She smiled more broadly and replied, "That's my business, Archie. It is not well for the young to depend on the old for help. Now get along with you. I want to give this matter more thought."

A couple of days later a note came in the mail addressed to me in a spidery, Spencerian script. The penmanship had the dignified flavor of the last century, and was the least bit shaky, as if the writer were unwell or very elderly. I had never seen the hand before, but guessed who it was before I opened it. It read:

*My dear Archibald: This is to introduce my esteemed friend, Dr. Royce Worthington. You will find him staying at the Belmont Hotel; he is expecting to hear from you. Dr. Worthington is exceptionally well qualified to deal with the matters that have been troubling you these few weeks past. You may repose every confidence in his judgment, especially where unusual measures are required.*

*Please to include your friend, Mr. Jedson, in this introduction, if you wish.*

*I am, sir,*
*Very sincerely yours,*
*Amanda Todd Jennings*

I rang up Joe Jedson and read the letter to him. He said that he would be over at once, and for me to telephone Worthington.

"Is Dr. Worthington there?" I asked as soon as the room clerk had put me through.

"Speaking," answered a cultured British voice with a hint of Oxford in it.

"This is Archibald Fraser, Doctor. Mrs. Jennings has written to me, suggesting that I look you up."

"Oh yes!" he replied, his voice warming considerably. "I shall be delighted. When will be a convenient time?"

"If you are free, I could come right over."

"Let me see——" He paused about long enough to consult a watch. "I have occasion to go to your side of the city. Might I stop by your office in thirty minutes, or a little later?"

"That will be fine, Doctor, if it does not discommode you——"

"Not at all. I will be there."

Jedson arrived a little later and asked me at once about Dr. Worthington. "I haven't seen him yet," I said, "but he sounds like something pretty swank in the way of an English-university don. He'll be here shortly."

My office girl brought in his card a half hour later. I got up to greet him and saw a tall, heavy-set man with a face of great dignity and evident intelligence. He was dressed in rather conservative, expensively tailored clothes and carried gloves, stick, and a large brief case, but he was black as draftsman's ink!

I tried not to show surprise. I hope I did not, for I have an utter horror of showing that kind of rudeness. There was no reason why the man should not be a Negro. I simply had not been expecting it.

Jedson helped me out. I don't believe he would show surprise if a fried egg winked at him. He took over the conversation for the first couple of minutes after I introduced him; we all found chairs, settled down, and spent a few minutes in the polite, meaningless exchanges that people make when they are sizing up strangers.

Worthington opened the matter. "Mrs. Jennings gave me to believe," he observed, "that there was some fashion in which I might possibly be of assistance to one, or both, of you——"

I told him that there certainly was, and sketched out the background for him from the time the racketeer contact man first showed up at my shop. He asked a few questions, and Jedson helped me out with some details. I got the impression that Mrs. Jennings had already told him most of it, and that he was simply checking.

"Very well," he said at last, his voice a deep, mellow rumble that seemed to echo in his big chest before it reached the air, "I am reasonably sure that we will find a way to cope with your problems, but first

I must make a few examinations before we can complete the diagnosis." He leaned over and commenced to unstrap his brief case.

"Uh . . . Doctor," I suggested, "hadn't we better complete our arrangements before you start to work?"

"Arrangements?" He looked momentarily puzzled, then smiled broadly. "Oh, you mean payment. My dear sir, it is a privilege to do a favor for Mrs. Jennings."

"But . . . but . . . see here, Doctor, I'd feel better about it. I assure you I am quite in the habit of paying for magic——"

He held up a hand. "It is not possible, my young friend, for two reasons: In the first place, I am not licensed to practice in your state. In the second place, I am not a magician."

I suppose I looked as inane as I sounded. "Huh? What's that? Oh! Excuse me, Doctor, I guess I just naturally assumed that since Mrs. Jennings had sent you, and your title, and all——"

He continued to smile, but it was a smile of understanding rather than amusement at my discomfiture. "That is not surprising; even some of your fellow citizens of my blood make that mistake. No, my degree is an honorary doctor of laws of Cambridge University. My proper pursuit is anthropology, which I sometimes teach at the University of South Africa. But anthropology has some odd bypaths; I am here to exercise one of them."

"Well, then, may I ask——"

"Certainly, sir. My avocation, freely translated from its quite unpronounceable proper name, is 'witch smeller.' "

I was still puzzled. "But doesn't that involve magic?"

"Yes and no. In Africa the hierarchy and the categories in these matters are not the same as in this continent. I am not considered a wizard, or witch doctor, but rather an antidote for such."

Something had been worrying Jedson. "Doctor," he inquired, "you were not originally from South Africa?"

Worthington gestured toward his own face. I suppose that Jedson read something there that was beyond my knowledge. "As you have discerned. No, I was born in a bush tribe south of the Lower Congo."

"From there, eh? That's interesting. By any chance, are you nganga?"

"Of the Ndembo, but not by chance." He turned to me and explained courteously. "Your friend asked me if I was a member of an occult fraternity which extends throughout Africa, but which has the bulk of its members in my native territory. Initiates are called nganga."

Jedson persisted in his interest. "It seems likely to me, Doctor, that Worthington is a name of convenience—that you have another name."

"You are again, right—naturally. My tribal name—do you wish to know it?"

"If you will."

"It is"—I cannot reproduce the odd clicking, lip-smacking noise he uttered—"or it is just as proper to state it in English, as the meaning is what counts—Man-Who-Asks-Inconvenient-Questions. Prosecuting attorney is another reasonably idiomatic, though not quite literal, translation, because of the tribal function implied. But it seems to me," he went on, with a smile of unmalicious humor, "that the name fits you even better than it does me. May I give it to you?"

Here occurred something that I did not understand, except that it must have its basis in some African custom completely foreign to our habits of thought. I was prepared to laugh at the doctor's witticism, and I am sure he meant it to be funny, but Jedson answered him quite seriously:

"I am deeply honored to accept."

"It is you who honor me, brother."

From then on, throughout our association with him, Dr. Worthington invariably addressed Jedson by the African name he had formerly claimed as his own, and Jedson called him "brother" or "Royce." Their whole attitude toward each other underwent a change, as if the offer and acceptance of a name had in fact made them brothers, with all the privileges and obligations of the relationship.

"I have not left you without a name," Jedson added. "You had a third name, your real name?"

"Yes, of course," Worthington acknowledged, "a name which we need not mention."

"Naturally," Jedson agreed, "a name which must not be mentioned. Shall we get to work, then?"

"Yes, let us do so." He turned to me. "Have you someplace here where I may make my preparations? It need not be large——"

"Will this do?" I offered, getting up and opening the door of cloak- and washroom which adjoins my office.

"Nicely, thank you," he said, and took himself and his brief case inside, closing the door after him. He was gone ten minutes at least.

Jedson did not seem disposed to talk, except to suggest that I caution my girl not to disturb us or let anyone enter from the outer office. We sat and waited.

Then he came out of the cloakroom, and I got my second big surprise of the day. The urbane Dr. Worthington was gone. In his place was an African personage who stood over six feet tall in his bare black feet, and whose enormous, arched chest was overlaid with thick, sleek muscles of polished obsidian. He was dressed in a loin skin of leopard, and carried certain accouterments, notably a pouch, which hung at his waist.

But it was not his equipment that held me, nor yet the John Henry-like proportions of that warrior frame, but the face. The eyebrows were painted white and the hairline had been outlined in the same color, but I hardly noticed these things. It was the expression—humorless, implacable, filled with dignity and strength which must be felt to be appreciated. The eyes gave a conviction of wisdom beyond my comprehension, and there was no pity in them—only a stern justice that I myself would not care to face.

We white men in this country are inclined to underestimate the black man—I know I do—because we see him out of his cultural matrix. Those we know have had their own culture wrenched from them some generations back and a servile pseudo culture imposed on them by force. We forget that the black man has a culture of his own, older than ours and more solidly grounded, based on character and the power of the mind rather than the cheap, ephemeral tricks of mechanical gadgets. But it is a stern, fierce culture with no sentimental concern for the weak and the unfit, and it never quite dies out.

I stood up in involuntary respect when Dr. Worthington entered the room.

"Let us begin," he said in a perfectly ordinary voice, and squatted down, his great toes spread and grasping the floor. He took several things out of the pouch—a dog's tail, a wrinkled black object the size of a man's fist, and other things hard to identify. He fastened the tail to his waist so that it hung down behind. Then he picked up one of the things that he had taken from the pouch—a small item wrapped and tied in red silk—and said to me, "Will you open your safe?"

I did so, and stepped back out of his way. He thrust the little bundle inside, clanged the door shut, and spun the knob. I looked inquiringly at Jedson.

"He has his . . . well . . . soul in that package, and has sealed it away behind cold iron. He does not know what dangers he may encounter," Jedson whispered. "See?" I looked and saw him pass his thumb carefully all around the crack that joined the safe to its door.

He returned to the middle of the floor and picked up the wrinkled black object and rubbed it affectionately. "This is my mother's father," he announced. I looked at it more closely and saw that it was a mummified human head with a few wisps of hair still clinging to the edge of the scalp! "He is very wise," he continued in a matter-of-fact voice, "and I shall need his advice. Grandfather, this is your new son and his friend." Jedson bowed, and I found myself doing so. "They want our help."

He started to converse with the head in his own tongue listening from time to time, and then answering. Once they seemed to get into an argument, but the matter must have been settled satisfactorily, for the palaver soon quieted down. After a few minutes he ceased talking and glanced around the room. His eye lit on a bracket shelf intended for an electric fan, which was quite high off the floor.

"There!" he said. "That will do nicely. Grandfather needs a high place from which to watch." He went over and placed the little head on the bracket so that it faced out into the room.

When he returned to his place in the middle of the room he dropped to all fours and commenced to cast around with his nose like a hunting dog trying to pick up a scent. He ran back and forth, snuffling and whining, exactly like a pack leader worried by mixed trails. The tail fastened to his waist stood up tensely and quivered, as if still part of a live animal. His gait and his mannerisms mimicked those of a hound so convincingly that I blinked my eyes when he sat down suddenly and announced:

"I've never seen a place more loaded with traces of magic. I can pick out Mrs. Jennings' very strongly and your own business magic. But after I eliminate them the air is still crowded. You must have had everything but a rain dance and a sabbat going on around you!"

He dropped back into his character of a dog without giving us a chance to reply, and started making his casts a little wider. Presently he appeared to come to some sort of an impasse, for he settled back, looked at the head, and whined vigorously. Then he waited.

The reply must have satisfied him; he gave a sharp bark and dragged open the bottom drawer of a file cabinet, working clumsily, as if with paws instead of hands. He dug into the back of the drawer eagerly and hauled out something which he popped into his pouch.

After that he trotted very cheerfully around the place for a short time, until he had poked his nose into every odd corner. When he had finished he returned to the middle of the floor, squatted down again, and said, "That takes care of everything here for the present. This place is the center of their attack, so grandfather has agreed to stay and watch here until I can bind a cord around your place to keep witches out."

I was a little perturbed at that. I was sure the head would scare my office girl half out of her wits if she saw it. I said so as diplomatically as possible.

"How about that?" he asked the head, then turned back to me after a moment of listening. "Grandfather says it's all right; he won't let anyone see him he has not been introduced to." It turned out that he was perfectly correct; nobody noticed it, not even the scrubwoman.

"Now then," he went on, "I want to check over my brother's place of business at the earliest opportunity, and I want to smell out both of your homes and insulate them against mischief. In the meantime, here is some advice for each of you to follow carefully: Don't let anything of yourself fall into the hands of strangers—nail parings, spittle, hair cuttings—guard it all. Destroy them by fire, or engulf them in running water. It will make our task much simpler. I am finished." He got up and strode back into the cloakroom.

Ten minutes later the dignified and scholarly Dr. Worthington was smoking a cigarette with us. I had to look up at his grandfather's head to convince myself that a jungle lord had actually been there.

BUSINESS WAS PICKING UP AT that time, and I had no more screwy accidents after Dr. Worthington cleaned out the place. I could see a net profit for the quarter and was beginning to feel cheerful again. I received a letter from Ditworth, dunning me about Biddle's phony claim, but I filed it in the wastebasket without giving it a thought.

One day shortly before noon Feldstein, the magicians' agent, dropped into my place. "Hi, Zack!" I said cheerfully when he walked in. "How's business?"

"Mr. Fraser, of all questions, that you should ask me that one," he said, shaking his head mournfully from side to side. "Business—it is terrible."

"Why do you say that?" I asked. "I see lots of signs of activity around——"

"Appearances are deceiving," he insisted, "especially in my business. Tell me—have you heard of a concern calling themselves 'Magic, Incorporated'?"

"That's funny," I told him. "I just did, for the first time. This just came in the mail"—and I held up an unopened letter. It had a return address on it of "Magic, Incorporated, Suite 700, Commonwealth Building."

Feldstein took it gingerly, as if he thought it might poison him, and inspected it. "That's the parties I mean," he confirmed. "The gonophs!"

"Why, what's the trouble, Zack?"

"They don't want that a man should make an honest living—Mr. Fraser," he interrupted himself anxiously, "you wouldn't quit doing business with an old friend who had always done right by you?"

"Of course not, Zack, but what's it all about?"

"Read it. Go ahead." He shoved the letter back to me.

I opened it. The paper was a fine quality, water-marked, rag bond, and the letterhead was chaste and dignified. I glanced over the stuffed-shirt committee and was quite agreeably impressed by the caliber of men they had as officers and directors—big men, all of them, except for a couple of names among the executives that I did not recognize.

The letter itself amounted to an advertising prospectus. It was a new idea; I suppose you could call it a holding company for magicians. They offered to provide any and all kinds of magical service. The customer could dispense with shopping around; he could call this one number, state his needs, and the company would supply the service and bill him. It seemed fair enough—no more than an incorporated agency.

I glanced on down. "—fully guaranteed service, backed by the entire assets of a responsible company—" "—surprisingly low standard fees, made possible by elimination of fee splitting with agents and by centralized administration—" "The gratifying response from the members of the great profession enables us to predict that Magic, Incorporated, will be the natural source to turn to for competent thaumaturgy in any line—probably the only source of truly first-rate magic——"

I put it down. "Why worry about it, Zack? It's just another agency. As for their claims—I've heard you say that you have all the best ones in your stable. You didn't expect to be believed, did you?"

"No," he conceded, "not quite, maybe—among us two. But this is really serious, Mr. Fraser. They've hired away most of my really first-class operators with salaries and bonuses I can't match. And now they offer magic to the pubic at a price that undersells those I've got left. It's ruin, I'm telling you."

It was hard lines. Feldstein was a nice little guy who grabbed the nickels the way he did for a wife and five beady-eyed kids, to whom he was devoted. But I felt he was exaggerating; he has a tendency to dramatize himself. "Don't worry," I said. "I'll stick by you, and so, I imagine, will most of your customers. This outfit can't get all the magicians together; they're too independent. Look at Ditworth. He tried with his association. What did it get him?"

"Ditworth—aagh!" He started to spit, then remembered he was in my office. "This *is* Ditworth—this company!"

"How do you figure that? He's not on the letterhead."

"I found out. You think he wasn't successful because you held out.

They held a meeting of the directors of the association—that's Ditworth and his two secretaries—and voted the contracts over to the new corporation. Then Ditworth resigns and his stooge steps in as front for the non-profit association, and Ditworth runs both companies. You will see! If we could open the books of Magic, Incorporated, you will find he has voting control, I know it!"

"It seems unlikely." I said slowly.

"You'll see! Ditworth with all his fancy talk about a no-profit service for the improvement of standards shouldn't be any place around Magic, Incorporated, should he, now? You call up and ask for him——"

I did not answer, but dialed the number on the letterhead. When a girl's voice said, "Good morning—Magic, Incorporated," I said:

"Mr. Ditworth, please."

She hesitated quite a long time, then said, "Who is calling, please?"

That made it my turn to hesitate. I did not want to talk to Ditworth; I wanted to establish a fact. I finally said, "Tell him it's Dr. Biddle's office."

Whereupon she answered readily enough, but with a trace of puzzlement in her voice, "But Mr. Ditworth is not in the suite just now; he was due in Dr. Biddle's office half an hour ago. Didn't he arrive?"

"Oh," I said, "perhaps he's with the chief and I didn't see him come in. Sorry." And I rang off.

"I guess you are right," I admitted, turning back to Feldstein.

He was too worried to be pleased about it. "Look," he said, "I want you should have lunch with me and talk about it some more."

"I was just on my way to the Chamber of Commerce luncheon. Come along and we'll talk on the way. You're a member."

"All right," he agreed dolefully. "Maybe I can't afford it much longer."

WE WERE A LITTLE LATE and had to take separate seats. The treasurer stuck the kitty under my nose and "twisted her tail." He wanted a ten-cent fine from me for being late. The kitty is an ordinary frying pan with a mechanical bicycle bell mounted on the handle. We pay all fines on the spot, which is good for the treasury and a source of innocent amusement. The treasurer shoves the pan at you and rings the bell until you pay up.

I hastily produced a dime and dropped it in. Steven Harris, who has an automobile agency, yelled, "That's right! Make the Scotchman pay up!" and threw a roll at me.

"Ten cents for disorder," announced our chairman, Norman Somers, without looking up. The treasurer put the bee on Steve. I heard the coin clink into the pan, then the bell was rung again.

"What's the trouble?" asked Somers.

"More of Steve's tricks," the treasurer reported in a tired voice. "Fairy gold, this time." Steve had chucked in a synthetic coin that some friendly magician had made up for him. Naturally, when it struck cold iron it melted away.

"Two bits more for counterfeiting," decided Somers, "then handcuff him and ring up the United States attorney." Steve is quite a card, but he does not put much over on Norman.

"Can't I finish my lunch first?" asked Steve, in tones that simply dripped with fake self-pity. Norman ignored him and he paid up.

"Steve, better have fun while you can," commented Al Donahue, who runs a string of drive-in restaurants. "When you sign up with Magic, Incorporated, you will have to cut out playing tricks with magic." I sat up and listened.

"Who said I was going to sign up with them?"

"Huh? Of course you are. It's the logical thing to do. Don't be a dope."

"Why should I?"

"Why should you? Why, it's the direction of progress, man. Take my case: I put out the fanciest line of vanishing desserts of any eating place in town. You can eat three of them if you like, and not feel full and not gain an ounce. Now I've been losing money on them, but kept them for advertising because of the way they bring in the women's trade. Now Magic, Incorporated, comes along and offers me the same thing at a price I can make money with them too. Naturally, I signed up."

"You would. Suppose they raise the prices on you after they have hired, or driven out of business, every competent wizard in town?"

Donahue laughed in a superior, irritating way. "I've got a contract."

"So? How long does it run? And did you read the cancellation clause?"

I knew what he was talking about, even if Donahue didn't; I had been through it. About five years ago a Portland cement firm came into town and began buying up the little dealers and cutting prices against the rest. They ran sixty-cent cement down to thirty-five cents a sack and broke their competitors. Then they jacked it back up by easy stages until cement sold for a dollar twenty-five. The boys took a whipping before they knew what had happened to them.

We all had to shut up about then, for the guest speaker, old B. J.

Timken, the big subdivider, started in. He spoke on "Cooperation and Service." Although he is not exactly a scintillating speaker, he had some very inspiring things to say about how businessmen could serve the community and help each other; I enjoyed it.

After the clapping died down, Norman Somers thanked B.J. and said, "That's all for today, gentlemen, unless there is some new business to bring before the house—"

Jedson got up. I was sitting with my back to him, and had not known he was present. "I think there is, Mr. Chairman—a very important matter. I ask the indulgence of the Chair for a few minutes of informal discussion."

Somers answered, "Certainly, Joe, if you've got something important."

"Thanks. I think it is. This is really an extension of the discussion between Al Donahue and Steve Harris earlier in the meeting. I think there has been a major change in business conditions going on in this city right under our noses and we haven't noticed it, except where it directly affected our own business. I refer to the trade in commercial magic. How many of you use magic in your business? Put your hands up." All the hands went up, except for a couple of lawyers'. Personally, I had always figured they were magicians themselves.

"O.K.," Jedson went on, "put them down. We knew that; we all use it. I use it for textiles. Hank Manning here uses nothing else for cleaning and pressing, and probably uses it for some of his dye jobs too. Wally Haight's Maple Shop uses it to assemble and finish fine furniture. Stan Robertson will tell you that Le Bon Marché's slick window displays are thrown together with spells, as well as two thirds of the merchandise in his store, especially in the kids' toy department. Now I want to ask you another question: In how many cases is the percentage of your cost charged to magic greater than your margin of profit? Think about it for a moment before answering." He paused, then said "All right—put up your hands."

Nearly as many hands went up as before.

"That's the point of the whole matter. We've got to have magic to stay in business. If anyone gets a strangle hold on magic in this community, we are all at his mercy. We would have to pay any prices that are handed us, charge the prices we are told to, and take what profits we are allowed to—or go out of business!"

The chairman interrupted him. "Just a minute, Joe. Granting that what you say is true—it is, of course—do you have any reason to feel that we are confronted with any particular emergency in the matter?"

"Yes, I do have." Joe's voice was low and very serious. "Little reasons, most of them, but they add up to convince me that someone is engaged in a conspiracy in restraint of trade." Jedson ran rapidly over the history of Ditworth's attempt to organize magicians and their clients into an association, presumably to raise the standards of the profession, and how alongside the non-profit association had suddenly appeared a capital corporation which was already in a fair way to becoming a monopoly.

"Wait a second, Joe," put in Ed Parmelee, who has a produce jobbing business. "I think that association is a fine idea. I was threatened by some rat who tried to intimidate me into letting him pick my magicians. I took it up with the association, and they took care of it; I didn't have any more trouble. I think an organization which can clamp down on racketeers is a pretty fine thing."

"You had to sign with the association to get their help, didn't you?"

"Why, yes, but that's entirely reasonable——"

"Isn't it possible that your gangster got what he wanted when you signed up?"

"Why, that seems pretty farfetched."

"I don't say," persisted Joe, "that is the explanation, but it is a distinct possibility. It would not be the first time that monopolists used goon squads with their left hands to get by coercion what their right hands could not touch. I wonder whether any of the rest of you have had similar experiences?"

It developed that several of them had. I could see them beginning to think.

One of the lawyers present formally asked a question through the chairman. "Mr. Chairman, passing for the moment from the association to Magic, Incorporated, is this corporation anything more than a union of magicians? If so, they have a legal right to organize."

Norman turned to Jedson. "Will you answer that, Joe?"

"Certainly. It is not a union at all. It is a parallel to a situation in which all the carpenters in town are employees of one contractor; you deal with that contractor or you don't build."

"Then it's a simple case of monopoly—if it is a monopoly. This state has a Little Sherman Act; you can prosecute."

"I think you will find that it is a monopoly. Have any of you noticed that there are no magicians present at today's meeting?"

We all looked around. It was perfectly true. "I think you can expect," he added, "to find magicians represented hereafter in this chamber by some executive of Magic, Incorporated. With respect to the possibility of prosecution"—he hauled a folded newspaper out of his hip pocket—"have any of you paid any attention to the governor's call for a special session of the legislature?"

Al Donahue remarked superciliously that he was too busy making a living to waste any time on the political game. It was a deliberate dig at Joe, for everybody knew that he was a committeeman, and spent quite a lot of time on civic affairs. The dig must have gotten under Joe's skin, for he said pityingly, "Al, it's a damn good thing for you that some of us are willing to spend a little time on government, or you would wake up some morning to find they had stolen the sidewalks in front of your house."

The chairman rapped for order; Joe apologized. Donahue muttered something under his breath about the whole political business being dirty, and that anyone associated with it was bound to turn crooked. I reached out for an ash tray and knocked over a glass of water, which spilled into Donahue's lap. It diverted his mind. Joe went on talking.

"Of course we knew a special session was likely for several reasons, but when they published the agenda of the call last night, I found tucked away toward the bottom an item 'Regulation of Thaumaturgy.' I couldn't believe that there was any reason to deal with such a matter in a special session unless something was up. I got on the phone last night and called a friend of mine at the capitol, a fellow committee member. She did not know anything about it, but she called me back later. Here's what she found out: The item was stuck into the agenda at the request of some of the governor's campaign backers; he has no special interest in it himself. Nobody seems to know what it is all about, but one bill on the subject has already been dropped in the hopper—" There was an interruption; somebody wanted to know what the bill said.

"I'm trying to tell you," Joe said patiently. "The bill was submitted by title alone; we won't be likely to know its contents until it is taken up in committee. But here is the title: 'A Bill to Establish Professional Standards for Thaumaturgists, Regulate the Practice of the Thaumaturgic Profession, Provide for the Appointment of a Commission to Examine, License, and Administer——' and so on. As you can see, it isn't even a proper title; it's just an omnibus onto which they can hang any sort of legislation regarding magic, including an abridgement of anti-monopoly regulation if they choose."

There was a short silence after this. I think all of us were trying to make up our minds on a subject that we were not really conversant with—politics. Presently someone spoke up and said, "What do you think we ought to do about it?"

"Well," he answered, "we at least ought to have our own representative at the capitol to protect us in the clinches. Besides that, we at least ought to be prepared to submit our own bill, if this one has any tricks in it, and bargain for the best compromise we can get. We should at least get an implementing amendment out of it that would put some real teeth into the state antitrust act, at least in so far as magic is concerned." He grinned. "That's four 'at leasts,' I think."

"Why can't the state Chamber of Commerce handle it for us? They maintain a legislative bureau."

"Sure, they have a lobby, but you know perfectly well that the state chamber doesn't see eye to eye with us little businessmen. We can't depend on them; we may actually be fighting them."

There was quite a powwow after Joe sat down. Everybody had his own ideas about what to do and tried to express them all at once. It became evident that there was no general agreement, whereupon Somers adjourned the meeting with the announcement that those interested in sending a representative to the capitol should stay. A few of the diehards like Donahue left, and the rest of us reconvened with Somers again in the chair. It was suggested that Jedson should be the one to go, and he agreed to do it.

Feldstein got up and made a speech with tears in his eyes. He wandered and did not seem to be getting anyplace, but finally he managed to get out that Jedson would need a good big war chest to do any good at the capitol, and also should be compensated for his expenses and loss of time. At that he astounded us by pulling out a roll of bills, counting out one thousand dollars, and shoving it over in front of Joe.

That display of sincerity caused him to be made finance chairman by general consent, and the subscriptions came in very nicely. I held down my natural impulses and matched Feldstein's donation, though I did wish he had not been quite so impetuous. I think Feldstein had a slight change of heart, a little later, for he cautioned Joe to be economical and not to waste a lot of money buying liquor for "those schlemiels at the capitol."

Jedson shook his head at this, and said that while he intended to pay his own expenses, he would have to have a free hand in the spending of the fund, particularly with respect to entertainment. He said the time was too short to depend on sweet reasonableness and disinterested patriotism alone—that some of those lunkheads had no more opinions than a weather vane and would vote to favor the last man they had had a drink with.

Someone made a shocked remark about bribery. "I don't intend to bribe anyone," Jedson answered with a brittle note in his voice. "If it comes to swapping bribes, we're licked to start with. I am just praying that there are still enough unpledged votes up there to make a little persuasive talking and judicious browbeating worth while."

He got his own way, but I could not help agreeing privately with Feldstein. And I made a resolution to pay a little more attention to politics thereafter; I did not even know the name of my own legislator. How did I know whether or not he was a high-caliber man or just a cheap opportunist?

And that is how Jedson, Bodie, and myself happened to find ourselves on the train, headed for the capitol.

Bodie went along because Jedson wanted a first-rate magician to play bird dog for him. He said he did not know what might turn up. I went along because I wanted to. I had never been to the capitol before, except to pass through, and was interested to see how this lawmaking business is done.

Jedson went straight to the Secretary of State's office to register as a lobbyist, while Jack and I took our baggage to the Hotel Constitution and booked some rooms. Mrs. Logan, Joe's friend the committeewoman, showed up before he got back.

Jedson had told us a great deal about Sally Logan during the train trip. He seemed to feel that she combined the shrewdness of Machiavelli with the greathearted integrity of Oliver Wendell Holmes. I was surprised at his enthusiasm, for I have often heard him grouse about women in politics.

"But you don't understand, Archie," he elaborated. "Sally isn't a woman politician, she is simply a politician, and asks no special consideration because of her sex. She can stand up and trade punches with the toughest manipulators on the Hill. What I said about women politicians is perfectly true, as a statistical generalization, but it proves nothing about any particular woman.

"It's like this: Most women in the Unites States have a shortsighted, peasant individualism resulting from the male-created romantic tradition of the last century. They were told that they were superior creatures, a little nearer to the angels than their menfolks. They were not encouraged to think, nor to assume social responsibility. It takes a strong mind to break out of that sort of conditioning, and most minds simply aren't up to it, male or female.

"Consequently, women as electors are usually suckers for romantic nonsense. They can be flattered into misusing their ballot even more easily than men. In politics their self-righteous feeling of virtue, combined with their essentially peasant training, resulted in their introducing a type of cut-rate, petty chiseling that should make Boss Tweed spin in his coffin.

"But Sally's not like that. She's got a tough mind which could reject the hokum."

"You're not in love with her, are you?"

"Who, me? Sally's happily married and has two of the best kids I know."

"What does her husband do?"

"Lawyer. One of the governor's supporters. Sally got started in politics through pinch-hitting for her husband one campaign."

"What is her official position up here"

"None. Right hand for the governor. That's her strength. Sally has never held a patronage job, nor been paid for her services."

After this build-up I was anxious to meet the paragon. When she called I spoke to her over the house phone and was about to say that I would come down to the lobby when she announced that she was coming up, and hung up. I was a little startled at the informality, not yet realizing that politicians did not regard hotel rooms as bedrooms, but as business offices.

When I let her in she said, "You're Archie Fraser, aren't you? I'm Sally Logan. Where's Joe?"

"He'll be back soon. Won't you sit down and wait?"

"Thanks." She plopped herself into a chair, took off her hat and shook out her hair. I looked her over.

I had unconsciously expected something pretty formidable in the way of a mannish matron. What I saw was a young, plump, cheerful-looking blonde, with an untidy mass of yellow hair and frank blue eyes. She was entirely feminine, not over thirty at the outside, and there was something about her that was tremendously reassuring.

She made me think of county fairs and well water and sugar cookies.

"I'm afraid this is going to be a tough proposition," she began at once. "I didn't think so, but just the same someone has a solid bloc lined up for Assembly Bill 22—that's the bill I wired Joe about. What do you boys plan to do, make a straight fight to kill it or submit a substitute bill?"

"Jedson drew up a fair-practices act with the aid of some of our Half World friends and a couple of lawyers. Would you like to see it?"

"Please. I stopped by the State Printing Office and got a few copies of the bill you are against—AB 22. We'll swap."

I was trying to translate the foreign language lawyers use when they write statutes when Jedson came in. He patted Sally's cheek without speaking, and she reached up and squeezed his hand and went on with her reading. He commenced reading over my shoulder. I gave up and let him have it. It made a set of building specifications look simple.

Sally asked, "What do you think of it, Joe?"

"Worse than I expected," he replied. "Take Paragraph 7——"

"I haven't read it yet."

"So? Well, in the first place it recognizes the association as a semi-public body like the Bar Association or the Community Chest, and permits it to initiate actions before the commission. That means that every magician had better by a damn sight belong to Ditworth's association and be careful not to offend it."

"But how can that be legal?" I asked. "It sounds unconstitutional to me—a private association like that——"

"Plenty of precedent, son. Corporations to promote world's fairs, for example. They're recognized, and even voted tax money. As for unconstitutionality, you'd have to prove that the law was not equal in application—which it isn't!—but awfully hard to prove."

"But, anyhow, a witch gets a hearing before the commission?"

"Sure, but there is the rub. The commission has very broad powers, almost unlimited powers over everything connected with magic. The bill is filled with phrases like 'reasonable and proper,' which means the sky's the limit, with nothing but the good sense and decency of the commissioners to restrain them. That's my objection to commissions in government—the law can never be equal in application under them. They have delegated legislative powers, and the law is what they say it is. You might as well face a drum-head court-martial.

"There are nine commissioners provided for in this case, six of which must be licensed magicians, first-class. I don't suppose it is necessary to point out that a few ill-advised appointments to the original commission will turn it into a tight little self-perpetuating oligarchy—through its power to license."

Sally and Joe were going over to see a legislator whom they thought might sponsor our bill, so they dropped me off at the capitol. I wanted to listen to some of the debate.

It gave me a warm feeling to climb up the big, wide steps of the statehouse. The old, ugly mass of masonry seemed to represent something tough in the character of the American people, the determination of free men to manage their own affairs. Our own current problem seemed a little smaller, not quite so overpoweringly important—still worth working on, but simply one example in a long history of the general problem of self-government.

I noticed something else as I was approaching the great bronze doors; the contractor for the outer construction of the building must have made his pile; the mix for the mortar was not richer than one to six!

I decided on the Assembly rather than the Senate because Sally said they generally put on a livelier show. When I entered the hall they were discussing a resolution to investigate the tarring and feathering the previous month of three agricultural-worker organizers up near the town of Six Points. Sally had remarked that it was on the calendar for the day, but that it would not take long because the proponents of the resolution did not really want it. However, the Central Labor Council had passed a resolution demanding it, and the labor-supported members were stuck with it.

The reason why they could only go through the motions of asking for an investigation was that the organizers were not really human beings at all, but mandrakes, a fact that the state council had not been aware of when they asked for an investigation. Since the making of mandrakes is the blackest kind of black magic, and highly illegal, they needed some way to drop it quietly. The use of mandrakes has always been opposed by organized labor, because it displaces real men—men with families to support. For the same reasons they oppose synthetic facsimiles and homunculi. But it is well known that the unions are not above using mandrakes, or mandragoras, as well as facsimiles, when it suits their purpose, such as for pickets, pressure groups, and the like. I suppose they feel justified in fighting fire with fire. Homunculi they can't use on account of their size, since they are too small to be passed off as men.

If Sally had not primed me, I would not have understood what took place. Each of the labor members got up and demanded in forthright terms a resolution to investigate. When they were all through, someone proposed that the matter be tabled until the grand jury of the county concerned held its next meeting. This motion was voted on without debate and without a roll call; although practically no members were present except those who had spoken in favor of the original resolution, the motion passed easily.

There was the usual crop of oil-industry bills on the agenda, such as you read about in the newspapers every time the legislature is in session. One of them was the next item on the day's calendar—a bill which proposed that the governor negotiate a treaty with the gnomes, under which the gnomes would aid the petroleum engineers in prospecting and, in addition, would advise humans in drilling methods so as to maintain the natural gas pressure underground needed to raise the oil to the surface. I think that is the idea, but I am no petroleum engineer.

The proponent spoke first. "Mr. Speaker," he said, "I ask for a 'Yes' vote on this bill, AB 79. It's purpose is quite simple and the advantages obvious. A very large part of the overhead cost of recovering crude oil from the ground lies in the uncertainties of prospecting and drilling. With the aid of the Little People this item can be reduced to an estimated 7 per cent of its present dollar cost, and the price of gasoline and other petroleum products to the people can be greatly lessened.

"The matter of underground gas pressure is a little more technical, but suffice it to say that it takes, in round numbers, a thousand cubic feet of natural gas to raise one barrel of oil to the surface. If we can get intelligent supervision of drilling operations far underground, where no human being can go, we can make the most economical use of this precious gas pressure.

"The only rational objection to this bill lies in whether or not we can deal with the gnomes on favorable terms. I believe that we can, for the Administration has some excellent connections in the Half World. The gnomes are willing to negotiate in order to put a stop to the present condition of chaos in which human engineers drill blindly, sometimes wrecking their homes and not infrequently violating their sacred places. They not unreasonably claim everything under the surface as their kingdom, but are willing to make any reasonable concession to abate what is to them an intolerable nuisance.

"If this treaty works out well, as it will, we can expect to arrange other treaties which will enable us to exploit all of the metal and mineral resources of this state under conditions highly advantageous to us and not hurtful to the gnomes. Imagine, if you please, having a gnome with his X-ray eyes peer into a mountainside and locate a rich vein of gold for you!"

It seemed very reasonable, except that, having once seen the king of the gnomes, I would not trust him very far, unless Mrs. Jennings did the negotiating.

As soon as the proponent sat down, another member jumped up and just as vigorously denounced it. He was older than most of the members, and I judged him to be a country lawyer. His accent placed him in the northern part of the state, well away from the oil country. "Mr. Speaker," he bellowed, "I ask for a vote of 'No'! Who would dream that an American legislature would stoop to such degrading nonsense? Have any of you ever seen a gnome? Have you any reason to believe that gnomes exist? This is just a cheap piece of political chicanery to do the public out of its proper share of the natural resources of our great state—"

He was interrupted by a question. "Does the honorable member from Lincoln County mean to imply that he has no belief in magic? Perhaps he does not believe in the radio or the telephone either."

"Not at all. If the Chair will permit, I will state my position so clearly that even my respected colleagues on the other side of the house will understand it. There are certain remarkable developments in human knowledge in general use which are commonly referred to by the laity as magic. These principles are well understood and are taught, I am happy to say, in our great publicly owned institutions for higher learning. I have every respect for the legitimate practitioners thereof. But, as I understand it, although I am not myself a practitioner of the great science, there is nothing in it that requires a belief in the Little People.

"But let us stipulate, for the sake of argument, that the Little People do exist. Is that any reason to pay them blackmail? Should the citizens of this commonwealth pay cumshaw to the denizens of the underworld—" He waited for his pun to be appreciated. It wasn't. "—for that which is legally and rightfully ours? If this ridiculous principle is pushed to its logical conclusion, the farmer and dairymen I am proud to number among my constituents will be required to pay toll to the elves before they can milk their cows!"

Someone slid into the seat beside me. I glanced around, saw that it was Jedson, and questioned him with my eyes. "Nothing doing now," he whispered. "We've got some time to kill and might as well do it here"—and he turned to the debate.

Somebody had gotten up to reply to the old duck with the Daniel Webster complex. "Mr. Speaker, if the honored member is quite through with his speech—I did not quite catch what office he is running for!—I would like to invite the attention of this body to the precedented standing in jurisprudence of elements of every nature, not only in Mosaic law, Roman law, the English common law, but also in the appellate court of our neighboring state to the south. I am confident that anyone possessing even an elementary knowledge of the law will recognize the case I have in mind without citation, but for the benefit of——"

"Mr. Speaker! I move to amend by striking out the last word."

"A strategem to gain the floor," Joe whispered.

"Is it the purpose of the honorable member who preceded me to imply——"

It went on and on. I turned to Jedson and asked, "I can't figure out this chap who is speaking; awhile ago he was hollering about cows. What's he afraid of, religious prejudices?"

"Partly that; he's from a very conservative district. But he's lined up with the independent oilmen. They don't want the state setting the terms; they think they can do better dealing with the gnomes directly."

"But what interest has he got in oil? There's no oil in his district."

"No. But there is outdoor advertising. The same holding company that controls the so-called independent oilmen holds a voting trust in the Countryside Advertising Corporation. And that can be awful important to him around election time."

The Speaker looked our way, and an assistant sergeant at arms threaded his way toward us. We shut up. Someone moved the order of the day, and the oil bill was put aside for one of the magic bills that had already come out of committee. This was a bill to outlaw every sort of magic, witchcraft, thaumaturgy.

No one spoke for it but the proponent, who launched into a diatribe that was more scholarly than logical. He quoted extensively from Blackstone's *Commentaries* and the records of the Massachusetts trials, and finished up with his head thrown back, one finger waving wildly to heaven and shouting. "'Thou shalt not suffer a witch to live!'"

No one bothered to speak against it; it was voted on immediately without roll call, and, to my complete bewilderment, passed without a single nay! I turned to Jedson and found him smiling at the expression on my face.

"It doesn't mean a thing, Archie," he said quietly.

"Huh?"

"He's a party wheel horse who had to introduce that bill to please a certain bloc of his constituents."

"You mean he doesn't believe in the bill himself?"

"Oh no, he believes in it all right, but he also knows it is hopeless. It has evidently been agreed to let him pass it over here in the Assembly this session so that he would have something to take home to his people. Now it will go to the senate committee and die there; nobody will ever hear of it again."

I guess my voice carries too well, for my reply got us a really dirty look from the Speaker. We got up hastily and left.

Once outside I asked what had happened that he was back so soon. "He would not touch it," he told me. "Said that he couldn't afford to antagonize the association."

"Does that finish us?"

"Not at all. Sally and I are going to see another member right after lunch. He's tied up in a committee meeting at the moment."

We stopped in a restaurant where Jedson had arranged to meet Sally Logan. Jedson ordered lunch, and I had a couple of cans of devitalized beer, insisting on their bringing it to the booth in the unopened containers. I don't like to get even a little bit tipsy, although I like to drink. On another occasion I had paid for the wizard-processed liquor and had received intoxicating liquor instead. Hence the unopened containers.

I sat there, staring into my glass and thinking about what I had heard that morning, especially about the bill to outlaw all magic. The more I thought about it the better the notion seemed. The country had gotten along all right in the old days before magic had become popular and commercially widespread. It was unquestionably a headache in many ways, even leaving out our present troubles with racketeers and monopolists. Finally I expressed my opinion to Jedson.

But he disagreed. According to him prohibition never does work in any field. He said that anything which can be supplied and which people want will be supplied—law or no law. To prohibit magic would simply be to turn over the field to the crooks and the black magicians.

"I see the drawbacks of magic as well as you do," he went on, "but it is like firearms. Certainly guns made it possible for almost anyone to commit murder and get away with it. But once they were invented the damage was done. All you can do is to try to cope with it. Things like the Sullivan Act—they didn't keep the crooks from carrying guns and using them; they simply took guns out of the hands of honest people.

"It's the same with magic. If you prohibit it, you take from decent people the enormous boons to be derived from a knowledge of the great arcane laws, while the nasty, harmful secrets hidden away in black grimoires and red grimoires will still be bootlegged to anyone who will pay the price and has no respect for law.

"Personally, I don't believe there was any less black magic practiced between, say, 1750 and 1950 than there is now, or was before then. Take a look at Pennsylvania and the hex country. Take a look at the Deep South. But since that time we have begun to have the advantages of white magic too."

Sally came in, spotted us, and slid into one side of the booth. "My," she said with a sigh of relaxation, "I've just fought my way across the lobby of the Constitution. The 'third house' is certainly out in full force this trip. I've never seen 'em so thick, especially the women."

"Third house?" I said.

"She means lobbyists, Archie," Jedson explained. "Yes, I noticed them. I'd like to make a small bet that two thirds of them are synthetic."

"I *thought* I didn't recognize many of them," Sally commented. "Are you sure, Joe?"

"Not entirely. But Bodie agrees with me. He says that the women are almost all mandrakes, or androids of some sort. Real women are never quite so perfectly beautiful—nor so tractable. I've got him checking on them now."

"In what way?"

"He says he can spot the work of most of the magicians capable of that high-powered stuff. If possible we want to prove that all these androids were made by Magic, Incorporated—though I'm not sure just what use we can make of the fact.

"Bodie has even located some zombies," he added.

"Not really!" exclaimed Sally. She wrinkled her nose and looked disgusted. "Some people have odd tastes."

They started discussing aspects of politics that I know nothing about, while Sally put away a very sizable lunch topped off by a fudge ice-cream cake slice. But I noticed that she ordered from the left-hand side of the menu—all vanishing items, like the alcohol in my beer.

I found out more about the situation as they talked. When a bill is submitted to the legislature, it is first referred to a committee for hearings. Ditworth's bill, AB 22, had been referred to the Committee on Professional Standards. Over in the Senate an identical bill had turned up and had been referred by the lieutenant governor, who presides in the Senate, to the Committee on Industrial Practices.

Our immediate object was to find a sponsor for our bill; if possible, one for each house, and preferably sponsors who were members, in their respective houses, of the committees concerned. All of this needed to be done before Ditworth's bills came up for hearing.

I went with them to see their second-choice sponsor for the Assembly. He was not on the Professional Standards Committee, but he was on the Ways and Means Committee, which meant that he carried a lot of weight in any committee.

He was a pleasant chap named Spence—Luther B. Spence—and I could see that he was quite anxious to please Sally—for past favors, I suppose. But they had no more luck with him than with their first-choice man. He said that he did not have time to fight for our bill, as the chairman of the Ways and Means Committee was sick and he was chairman pro tem.

Sally put it to him flatly. "Look here, Luther, when you have needed a hand in the past, you've gotten it from me. I hate to remind a man of obligations, but you will recall that matter of the vacancy last year on the Fish and Game Commission. Now I want action on this matter, and not excuses!"

Spence was plainly embarrassed. "Now, Sally, please don't feel like that. You're getting your feathers up over nothing. You know I'll always do anything I can for you, but you don't really need this, and it would necessitate my neglecting things that I can't afford to neglect."

"What do you mean, I don't need it?"

"I mean you should not worry about AB 22. It's a cinch bill."

Jedson explained that term to me later. A cinch bill, he said, was a bill introduced for tactical reasons. The sponsors never intended to try to get it enacted into law, but simply used it as a bargaining point. It's like an "asking price" in a business deal.

"Are you sure of that?"

"Why, yes, I think so. The word has been passed around that there is another bill coming up that won't have the bugs in it that this bill has."

After we left Spence's office, Jedson said, "Sally, I hope Spence is right, but I don't trust Ditworth's intentions. He's out to get a stranglehold on the industry. I know it!"

"Luther usually has the correct information, Joe."

"Yes, that is no doubt true, but this is a little out of his line. Anyhow, thanks, kid. You did your best."

"Call on me if there is anything else, Joe. And come out to dinner before you go; you haven't seen Bill or the kids yet."

"I won't forget."

Jedson finally gave up as impractical trying to submit our bill, and concentrated on the committees handling Ditworth's bills. I did not see much of him. He would go out at four in the afternoon to a cocktail party and get back to the hotel at three in the morning, bleary-eyed, with progress to report.

He woke me up the fourth night and announced jubilantly, "It's in the bag, Archie!"

"You killed those bills?"

"Not quite. I couldn't manage that. But they will be reported out of committee so amended that we won't care if they do pass. Furthermore, the amendments are different in each committee."

"Well, what of that?"

"That means that even if they do pass their respective houses they will have to go to conference committee to have their differences ironed out, then back for final passage in each house. The chances of that this late in a short session are negligible. Those bills are dead."

Jedson's predictions were justified. The bills came out of committee with a "do pass" recommendation late Saturday evening. That was the actual time; the statehouse clock had been stopped forty-eight hours before to permit first and second readings of an administration "must" bill. Therefore it was officially Thursday. I know that sounds cockeyed, and it is, but I am told that every legislature in the country does it toward the end of a crowded session.

The important point is that, Thursday or Saturday, the session would adjourn sometime that night. I watched Ditworth's bill come up in the Assembly. It was passed, without debate, in the amended form. I sighed with relief. About midnight Jedson joined me and reported that the same thing had happened in the Senate. Sally was on watch in the conference committee room, just to make sure that the bills stayed dead.

Joe and I remained on watch in our respective houses. There was probably no need for it, but it made us feel easier. Shortly before two in the morning Bodie came in and said we were to meet Jedson and Sally outside the conference committee room.

"What's that?" I said, immediately all nerves. "Has something slipped?"

"No, it's all right and it's all over. Come on."

Joe answered my question, as I hurried up with Bodie trailing, before I could ask it. "It's O.K., Archie. Sally was present when the committee adjourned *sine die,* without acting on those bills. It's all over; we've won!"

We went over to the bar across the street to have a drink in celebration.

In spite of the late hour the bar was moderately crowded. Lobbyists, local politicians, legislative attachés, all the swarm of camp followers who throng the capitol whenever the legislature is sitting—all such were still up and around, and many of them had picked this bar as a convenient place to wait for news of adjournment.

We were lucky to find a stool at the bar for Sally. We three men made a tight little cluster around her and tried to get the attention of the overworked bartender. We had just managed to place our orders when a young man tapped on the shoulder of the customer on the stool to the right of Sally. He immediately got down and left. I nudged Bodie to tell him to take the seat.

Sally turned to Joe. "Well, it won't be long now. There go the sergeants at arms." She nodded toward the young man, who was repeating the process farther down the line.

"What does that man?" I asked Joe.

"It means they are getting along toward the final vote on the bill they were waiting on. They've gone to 'call of the house' now, and the Speaker has ordered the sergeant at arms to send his deputies out to arrest absent members."

"Arrest them?" I was a little bit shocked.

"Only technically. You see, the Assembly has had to stall until the Senate was through with this bill, and most of the members have wandered out for a bit to eat, or drink. Now they are ready to vote, so they round them up."

A fat man took a stool near us which had just been vacated by a member. Sally said, "Hello, Don."

He took a cigar from his mouth and said, "How are yuh, Sally? What's new? Say, I thought you were interested in that bill on magic?"

We were all four alert at once. "I am," Sally admitted. "What about it?"

"Well, then, you had better get over there. They're voting on it right away. Didn't you notice the 'call of the house'?"

I think we set a new record getting across the street, with Sally leading the field in spite of her plumpness. I was asking Jedson how it could be possible, and he shut me up with, "I don't know, man! We'll have to see."

We managed to find seats on the main floor back of the rail. Sally beckoned to one of the pages she knew and sent him up to the clerk's desk for a copy of the bill that was pending. In front of the rail the Assemblymen gathered in groups. There was a crowd around the desk of the administration floor leader and a smaller cluster around the floor leader of the opposition. The whips had individual members buttonholed here and there, arguing with them in tense whispers.

The page came back with the copy of the bill. It was an appropriation bill for the Middle Counties Improvement Project—the last of the "must" bills for which the session had been called—but pasted to it, as a rider, *was Ditworth's bill in its original, most damnable form!*

It had been added as an amendment in the Senate, probably as a concession to Ditworth's stooges in order to obtain their votes to make up the two-thirds majority necessary to pass the appropriation bill to which it had been grafted.

The vote came almost at once. It was evident, early in the roll call, that the floor leader had his majority in hand and that the bill would pass. When the clerk announced its passage, a motion to adjourn *sine die* was offered by the opposition floor leader and it was carried unanimously. The Speaker called the two floor leaders to his desk and instructed them to wait on the governor and the presiding officer of the Senate with notice of adjournment.

The crack of his gavel released us from stunned immobility. We shambled out.

We got in to see the governor late the next morning. The appointment, squeezed into an overcrowded calendar, was simply a concession to Sally and another evidence of the high regard in which she was held around the capitol. For it was evident that he did not want to see us and did not have time to see us.

But he greeted Sally affectionately and listened patiently while Jedson explained in a few words why we thought the combined Ditworth-Middle Counties bill should be vetoed.

The circumstances were not favorable to reasoned exposition. The governor was interrupted by two calls that he had to take, one from his director of finance and one from Washington. His personal secretary came in once and shoved a memorandum under his eyes, at which the old man looked worried, then scrawled something on it and handed it back. I could tell that his attention was elsewhere for some minutes after that.

When Jedson stopped talking, the governor sat for a moment, looking down at his blotter pad, an expression of deep-rooted weariness on his face. Then he answered in slow words, "No, Mr. Jedson, I can't see it. I regret as much as you do that this business of the regulation of magic has been tied in with an entirely different matter. But I cannot veto part of a bill and sign the rest—even though the bill includes two widely separated subjects.

"I appreciate the work you did to help elect my administration"—I could see Sally's hand in that remark—"and wish that we could agree in this. But the Middle Counties Project is something that I have worked toward since my inauguration. I hope and believe that it will be the means whereby the most depressed area in our state can work out its economic problems without further grants of public money. If I thought that the amendment concerning magic would actually do a grave harm to the state——"

He paused for a moment. "But I don't. When Mrs. Logan called me this morning I had my legislative counsel analyze the bill. I agree that the bill is unnecessary, but it seems to do nothing more than add a little more bureaucratic red tape. That's not good, but we manage to do business under a lot of it; a little more can't wreck things."

I butted in—rudely, I suppose—but I was all worked up. "But, Your Excellency, if you would just take time to examine this matter yourself, in detail, you would see how much damage it will do!"

I would not have been surprised if he had flared back at me. Instead, he indicated a file basket that was stacked high and spilling over. "Mr. Fraser, there you see fifty-seven bills passed by this session of the legislature. Every one of them has some defect. Every one of them is of vital importance to some, or all, of the people of this state. Some of them are as long to read as an ordinary novel. In the next nine days I must decide what ones shall become law and what ones must wait for revision at the next regular session. During that nine days at least a thousand people will want me to see them about some one of those bills——"

His aide stuck his head in the door. "Twelve-twenty, chief! You're on the air in forty minutes."

The governor nodded absently and stood up. "You will excuse me? I'm expected at a luncheon." He turned to his aide, who was getting out his hat and gloves from a closet. "You have the speech, Jim?"

"Of course, sir."

"Just a minute!" Sally had cut in. "Have you taken your tonic?"

"Not yet."

"You're not going off to one of those luncheons without it!" She ducked into his private washroom and came out with a medicine bottle. Joe and I bowed out as quickly as possible.

Outside I started fuming to Jedson about the way we had been given the run-around, as I saw it. I made some remark about dunderheaded, compromising politicians when Joe cut me short.

"Shut up, Archie! Try running a state sometime instead of a small business and see how easy you find it!"

I shut up.

Bodie was waiting for us in the lobby of the capitol. I could see that he was excited about something, for he flipped away a cigarette and rushed toward us. "Look!" he commanded. "Down there!"

We followed the direction of his finger and saw two figures just going out the big doors. One was Ditworth, the other was a well-known lobbyist with whom he had worked. "What about it?" Joe demanded.

"I was standing here behind this phone booth, leaning against the wall and catching a cigarette. As you can see, from here that big mirror reflects the bottom of the rotunda stairs. I kept an eye on it for you fellows. I noticed this lobbyist, Sims, coming downstairs by himself, but he was gesturing as if he were talking to somebody. That made me curious, so I looked around the corner of the booth and saw him directly. He was not alone; he was with Ditworth. I looked back at the mirror and he appeared to be alone. *Ditworth cast no reflection in the mirror!*"

Jedson snapped his fingers. "A demon!" he said in an amazed voice. "And I never suspected it!"

I AM SURPRISED THAT MORE suicides don't occur on trains. When a man is down, I know of nothing more depressing than staring at the monotonous scenery and listening to the maddening *lickety-tock* of the rails. In a way I was glad to have this new development of Ditworth's inhuman status to think about; it kept my mind off poor old Feldstein and his thousand dollars.

Startling as it was to discover that Ditworth was a demon, it made no real change in the situation except to explain the efficiency and speed with which we had been outmaneuvered and to confirm as a certainty our belief that the racketeers and Magic, Incorporated, were two heads of the same beast. But we had no way of proving that Ditworth was a Half World monster. If we tried to haul him into court for a test, he was quite capable of lying low and sending out a facsimile, or a mandrake, built to look like him and immune to the mirror test.

We dreaded going back and reporting our failure to the committee—at least I did. But at least we were spared that. The Middle Counties Act carried an emergency clause which put it into effect the day it was signed. Ditworth's bill, as an amendment, went into action with the same speed. The newspapers on sale at the station when we got off the train carried the names of the new commissioners for thaumaturgy.

Nor did the commission waste any time in making its power felt. They announced their intention of raising the standards of magical practice in all fields, and stated that new and more thorough examinations would be prepared at once. The association formerly headed by Ditworth opened a coaching school in which practicing magicians could take a refresher course in thaumaturgic principles and arcane law. In accordance with the high principles set forth in their charter, the school was not restricted to members of the association.

That sounds bighearted of the association. It wasn't. They managed to convey a strong impression in their classes that membership in the association would be a big help in passing the new examinations. Nothing you could put your finger on to take into court—just a continuous impression. The association grew.

A couple of weeks later all licenses were canceled and magicians were put on a day-to-day basis in their practice, subject to call for reexamination at a day's notice. A few of the outstanding holdouts against signing up with Magic, Incorporated, were called up, examined, and licenses refused them. The squeeze was on. Mrs. Jennings quietly withdrew from any practice. Bodie came around to see me; I had an uncompleted contract with him involving some apartment houses.

"Here's your contract, Archie," he said bitterly. "I'll need some time to pay the penalties for noncompletion; my bond was revoked when they canceled the licenses."

I took the contract and tore it in two. "Forget that talk about penalties," I told him. "You take your examinations and we'll write a new contract."

He laughed unhappily. "Don't be a Pollyanna."

I changed my tack. "What are you going to do? Sign up with Magic, Incorporated?"

He straightened himself up. "I've never temporized with demons; I won't start now."

"Good boy," I said. "Well, if the eating gets uncertain, I reckon we can find a job of some sort here for you."

IT WAS A GOOD THING that Bodie had some money saved, for I was a little too optimistic in my offer. Magic, Incorporated, moved quickly into the second phase of their squeeze, and it began to be a matter of speculation as to whether I myself would eat regularly. There were still quite a number of licensed magicians in town who were not employed by Magic, Incorporated—it would have been an evident, actionable frame-up to freeze out everyone—but those available were all incompetent bunglers, not fit to mix a philter. There was no competent, legal magical assistance to be gotten at any price—except through Magic, Incorporated.

I was forced to fall back on old-fashioned methods in every respect. Since I don't use much magic in any case, it was possible for me to do that, but it was the difference between making money and losing money.

I had put Feldstein on as a salesman after his agency folded up under him. He turned out to be a crackajack and helped to reduce the losses. He could smell a profit even farther than I could—farther than Dr. Worthington could smell a witch.

But most of the other businessmen around me were simply forced to capitulate. Most of them used magic in at least one phase of their business; they had their choice of signing a contract with Magic, Incorporated, or closing their doors. They had wives and kids—they signed.

The fees for thaumaturgy were jacked up until they were all the traffic would bear, to the point where it was just cheaper to do business with magic than without it. The magicians got none of the new profits; it all stayed with the corporation. As a matter of fact, the magicians got less of the proceeds than when they had operated independently, but they took what they could get and were glad of the chance to feed their families.

Jedson was hard hit—disastrously hit. He held out, naturally, preferring honorable bankruptcy to dealing with demons, but he used magic throughout his business. He was through. They started by disqualifying August Welker, his foreman, then cut off the rest of his resources. It was intimated that Magic, Incorporated, did not care to deal with him, even had he wished it.

WE WERE ALL OVER AT Mrs. Jennings's late one afternoon for tea—myself, Jedson, Bodie, and Dr. Royce Worthington, the witch smeller. We tried to keep the conversation away from our troubles, but we just could not do it. Anything that was said led back somehow to Ditworth and his damnable monopoly.

After Jack Bodie had spent ten minutes explaining carefully and mendaciously that he really did not mind being out of witchcraft, that he did not have any real talent for it, and had only taken it up to please his old man, I tried to change the subject. Mrs. Jennings had been listening to Jack with such pity and compassion in her eyes that I wanted to bawl myself.

I turned to Jedson and said inanely, "How is Miss Megeath?"

She was the white witch from Jersey City, the one who did creative magic in textiles. I had no special interest in her welfare.

He looked up with a start. "Ellen? She's . . . she's all right. They took her license away a month ago," he finished lamely.

That was not the direction I wanted the talk to go. I turned it again. "Did she ever manage to do that whole-garment stunt?"

He brightened a little. "Why, yes, she did—once. Didn't I tell you about it?" Mrs. Jennings showed polite curiosity, for which I silently thanked her. Jedson explained to the others what they had been trying to accomplish. "She really succeeded too well," he continued. "Once she had started, she kept right on, and we could not bring her out of her trance. She turned out over thirty thousand little striped sports dresses, all the same size and pattern. My lofts were loaded with them. Nine tenths of them will melt away before I dispose of them.

"But she won't try it again," he added. "Too hard on her health."

"How?" I inquired.

"Well, she lost ten pounds doing that one stunt. She's not hardy enough for magic. What she really needs is to go out to Arizona and lie around in the sun for a year. I wish to the Lord I had the money. I'd send her."

I cocked an eyebrow at him. "Getting interested, Joe?" Jedson is an inveterate bachelor, but it pleases me to pretend otherwise. He generally plays up, but this time he was downright surly. It showed the abnormal state of nerves he was in.

"Oh, for cripes' sake, Archie! Excuse me, Mrs. Jennings! But can't I take a normal humane interest in a person without you seeing an ulterior motive in it?"

"Sorry."

"That's all right." He grinned. "I shouldn't be so touchy. Anyhow, Ellen and I have cooked up an invention between us that might be a solution for all of us. I'd been intending to show it to all of you just as soon as we had a working model. Look, folks!" He drew what appeared to be a fountain pen out of a vest pocket and handed it to me.

"What is it? A pen?"

"No."

"A fever thermometer?"

"No. Open it up."

I unscrewed the cap and found that it contained a miniature parasol. It opened and closed like a real umbrella, and was about three inches across when opened. It reminded me of one of those clever little Japanese favors one sometimes gets at parties, except that it seemed to be made of oiled silk and metal instead of tissue paper and bamboo.

"Pretty," I said, "and very clever. What's it good for?"

"Dip it in water."

I looked around for some. Mrs. Jennings poured some into an empty cup, and I dipped it in.

It seemed to crawl in my hands.

In less than thirty seconds I was holding a full-sized umbrella in my hands and looking as silly as I felt. Bodie smacked a palm with a fist.

"It's a lulu, Joe! I wonder why someone didn't think of it before."

Jedson accepted congratulations with a fatuous grin, then added, "That's not all—look." He pulled a small envelope out of a pocket and produced a tiny transparent raincoat, suitable for a six-inch doll. "This is the same gag. And this." He hauled out a pair of rubber overshoes less than an inch long. "A man could wear these as a watch fob, or a woman could carry them on a charm bracelet. Then, with either the umbrella or the raincoat, one need never be caught in the rain. The minute the rain hits them, presto!—full size. When they dry out they shrink up."

We passed them around from hand to hand and admired them. Joe went on. "Here's what I have in mind. This business needs a magician—that's you, Jack—and a merchandiser—that's you, Archie. It has two major stockholders: that's Ellen and me. She can go take the rest cure she needs, and I'll retire and resume my studies, same as I always wanted to do."

My mind immediately started turning over the commercial possibilities, then I suddenly saw the hitch. "Wait a minute, Joe. We can't set up business in this state."

"No."

"It will take some capital to move out of the state. How are you fixed? Frankly, I don't believe I could raise a thousand dollars if I liquidated."

He made a wry face. "Compared with me you are rich."

I got up and began wandering nervously around the room. We would just have to raise the money somehow. It was too good a thing to be missed, and would rehabilitate all of us. It was clearly patentable, and I could see commercial possibilities that would never occur to Joe. Tents for camping, canoes, swimming suits, traveling gear of every sort. We had a gold mine.

Mrs. Jennings interrupted in her sweet and gentle voice. "I am not sure it will be too easy to find a state in which to operate."

"Excuse me, what did you say?"

"Dr. Royce and I have been making some inquiries. I am afraid you will find the rest of the country about as well sewed up as this state."

"What! Forty-eight states?"

"Demons don't have the same limitations in time that we have."

That brought me up short. Ditworth again.

Gloom settled down on us like fog. We discussed it from every angle and came right back to where we had started. It was no help to have a clever, new business; Ditworth had us shut out of every business. There was an awkward silence.

I finally broke it with an outburst that surprised myself. "Look here!" I exclaimed. "This situation is intolerable. Let's quit kidding ourselves and admit it. As long as Ditworth is in control we're whipped. Why don't we do something?"

Jedson gave me a pained smile. "God knows I'd like to, Archie, if I could think of anything useful to do."

"But we know who our enemy is—Ditworth! Let's tackle him—legal or not, fair means or dirty!"

"But that is just the point. Do we know our enemy? To be sure, we know he is a demon, but what demon, and where? Nobody has seen him in weeks."

"Huh? But I thought just the other day——"

"Just a dummy, a hollow shell. The real Ditworth is somewhere out of sight."

"But, look, if he is a demon, can't he be invoked, and compelled—"

Mrs. Jennings answered this time. "Perhaps—though it's uncertain and dangerous. But we lack one essential—his name. To invoke a demon you must know his real name, otherwise he will not obey you, no matter how powerful the incantation. I have been searching the Half World for weeks, but I have not learned that necessary name."

Dr. Worthington cleared his throat with a rumble as deep as a cement mixer, and volunteered, "My abilities are at your disposal, if I can help abate this nuisance——"

Mrs. Jennings thanked him. "I don't see how we can use you as yet, Doctor. I knew we could depend on you."

Jedson said suddenly, "White prevails over black."

She answered, "Certainly."

"Everywhere?"

"Everywhere, since darkness is the absence of light."

He went on, "It is not good for the white to wait on the black."

"It is not good."

"With my brother Royce to help, we might carry light into darkness."

She considered this. "It is possible, yes. But very dangerous."

"You have been there?"

"On occasion. But you are not I, nor are these others."

Everyone seemed to be following the thread of the conversation but me. I interrupted with, "Just a minute, please. Would it be too much to explain what you are talking about?"

"There was no rudeness intended, Archibald," said Mrs. Jennings in a voice that made it all right. "Joseph has suggested that, since we are stalemated here, we make a sortie into the Half World, smell out this demon, and attack him on his home ground."

It took me a moment to grasp the simple audacity of the scheme. Then I said, "Fine! Let's get on with it. When do we start?"

They lapsed back into a professional discussion that I was unable to follow. Mrs. Jennings dragged out several musty volumes and looked up references on points that were sheer Sanskrit to me. Jedson borrowed her almanac, and he and the doctor stepped out into the back yard to observe the moon.

Finally it settled down into an argument—or rather discussion; there could be no argument, as they all deferred to Mrs. Jennings's judgment concerning liaison. There seemed to be no satisfactory way to maintain contact with the real world, and Mrs. Jennings was unwilling to start until it was worked out. The difficulty was this: not being black magicians, not having signed a compact with Old Nick, they were not citizens of the Dark Kingdom and could not travel through it with certain impunity.

Bodie turned to Jedson. "How about Ellen Megeath?" he inquired doubtfully.

"Ellen? Why, yes, of course. She would do it. I'll telephone her. Mrs. Jennings, do any of your neighbors have a phone?"

"Never mind," Bodie told him, "just think about her for a few minutes so that I can get a line—" He stared at Jedson's face for a moment, then disappeared suddenly.

Perhaps three minutes later Ellen Megeath dropped lightly out of nothing. "Mr. Bodie will be along in a few minutes," she said. "He stopped to buy a pack of cigarettes." Jedson took her over and presented her to Mrs. Jennings. She did look sickly, and I could understand Jedson's concern. Every few minutes she would swallow and choke a little, as if bothered by an enlarged thyroid.

As soon as Jack was back they got right down to details. He had explained to Ellen what they planned to do, and she was entirely willing. She insisted that one more session of magic would do her no harm. There was no advantage in waiting; they prepared to depart at once. Mrs. Jennings related the marching orders. "Ellen, you will need to follow me in trance, keeping in close rapport. I think you will find that couch near the fireplace a good place to rest your body. Jack, you will remain here and guard the portal." The chimney of Mrs. Jennings's livingroom fireplace was to be used as most convenient. "You will keep in touch with us through Ellen."

"But, Granny, I'll be needed in the Half——"

"No, Jack." She was gently firm. "You are needed here much more. Someone has to guard the way and help us back, you know. Each to his task."

He muttered a bit, but gave in. She went on, "I think that is all. Ellen and Jack here; Joseph, Royce, and myself to make the trip. You will have nothing to do but wait, Archibald, but we won't be longer than ten minutes, world time, if we are to come back." She bustled away toward the kitchen, saying something about the unguent and calling back to Jack to have the candles ready. I hurried after her.

"What do you mean," I demanded, "about me having nothing to do but wait? I'm going along!"

She turned and looked at me before replying, troubled concern in her magnificent eyes. "I don't see how that can be, Archibald."

Jedson had followed us and now took me by the arm. "See here, Archie, do be sensible. It's utterly out of the question. You're not a magician."

I pulled away from him. "Neither are you."

"Not in a technical sense, perhaps, but I know enough to be useful. Don't be a stubborn fool, man; if you come, you'll simply handicap us."

That kind of argument is hard to answer and manifestly unfair. "How?" I persisted.

"Hell's bells, Archie, you're young and strong and willing, and there is no one I would rather have at my back in a roughhouse, but this is not a job for courage, or even intelligence alone. It calls for special knowledge and experience."

"Well," I answered, "Mrs. Jennings has enough of that for a regiment. But—if you'll pardon me, Mrs. Jennings!—she is old and feeble. I'll be her muscles if her strength fails."

Joe looked faintly amused, and I could have kicked him. "But that is not what is required in——"

Dr. Worthington's double-bass rumble interrupted him from somewhere behind us. "It occurs to me, brother, that there may possibly be a use for our young friend's impetuous ignorance. There are times when wisdom is too cautious."

Mrs. Jennings put a stop to it. "Wait—all of you," she commanded, and trotted over to a kitchen cupboard. This she opened, moved aside a package of rolled oats, and took down a small leather sack. It was filled with slender sticks.

She cast them on the floor, and the three of them huddled around the litter, studying the patterns. "Cast them again," Joe insisted. She did so.

I saw Mrs. Jennings and the doctor nod solemn agreement to each other. Jedson shrugged and turned away. Mrs. Jennings addressed me, concern in her eyes. "You will go," she said softly. "It is not safe, but you will go."

We wasted no more time. The unguent was heated and we took turns rubbing it on each other's backbone. Bodie, as gatekeeper, sat in the midst of his penacles, mekagrans, and runes, and intoned monotonously from the great book. Worthington elected to go in his proper person, ebony in a breechcloth, parasymbols scribed on him from head to toe, his grandfather's head cradled in an elbow.

There was some discussion before they could decide on a final form for Joe, and the metamorphosis was checked and changed several times. He finished up with paper-thin gray flesh stretched over an obscenely distorted skull, a sloping back, the thin flanks of an animal, and a long, bony tail, which he twitched incessantly. But the whole composition was near enough to human to create a revulsion much greater than would be the case for a more outlandish shape. I gagged at the sight of him, but he was pleased. "There!" he exclaimed in a voice like scratched tin. "You'd done a beautiful job, Mrs. Jennings. Asmodeus would not know me from his own nephew."

"I trust not," she said. "Shall we go?"

"How about Archie?"

"It suits me to leave him as he is."

"Then how about your own transformation?"

"I'll take care of that," she answered, somewhat tartly. "Take your places."

Mrs. Jennings and I rode double on the same broom, with me in front, facing the candle stuck in the straws. I've noticed All Hallow's Eve decorations which show the broom with the handle forward and the brush trailing. That is a mistake. Custom is important in these matters. Royce and Joe were to follow close behind us. Seraphin leaped quickly to his mistress' shoulder and settled himself, his whiskers quivering with eagerness.

Bodie pronounced the word, our candle flared up high, and we were off. I was frightened nearly to panic, but tried not to show it as I clung to the broom. The fireplace gaped at us, and swelled to a monster arch. The fire within roared up like a burning forest and swept us along with it. As we swirled up I caught a glimpse of a salamander dancing among the flames, and felt sure that it was my own—the one that had honored me with its approval and sometimes graced my new fireplace. It seemed a good omen.

We had left the portal far behind—if the word "behind" can be used in a place where directions are symbolic—the shrieking din of the fire was no longer with us, and I was beginning to regain some part of my nerve. I felt a reassuring hand at my waist, and turned my head to speak to Mrs. Jennings.

I nearly fell off the broom.

When we left the house there had mounted behind me an old, old woman, a shrunken, wizened body kept alive by an indomitable spirit. She whom I now saw was a young woman, strong, perfect, and vibrantly beautiful. There is no way to describe her; she was without defect of any sort, and imagination could suggest no improvement.

Have you ever seen the bronze Diana of the Woods? She was something like that, except that metal cannot catch the live, dynamic beauty that I saw.

But it was the same woman!

Mrs. Jennings—Amanda Todd, that was—at perhaps her twenty-fifth year, when she had reached the full maturity of her gorgeous womanhood, and before time had softened the focus of perfection.

I forgot to be afraid. I forgot everything except that I was in the presence of the most compelling and dynamic female I had ever known. I forgot that she was at least sixty years older than myself, and that her present form was simply a triumph of sorcery. I suppose if anyone had asked me at that time if I were in love with Amanda Jennings, I would have answered, "Yes!" But at the time my thoughts were much too confused to be explicit. She was there, and that was sufficient.

She smiled, and her eyes were warm with understanding. She spoke, and her voice was the voice I knew, even though it was rich contralto in place of the accustomed clear, thin soprano. "Is everything all right, Archie?"

"Yes," I answered in a shaky voice. "Yes, Amanda, everything is all right!"

As for the Half World——How can I describe a place that has no single matching criterion with what I have known? How can I speak of things for which no words have been invented? One tells of things unknown in terms of things which are known. Here there is no relationship by which to link; all is irrelevant. All I can hope to do is tell how matters affected my human senses, how events influenced my human emotions, knowing that there are two falsehoods involved—the falsehood I saw and felt, and the falsehood that I tell.

I have discussed this matter with Jedson, and he agrees with me that the difficulty is insuperable, yet some things may be said with a partial element of truth—truth of a sort, with respect to how the Half World impinged on me.

There is one striking difference between the real world and the Half World. In the real world there are natural laws which persist through changes of custom and culture; in the Half World only custom has any degree of persistence, and of natural law there is none. Imagine, if you please, a condition in which the head of a state might repeal the law of gravitation and have his decree really effective—a place where King

Canute could order back the sea and have the waves obey him. A place where "up" and "down" were matters of opinion, and directions might read as readily in days or colors as in miles.

And yet it was not a meaningless anarchy, for they were constrained to obey their customs as unavoidably as we comply with the rules of natural phenomena.

We made a sharp turn to the left in the formless grayness that surrounded us in order to survey the years for a sabbat meeting. It was Amanda's intention to face the Old One with the matter directly rather than to search aimlessly through ever changing mazes of the Half World for a being hard to identify at best.

Royce picked out the sabbat, though I could see nothing until we let the ground come up to meet us and proceeded on foot. Then there was light and form. Ahead of us, perhaps a quarter of a mile away, was an eminence surmounted by a great throne which glowed red through the murky air. I could not make out clearly the thing seated there, but I knew it was "himself"—our ancient enemy.

We were no longer alone. Life—sentient, evil undeadness—boiled around us and fogged the air and crept out of the ground. The ground itself twitched and pulsated as we walked over it. Faceless things sniffed and nibbled at our heels. We were aware of unseen presences about us in the fog-shot gloom: beings that squeaked, grunted, and sniggered; voices that were slobbering whimpers, that sucked and retched and bleated.

They seemed vaguely disturbed by our presence—Heaven knows that I was terrified by them!—for I could hear them flopping and shuffling out of our path, then closing cautiously in behind, as they bleated warnings to one another.

A shape floundered into our path and stopped, a shape with a great bloated head and moist, limber arms. "Back!" it wheezed. "Go back! Candidates for witchhood apply on the lower level." It did not speak English, but the words were clear.

Royce smashed it in the face and we stamped over it, its chalky bones crunching underfoot. It pulled itself together again, whining its submission, then scurried out in front of us and thereafter gave us escort right up to the great throne.

"That's the only way to treat these beings," Joe whispered in my ear. "Kick 'em in the teeth first, and they'll respect you."

There was a clearing before the throne which was crowded with black witches, black magicians, demons in every foul guise, and lesser unclean things. On the left side the caldron boiled. On the right some of the company were partaking of the witches' feast. I turned my head away from that. Directly before the throne, as custom calls for, the witches' dance was being performed for the amusement of the Goat. Some dozens of men and women, young and old, comely and hideous, cavorted and leaped in impossible acrobatic adagio.

The dance ceased and they gave way uncertainly before us as we pressed up to the throne. "What's this? What's this?" came a husky, phlegm-filled voice. "It's my little sweetheart! Come up and sit beside me, my sweet! Have you come at last to sign my compact?"

Jedson grasped my arm; I checked my tongue.

"I'll stay where I am," answered Amanda in a voice crisp with contempt. "As for your compact, you know better."

"Then why are you here? And why such *odd* companions." He looked down at us from the vantage of his throne, slapped his hairy thigh and laughed immoderately. Royce stirred and muttered; his grandfather's head chattered in wrath. Seraphin spat.

Jedson and Amanda put their heads together for a moment, then she answered, "By the treaty with Adam, I claim the right to examine."

He chuckled, and the little devils around him covered their ears. "You claim privileges here? With no compact?"

"Your customs," she answered sharply.

"Ah yes, the customs! Since you invoke them, so let it be. And whom would you examine?"

"I do not know his name. He is one of your demons who has taken improper liberties outside your sphere."

"One of my demons, and you know not his name? I have seven million demons, my pretty. Will you examine them one by one, or all together?" His sarcasm was almost the match of her contempt.

"All together."

"Never let it be said that I would not oblige a guest. If you will go forward—let me see—exactly five months and three days, you will find my gentlemen drawn up for inspection."

I do not recollect how we got there. There was a great, brown plain, and no sky. Drawn up in military order for review by their evil lord were all the fiends of the Half World, legion on legion, wave after wave. The Old One was attended by his cabinet; Jedson pointed them out to me—Lucifugé, the prime minister; Sataniacha, field marshal; Beelzebub and Leviathan, wing commanders; Ashtoreth, Abaddon, Mammon, Theutus, Asmodeus, and Incubus, the Fallen Thrones. The seventy princes each commanded a division, and each remained with his command, leaving only the dukes and the thrones to attend their lord, Satan Mekratrig.

He himself still appeared as the Goat, but his staff took every detestable shape they fancied. Asmodeus sported three heads, each evil and each different, rising out of the hind quarters of a swollen dragon. Mammon resembled, very roughly, a particularly repulsive tarantula. Ashtoreth I cannot describe at all. Only the Incubus affected a semblance of human form, as the only vessel adequate to display his lecherousness.

The Goat glanced our way. "Be quick about it," he demanded. "We are not here for your amusement."

Amanda ignored him, but led us toward the leading squadron. "Come back!" he bellowed. And indeed we were back; our steps had led us no place. "You ignore the customs. Hostages first!"

Amanda bit her lip. "Admitted," she retorted, and consulted briefly with Royce and Jedson. I caught Royce's answer to some argument.

"Since I am to go," he said, "it is best that I choose my companion, for reasons that are sufficient to me. My grandfather advises me to take the youngest. That one, of course, is Fraser."

"What's that?" I said when my name was mentioned. I had been rather pointedly left out of all the discussions, but this was surely my business.

"Royce wants you to go with him to smell out Ditworth," explained Jedson.

"And leave Amanda here with these fiends? I don't like it."

"I can look out for myself, Archie," she said quietly. "If Dr. Worthington wants you, you can help me most by going with him."

"What is this hostage stuff?"

"Having demanded the right of examination," she explained, "you must bring back Ditworth—or the hostages are forfeit."

Jedson spoke up before I could protest. "Don't be a hero, son. This is serious. You can serve us all best by going. If you two don't come back, you can bet that they'll have a fight on their hands before they claim their forfeit!"

I went. Worthington and I had hardly left them before I realized acutely that what little peace of mind I had come from the nearness of Amanda. Once out of her immediate influence the whole mind-twisting horror of the place and its grisly denizens hit me. I felt something rub against my ankles and nearly jumped out of my shoes. But when I looked down I saw that Seraphin, Amanda's cat, had chosen to follow me. After that things were better with me.

Royce assumed his dog pose when we came to the first rank of demons. He first handed me his grandfather's head. Once I would have found that mummified head repulsive to touch; it seemed a friendly, homey thing here. Then he was down on all fours, scalloping in and out of the ranks of infernal warriors. Seraphin scampered after him, paired up and hunted with him. The hound seemed quite content to let the cat do half the work, and I have no doubt he was justified. I walked as rapidly as possible down the aisles between adjacent squadrons while the animals cast out from side to side.

It seems to me that this went on for many hours, certainly so long that fatigue changed to a wooden automatism and horror died down to a dull unease. I learned not to look at the eyes of the demons, and was no longer surprised at any *outré* shape.

Squadron by squadron, division by division, we combed them, until at last, coming up the left wing, we reached the end. The animals had been growing increasingly nervous. When they had completed the front rank of the leading squadron, the hound trotted up to me and whined. I suppose he sought his grandfather, but I reached down and patted his head.

"Don't despair, old friend," I said, "we have still these." I motioned toward the generals, princess all, who were posted before their divisions. Coming up from the rear as we had, we had yet to examine the generals of the leading divisions on the left wing. But despair already claimed me; what were half a dozen possibilities against an eliminated seven million?

The dog trotted away to the post of the nearest general, the cat close beside him, while I followed as rapidly as possible. He commenced to yelp before he was fairly up to the demon, and I broke into a run. The demon stirred and commenced to metamorphose. But even in this strange shape there was something familiar about it. "Ditworth!" I yelled, and dived for him.

I felt myself buffeted by leather wings, raked by claws. Royce came to my aid, a dog no longer, but two hundred pounds of fighting Negro. The cat was a ball of fury, teeth and claws. Nevertheless, we would have been lost, done in completely, had not an amazing thing happened. A demon broke ranks and shot toward us. I sensed him rather than saw him, and thought that he had come to succor his master, though I had been assured that their customs did not permit it. But he helped us—us, his natural enemies—and attacked with such vindictive violence that the gage was turned to our favor.

Suddenly it was all over. I found myself on the ground, clutching at not a demon prince but Ditworth in his pseudo-human form—a little mild businessman, dressed with restrained elegance, complete to brief case, spectacles, and thinning hair.

"Take that thing off me," he said testily. "That thing" was grandfather, who was clinging doggedly with toothless gums to his neck.

Royce spared a hand from the task of holding Ditworth and resumed possession of his grandfather. Seraphin stayed where he was, claws dug into our prisoner's leg.

The demon who had rescued us was still with us. He had Ditworth by the shoulders, talons dug into their bases. I cleared my throat and said, "I believe we owe this to you——" I had not the slightest notion of the proper thing to say. I think the situation was utterly without precedent.

The demon made a grimace that may have been intended to be friendly, but which I found frightening. "Let me introduce myself," he said in English. "I'm Federal Agent William Kane, Bureau of Investigation."

I think that was what made me faint.

I came to, lying on my back. Someone had smeared a salve on my wounds and they were hardly stiff, and not painful in the least, but I was mortally tired. There was talking going on somewhere near me. I turned my head and saw all the members of my party gathered together. Worthington and the friendly demon who claimed to be a G-man held Ditworth between them, facing Satan. Of all the mighty infernal army I saw no trace.

"So it was my nephew Nebiros," mused the Goat, shaking his head and clucking. "Nebiros, you are a bad lad and I'm proud of you, but I'm afraid you will have to try your strength against their champion now that they have caught you." He addressed Amanda. "Who is your champion, my dear?"

The friendly demon spoke up. "That sounds like my job."

"I think not," countered Amanda. She drew him to one side and whispered intently. Finally he shrugged his wings and gave in.

Amanda rejoined the group. I struggled to my feet and came up to them. "A trial to the death, I think," she was saying. "Are you ready, Nebiros?" I was stretched between heart-stopping fear for Amanda and a calm belief that she could do anything she attempted. Jedson saw my face and shook his head. I was not to interrupt.

But Nebiros had no stomach for it. Still in his Ditworth form and looking ridiculously human, he turned to the Old One. "I dare not, Uncle. The outcome is certain. Intercede for me."

"Certainly, Nephew. I had rather hoped she would destroy you. You'll trouble me someday." Then to Amanda, "Shall we say . . . ah . . . ten thousand thousand years?"

Amanda gathered our votes with her eyes, including me, to my proud pleasure, and answered, "So be it." It was not a stiff sentence as such things go, I'm told—about equal to six months in jail in the real world—but he had not offended their customs; he had simply been defeated by white magic.

Old Nick brought down one arm in an emphatic gesture. There was a crashing roar and a burst of light and Ditworth-Nebiros was spread-eagled before us on a mighty boulder, his limbs bound with massive iron chains. He was again in demon form. Amanda and Worthington examined the bonds. She pressed a seal ring against each hasp and nodded to the Goat. At once the boulder receded with great speed into the distance until it was gone from sight.

"That seems to be about all, and I suppose you will be going now," announced the Goat. "All except this one——" He smiled at the demon G-man. "I have plans for him."

"No." Amanda's tone was flat.

"What's that, my little one? He has not the protection of your party, and he has offended our customs."

"No!"

"Really, I must insist."

"Satan Mekratrig," she said slowly, "do you wish to try your strength with me?"

"With you, madame?" He looked at her carefully, as if inspecting her for the first time. "Well, it's been a trying day, hasn't it? Suppose we say no more about it. Till another time, then——"

He was gone.

The demon faced her. "Thanks," he said simply. "I wish I had a hat to take off." He added anxiously, "Do you know your way out of here?"

"Don't you?"

"No, that's the trouble. Perhaps I should explain myself. I'm assigned to the antimonopoly division; we got a line on this chap Ditworth, or Nebiros. I followed him in here, thinking he was simply a black wizard and that I could use his portal to get back. By the time I knew better it was too late, and I was trapped. I had about resigned myself to an eternity as a fake demon."

I was very much interested in his story. I knew, of course, that all G-men are either lawyers, magicians, or accountants, but all that I had ever met were accountants. This calm assumption of incredible dangers impressed me and increased my already high opinion of Federal agents.

"You may use our portal to return," Amanda said. "Stick close to us." Then to the rest of us, "Shall we go now?"

Jack Bodie was still intoning the lines from the book when we landed. "Eight and a half minutes," he announced, looking at his wrist watch. "Nice work. Did you turn the trick?"

"Yes, we did," acknowledged Jedson, his voice muffled by the throes of his remetamorphosis. "Everything that——"

But Bodie interrupted. "Bill Kane—you old scoundrel!" he shouted. "How did you get in on this party?" Our demon had shucked his transformation on the way and landed in his natural form—lean, young, and hard-bitten, in a quiet gray suit and snap-brim hat.

"Hi, Jack," he acknowledged. "I'll look you up tomorrow and tell you all about it. Got to report in now." With which he vanished.

Ellen was out of her trance, and Joe was bending solicitously over her to see how she had stood up under it. I looked around for Amanda.

Then I heard her out in the kitchen and hurried out there. She looked up and smiled at me, her lovely face serene and coolly beautiful. "Amanda," I said, "Amanda——"

I suppose I had the subconscious intention of kissing her, making love to her. But it is very difficult to start anything of that sort unless the woman in the case in some fashion indicates her willingness. She did not. She was warmly friendly, but there was a barrier of reserve I could not cross. Instead, I followed her around the kitchen, talking inconsequentially, while she made hot cocoa and toast for all of us.

When we rejoined the others I sat and let my coca get cold, staring at her with vague frustration in my heart while Jedson told Ellen and Jack about our experiences. He took Ellen home shortly thereafter, and Jack followed them out.

When Amanda came back from telling them good night at the door, Dr. Royce was stretched out on his back on the hearthrug, with Seraphin curled up on his broad chest. They were both snoring softly. I realized suddenly that I was wretchedly tired. Amanda saw it, too, and said, "Lie down on the couch for a little and nap if you can."

I needed no urging. She came over and spread a shawl over me and kissed me tenderly. I heard her going upstairs as I fell asleep.

I was awakened by sunlight striking my face. Seraphin was sitting in the window, cleaning himself. Dr. Worthington was gone, but must have just left, for the nap on the hearthrug had not yet straightened up. The house seemed deserted. Then I heard her light footsteps in the kitchen. I was up at once and quickly out there.

She had her back toward me and was reaching up to the old-fashioned pendulum clock that hung on her kitchen wall. She turned as I came in—tiny, incredibly aged, her thin white hair brushed neatly into a bun.

It was suddenly clear to me why a motherly good-night kiss was all that I had received the night before; she had had enough sense for two of us, and had refused to permit me to make a fool of myself.

She looked up at me and said in a calm, matter-of-fact voice, "See, Archie, my old clock stopped yesterday"—she reached up and touched the pendulum—"but it is running again this morning."

THERE IS NOT ANYTHING MORE to tell. With Ditworth gone, and Kane's report, Magic, Incorporated, folded up almost overnight. The new licensing laws were an unenforced dead letter even before they were repealed.

We all hang around Mrs. Jennings's place just as much as she will let us. I'm really grateful that she did not let me get involved with her younger self, for our present relationship is something solid, something to tie to. Just the same, if I had been born sixty years sooner, Mr. Jennings would have had some rivalry to contend with.

I helped Ellen and Joe organize their new business, then put Bodie in as manager, for I decided that I did not want to give up my old line. I've built the new wing and bought those two trucks, just as Mrs. Jennings predicted. Business is good.

# "—And He Built a Crooked House"

A*mericans are considered crazy anywhere* in the world.

They will usually concede a basis for the accusation but point to California as the focus of the infection. Californians stoutly maintain that their bad reputation is derived solely from the acts of the inhabitants of Los Angeles County. Angelenos will, when pressed, admit the charge but explain hastily, "It's Hollywood. It's not our fault—we didn't ask for it; Hollywood just grew."

The people in Hollywood don't care; they glory in it. If you are interested, they will drive you up Laurel Canyon "—where we keep the violent cases." The Canyonites—the brown-legged women, the trunks-clad men constantly busy building and rebuilding their slaphappy unfinished houses—regard with faint contempt the dull creatures who live down in the flats, and treasure in their hearts the secret knowledge that they, and only they, know how to live.

Lookout Mountain Avenue is the name of a side canyon which twists up from Laurel Canyon. The other Canyonites don't like to have it mentioned; after all, one must draw the line somewhere!

High up on Lookout Mountain at number 8775, across the street from the Hermit—the original Hermit of Hollywood—lived Quintus Teal, graduate architect.

Even the architecture of southern California is different. Hot dogs are sold from a structure built like and designated "The Pup." Ice cream cones come from a giant stucco ice cream cone, and neon proclaims "Get the Chili Bowl Habit!" from the roofs of buildings which are indisputably chili bowls. Gasoline, oil, and free road maps are dispensed beneath the wings of tri-motored transport planes, while the certified rest rooms, inspected hourly for your comfort, are located in the cabin of the plane itself. These things may surprise, or amuse, the tourist, but the local residents, who walk bareheaded in the famous California noonday sun, take them as a matter of course.

Quintus Teal regarded the efforts of his colleagues in architecture as faint-hearted, fumbling, and timid.

"WHAT IS A HOUSE?" TEAL demanded of his friend, Homer Bailey.

"Well—" Bailey admitted cautiously, "speaking in broad terms, I've always regarded a house as a gadget to keep off the rain."

"Nuts! You're as bad as the rest of them."

"I didn't say the definition was complete—"

"Complete! It isn't even in the right direction. From that point of view we might just as well be squatting in caves. But I don't blame you," Teal went on magnanimously, "you're no worse than the lugs you find practicing architecture. Even the Moderns—all they've done is to abandon the Wedding Cake School in favor of the Service Station School, chucked away the gingerbread and slapped on some chromium, but at heart they are as conservative and traditional as a county courthouse. Neutra! Schindler! What have those bums got? What's Frank Lloyd Wright got that I haven't got?"

"Commissions," his friend answered succinctly.

"Huh? Wha' d'ju say?" Teal stumbled slightly in his flow of words, did a slight double take, and recovered himself. "Commissions. Correct. And why? Because I don't think of a house as an upholstered cave; I think of it as a machine for living, a vital process, live dynamic thing, changing with the mood of the dweller—not a dead, static, oversized coffin. Why should we be held down by the frozen concepts of our ancestors? Any fool with a little smattering of descriptive geometry can design a house in the ordinary way. Is the static geometry of Euclid the only mathematics? Are we to completely disregard the Picard-Vessiot theory? How about modular system?—to say nothing of the rich suggestions of stereochemistry. Isn't there a place in architecture for transformation, for homomorphology, for actional structures?"

"Blessed if I know," answered Bailey. "You might just as well be talking about the fourth dimension for all it means to me."

"And why not? Why should we limit ourselves to the—Say!" He interrupted himself and stared into distances. "Homer, I think you've really got something. After all, why not? Think of the infinite richness of articulation and relationship in four dimensions. What a house, what a house—" He stood quite still, his pale bulging eyes blinking thoughtfully.

Bailey reached up and shook his arm. "Snap out of it. What the hell are you talking about, four dimensions? Time is the fourth dimension; you can't drive nails into *that.*"

Teal shrugged him off. "Sure. Sure. Time is *a* fourth dimension, but I'm thinking about a fourth spatial dimension, like length, breadth and thickness. For economy of materials and convenience of arrangement you couldn't beat it. To say nothing of the saving of ground space—you could put an eight-room house on the land now occupied by a one-room house. Like a tesseract—"

"What's a tesseract?"

"Didn't you go to school? A tesseract is a hypercube, a square figure with four dimensions to it, like a cube has three, and a square has two. Here, I'll show you." Teal dashed out into the kitchen of his apartment and returned with a box of toothpicks which he spilled on the table between them, brushing glasses and a nearly empty Holland gin bottle carelessly aside. "I'll need some plasticine. I had some around here last week." He burrowed into a drawer of the littered desk which crowded one corner of his dining room and emerged with a lump of oily sculptor's clay. "Here's some."

"What are you going to do?"

"I'll show you." Teal rapidly pinched off small masses of the clay and rolled them into pea-sized balls. He stuck toothpicks into four of these and hooked them together into a square. "There! That's a square."

"Obviously."

"Another one like it, four more toothpicks, and we make a cube." The toothpicks were now arranged in the framework of a square box, a cube, with the pellets of clay holding the corners together. "Now we make another cube just like the first one, and the two of them will be two sides of the tesseract."

Bailey started to help him roll the little balls of clay for the second cube, but became diverted by the sensuous feel of the docile clay and started working and shaping it with his fingers.

"Look," he said, holding up his effort, a tiny figurine, "Gypsy Rose Lee."

"Looks more like Gargantua; she ought to sue you. Now pay attention. You open up one corner of the first cube, interlock the second cube at the corner, and then close the corner. Then take eight more toothpicks and join the bottom of the first cube to the bottom of the second, on a slant, and the top of the first to the top of the second, the same way." This he did rapidly, while he talked.

"What's that supposed to be?" Bailey demanded suspiciously.

"That's a tesseract, eight cubes forming the sides of a hypercube in four dimensions."

"It looks more like a cat's cradle to me. You've only got two cubes there anyhow. Where are the other six?"

"Use your imagination, man. Consider the top of the first cube in relation to the top of the second; that's cube number three. Then the two bottom squares, then the front faces of each cube, the back faces, the right hand, the left hand—eight cubes." He pointed them out.

"Yeah, I see 'em. But they still aren't cubes; they're whatchamu-callems—prisms. They are not square, they slant."

"That's just the way you look at it, in perspective. If you drew a picture of a cube on a piece of paper, the side squares would be slaunchwise, wouldn't they? That's perspective. When you look at a four-dimensional figure in three dimensions, naturally it looks crooked. But those are all cubes just the same."

"Maybe they are to you, brother, but they still look crooked to me."

Teal ignored the objections and went on. "Now consider this as the framework of an eight-room house; there's one room on the ground floor—that's for service, utilities, and garage. There are six rooms opening off it on the next floor, living room, dining room, bath, bedrooms, and so forth. And up at the top, completely enclosed and with windows on four sides, is your study. There! How do you like it?"

"Seems to me you have the bathtub hanging out of the living room ceiling. Those rooms are interlaced like an octopus."

"Only in perspective, only in perspective. Here, I'll do it another way so you can see it." This time Teal made a cube of toothpicks, then made a second of halves of toothpicks, and set it exactly in the center of the first by attaching the corners of the small cube to the large cube by short lengths of toothpick. "Now—the big cube is your ground floor, the little cube inside is your study on the top floor. The six cubes joining them are the living rooms. See?"

Bailey studied the figure, then shook his head. "I still don't see but two cubes, a big one and a little one. Those other six things, they look like pyramids this time instead of prisms, but they still aren't cubes."

"Certainly, certainly, you are seeing them in different perspective. Can't you see that?"

"Well, maybe. But that room on the inside, there. It's completely surrounded by the thingamujigs. I thought you said it had windows on four sides."

"It has—it just looks like it was surrounded. That's the grand feature about a tesseract house, complete outside exposure for every room, yet every wall serves two rooms and an eight-room house requires only a one-room foundation. It's revolutionary."

"That's putting it mildly. You're crazy, bud; you can't build a house like that. That inside room is on the inside, and there she stays."

Teal looked at his friend in controlled exasperation. "It's guys like you that keep architecture in its infancy. How many square sides has a cube?"

"Six."

"How many of them are inside?"

"Why, none of 'em. They're all on the outside."

"All right. Now listen—a tesseract has eight cubical sides, *all on the outside.* Now watch me. I'm going to open up this tesseract like you can open up a cubical pasteboard box, until it's flat. That way you'll be able to see all eight of the cubes." Working very rapidly he constructed four cubes, piling one on top of the other in an unsteady tower. He then built out four more cubes from the four exposed faces of the second cube in the pile. The structure swayed a little under the loose coupling of the clay pellets, but it stood, eight cubes in an inverted cross, a double cross, as the four additional cubes stuck out in four directions. "Do you see it now? It rests on the ground floor room, the next six cubes are the living rooms, and there is your study, up at the top."

Bailey regarded it with more approval than he had the other figures. "At least I can understand it. You say that is a tesseract, too?"

"That is a tesseract unfolded in three dimensions. To put it back together you tuck the top cube onto the bottom cube, fold those side cubes in till they meet the top cube and there you are. You do all this folding through a fourth dimension of course; you don't distort any of the cubes, or fold them into each other."

Bailey studied the wobbly framework further. "Look here," he said at last, "why don't you forget about folding this thing up through a fourth dimension—you can't anyway—and build a house like this?"

"What do you mean, I can't? It's a simple mathematical problem—"

"Take it easy, son. It may be simple in mathematics, but you could never get your plans approved for construction. There isn't any fourth dimension; forget it. But this kind of a house—it might have some advantages."

Checked, Teal studied the model. "Hm-m-m—Maybe you got something. We could have the same number of rooms, and we'd save the same amount of ground space. Yes, and we would set that middle cross-shaped floor northeast, southwest, and so forth, so that every room would get sunlight all day long. That central axis lends itself nicely to central heating. We'll put the dining room on the northeast and the kitchen on the southeast, with big view windows in every room. O.K., Homer, I'll do it! Where do you want it built?"

"Wait a minute! Wait a minute! I didn't say you were going to build it for me—"

"Of course I am. Who else? Your wife wants a new house; this is it."

"But Mrs. Bailey wants a Georgian house—"

"Just an idea she has. Women don't know what they want—"

"Mrs. Bailey does."

"Just some idea an out-of-date architect has put in her head. She drives a new car, doesn't she? She wears the very latest styles—why should she live in an eighteenth century house? This house will be even later than this year's model; it's years in the future. She'll be the talk of the town."

"Well—I'll have to talk to her."

"Nothing of the sort. We'll surprise her with it. Have another drink."

"Anyhow, we can't do anything about it now. Mrs. Bailey and I are driving up to Bakersfield tomorrow. The company's bringing in a couple of wells tomorrow."

"Nonsense. That's just the opportunity we want. It will be a surprise for her when you get back. You can just write me a check right now, and your worries are over."

"I oughtn't to do anything like this without consulting her. She won't like it."

"Say, who wears the pants in your family anyhow?"

The check was signed about halfway down the second bottle.

THINGS ARE DONE FAST IN southern California. Ordinary houses there are usually built in a month's time. Under Teal's impassioned heckling the tesseract house climbed dizzily skyward in days rather than weeks, and its cross-shaped second story came jutting out at the four corners of the world. He had some trouble at first with the inspectors over these four projecting rooms but by using strong girders and folding money he had been able to convince them of the soundness of his engineering.

By arrangement, Teal drove up in front of the Bailey residence the morning after their return to town. He improvised on his two-tone horn. Bailey stuck his head out the front door. "Why don't you use the bell?"

"Too slow," answered Teal cheerfully. "I'm a man of action. Is Mrs.

Bailey ready? Ah, there you are, Mrs. Bailey! Welcome home, welcome home. Jump in, we've got a surprise for you!"

"You know Teal, my dear," Bailey put in uncomfortably.

Mrs. Bailey sniffed. "I know him. We'll go in our own car, Homer."

"Certainly, my dear."

"Good idea," Teal agreed; " 'sgot more power than mine; we'll get there faster. I'll drive, I know the way." He took the keys from Bailey, slid into the driver's seat, and had the engine started before Mrs. Bailey could rally her forces.

"Never have to worry about my driving," he assured Mrs. Bailey, turning his head as he did so, while he shot the powerful car down the avenue and swung onto Sunset Boulevard, "it's a matter of power and control, a dynamic process, just my meat—I've never had a serious accident."

"You won't have but one," she said bitingly. "Will you *please* keep your eyes on the traffic?"

He attempted to explain to her that a traffic situation was a matter, not of eyesight, but intuitive integration of courses, speeds, and probabilities, but Bailey cut him short. "Where is the house, Quintus?"

"House?" asked Mrs. Bailey suspiciously. "What's this about a house, Homer? Have you been up to something without telling me?"

Teal cut in with his best diplomatic manner. "It certainly is a house, Mrs. Bailey. And what a house! It's a surprise for you from a devoted husband. Just wait till you see it—"

"I shall," she agreed grimly. "What style is it?"

"This house sets a new style. It's later than television, newer than next week. It must be seen to be appreciated. By the way," he went on rapidly, heading off any retort, "did you folks feel the earthquake last night?"

"Earthquake? What earthquake? Homer, was there an earthquake?"

"Just a little one," Teal continued, "about two A.M. If I hadn't been awake, I wouldn't have noticed it."

Mrs. Bailey shuddered. "Oh, this awful country! Do you hear that, Homer? We might have been killed in our beds and never have known it. Why did I ever let you persuade me to leave Iowa?"

"But my dear," he protested hopelessly, "you wanted to come out to California; you didn't like Des Moines."

"We needn't go into that," she said firmly. "You are a man; you should anticipate such things. Earthquakes!"

"That's one thing you needn't fear in your new home, Mrs. Bailey,"

Teal told her. "It's absolutely earthquake-proof; every part is in perfect dynamic balance with every other part."

"Well, I hope so. Where is this house?"

"Just around this bend. There's the sign now." A large arrow sign, of the sort favored by real estate promoters, proclaimed in letters that were large and bright even for southern California:

THE HOUSE OF THE FUTURE!!!

COLOSSAL—AMAZING—REVOLUTIONARY

*See How Your Grandchildren Will Live!*

Q. TEAL, ARCHITECT

"Of course that will be taken down," he added hastily, noting her expression, "as soon as you take possession." He slued around the corner and brought the car to a squealing halt in front of the House of the Future. "*Voilà!*" He watched their faces for response.

Bailey stared unbelievingly, Mrs. Bailey in open dislike. They saw a simple cubical mass, possessing doors and windows, but no other architectural features, save that it was decorated in intricate mathematical designs. "Teal," Bailey asked slowly, "what have you been up to?"

Teal turned from their faces to the house. Gone was the crazy tower with its jutting second-story rooms. No trace remained of the seven rooms above ground floor level. Nothing remained but the single room that rested on the foundations. "Great jumping cats!" he yelled, "I've been robbed!"

He broke into a run.

But it did him no good. Front or back, the story was the same: the other seven rooms had disappeared, vanished completely. Bailey caught up with him, and took his arm. "Explain yourself. What is this about being robbed? How come you built anything like this—it's not according to agreement."

"But I didn't. I built just what we had planned to build, an eight-room house in the form of a developed tesseract. I've been sabotaged; that's what it is! Jealously! The other architects in town didn't dare let me finish this job; they knew they'd be washed up if I did."

"When were you last here?"

"Yesterday afternoon."

"Everything all right then?"

"Yes. The gardeners were just finishing up."

Bailey glanced around at the faultlessly manicured landscaping. "I don't see how seven rooms could have been dismantled and carted away from here in a single night without wrecking this garden."

Teal looked around, too. "It doesn't look it. I don't understand it."

Mrs. Bailey joined them. "Well? Well? Am I to be left to amuse myself? We might as well look it over as long as we are here, though I'm warning you, Homer, I'm not going to like it."

"We might as well," agreed Teal, and drew a key from his pocket with which he let them in the front door. "We may pick up some clues."

The entrance hall was in perfect order, the sliding screens that separated it from the garage space were back, permitting them to see the entire compartment. "This looks all right," observed Bailey. "Let's go up on the roof and try to figure out what happened. Where's the staircase? Have they stolen that, too?"

"Oh, no," Teal denied, "look—" He pressed a button below the light switch; a panel in the ceiling fell away and a light, graceful flight of stairs swung noiselessly down. Its strength members were the frosty silver of duralumin, its treads and risers transparent plastic. Teal wriggled like a boy who has successfully performed a card trick, while Mrs. Bailey thawed perceptibly.

It was beautiful.

"Pretty slick," Bailey admitted. "Howsomever it doesn't seem to go any place—"

"Oh, that—" Teal followed his gaze. "The cover lifts up as you approach the top. Open stair wells are anachronisms. Come on." As predicted, the lid of the staircase got out of their way as they climbed the flight and permitted them to debouch at the top, but not, as they had expected, on the roof of the single room. They found themselves standing in the middle one of the five rooms which constituted the second floor of the original structure.

For the first time on record Teal had nothing to say. Bailey echoed him, chewing on his cigar. Everything was in perfect order. Before them, through open doorway and translucent partition lay the kitchen, a chef's dream of up-to-the-minute domestic engineering, monel metal, continuous counter space, concealed lighting, functional arrangement. On the left the formal, yet gracious and hospitable dining room awaited guests, its furniture in parade-ground alignment.

Teal knew before he turned his head that the drawing room and lounge would be found in equally substantial and impossible existence.

"Well, I must admit this *is* charming," Mrs. Bailey approved, "and the kitchen is just *too* quaint for words—though I would never have guessed from the exterior that this house had so much room upstairs. Of course *some* changes will have to be made. That secretary now—if we moved it over *here* and put the settle over *there*—"

"Stow it, Matilda," Bailey cut in brusquely. "Wha'd' yuh make of it, Teal?"

"Why, Homer Bailey! The very id—"

"Stow it, I said. Well, Teal?"

The architect shuffled his rambling body. "I'm afraid to say. Let's go on up."

"How?"

"Like this." He touched another button; a mate, in deeper colors, to the fairy bridge that had let them up from below offered them access to the next floor. They climbed it, Mrs. Bailey expostulating in the rear, and found themselves in the master bedroom. Its shades were drawn, as had been those on the level below, but the mellow lighting came on automatically. Teal at once activated the switch which controlled still another flight of stairs, and they hurried up into the top floor study.

"Look, Teal," suggested Bailey when he had caught his breath, "can we get to the roof above this room? Then we could look around."

"Sure, it's an observatory platform." They climbed a fourth flight of stairs, but when the cover at the top lifted to let them reach the level above, they found themselves, not on the roof, but *standing in the ground floor room where they had entered the house.*

Mr. Bailey turned a sickly gray. "Angels in heaven," he cried, "this place is haunted. We're getting out of here." Grabbing his wife he threw open the front door and plunged out.

Teal was too much preoccupied to bother with their departure. There was an answer to all this, an answer that he did not believe. But he was forced to break off considering it because of hoarse shouts from somewhere above him. He lowered the staircase and rushed upstairs. Bailey was in the central room leaning over Mrs. Bailey, who had fainted. Teal took in the situation, went to the bar built into the lounge, and poured three fingers of brandy, which he returned with and handed to Bailey. "Here—this'll fix her up."

Bailey drank it.

"That was for Mrs. Bailey," said Teal.

"Don't quibble," snapped Bailey. "Get her another." Teal took the precaution of taking one himself before returning with a dose earmarked for his client's wife. He found her just opening her eyes.

"Here, Mrs. Bailey," he soothed, "this will make you feel better."

"I never touch spirits," she protested, and gulped it.

"Now tell me what happened," suggested Teal. "I thought you two had left."

"But we did—we walked out the front door and found ourselves up here, in the lounge."

"The hell you say! Hm-m-m—wait a minute." Teal went into the lounge. There he found that the big view window at the end of the room was open. He peered cautiously through it. He stared, not out at the California countryside, but into the ground floor room—or a reasonable facsimile thereof. He said nothing, but went back to the stair well which he had left open and looked down it. The ground floor room was still in place. Somehow, it managed to be in two different places at once, on different levels.

He came back into the central room and seated himself opposite Bailey in a deep, low chair, and sighted him past his upthrust bony knees. "Homer," he said impressively, "do you know what has happened?"

"No, I don't—but if I don't find out pretty soon, something is going to happen and pretty drastic, too!"

"Homer, this is a vindication of my theories. This house is a real tesseract."

"What's he talking about, Homer?"

"Wait, Matilda—now Teal, that's ridiculous. You've pulled some hanky-panky here and I won't have it—scaring Mrs. Bailey half to death, and making me nervous. All I want is to get out of here, with no more of your trapdoors and silly practical jokes."

"Speak for yourself, Homer," Mrs. Bailey interrupted, "I was *not* frightened; I was just took all over queer for a moment. It's my heart; all of my people are delicate and highstrung. Now about this tessy thing—explain yourself, Mr. Teal. Speak up."

He told her as well as he could in the face of numerous interruptions the theory back of the house. "Now as I see it, Mrs. Bailey," he concluded, "this house, while perfectly stable in three dimensions, was not stable in four dimensions. I had built a house in the shape of an unfolded tesseract; something happened to it, some jar or side thrust, and it collapsed into its normal shape—it folded up." He snapped his fingers suddenly. "I've got it! The earthquake!"

"Earthquake?"

"Yes, yes, the little shake we had last night. From a four dimensional standpoint this house was like a plane balanced on edge. One little push and it fell over, collapsed along its natural joints into a stable four-dimensional figure."

"I thought you boasted about how safe this house was."

"It *is* safe—three-dimensionally."

"I don't call a house safe," commented Bailey edgily, "that collapses on the first little temblor."

"But look around you, man!" Teal protested. "Nothing has been disturbed, not a piece of glassware cracked. Rotation through a fourth dimension can't effect a three-dimensional figure any more than you can shake letters off a printed page. If you had been sleeping in here last night, you would never have awakened."

"That's just what I'm afraid of. Incidentally, has your great genius figured out any way for us to get out of this booby trap?"

"Huh? Oh, yes, you and Mrs. Bailey started to leave and landed back up here, didn't you? But I'm sure there is no real difficulty—we came in, we can go out. I'll try it." He was up and hurrying downstairs before he had finished talking. He flung open the front door, stepped through, and found himself staring at his companions, down the length of the second floor lounge. "Well, there does seem to be some slight problem," he admitted blandly. "A mere technicality, though—we can always go out a window." He jerked aside the long drapes that covered the deep French windows set in one side wall of the lounge. He stopped suddenly.

"Hm-m-m," he said, "this is interesting—very."

"What is?" asked Bailey, joining him.

"This." The window stared directly into the dining room, instead of looking outdoors. Bailey stepped back to the corner where the lounge and the dining room joined the central room at ninety degrees.

"But that can't be," he protested, "that window is maybe fifteen, twenty feet from the dining room."

"Not in a tesseract," corrected Teal. "Watch." He opened the window and stepped through, talking back over his shoulder as he did so.

From the point of view of the Baileys he simply disappeared.

But not from his own viewpoint. It took him some seconds to catch his breath. Then he cautiously disentangled himself from the rosebush to which he had become almost irrevocably wedded, making a mental note the while never again to order landscaping which involved plants with thorns, and looked around him.

He was outside the house. The massive bulk of the ground floor room thrust up beside him. Apparently he had fallen off the roof.

He dashed around the corner of the house, flung open the front door and hurried up the stairs. "Homer!" he called out, "Mrs. Bailey! I've found a way out!"

Bailey looked annoyed rather than pleased to see him. "What happened to you?"

"I fell out. I've been outside the house. You can do it just as easily—just step through those French windows. Mind the rosebush, though—we may have to build another stairway."

"How did you get back in?"

"Through the front door."

"Then we shall leave the same way. Come, my dear." Bailey set his hat firmly on his head and marched down the stairs, his wife on his arm.

Teal met them in the lounge. "I could have told you that wouldn't work," he announced. "Now here's what we have to do: As I see it, in a four-dimensional figure a three-dimensional man has two choices every time he crosses a line of juncture, like a wall or a threshold. Ordinarily he will make a ninety-degree turn through the fourth dimension, only he doesn't feel it with his three dimensions. Look." He stepped through the very window that he had fallen out of a moment before. Stepped through and arrived in the dining room, where he stood, still talking.

"I watched where I was going and arrived where I intended to." He stepped back into the lounge. "The time before I didn't watch and I moved on through normal space and fell out of the house. It must be a matter of subconscious orientation."

"I'd hate to depend on subconscious orientation when I step out for the morning paper."

"You won't have to; it'll become automatic. Now to get out of the house this time—Mrs. Bailey, if you will stand here with your back to the window, and jump backward, I'm pretty sure you will land in the garden."

Mrs. Bailey's face expressed her opinion of Teal and his ideas. "Homer Bailey," she said shrilly, "are you going to stand there and let him suggest such—"

"But Mrs. Bailey," Teal attempted to explain, "we can tie a rope on you and lower you down eas—"

"Forget it, Teal," Bailey cut him off brusquely. "We'll have to find a better way than that. Neither Mrs. Bailey nor I are fitted for jumping."

Teal was temporarily nonplused; there ensued a short silence. Bailey broke it with, "Did you hear that, Teal?"

"Hear what?"

"Someone talking off in the distance. D'you s'pose there could be someone else in the house, playing tricks on us, maybe?"

"Oh, not a chance. I've got the only key."

"But I'm sure of it," Mrs. Bailey confirmed. "I've heard them ever since we came in. Voices. Homer, I can't stand much more of this. Do something."

"Now, now, Mrs. Bailey," Teal soothed, "don't get upset. There can't be anyone else in the house, but I'll explore and make sure. Homer, you stay here with Mrs. Bailey and keep an eye on the rooms on this floor." He passed from the lounge into the ground floor room and from there to the kitchen and on into the bedroom. This led him back to the lounge by a straight-line route, that is to say, by going straight ahead on the entire trip he returned to the place from which he started.

"Nobody around," he reported. "I opened all of the doors and windows as I went—all except this one." He stepped to the window opposite the one through which he had recently fallen and thrust back the drapes.

He saw a man with his back toward him, four rooms away. Teal snatched open the French window and dived through it, shouting, "There he goes now! Stop thief!"

The figure evidently heard him; it fled precipitately. Teal pursued, his gangling limbs stirred to unanimous activity, through drawing room, kitchen, dining room, lounge—room after room, yet in spite of Teal's best efforts he could not seem to cut down the four-room lead that the interloper had started with.

He saw the pursued jump awkwardly but actively over the low sill of a French window and in so doing knock off the hat. When he came up to the point where his quarry had lost his headgear, he stopped and picked it up, glad of an excuse to stop and catch his breath. He was back in the lounge.

"I guess he got away from me," he admitted. "Anyhow, here's his hat. Maybe we can identify him."

Bailey took the hat, looked at it, then snorted, and slapped it on Teal's head. It fitted perfectly. Teal looked puzzled, took the hat off, and examined it. On the sweat band were the initials "Q.T." It was his own.

Slowly comprehension filtered through Teal's features. He went back to the French window and gazed down the series of rooms through which he had pursued the mysterious stranger. They saw him wave his arms semaphore fashion. "What are you doing?" asked Bailey.

"Come see." The two joined him and followed his stare with their own. Four rooms away they saw the backs of three figures, two male and one female. The taller, thinner of the men was waving his arms in a silly fashion.

Mrs. Bailey screamed and fainted again.

Some minutes later, when Mrs. Bailey had been resuscitated and somewhat composed, Bailey and Teal took stock. "Teal," said Bailey, "I won't waste any time blaming you; recriminations are useless and I'm sure you didn't plan for this to happen, but I suppose you realize we are in a pretty serious predicament. How are we going to get out of here? It looks now as if we would stay until we starve; every room leads into another room."

"Oh, it's not that bad. I got out once, you know."

"Yes, but you can't repeat it—you tried."

"Anyhow we haven't tried all the rooms. There's still the study."

"Oh, yes, the study. We went through there when we first came in, and didn't stop. Is it your idea that we might get out through its windows?"

"Don't get your hopes up. Mathematically, it ought to look into the four side rooms on this floor. Still we never opened the blinds; maybe we ought to look."

" 'Twon't do any harm anyhow. Dear, I think you had best just stay here and rest—"

"Be left alone in this horrible place? I should say not!" Mrs. Bailey was up off the couch where she had been recuperating even as she spoke.

They went upstairs. "This is the inside room, isn't it, Teal?" Bailey inquired as they passed through the master bedroom and climbed on up toward the study. "I mean it was the little cube in your diagram that was in the middle of the big cube, and completely surrounded."

"That's right," agreed Teal. "Well, let's have a look. I figure this window ought to give into the kitchen." He grasped the cords of Venetian blinds and pulled them.

It did not. Waves of vertigo shook them. Involuntarily they fell to the floor and grasped helplessly at the pattern on the rug to keep from falling. "Close it! Close it!" moaned Bailey.

Mastering in part a primitive atavistic fear, Teal worked his way back to the window and managed to release the screen. The window had looked *down* instead of *out,* down from a terrifying height.

Mrs. Bailey had fainted again.

Teal went back after more brandy while Bailey chafed her wrists.

When she had recovered, Teal went cautiously to the window and raised the screen a crack. Bracing his knees, he studied the scene. He turned to Bailey. "Come look at this, Homer. See if you recognize it."

"You stay away from there, Homer Bailey!"

"Now, Matilda, I'll be careful." Bailey joined him and peered out.

"See up there? That's the Chrysler Building, sure as shooting. And there's the East River, and Brooklyn." They gazed straight down the sheer face of an enormously tall building. More than a thousand feet away a toy city, very much alive, was spread out before them. "As near as I can figure it out, we are looking down the side of the Empire State Building from a point just above its tower."

"I don't think so—it's too perfect. I think space is folded over through the fourth dimension here and we are looking past the fold."

"You mean we aren't really seeing it?"

"No, we're seeing it all right. I don't know what would happen if we climbed out this window, but I for one don't want to try. But what a view! Oh, boy, what a view! Let's try the other windows."

They approached the next window more cautiously, and it was well that they did, for it was even more disconcerting, more reason-shaking, than the one looking down the gasping height of the sky-scraper. It was a simple seascape, open ocean and blue sky—but the ocean was where the sky should have been, and contrariwise. This time they were somewhat braced for it, but they both felt seasickness about to overcome them at the sight of waves rolling overhead; they lowered the blind quickly without giving Mrs. Bailey a chance to be disturbed by it.

Teal looked at the third window. "Game to try it, Homer?"

"Hrrumph—well, we won't be satisfied if we don't. Take it easy." Teal lifted the blind a few inches. He saw nothing, and raised it a little more—still nothing. Slowly he raised it until the window was fully exposed. They gazed out at—nothing.

Nothing, nothing at all. What color is nothing? Don't be silly! What shape is it? Shape is an attribute of *something*. It had neither depth nor form. It had not even blackness. It was *nothing*.

Bailey chewed at his cigar. "Teal, what do you make of that?"

Teal's insouciance was shaken for the first time. "I don't know, Homer, I don't rightly know—but I think that window ought to be walled up." He stared at the lowered blind for a moment. "I think maybe we looked at a place where space *isn't*. We looked around a fourth-dimensional corner and there wasn't anything there." He rubbed his eyes. "I've got a headache."

They waited for a while before tackling the fourth window. Like an unopened letter, it might *not* contain bad news. The doubt left hope. Finally the suspense stretched too thin and Bailey pulled the cord himself, in the face of his wife's protests.

It was not so bad. A landscape stretched away from them, right side up, and on such a level that the study appeared to be a ground floor room. But it was distinctly unfriendly.

A hot, hot sun beat down from lemon-colored sky. The flat ground seemed burned a sterile, bleached brown and incapable of supporting life. Life there was, strange stunted trees that lifted knotted, twisted arms to the sky. Little clumps of spiky leaves grew on the outer extremities of these misshapen growths.

"Heavenly day," breathed Bailey, "Where is that?"

Teal shook his head, his eyes troubled. "It beats me."

"It doesn't look like anything on Earth. It looks more like another planet—Mars, maybe."

"I wouldn't know. But, do you know, Homer, it might be worse than that, worse than another planet, I mean."

"Huh? What's that you say?"

"It might be clear out of space entirely. I'm not sure that that is our sun at all. It seems too bright."

Mrs. Bailey had somewhat timidly joined them and now gazed out at the outré scene. "Homer," she said in a subdued voice, "those hideous trees—they frighten me."

He patted her hand.

Teal fumbled with the window catch.

"What are you doing?" Bailey demanded.

"I thought if I stuck my head out the window I might be able to look around and tell a bit more."

"Well—all right," Bailey grudged, "but be careful."

"I will." He opened the window a crack and sniffed. "The air is all right, at least." He threw it open wide.

His attention was diverted before he could carry out his plan. An uneasy tremor, like the first intimation of nausea, shivered the entire building for a long second, and was gone.

"Earthquake!" They all said at once. Mrs. Bailey flung her arms around her husband's neck.

Teal gulped and recovered himself, saying:

"It's all right, Mrs. Bailey. This house is perfectly safe. You know you can expect settling tremors after a shock like last night." He had just settled his features into an expression of reassurance when the second shock came. This one was no mild shimmy but the real seasick roll.

In every Californian, native born or grafted, there is a deep-rooted primitive reflex. An earthquake fills him with soul-shaking claustrophobia which impels him blindly to *get outdoors!* Model Boy Scouts will push aged grandmothers aside to obey it. It is a matter of record that Teal and Bailey landed on top of Mrs. Bailey. Therefore, she must have jumped through the window first. The order of precedence cannot be attributed to chivalry; it must be assumed that she was in readier position to spring.

They pulled themselves together, collected their wits a little, and rubbed sand from their eyes. Their first sensations were relief at feeling the solid sand of the desert land under them. Then Bailey noticed something that brought them to their feet and checked Mrs. Bailey from bursting into the speech that she had ready.

"Where's the house?"

It was gone. There was no sign of it at all. They stood in the center of flat desolation, the landscape they had seen from the window. But, aside from the tortured, twisted trees there was nothing to be seen but the yellow sky and the luminary overhead, whose furnacelike glare was already almost insufferable.

Bailey looked slowly around, then turned to the architect.

"Well, Teal?" His voice was ominous.

Teal shrugged helplessly. "I wish I knew. I wish I could even be sure that we were on Earth."

"Well, we can't stand here. It's sure death if we do. Which direction?"

"Any, I guess. Let's keep a bearing on the sun."

THEY HAD TRUDGED ON FOR an undetermined distance when Mrs. Bailey demanded a rest. They stopped. Teal said in an aside to Bailey, "Any ideas?"

"No . . . no, none. Say, do you hear anything?"

Teal listened. "Maybe—unless it's my imagination."

"Sounds like an automobile. Say, it *is* an automobile!"

They came to the highway in less than another hundred yards. The automobile, when it arrived, proved to be an elderly, puffing light truck, driven by a rancher. He crunched to a stop at their hail. "We're stranded. Can you help us out?"

"Sure. Pile in."

"Where are you headed?"

"Los Angeles."

"Los Angeles? Say, where is this place?"

"Well, you're right in the middle of the Joshua-Tree National Forest."

THE RETURN WAS AS DISPIRITING as the Retreat from Moscow. Mr. and Mrs. Bailey sat up in front with the driver while Teal bumped along in the body of the truck, and tried to protect his head from the sun. Bailey subsidized the friendly rancher to detour to the tesseract house, not because they wanted to see it again, but in order to pick up their car.

At last the rancher turned the corner that brought them back to where they had started. But the house was no longer there.

There was not even the ground floor room. It had vanished. The Baileys, interested in spite of themselves, poked around the foundations with Teal.

"Got any answers for this one, Teal?" asked Bailey.

"It must be that on that last shock it simply fell through into another section of space. I can see now that I should have anchored it at the foundations."

"That's not all you should have done."

"Well, I don't see that there is anything to get down-hearted about. The house was insured, and we've learned an amazing lot. There are possibilities, man, possibilities! Why, right now I've got a great new revolutionary idea for a house—"

Teal ducked in time. He was always a man of action.

# "THEY—"

T*hey would not let him* alone.

They never would let him alone. He realized that that was part of the plot against him—never to leave him in peace, never to give him a chance to mull over the lies they had told him, time enough to pick out the flaws, and to figure out the truth for himself.

That damned attendant this morning! He had come busting in with his breakfast tray, waking him, and causing him to forget his dream. If only he could remember that dream—

Someone was unlocking the door. He ignored it.

"Howdy, old boy. They tell me you refused your breakfast?" Dr. Hayward's professionally kindly mask hung over his bed.

"I wasn't hungry."

"But we can't have that. You'll get weak, and then I won't be able to get you well completely. Now get up and get your clothes on and I'll order an eggnog for you. Come on, that's a good fellow!"

Unwilling, but still willing at that moment to enter into any conflict of wills, he got out of bed and slipped on his bathrobe. "That's better," Hayward approved. "Have a cigarette?"

"No, thank you."

The doctor shook his head in a puzzled fashion. "Darned if I can figure you out. Loss of interest in physical pleasure does not fit your type of case."

"What is my type of case?" he inquired in flat tones.

"Tut! Tut!" Hayward tried to appear roguish. "If medicos told their professional secrets, they might have to work for a living."

"What is my type of case?"

"Well—the label doesn't matter, does it? Suppose you tell me. I really know nothing about your case as yet. Don't you think it is about time you talked?"

"I'll play chess with you."

"All right, all right." Hayward made a gesture of impatient concession. "We've played chess every day for a week. If you will talk, I'll play chess."

What could it matter? If he was right, they already understood perfectly that he had discovered their plot; there was nothing to be gained by concealing the obvious. Let them try to argue him out of it. Let the tail go with the hide! To hell with it!

He got out the chessmen and commenced setting them up. "What do you know of my case so far?"

"Very little. Physical examination, negative. Past history, negative. High intelligence, as shown by your record in school and your success in your profession. Occasional fits of moodiness, but nothing exceptional. The only positive information was the incident that caused you to come here for treatment."

"To be brought here, you mean. Why should it cause comment?"

"Well, good gracious, man—if you barricade yourself in your room and insist that your wife is plotting against you, don't you expect people to notice?"

"But she was plotting against me—and so are you. White, or black?"

"Black—it's your turn to attack. Why do you think we are plotting against you?"

"It's an involved story, and goes way back into my early childhood. There was an immediate incident, however—" He opened by advancing the white king's knight to KB3. Hayward's eyebrows raised.

"You make a piano attack?"

"Why not? You know that it is not safe for me to risk a gambit with you."

The doctor shrugged his shoulders and answered the opening. "Suppose we start with your early childhood. It may shed more light than more recent incidents. Did you feel that you were being persecuted as a child?"

"No!" He half rose from his chair. "When I was a child I was sure of myself. I knew then, I tell you; I knew! Life was worth while, and I knew it. I was at peace with myself and my surroundings. Life was good and I was good and I assumed that the creatures around me were like myself."

"And weren't they?"

"Not at all! Particularly the children. I didn't know what viciousness was until I was turned loose with other children. The little devils! And I was expected to be like them and play with them."

The doctor nodded. "I know. The herd compulsion. Children can be pretty savage at times."

"You've missed the point. This wasn't any healthy roughness; these creatures were different—not like myself at all. They looked like me, but they were not like me. If I tried to say anything to one of them about anything that mattered to me, all I could get was a stare and a scornful laugh. Then they would find some way to punish me for having said it."

Hayward nodded. "I see what you mean. How about grownups?"

"That is somewhat different. Adults don't matter to children at first—or, rather they did not matter to me. They were too big, and they did not bother me, and they were busy with things that did not enter into my considerations. It was only when I noticed that my presence affected them that I began to wonder about them."

"How do you mean?"

"Well, they never did the things when I was around that they did when I was not around."

Hayward looked at him carefully. "Won't that statement take quite a lot of justifying? How do you know what they did when you weren't around?"

He acknowledged the point. "But I used to catch them just stopping. If I came into a room, the conversation would stop suddenly, and then it would pick up about the weather or something equally inane. Then I took to hiding and listening and looking. Adults did not behave the same way in my presence as out of it."

"Your move, I believe. But see here, old man—that was when you were a child. Every child passes through that phase. Now that you are a man, you must see the adult point of view. Children are strange creatures and have to be protected—at least, we do protect them—from many adult interests. There is a whole code of conventions in the matter that—"

"Yes, yes," he interrupted impatiently, "I know all that. Nevertheless, I noticed enough and remembered enough that was never clear to me later. And it put me on my guard to notice the next thing."

"Which was?" He noticed that the doctor's eyes were averted as he adjusted a castle's position.

"The things I saw people doing and heard them talking about were never of any importance. They must be doing something else."

"I don't follow you."

"You don't choose to follow me. I'm telling this to you in exchange for a game of chess."

"Why do you like to play chess so well?"

"Because it is the only thing in the world where I can see all the factors and understand all the rules. Never mind—I saw all around me this enormous plant, cities, farms, factories, churches, schools, homes, railroads, luggage, roller coaster, trees, saxophones, libraries, people and animals. People that looked like me and who should have felt very much like me, if what I was told was the truth. But what did they appear to be doing? 'They went to work to earn the money to buy the food to get the strength to go to work to earn the money to buy the food to get the strength to go to work to get the strength to buy the food to earn the money to go to—' until they fell over dead. Any slight variation in the basic pattern did not matter, for they always fell over dead. And everybody tried to tell me that I should be doing the same thing. I knew better!"

The doctor gave him a look apparently intended to denote helpless surrender and laughed. "I can't argue with you. Life does look like that, and maybe it is just that futile. But it is the only life we have. Why not make up your mind to enjoy it as much as possible?"

"Oh, no!" He looked both sulky and stubborn. "You can't peddle nonsense to me by claiming to be fresh out of sense. How do I know? Because all this complex stage setting, all these swarms of actors, could not have been put here just to make idiot noises at each other. Some other explanation, but not that one. An insanity as enormous, as complex, as the one around me had to be planned. I've found the plan!"

"Which is?"

He noticed that the doctor's eyes again averted.

"It is a play intended to divert me, to occupy my mind and confuse me, to keep me so busy with details that I will not have time to think about the meaning. You are all in it, every one of you." He shook his finger in the doctor's face. "Most of them may be helpless automatons, but you're not. You are one of the conspirators. You've been sent in as a troubleshooter to try to force me to go back to playing the role assigned to me!"

He saw that the doctor was waiting for him to quiet down.

"Take it easy," Hayward finally managed to say. "Maybe it is all a conspiracy, but why do you think that you have been singled out for special attention? Maybe it is a joke on all of us. Why couldn't I be one of the victims as well as yourself?"

"Got you!" He pointed a long finger at Hayward. "That is the essence of the plot. All of these creatures have been set up to look like me in order to prevent me from realizing that I was the center of the arrangements. But I have noticed the key fact, the mathematically inescapable fact, that I am unique. Here am I, sitting on the inside. The world extends outward from me. I am the center—"

"Easy, man, easy! Don't you realize that the world looks that way to me, too. We are each the center of the universe—"

"Not so! That is what you have tried to make me believe, that I am just one of millions more just like me. Wrong! If they were like me, then I could get into communication with them. I can't. I have tried and tried and I can't. I've sent out my inner thoughts, seeking some one other being who has them, too. What have I gotten back? Wrong answers, jarring incongruities, meaningless obscenity. I've tried, I tell you. God!—how I've tried! But there is nothing out there to speak to me—nothing but emptiness and otherness!"

"Wait a minute. Do you mean to say that you think there is nobody home at my end of the line? Don't you believe that I am alive and conscious?"

He regarded the doctor soberly. "Yes, I think you are probably alive, but you are one of the others—my antagonists. But you have set thousands of others around me whose faces are blank, not lived in, and whose speech is a meaningless reflex of noise."

"Well, then, if you concede that I am an ego, why do you insist that I am so very different from yourself?"

"Why? Wait!" He pushed back from the chess table and strode over to the wardrobe, from which he took out a violin case.

While he was playing, the lines of suffering smoothed out of his face and his expression took a relaxed beatitude. For a while he recaptured the emotions, but not the knowledge, which he had possessed in dreams. The melody proceeded easily from proposition to proposition with inescapable, unforced logic. He finished with a triumphant statement of the essential thesis and turned to the doctor. "Well?"

"Hm-m-m." He seemed to detect an even greater degree of caution in the doctor's manner. "It's an odd bit, but remarkable. 'S pity you didn't take up the violin seriously. You could have made quite a reputation. You could even now. Why don't you do it? You could afford to, I believe."

He stood and stared at the doctor for a long moment, then shook his head as if trying to clear it. "It's no use," he said slowly, "no use at all. There is no possibility of communication. I am alone." He replaced the instrument in its case and returned to the chess table. "My move, I believe?"

"Yes. Guard your queen."

He studied the board. "Not necessary. I no longer need my queen. Check."

The doctor interposed a pawn to parry the attack.

He nodded. "You use your pawns well, but I have learned to anticipate your play. Check again—and mate, I think."

The doctor examined the new situation. "No," he decided, "no—not quite." He retreated from the square under attack. "Not checkmate—stalemate at the worst. Yes, another stalemate."

He was upset by the doctor's visit. He couldn't be wrong, basically, yet the doctor had certainly pointed out logical holes in his position. From a logical standpoint the whole world might be a fraud perpetrated on everybody. But logic meant nothing—logic itself was a fraud, starting with unproved assumptions and capable of proving anything. The world is what it is!—and carries its own evidence of trickery.

But does it? What did he have to go on? Could he lay down a line between known facts and everything else and then make a reasonable interpretation of the world, based on facts alone—an interpretation free from complexities of logic and no hidden assumptions of points not certain. Very well—

First fact, himself. He knew himself directly. He existed.

Second facts, the evidence of his "five senses," everything that he himself saw and heard and smelled and tasted with his physical senses. Subject to their limitations, he must believe his senses. Without them he was entirely solitary, shut up in a locker of bone, blind, deaf, cutoff, the only being in the world.

And that was not the case. He knew that he did not invent the information brought to him by his senses. There had to be something else out there, some otherness that produced the things his senses recorded. All philosophies that claimed that the physical world around him did not exist except in his imagination were sheer nonsense.

But beyond that, what? Were there any third facts on which he could rely? No, not at this point. He could not afford to believe anything that he was told, or that he read, or that was implicitly assumed to be true about the world around him. No, he could not believe any of it, for the sum total of what he had been told and read and been taught in school was so contradictory, so senseless, so wildly insane that none of it could be believed unless he personally confirmed it.

Wait a minute—The very telling of these lies, these senseless contradictions, was a fact in itself, known to him directly. To that extent they were data, probably very important data.

The world as it had been shown to him was a piece of unreason, an idiot's dream. Yet it was on too mammoth a scale to be without some reason. He came wearily back to his original point: Since the world could not be as crazy as it appeared to be, it must necessarily have been arranged to appear crazy in order to deceive him as to the truth.

Why had they done it to him? And what was the truth behind the sham? There must be some clue in the deception itself. What thread ran through it all? Well, in the first place he had been given a superabundance of explanations of the world around him, philosophies, religions, "common sense" explanations. Most of them were so clumsy, so obviously inadequate, or meaningless, that they could hardly have expected him to take them seriously. They must have intended them simply as misdirection.

But there were certain basic assumptions running through all the hundreds of explanations of the craziness around him. It must be these basic assumptions that he was expected to believe. For example, there was the deepseated assumption that he was a "human being," essentially like millions of others around him and billions more in the past and the future.

That was nonsense! He had never once managed to get into real communication with all those things that looked so much like him but were so different. In the agony of his loneliness, he had deceived himself that Alice understood him and was a being like him. He knew now that he had suppressed and refused to examine thousands of little discrepancies because he could not bear the thought of returning to complete loneliness. He had needed to believe that his wife was a living, breathing being of his own kind who understood his inner thoughts. He had refused to consider the possibility that she was simply a mirror, an echo—or something unthinkably worse.

He had found a mate, and the world was tolerable, even though dull, stupid, and full of petty annoyance. He was moderately happy and had put away his suspicions. He had accepted, quite docilely, the treadmill he was expected to use, until a slight mischance had momentarily cut through the fraud—then his suspicions had returned with impounded force; the bitter knowledge of his childhood had been confirmed.

He supposed that he had been a fool to make a fuss about it. If he had kept his mouth shut they would not have locked him up. He should have been as subtle and as shrewd as they, kept his eyes and ears open and learned the details of and the reasons for the plot against him. He might have learned how to circumvent it.

But what if they had locked him up—the whole world was an asylum and all of them his keepers.

A key scraped in the lock, and he looked up to see an attendant entering with a tray. "Here's your dinner, sir."

"Thanks, Joe," he said gently. "Just put it down."

"Movies tonight, sir," the attendant went on. "Wouldn't you like to go? Dr. Hayward said you could—"

"No, thank you. I prefer not to."

"I wish you would, sir." He noticed with amusement the persuasive intentness of the attendant's manner. "I think the doctor wants you to. It's a good movie. There's a Mickey Mouse cartoon—"

"You almost persuade me, Joe," he answered with passive agreeableness. "Mickey's trouble is the same as mine, essentially. However, I'm not going. They need not bother to hold movies tonight."

"Oh, there will be movies in any case, sir. Lots of our other guests will attend."

"Really? Is that an example of thoroughness, or are you simply keeping up the pretense in talking to me? It isn't necessary, Joe, if it's any strain on you. I know the game. If I don't attend, there is no point in holding movies."

He liked the grin with which the attendant answered this thrust. Was it possible that this being was created just as he appeared to be—big muscles, phlegmatic disposition, tolerant, doglike? Or was there nothing going on behind those kind eyes, nothing but robot reflex? No, it was more likely that he was one of them, since he was so closely in attendance on him.

The attendant left and he busied himself at his supper tray, scooping up the already-cut bites of meat with a spoon, the only implement provided. He smiled again at their caution and thoroughness. No danger of that—he would not destroy this body as long as it served him in investigating the truth of the matter. There were still many different avenues of research available before taking that possibly irrevocable step.

After supper he decided to put this thoughts in better order by writing them; obtained paper. He should start with a general statement of some underlying postulate of the credos that had been drummed into him all his "life." Life? Yes, that was a good one. He wrote:

"I am told that I was born a certain number of years ago and that I will die a similar number of years hence. Various clumsy stories have been offered me to explain to me where I was before birth and what becomes of me after death, but they are rough lies, not intended to deceive, except as misdirection. In every other possible way the world around me assures me that I am mortal, here but a few years, and a few years hence gone completely—nonexistent.

"WRONG—I am immortal. I transcend this little time axis; a seventy-year span on it is but a casual phase in my experience. Second only to the prime datum of my own existence is the emotionally convincing certainty of my own continuity. I may be a closed curve, but, closed or open, I neither have a beginning nor an end. Self-awareness is not relational; it is absolute, and cannot be reached to be destroyed, or created. Memory, however, being a relational aspect of consciousness, may be tampered with and possibly destroyed.

"It is true that most religions which have been offered me teach immortality, but note the fashion in which they teach it. The surest way to lie convincingly is to tell the truth unconvincingly. They did not wish me to believe.

"Caution: Why have they tried so hard to convince me that I am going to die in a few years? There must be a very important reason. I infer that they are preparing me for some sort of a major change. It may be crucially important for me to figure out their intentions about this—probably I have several years in which to reach a decision. Note: Avoid using the types of reasoning they have taught me."

The attendant was back. "Your wife is here, sir."

"Tell her to go away."

"Please, sir—Dr. Hayward is most anxious that you should see her."

"Tell Dr. Hayward that I said that he is an excellent chess player."

"Yes, sir." The attendant waited for a moment. "Then you won't see her, sir?"

"No, I won't see her."

He wandered around the room for some minutes after the attendant had left, too distrait to return to his recapitulation. By and large they had played very decently with him since they had brought him here. He was glad that they had allowed him to have a room alone, and he certainly had more time free for contemplation than had ever been possible on the outside. To be sure, continuous effort to keep him busy and to distract him was made, but, by being stubborn, he was able to circumvent the rules and gain some hours each day for introspection.

But, damnation!—he did wish they would not persist in using Alice in their attempts to divert his thoughts. Although the intense terror and revulsion which she had inspired in him when he had first rediscovered the truth had now aged into a simple feeling of repugnance and distaste for her company, nevertheless it was emotionally upsetting to be reminded of her, to be forced into making decisions about her.

After all, she had been his wife for many years. Wife? What was a wife? Another soul like one's own, a complement, the other necessary pole to the couple, a sanctuary of understanding and sympathy in the boundless depths of aloneness. That was what he had thought, what he had needed to believe and had believed fiercely for years. The yearning need for companionship of his own kind had caused him to see himself reflected in those beautiful eyes and had made him quite uncritical of occasional incongruities in her responses.

He sighed. He felt that he had sloughed off most of the typed emotional reactions which they had taught him by precept and example, but Alice had gotten under his skin, 'way under, and it still hurt. He had been happy—what if it had been a dope dream? They had given him an excellent, a beautiful mirror to play with—the more fool he to have looked behind it!

Wearily he turned back to his summing up:

"The world is explained in either one of two ways; the common-sense way which says that the world is pretty much as it appears to be and that ordinary human conduct and motivations are reasonable, and the religio-mystic solution which states that the world is dream stuff, unreal, insubstantial, with reality somewhere beyond.

"WRONG—both of them. The common-sense scheme has no sense to it of any sort. Life is short an full of trouble. Man born of woman is born to trouble as the sparks fly upward. His days are few and they are numbered. All is vanity and vexation. Those quotations may be jumbled and incorrect, but that is a fair statement of the common-sense world-is-as-it-seems in its only possible evaluation. In such a world, human striving is about as rational as the blind dartings of a moth against a light bulb. The common-sense world is a blind insanity, out of nowhere, going nowhere, to no purpose.

"As for the other solution, it appears more rational on the surface, in that it rejects the utterly irrational world of common sense. But it is not a rational solution, it is simply a flight from reality of any sort, for it refuses to believe the results of the only available direct communication between the ego and the Outside. Certainly the 'five senses' are poor enough channels of communication, but they are the only channels."

He crumpled up the paper and flung himself from the chair. Order and logic were no good—his answer was right because it smelled right. But he still did not know all the answer. Why the grand scale to the deception, countless creatures, whole continents, an enormously involved and minutely detailed matrix of insane history, insane tradition, insane culture? Why bother with more than a cell and a strait jacket?

It must be, it had to be, because it was supremely important to deceive him completely, because a lesser deception would not do. Could it be that they dare not let him suspect his real identity no matter how difficult and involved the fraud?

He had to know. In some fashion he must get behind the deception and see what went on when he was not looking. He had had one glimpse; this time he must see the actual workings, catch the puppet masters in their manipulations.

Obviously the first step must be to escape from this asylum, but to do it so craftily that they would never see him, never catch up with him, not have a chance to set the stage before him. That would be hard to do. He must excel them in shrewdness and subtlety.

Once decided, he spent the rest of the evening in considering the means by which he might accomplish his purpose. It seemed almost impossible—he must get away without once being seen and remain in strict hiding. They must lose track of him completely in order that they would not know where to center their deceptions. That would mean going without food for several days. Very well—he could do it. He must not give them any warning by unusual action or manner.

The lights blinked twice. Docilely he go up and commenced preparations for bed. When the attendant looked through the peephole he was already in bed, with his face turned to the wall.

Gladness! Gladness everywhere! It was good to be with his own kind, to hear the music swelling out of every living thing, as it always had and always would—good to know that everything was living and aware of him, participating in him, as he participated in them. It was good to be, good to know the unity of many and the diversity of one. There had been one bad thought—the details escaped him—but it was gone—it had never been; there was no place for it.

THE EARLY-MORNING SOUNDS FROM the adjacent ward penetrated the sleepladen body which served him here and gradually recalled him to awareness of the hospital room. The transition was so gentle that he carried over full recollection of what he had been doing and why. He lay still, a gentle smile on his face, and savored the uncouth, but not unpleasant, languor of the body he wore. Strange that he had ever forgotten despite their tricks and stratagems. Well, now that he had recalled the key, he would quickly set things right in this odd place. He would call them in at once and announce the new order. It would be amusing to see old Glaroon's expression when he realized that the cycle had ended—

The click of the peephole and rasp of the door being unlocked guillotined his line of thought. The morning attendant pushed briskly in with the breakfast tray and placed it on the tip table. "Morning, sir. Nice, bright day—want it in bed, or will you get up?"

Don't answer! Don't listen! Suppress this distraction! This is part of their plan—But it was too late, too late. He felt himself slipping, falling, wrenched from reality back into the fraud world in which they had kept him. It was gone, gone completely, with no single association around him to which to anchor memory. There was nothing left but the sense of heartbreaking loss and the acute ache of unsatisfied catharsis.

"Leave it where it is. I'll take care of it."

"Okey-doke." The attendant bustled out, slamming the door, and noisily locked it.

He lay quite still for a long time, every nerve end in his body screaming for relief.

At last he got out of bed, still miserably unhappy, and attempted to concentrate on his plans for escape. But the psychic wrench he had received in being recalled so suddenly from his plane of reality had left him bruised and emotionally disturbed. His mind insisted on rechewing its doubts, rather than engage in constructive thought. Was it possible that the doctor was right, that he was not alone in his miserable dilemma? Was he really simply suffering from paranoia, delusion of self-importance?

Could it be that each unit in this yeasty swarm around him was the prison of another lonely ego-helpless, blind, and speechless, condemned to an eternity of miserable loneliness? Was the look of suffering which he had brought to Alice's face a true reflection of inner torment and not simply a piece of play acting intended to maneuver him into compliance with their plans?

A knock sounded at the door. He said "Come in," without looking up. Their comings and goings did not matter to him.

"Dearest—" A well-known voice spoke slowly and hesitantly.

"Alice!" He was on his feet at once, and facing her. "Who let you in here?"

"Please, dear, please—I had to see you."

"It isn't fair. It isn't fair." He spoke more to himself than to her. Then: "Why did you come?"

She stood up to him with a dignity he had hardly expected. The beauty of her childlike face had been marred by line and shadow, but it shone with an unexpected courage. "I love you," she answered quietly. "You can tell me to go away, but you can't make me stop loving you and trying to help you."

He turned away from her in an agony of indecision. Could it be possible that he had misjudged her? Was there, behind that barrier of flesh and sound symbols, a spirit that truly yearned toward his? Lovers whispering in the dark—*"You do understand, don't you?"*

*"Yes, dear heart, I understand."*

*"Then nothing that happens to us can matter, as long as we are together and understand—"* Words, words, rebounding hollowly from an unbroken wall—

No, he couldn't be wrong! Test her again—"Why did you keep me on that job in Omaha?"

"But I didn't make you keep that job. I simply pointed out that we should think twice before—"

"Never mind. Never mind." Soft hands and a sweet face preventing him with mild stubbornness from ever doing the thing that his heart told him to do. Always with the best of intentions, the best of intentions, but always so that he had never quite managed to do the silly, unreasonable things that he knew were worth while. Hurry, hurry, hurry, and strive, with an angel-faced jockey to see that you don't stop long enough to think for yourself—

"Why did you try to stop me from going back upstairs that day?"

She managed to smile, although her eyes were already spilling over with tears. "I didn't know it really mattered to you. I didn't want us to miss the train."

It had been a small thing, an unimportant thing. For some reason not clear to him he had insisted on going back upstairs to his study when they were about to leave the house for a short vacation. It was raining, and she had pointed out that there was barely enough time to get to the station. He had surprised himself and her, too, by insisting on his own way in circumstances in which he had never been known to be stubborn.

He had actually pushed her to one side and forced his way up the stairs. Even then nothing might have come of it had he not—quite unnecessarily—raised the shade of the window that faced toward the rear of the house.

It was a very small matter. It had been raining, hard, out in front. From this window the weather was clear and sunny, with no sign of rain.

He had stood there quite a long while, gazing out at the impossible sunshine and rearranging his cosmos in his mind. He re-examined long-suppressed doubts in the light of this one small but totally unexplainable discrepancy. Then he had turned and had found that she was standing behind him.

He had been trying ever since to forget the expression that he had surprised on her face.

"What about the rain?"

"The rain?" she repeated in a small, puzzled voice. "Why, it was raining, of course. What about it?"

"But it was not raining out my study window."

"What? But of course it was. I did notice the sun break through the clouds for a moment, but that was all."

"Nonsense!"

"But darling, what has the weather to do with you and me? What difference does it make whether it rains or not—to us?" She approached him timidly and slid a small hand between his arm and side. "Am I responsible for the weather?"

"I think you are. Now please go."

She withdrew from him, brushed blindly at her eyes, gulped once, then said in a voice held steady: "All right, I'll go. But remember—you can come home if you want to. And I'll be there, if you want me." She waited a moment, then added hesitantly: "Would you . . . would you kiss me good-by?"

He made no answer of any sort, neither with voice nor eyes. She looked at him, then turned, fumbled blindly for the door, and rushed through it.

The creature he knew as Alice went to the place of assembly without stopping to change form. "It is necessary to adjourn this sequence. I am no longer able to influence his decisions."

They had expected it, nevertheless they stirred with dismay.

The Glaroon addressed the First for Manipulation. "Prepare to graft the selected memory track at once."

Then, turning to the First for Operations, the Glaroon said: "The extrapolation shows that he will tend to escape within two of his days. This sequence degenerated primarily through your failure to extend that rainfall all around him. Be advised."

"It would be simpler if we understood his motives."

"In my capacity as Dr. Hayward, I have often thought so," commented the Glaroon acidly, "but if we understood his motives, we would be part of him. Bear in mind the Treaty! He almost remembered."

The creature known as Alice spoke up. "Could he not have the Taj Mahal next sequence? For some reason he values it."

"You are becoming assimilated!"

"Perhaps. I am not in fear. Will he receive it?"

"It will be considered."

The Glaroon continued with orders: "Leave structures standing until adjournment. New York City and Harvard University are now dismantled. Divert him from those sectors.

"Move!"

# Waldo

*The act was billed as* ballet tap—which does not describe it.

His feet created an intricate tympany of crisp, clean taps. There was a breath-catching silence as he leaped high into the air, higher than a human being should—and performed, while floating there, a fantastically improbable *entrechats douze.*

He landed on his toes, apparently poised, yet producing a fortissimo of thunderous taps.

The spotlights cut, the stage lights came up. The audience stayed silent a long moment, then realized it was time to applaud, and *gave.*

He stood facing them, letting the wave of their emotion sweep through him. He felt as if he could lean against it; it warmed him through to his bones.

It was wonderful to dance, glorious to be applauded, to be *liked,* to be *wanted.*

When the curtain rang down for the last time he let his dresser lead him away. He was always a little bit drunk at the end of a performance; dancing was a joyous intoxication even in rehearsal, but to have an audience lifting him, carrying him along, applauding him—he never grew jaded to it. It was always new and heartbreakingly wonderful.

"This way, chief. Give us a little smile." The flash bulb flared. "Thanks."

"Thank *you.* Have a drink." He motioned toward one end of his dressing room. They were all such nice fellows, such grand guys—the reporters, the photographers—all of them.

"How about one standing up?" He started to comply, but his dresser, busy with one slipper, warned him:

"You operate in half an hour."

"Operate?" the news photographer said. "What's it this time?"

"A left cerebrectomy," he answered.

"Yeah? How about covering it?"

"Glad to have you—if the hospital doesn't mind."

"We'll fix that."

Such grand guys.

"—trying to get a little different angle on a feature article." It was a feminine voice, near his ear. He looked around hastily, slightly confused. "For example, what made you decide to take up dancing as a career?"

"I'm sorry," he apologized. "I didn't hear you. I'm afraid it's pretty noisy in here."

"I said, why did you decide to take up dancing?"

"Well, now, I don't quite know how to answer that. I'm afraid we would have to go back quite a way—"

JAMES STEVENS SCOWLED AT HIS assistant engineer. "What have you got to look happy about?" he demanded.

"It's just the shape of my face," his assistant apologized. "Try laughing at this one: there's been another crash."

"Oh, cripes! Don't tell me—let me guess. Passenger or freight?"

"A Climax duo-freighter on the Chicago-Salt Lake shuttle, just west of North Platte. And, chief——"

"Yes?"

"The Big Boy wants to see you."

"That's interesting. That's very, very interesting. Mac——"

"Yeah, chief."

"How would you like to be Chief Traffic Engineer of North American Power-Air? I hear there's going to be a vacancy."

Mac scratched his nose. "Funny that you should mention that, chief. I was just going to ask you what kind of recommendation you could give me in case I went back into civil engineering. Ought to be worth something to you to get rid of me."

"I'll get rid of you—right now. You bust out to Nebraska, find that heap before the souvenir hunters tear it apart, and bring back its deKalbs and its control board."

"Trouble with cops, maybe?"

"You figure it out. Just be sure you come back."

Stevens's office was located immediately adjacent to the zone power plant; the business offices of North American were located in a hill, a good three quarters of a mile away. There was the usual interconnecting tunnel; Stevens entered it and deliberately chose the low-speed slide in order to have more time to think before facing the boss.

By the time he arrived he had made up his mind, but he did not like the answer.

The Big Boy—Stanley F. Gleason, Chairman of the Board—greeted him quietly. "Come in, Jim. Sit down. Have a cigar."

Stevens slid into a chair, declined the cigar and pulled out a cigarette, which he lit while looking around. Besides the chief and himself, there were present Harkness, head of the legal staff, Dr. Rambeau, Stevens's opposite number for research, and Striebel, the chief engineer for city power. Us five and no more, he thought grimly—all the heavyweights and none of the middleweights. Heads will roll!—starting with mine.

"Well," he said, almost belligerently, "we're all here. Who's got the cards? Do we cut for deal?"

Harkness looked faintly distressed by the impropriety; Rambeau seemed too sunk in some personal gloom to pay any attention to wisecracks in bad taste. Gleason ignored it. "We've been trying to figure a way out of our troubles, James. I left word for you on the chance that you might not have left."

"I stopped by simply to see if I had any personal mail," Stevens said bitterly. "Otherwise I'd be on the beach at Miami, turning sunshine into vitamin D."

"I know," said Gleason, "and I'm sorry. You deserve that vacation, Jimmie. But the situation has gotten worse instead of better. Any ideas?"

"What does Dr. Rambeau say?"

Rambeau looked up momentarily. "The deKalb receptors can't fail," he stated.

"But they do."

"They can't. You've operated them improperly." He sunk back into his personal prison.

Stevens turned back to Gleason and spread his hands. "So far as I know, Dr. Rambeau is right—but if the fault lies in the engineering department, I haven't been able to locate it. You can have my resignation."

"I don't want your resignation," Gleason said gently. "What I want is results. We have a responsibility to the public."

"And to the stockholders," Harkness put in.

"That will take care of itself if we solve the other," Gleason observed. "How about it, Jimmie? Any suggestions?"

Stevens bit his lip. "Just one," he announced, "and one I don't like to make. Then I look for a job peddling magazine subscriptions."

"So? Well, what is it?"

*"We've got to consult Waldo."*

Rambeau suddenly snapped out of his apathy. "What! That charlatan? This is a matter of *science.*"

Harkness said, "Really, Dr. Stevens——"

Gleason held up a hand. "Dr. Stevens' suggestion is logical. But I'm afraid it's a little late, Jimmie. I talked with him last week."

Harkness looked surprised; Stevens looked annoyed as well. "Without letting me know?"

"Sorry, Jimmie. I was just feeling him out. But it's no good. His terms, to us, amount to confiscation."

"Still sore over the Hathaway patents?"

"Still nursing his grudge."

"You should have let me handle the matter," Harkness put in. "He can't do this to us—there is public interest involved. Retain him, if need be, and let the fee be adjudicated in equity. I'll arrange the details."

"I'm afraid you would," Gleason said dryly. "Do you think a court order will make a hen lay an egg?"

Harkness looked indignant, but shut up.

Stevens continued, "I would not have suggested going to Waldo if I had not had an idea as how to approach him. I know a friend of his——"

"A friend of *Waldo*? I didn't know he had any."

"This man is sort of an uncle to him—his first physician. With his help I might get on Waldo's good side."

Dr. Rambeau stood up. "This is intolerable," he announced. "I must ask that you excuse me." He did not wait for an answer, but strode out, hardly giving the door time to open in front of him.

Gleason followed his departure with worried eyes. "Why does he take it so hard, Jimmie? You would think he hated Waldo personally."

"Probably he does, in a way. But it's more than that; his whole universe is toppling. For the last twenty years, ever since Pryor's reformulation of the General Field Theory did away with Heisenberg's Uncertainty Principle, physics has been considered an exact science. The power failures and transmission failures we have been suffering are a terrific nuisance to you and to me, but to Dr. Rambeau they amount to an attack on his faith. Better keep an eye on him."

"Why?"

"Because he might come unstruck entirely. It's a pretty serious matter for a man's religion to fail him."

"Hm-m-m. How about yourself? Doesn't it hit you just as hard?"

"Not quite. I'm an engineer—from Rambeau's point of view just a high-priced tinker. Difference in orientation. Not but what I'm pretty upset."

The audio circuit of the communicator on Gleason's desk came to life. "Calling Chief Engineer Stevens—calling Chief Engineer Stevens." Gleason flipped the tab.

"He's here. Go ahead."

"Company code, translated. Message follows: 'Cracked up four miles north of Cincinnati. Shall I go on to Nebraska, or bring in the you-know-what from my own crate?' Message ends. Signed 'Mac.'"

"Tell him to *walk* back!" Stevens said savagely.

"Very well, sir." The instrument cut off.

"Your assistant?" asked Gleason.

"Yes. That's about the last straw, chief. Shall I wait and try to analyze this failure, or shall I try to see Waldo?"

"Try to see Waldo."

"O.K. If you don't hear from me, just send my severance pay care of Palmdale Inn, Miami. I'll be the fourth beachcomber from the right."

Gleason permitted himself an unhappy smile. "If you *don't* get results, I'll be the fifth. Good luck."

"So long."

When Stevens had gone, Chief Stationary Engineer Striebel spoke up for the first time. "If the power to the cities fails," he said softly, "you know where I'll be, don't you?"

"Where? Beachcomber number six?"

"Not likely. I'll be number one in my spot—first man to be lynched."

"But the power to the cities *can't* fail. You've got too many cross-connects and safety devices."

"Neither can the deKalbs fail, supposedly. Just the same—think about Sublevel 7 in Pittsburgh, with the lights out. Or, rather, don't think about it!"

DOC GRIMES LET HIMSELF INTO the aboveground access which led into his home, glanced at the announcer, and noted with mild, warm interest that someone close enough to him to possess his house combination was inside. He moved ponderously downstairs, favoring his game leg, and entered the lounging room.

"Hi, Doc!" James Stevens got up when the door snapped open and came forward to greet him.

"H'lo, James. Pour yourself a drink. I see you have. Pour me one."

"Right."

While his friend complied, Grimes shucked himself out of the outlandish anachronistic greatcoat he was wearing and threw it more or less in the direction of the robing alcove. It hit the floor heavily, much more heavily than its appearance justified, despite its unwieldy bulk. It clunked.

Stooping, he peeled off thick overtrousers as massive as the coat. He was dressed underneath in conventional business tights in blue and sable. It was not a style that suited him. To an eye unsophisticated in matters of civilized dress—let us say the mythical man-from-Antares—he might have seemed uncouth, even unsightly. He looked a good bit like an elderly fat beetle.

James Stevens's eye made no note of the tights, but he looked with disapproval on the garments which had just been discarded. "Still wearing that fool armor," he commented.

"Certainly."

"Damn it, Doc—you'll make yourself sick, carrying that junk around. It's unhealthy."

"Danged sight sicker if I don't."

"Rats! *I* don't get sick, and *I* don't wear armor—outside the lab."

"You should." Grimes walked over to where Stevens had reseated himself. "Cross your knees." Stevens complied; Grimes struck him smartly below the kneecap with the edge of his palm. The reflex jerk was barely perceptible. "Lousy," he remarked, then peeled back his friend's right eyelid.

"You're in poor shape," he added after a moment.

Stevens drew away impatiently. "*I'm* all right. It's you we're talking about."

"What about me?"

"Well—Damnation, Doc, you're throwing away your reputation. They talk about you."

Grimes nodded. "I know. 'Poor old Gus Grimes—a slight touch of cerebral termites.' Don't worry about my reputation; I've always been out of step. What's your fatigue index?"

"I don't know. It's all right."

"It is, eh? I'll wrestle you, two falls out of three."

Stevens rubbed his eyes. "Don't needle me, Doc. I'm run-down. I know that, but it isn't anything but overwork."

"Humph! James, you are a fair-to-middlin' radiation physicist——"

"Engineer."

"—engineer. But you're no medical man. You can't expect to pour every sort of radiant energy through the human system year after year and not pay for it. It wasn't designed to stand it."

"But I wear armor in the lab. You know that."

"Surely. But how about outside the lab?"

"But——Look, Doc—I hate to say it, but your whole thesis is ridiculous. Sure there is radiant energy in the air these days, but nothing harmful. All the colloidal chemists agree——"

"Colloidal, fiddlesticks!"

"But you've got to admit that biological economy is a matter of colloidal chemistry."

"I've got to admit nothing. I'm not contending that colloids are not the fabric of living tissue—they are. But I've maintained for forty years that it was dangerous to expose living tissue to assorted radiation without being sure of the effect. From an evolutionary standpoint the human animal is habituated to and adapted to only the natural radiation of the sun—and he can't stand that any too well, even under a thick blanket of ionization. Without that blanket——Did you ever see a solar-X type cancer?"

"Of course not."

"No, you're too young. *I* have. Assisted at the autopsy of one, when I was an intern. Chap was on the Second Venus Expedition. Four hundred and thirty-eight cancers we counted in him, then gave up."

"Solar-X is whipped."

"Sure it is. But it ought to be a warning. You bright young squirts can cook up things in your labs that we medicos can't begin to cope with. We're behind—bound to be. We usually don't know what's happened until the damage is done. This time you've torn it." He sat down heavily and suddenly looked as tired and whipped as did his younger friend.

Stevens felt the sort of tongue-tied embarrassment a man may feel when a dearly beloved friend falls in love with an utterly worthless person. He wondered what he could say that would not seem rude.

He changed the subject. "Doc, I came over because I had a couple of things on my mind—"

"Such as?"

"Well, a vacation for one. I know I'm run-down. I've been overworked, and a vacation seems in order. The other is your pal, Waldo."

"Huh?"

"Yeah. Waldo Farthingwaite-Jones, bless his stiff-necked, bad-tempered heart."

"Why Waldo? You haven't suddenly acquired an interest in *myasthenia gravis,* have you?"

"Well, no. I don't care what's wrong with him physically. He can have hives, dandruff, or the galloping never-get-overs, for all I care. I hope he has. What I want is to pick his brains."

"So?"

"I can't do it alone. Waldo doesn't help people; he *uses* them. You're his only normal contact with people."

"That is not entirely true—"

"Who else?"

"You misunderstand me. He has *no* normal contacts. I am simply the only person who dares to be rude to him."

"But I thought— Never mind. D'you know, this is an inconvenient setup? Waldo is the man we've got to have. Why should it come about that a genius of his caliber should be so unapproachable, so immune to ordinary social demands? Oh, I know his disease has a lot to do with it, but why should *this* man have *this* disease? It's an improbable coincidence."

"It's not a matter of his infirmity," Grimes told him. "Or, rather, not in the way you put it. His weakness *is* his genius, in a way——"

"Huh?"

"Well——" Grimes turned his sight inward, let his mind roam back over his long association—lifelong, for Waldo—with this particular patient. He remembered his subliminal misgivings when he delivered the child. The infant had been sound enough, superficially, except for a slight blueness. But then lots of babies were somewhat cyanotic in the delivery room. Nevertheless, he had felt a slight reluctance to give it the tunk on the bottom, the slap which would shock it into taking its first lungful of air.

But he had squelched his own feelings, performed the necessary "laying on of hands," and the freshly born human had declared its independence with a satisfactory squall. There was nothing else he could have done; he was a young G.P. then, who took his Hippocratic oath seriously. He still took it seriously, he supposed, even though he sometimes referred to it as the "hypocritical" oath. Still, he had been right in his feelings; there *had* been something rotten about that child—something that was not entirely *myasthenia gravis.*

He had felt sorry for the child at first, as well as having an irrational feeling of responsibility for its condition. Pathological muscular weakness is an almost totally crippling condition, since the patient has no unaffected limbs to retrain into substitutes. There the victim must lie, all organs, limbs, and functions present, yet so pitifully, completely weak as to be unable to perform any normal function. He must spend his life in a condition of exhausted collapse, such as you or I might reach at the finish line of a grueling cross-country run. No help for him, and no relief.

During Waldo's childhood he had hoped constantly that the child would die, since he was so obviously destined for tragic uselessness, while simultaneously, as a physician, doing everything within his own skill and the skill of numberless consulting specialists to keep the child alive and cure it.

Naturally, Waldo could not attend school; Grimes ferreted out sympathetic tutors. He could indulge in no normal play; Grimes invented sickbed games which would not only stimulate Waldo's imagination but encourage him to use his flabby muscles to the full, weak extent of which he was capable.

Grimes had been afraid that the handicapped child, since it was not subjected to the usual maturing stresses of growing up, would remain infantile. He knew now—had known for a long time—that he need not have worried. Young Waldo grasped at what little life was offered him, learned thirstily, tried with a sweating tenseness of will to force his undisciplined muscles to serve him.

He was clever in thinking of dodges whereby to circumvent his muscular weakness. At seven he devised a method of controlling a spoon with two hands, which permitted him—painfully—to feed himself. His first mechanical invention was made at ten.

It was a gadget which held a book for him, at any angle, controlled lighting for the book, and turned its pages. The gadget responded to finger tip pressure on a simple control panel. Naturally, Waldo could not build it himself, but he could conceive it, and explain it; Farthingwaite-Joneses could well afford the services of a designing engineer to build the child's conception.

Grimes was inclined to consider this incident, in which the child Waldo acted in a role of intellectual domination over a trained mature adult neither blood relation nor servant, as a landmark in the psychological process whereby Waldo eventually came to regard the entire human race as his servants, his *hands,* present or potential.

"WHAT'S EATING YOU, DOC?"

"Eh? Sorry, I was daydreaming. See here, son—you mustn't be too harsh on Waldo. I don't *like* him myself. But you must take him as a whole."

"*You* take him."

"*Shush*. You spoke of needing his genius. He wouldn't have a genius if he had not been crippled. You didn't know his parents. They were good stock—fine, intelligent people—but nothing spectacular. Waldo's potentialities weren't any greater than theirs, but he had to do more with them to accomplish anything. He had to do everything the hard way. He *had* to be clever."

"Sure. Sure, but why should he be so utterly poisonous? Most big men aren't."

"Use your head. To get anywhere in his condition he had to develop a will, a driving one-track mind, with a total disregard for any other considerations. What would you expect him to be but stinking selfish?"

"I'd—Well, never mind. We need him and that's that."

"Why?"

Stevens explained.

IT MAY PLAUSIBLY BE URGED that the shape of a culture—its mores, evaluations, family organizations, eating habits, living patterns, pedagogical methods, institutions, forms of government, and so forth—arise from the economic necessities of its technology. Even though the thesis be too broad and much oversimplified, it is nonetheless true that much which characterized the long peace which followed the constitutional establishment of the United Nations grew out of the technologies which were hothouse-forced by the needs of the belligerents in the war of the forties. Up to that time broadcast and beamcast were used only for commercial radio, with rare exceptions. Even telephony was done almost entirely by actual metallic connection from one instrument to another. If a man in Monterey wished to speak to his wife or partner in Boston, a physical, copper neuron stretched bodily across the continent from one to the other.

Radiant power was then a hop dream, found in Sunday supplements and comic books.

A concatenation—no, a meshwork—of new developments was necessary before the web of copper covering the continent could be dispensed with. Power could not broadcast economically; it was necessary to wait for the co-axial beam—a direct result of the imperative military shortages of the Great War. Radio telephony could not replace wired telephony until ultra micro-wave techniques made room in the ether, so to speak, for the traffic load. Even then it was necessary to invent a tuning device which could be used by a nontechnical person—a ten-year-old child, let us say—as easily as the dial selector which was characteristic of the commercial wired telephone of the era then terminating.

Bell Laboratories cracked that problem; the solution led directly to the radiant power receptor, domestic type, keyed, sealed, and metered. The way was open for commercial radio power transmission—except in on respect: efficiency. Aviation waited on the development of the Otto-cycle engine; the Industrial Revolution waited on the steam engine; radiant power waited on a really cheap, plentiful power source. Since radiation of power is inherently wasteful, it was necessary to have power cheap and plentiful enough to waste.

The same year brought atomic energy. The physicists working for the United States Army—the United States of North America had its own army then—produced a superexplosive; the notebooks recording their tests contained, when properly correlated, everything necessary to produce almost any other sort of nuclear reaction, even the so-called Solar Phoenix, the hydrogen-helium cycle, which is the source of the sun's power.

Radiant power became economically feasible—and inevitable.

The reaction whereby copper is broken down into phosphorus, silicon29 and helium3, plus degenerating chain reactions, was one of the several cheap and convenient means developed for producing unlimited and practically free power.

Of course Stevens included none of this in his explanation to Grimes. Grimes was absentmindedly aware of the whole dynamic process; he had seen radiant power grow up, just as his grandfather had seen the development of aviation. He had seen the great transmission lines removed from the sky—"mined" for their copper; he had seen the heavy cables being torn from the dug-up streets of Manhattan. He might even recall his first independent-unit radiotelephone with its somewhat disconcerting double dial—he had gotten a lawyer in Buenos Aires on it when attempting to reach his neighborhood delicatessen. For two weeks he made all his local calls by having them relayed back from South America before he discovered that it made a difference which dial he used first.

At that time Grimes had not yet succumbed to the new style in architecture. The London Plan did not appeal to him; he liked a house aboveground, where he could see it. When it became necessary to increase the floor space in his offices, he finally gave in and went subsurface, not so much for the cheapness, convenience, and general all-around practicability of living in a tri-conditioned cave, but because he had already become a little worried about the possible consequences of radiation pouring through the human body. The fused-earth walls of his new residence were covered with lead; the roof of the cave had a double thickness. His hole in the ground was as near radiationproof as he could make it.

"—THE MEAT OF THE MATTER," Stevens was saying, "is that the delivery of power to transportation units has become erratic as the devil. Not enough yet to tie up traffic, but enough to be very disconcerting. There have been some nasty accidents; we can't keep hushing them up forever. I've got to do something about it."

"Why?"

"'Why?' Don't be silly. In the first place as traffic engineer for NAPA my bread and butter depends on it. In the second place the problem is upsetting in itself. A properly designed piece of mechanism ought to work—all the time, every time. These don't, and we can't find out why not. Our staff mathematical physicists have about reached the babbling stage."

Grimes shrugged. Stevens felt annoyed by the gesture. "I don't think you appreciate the importance of this problem, Doc. Have you any idea of the amount of horsepower involved in transportation? Counting both private and commercial vehicles and common carriers, North American Power-Air supplies more than half the energy used in this continent. We *have* to be right. You can add to that our city-power affiliate. No trouble there—yet. But we don't *dare* think what a city-power breakdown would mean."

"I'll give you a solution."

"Yeah? Well, give."

"Junk it. Go back to oil-powered and steam-powered vehicles. Get rid of these damned radiant-powered deathtraps."

"Utterly impossible. You don't know what you're saying. It took more than fifteen years to make the changeover. Now we're geared to it. Gus, if NAPA closed up shop, half the population of the northwest seaboard would starve, to say nothing of the lake states and the Philly-Boston axis."

"Hrrmph——Well, all I've got to say is that that might be better than the slow poisoning that is going on now."

Stevens brushed it away impatiently. "Look, Doc, nurse a bee in your bonnet if you like, but don't ask me to figure it into my calculations. Nobody else sees any danger in radiant power."

Grimes answered mildly. "Point is, son, they aren't looking in the right place. Do you know what the high jump record was last year?"

"I never listen to the sport news."

"Might try it sometime. The record leveled off at seven foot two, 'bout twenty years back. Been dropping ever since. You might try graphing athletic records against radiation in the air—artificial radiation. Might find some results that would surprise you."

"Shucks, everybody knows there has been a swing away from heavy sports. The sweat-and-muscles fad died out, that's all. We've simply advanced into a more intellectual culture."

"Intellectual, hogwash! People quite playing tennis and such because they are tired all the time. Look at you. You're a mess."

"Don't needle me, Doc."

"Sorry. But there has been a clear deterioration in the performance of the human animal. If we had decent records on such things I could prove it, but any physician who's worth his salt can *see* it, if he's got eyes in him and isn't wedded to a lot of fancy instruments. I can't prove what causes it, not yet, but I've a damned good hunch that it's caused by the stuff you peddle."

"Impossible. There isn't a radiation put on the air that hasn't been tested very carefully in the bio labs. We're neither fools nor knaves."

"Maybe you don't test 'em long enough. I'm not talking about a few hours, or a few weeks; I'm talking about the cumulative effects of years of radiant frequencies pouring through the tissues. What does that do?"

"Why, nothing—I believe."

"You believe, but you don't know. Nobody has ever tried to find out. F'rinstance—what effect does sunlight have on silicate glass? Ordinarily you would say 'none,' but you've seen desert glass?"

"That bluish-lavender stuff? Of course."

"Yes. A bottle turns colored in a few months in the Mojave Desert. But have you ever seen the windowpanes in the old houses on Beacon Hill?"

"I've never been on Beacon Hill."

"O.K., then I'll tell you. Same phenomena—only it takes a century or more, in Boston. Now tell me—you savvy physics—could you measure the change taking place in those Beacon Hill windows?"

"Mm-m-m—probably not."

"But it's going on just the same. Has anyone ever tried to measure the changes produced in human tissue by thirty years of exposure to ultra short-wave radiation?"

"No, but——"

"No 'buts.' I see an effect. I've made a wild guess at a cause. Maybe I'm wrong. But I've felt a bit more spry since I've taken to invariably wearing my lead overcoat whenever I go out."

Stevens surrendered the argument. "Maybe you're right, Doc. I won't fuss with you. How about Waldo? Will you take me to him and help me handle him?"

"When do you want to go?"

"The sooner the better."

"Now?"

"Suits."

"Call your office."

"Are you ready to leave right now? It would suit me. As far as the front office is concerned, I'm on vacation; nevertheless, I've got this on my mind so I want to get at it."

"Quit talking and git."

They went topside to where their cars were parked. Grimes headed toward his, a big-bodied old-fashioned Boeing family landau. Stevens checked him. "You aren't planning to go in that? It 'u'd take us the rest of the day."

"Why not? She's got an auxiliary space drive and she's tight. You could fly from here to the Moon and back."

"Yes, but she's so infernal slow. We'll use my 'broomstick.'"

Grimes let his eyes run over his friend's fusi-formed little speedster. Its body was as nearly invisible as the plastic industry could achieve. A surface layer, two molecules thick, gave it a refractive index sensibly identical with that of air. When perfectly clean it was very difficult to see. At the moment it had picked up enough casual dust and water vapor to be faintly seen—a ghost of a soap bubble of a ship.

Running down the middle, clearly visible through the walls, was the only metal part of the ship—the shaft, or, more properly, the axis core, and the spreading sheaf of deKalb receptors at its terminus. The appearance was enough like a giant witch's broom to justify the nickname. Since the saddles, of transparent plastic, were mounted tandem over the shaft so that the metal rod passed between the legs of the pilot and passengers, the nickname was doubly apt.

"Son," Grimes remarked, "I know I ain't pretty, nor am I graceful. Nevertheless, I retain a certain residuum of self-respect and some shred of dignity. I am *not* going to tuck that thing between my shanks and go scooting through the air on it."

"Oh, rats! You're old-fashioned."

"I may be. Nevertheless, any peculiarities I have managed to retain to my present age I plan to hang onto. No."

"Look—I'll polarize the hull before we raise. How about it?"

"Opaque?"

"Opaque."

Grimes slid a regretful glance at his own frumpish boat, but assented by fumbling for the barely visible port of the speedster. Stevens assisted him; they climbed in and straddled the stick.

"Atta boy, Doc," Stevens commended, "I'll have you there in three shakes. That tub of yours probably won't do over five hundred, and Wheelchair must be all of twenty-five thousand miles up."

"I'm never in a hurry," Grimes commented, "and don't call Waldo's house 'Wheelchair'—not to his face."

"I'll remember," Stevens promised. He fumbled, apparently in empty air; the hull suddenly became dead black, concealing them. It changed as suddenly to mirror bright; the car quivered, then shot up out of sight.

WALDO F. JONES SEEMED TO be floating in thin air at the center of a spherical room. The appearance was caused by the fact that he was indeed floating in air. His house lay in a free orbit, with a period of just over twenty-four hours. No spin had been impressed on his home; the pseudo gravity of centrifugal force was the thing he wanted least. He had left earth to get away from its gravitational field; he had not been down to the surface one in the seventeen years since his house was built and towed into her orbit; he never intended to do so for any purpose whatsoever.

Here, floating free in space in his own air-conditioned shell, he was almost free of the unbearable lifelong slavery to his impotent muscles. What little strength he had he could spend economically, in movement, rather than in fighting against the tearing, tiring weight of the Earth's thick field.

Waldo had been acutely interested in space flight since early boyhood, not from any desire to explore the depths, but because his boyish, overtrained mind had seen the enormous advantage—to him—in weightlessness. While still in his teens he had helped the early experimenters in space flight over a hump by supplying them with a control system which a pilot could handle delicately while under the strain of two or three gravities.

Such an invention was no trouble at all to him; he had simply adapted manipulating devices which he himself used in combating the overpowering weight of one gravity. The first successful and safe rocket ship contained relays which had once aided Waldo in moving himself from bed to wheelchair.

The deceleration tanks, which are now standard equipment for the lunar mail ships, traced their parentage to a flotation tank in which Waldo habitually had eaten and slept up to the time when he left the home of his parents for his present, somewhat unique, home. Most of his basic inventions had originally been conceived for his personal convenience, and only later adapted for commercial exploitation. Even the ubiquitous and grotesquely humanoid gadgets known universally as "waldoes"—Waldo F. Jones's Synchronous Reduplicating Pantograph, Pat. #296,001,437, new series, *et al*—passed through several generations of development and private use in Waldo's machine shop before he redesigned them for mass production. The first of them, a primitive gadget compared with the waldoes now to be found in every shop, factory, plant, and warehouse in the country, had been designed to enable Waldo to operate a metal lathe.

Waldo had resented the nickname the public had fastened on them—it struck him as overly familiar—but he had coldly recognized the business advantage to himself in having the public identify him verbally with a gadget so useful and important.

When the newscasters tagged his spacehouse "Wheelchair," one might have expected him to regard it as more useful publicity. That he did not so regard it, that he resented it and tried to put a stop to it, arose from another and peculiarly Waldo-ish fact: Waldo did not think of himself as a cripple.

He saw himself not as a crippled human being, but as something higher than human, the next step up, a being so superior as not to need the coarse, brutal strength of the smooth apes. Hairy apes, smooth apes, then Waldo—so the progression ran in his mind. A chimpanzee, with muscles that hardly bulge at all, can tug as high as fifteen hundred pounds with one hand. This Waldo had proved by obtaining one and patiently enraging it into full effort. A well-developed man can grip one hundred and fifty pounds with one hand. Wadlo's own grip, straining until the sweat sprang out, had never reached fifteen pounds.

Whether the obvious inference were fallacious or true, Waldo believed in it, evaluated by it. Men were overmuscled canaille, smooth chimps. He felt himself at least ten times superior to them.

He had much to go on.

Though floating in air, he was busy, quite busy. Although he never went to the surface of the Earth his business was there. Aside from managing his many properties he was in regular practice as a consulting engineer, specializing in motion analysis. Hanging close to him in the room were the paraphernalia necessary to the practice of his profession. Facing him was a four-by-five color-stereo television receptor. Two sets of co-ordinates, rectilinear and polar, crosshatched it. Another smaller receptor hung above it and to the right. Both receptors were fully recording, by means of parallel circuits conveniently out of the way in another compartment.

The smaller receptor showed the faces of two men watching him. The larger showed a scene inside a large shop, hangarlike in its proportions. In the immediate foreground, almost full size, was a grinder in which was being machined a large casting of some sort. A workman stood beside it, a look of controlled exasperation on his face.

"He's the best you've got," Waldo stated to the two men in the smaller screen. "To be sure, he is clumsy and does not have the touch for fine work, but he is superior to the other morons you call machinists."

The workman looked around, as if trying to locate the voice. It was evident that he could hear Waldo, but that no vision receptor had been provided for him. "Did you mean that crack for me?" he said harshly.

"You misunderstand me, my good man," Waldo said sweetly. "I was complimenting you. I actually have hopes of being able to teach you the rudiments of precision work. Then we shall expect you to teach those butterbrained oafs around you. The gloves, please."

Near the man, mounted on the usual stand, were a pair of primary waldoes, elbow length and human digited. They were floating on the line, in parallel with a similar pair physically in front of Waldo. The secondary waldoes, whose actions could be controlled by Waldo himself by means of his primaries, were mounted in front of the power tool in the position of the operator.

Waldo's remark had referred to the primaries near the workman. The machinist glanced at them, but made no move to insert his arms in them. "I don't take no orders from nobody I can't see," he said flatly. He looked sidewise out of the scene as he spoke.

"Now, Jenkins," commenced one of the two men in the smaller screen.

Waldo sighed. "I really haven't the time or the inclination to solve your problems of shop discipline. Gentlemen, please turn your pickup, so that our petulant friend may see me."

The change was accomplished; the workman's face appeared in the background of the smaller of Waldo's screens, as well as in the larger. "There—is that better?" Waldo said gently. The workman grunted.

"Now . . . your name, please?"

"Alexander Jenkins."

"Very well, friend Alec—the gloves."

Jenkins thrust his arms into the waldoes and waited. Waldo put his arms into the primary pair before him; all three pairs, including the secondary pair mounted before the machine, came to life. Jenkins bit his lip, as if he found unpleasant the sensation of having his fingers manipulated by the gauntlets he wore.

Waldo flexed and extended his fingers gently; the two pairs of waldoes in the screen followed in exact, simultaneous parallelism. "Feel it, my dear Alec," Waldo advised. "Gently, gently—the sensitive touch. Make your muscles work for you." He then started hand movements of definite pattern; the waldoes at the power tool reached up, switched on the power, and began gently, gracefully, to continue the machining of the casting. A mechanical hand reached down, adjusted a vernier, while the other increased the flow of oil cooling the cutting edge. "Rhythm, Alec, rhythm. No jerkiness, no unnecessary movement. Try to get in time with me."

The casting took shape with deceptive rapidity, disclosed what it was—the bonnet piece for an ordinary three-way nurse. The chucks drew back from it; it dropped to the belt beneath, and another rough casting took its place. Waldo continued with unhurried skill, his finger motions within his waldoes exerting pressure which would need to be measured in fractions of ounces, but the two sets of waldoes, paralleled to him thousands of miles below, followed his motions accurately and with force appropriate to heavy work at hand.

Another casting landed on the belt—several more. Jenkins, although not called upon to do any work in his proper person, tired under the strain of attempting to anticipate and match Waldo's motions. Sweat dripped down his forehead, ran off his nose, accumulated on his chin. Between castings he suddenly withdrew his arms from the paralleled primaries. "That's enough," he announced.

"One more, Alec. You are improving."

"No!" He turned as if to walk off. Waldo made a sudden movement—so sudden as to strain him, even in his weight-free environment. One steel hand of the secondary waldoes lashed out, grasped Jenkins by the wrist.

"Not so fast, Alec."

"Let go of me!"

"Softly, Alec, softly. You'll do as you are told, *won't you*?" The steel hand clamped down hard, twisted. Waldo had exerted all of two ounces of pressure.

Jenkins grunted. The one remaining spectator—one had left soon after the lesson started—said, "Oh, I say, Mr. Jones!"

"Let him obey, or fire him. You know the terms of my contract."

There was a sudden cessation of stereo and sound, cut from the Earth end. It came back on a few seconds later. Jenkins was surly, but no longer recalcitrant. Waldo continued as if nothing had happened. "Once more, my dear Alec."

When the repetition had been completed, Waldo directed, "Twenty times, wearing the wrist and elbow lights with the chronanalyzer in the picture. I shall expect the superposed strips to match, Alec." He cut off the larger screen without further words and turned to the watcher in the smaller screen. "Same time tomorrow, McNye. Progress is satisfactory. In time we'll turn this madhouse of yours into a modern plant." He cleared that screen without saying good-by.

Waldo terminated the business interview somewhat hastily, because he had been following with one eye certain announcements on his own local information board. A craft was approaching his house. Nothing strange about that; tourists were forever approaching and being pushed away by his autoguardian circuit. But this craft had the approach signal, was now clamping to his threshold flat. It was a broomstick, but he could not place the license number. Florida license. Whom did he know with a Florida license?

He immediately realized the he knew no one who possessed his approach signal—that list was *very* short—and who could also reasonably be expected to sport a Florida license. The suspicious defensiveness with which he regarded the entire world asserted itself; he cut in the circuit whereby he could control by means of his primary waldoes the strictly illegal but highly lethal inner defenses of his home. The craft was opaqued; he did not like that.

A youngish man wormed his way out. Waldo looked him over. A stranger—face vaguely familiar perhaps. An ounce of pressure in the primaries and the face would cease to be a face, but Waldo's actions were under cold cortical control; he held his fire. The man turned, as if to assist another passenger. Yes, there was another. Uncle Gus!—but the doddering old fool had brought a stranger with him. He knew better than that. He knew how Waldo felt about strangers!

Nevertheless, he released the outer lock of the reception room and let them in.

Gus Grimes snaked his way through the lock, pulling himself from one handrail to the next, and panting a little as he always did when forced to move weight free. Matter of diaphragm control, he told himself as he always did; can't be the exertion. Stevens streaked in after him, displaying a groundhog's harmless pride in handling himself well in space conditions. Grimes arrested himself just inside the reception room, grunted, and spoke to a man-sized dummy waiting there. "Hello, Waldo."

The dummy turned his eyes and head slightly. "Greetings, Uncle

Gus. I do wish you would remember to phone before dropping in. I would have had your special dinner ready."

"Never mind. We may not be here that long. Waldo, this is my friend, Jimmie Stevens."

The dummy faced Stevens. "How do you do, Mr. Stevens," the voice said formally. "Welcome to Freehold."

"How do you do, Mr. Jones," Stevens replied, and eyed the dummy curiously. It was surprisingly lifelike; he had been taken in by it at first, a "reasonable facsimile." Come to think of it, he had heard of this dummy. Except in vision screen few had seen Waldo in his own person. Those who had business at Wheelchair—no, "Freehold," he must remember that—those who had business at Freehold heard a voice and saw this simulacrum.

"But you *must* stay for dinner, Uncle Gus," Waldo continued. "You can't run out on me like that; you don't come often enough for that. I can stir something up."

"Maybe we will," Grimes admitted. "Don't worry about the menu. You know me. I can eat a turtle *with* the shell."

It had really been a bright idea, Stevens congratulated himself, to get Doc Grimes to bring him. Not here five minutes and Waldo was insisting on them staying for dinner. Good omen!

He had not noticed that Waldo had addressed the invitation to Grimes alone, and that it had been Grimes who had assumed the invitation to be for both of them.

"Where are you, Waldo?" Grimes continued. "In the lab?" He made a tentative movement, as if to leave the reception room.

"Oh, don't bother," Waldo said hastily. "I'm sure you will be more comfortable where you are. Just a moment and I will put some spin on the room so that you may sit down."

"What's eating you, Waldo?" Grimes said testily. "You know I don't insist on weight. And I don't care for the company of your talking doll. I want to see you." Stevens was a little surprised by the older man's insistence; he had thought it considerate of Waldo to offer to supply acceleration. Weightlessness put him a little on edge.

Waldo was silent for an uncomfortable period. At last he said frigidly, "Really, Uncle Gus, what you ask is out of the question. You must be aware of that."

Grimes did not answer him. Instead, he took Steven's arm. "Come on, Jimmie. We're leaving."

"Why, Doc! What's the matter?"

"Waldo wants to play games. I don't play games."

"But—"

"Ne' mind! Come along. Waldo, open the lock."

"Uncle Gus!"

"Yes, Waldo?"

"Your guest—you vouch for him?"

"Naturally, you dumb fool, else I wouldn't have brought him."

"You will find me in my workshop. The way is open."

Grimes turned to Stevens. "Come along, son."

Stevens trailed after Grimes as one fish might follow another, while taking in with his eyes as much of Waldo's fabulous house as he could see. The place was certainly unique, he conceded to himself—unlike anything he had ever seen. It completely lacked up-and-down orientation. Space craft, even space stations, although always in free fall with respect to any but internally impressed accelerations, invariably are designed with up-and-down; the up-and-down axis of a ship is determined by the direction of its accelerating drive; the up-and-down of a space station is determined by its centrifugal spin.

Some few police and military craft use more that one axis of acceleration; their up-and-down shifts, therefore, and their personnel, must be harnessed when the ship maneuvers. Some space stations apply spin only to living quarters. Nevertheless, the rule is general; human beings are used to weight; all their artifacts have that assumption implicit in their construction—except Waldo's house.

It is hard for a groundhog to dismiss the notion of weight. We seem to be born with an instinct which demands it. If one thinks of a vessel in a free orbit around the Earth, one is inclined to think of the direction toward the Earth as "down," to think of oneself as standing or sitting on that wall of the ship, using it as a floor. Such a concept is completely mistaken. To a person inside a freely falling body there is no sensation of weight whatsoever and no direction of up-and-down, except that which derives from the gravitational field of the vessel itself. As for the latter, neither Waldo's house nor any space craft as yet built is massive enough to produce a field dense enough for the human body to notice it. Believe it or not, that is true. It takes a mass as gross as a good-sized planetoid to give the human body a feeling of weight.

It may be objected that a body in a free orbit around the Earth is not a freely falling body. The concept involved is human, Earth surface in type, and completely erroneous. Free flight, free fall, and free orbit are equivalent terms. The Moon falls constantly toward the Earth; the Earth falls constantly toward the Sun, but the sidewise vector of their several motions prevents them from approaching their primaries. It is free fall nonetheless. Consult any ballistician or any astrophysicist.

When there is free fall there is no sensation of weight. A gravitational field must be opposed to be detected by the human body.

Some of these considerations passed through Stevens's mind as he handwalked his way to Waldo's workshop. Waldo's home had been constructed without any consideration being given to up-and-down. Furniture and apparatus were affixed to any wall; there was no "floor." Decks and platforms were arranged at any convenient angle and of any size or shape, since they had nothing to do with standing or walking. Properly speaking, they were bulkheads and working surfaces rather than decks. Furthermore, equipment was not necessarily placed close to such surfaces; frequently it was more convenient to locate it with space all around it, held in place by light guys or slender stanchions.

The furniture and equipment was all odd in design and frequently odd in purpose. Most furniture on Earth is extremely rugged, and at least 90 per cent of it has a single purpose—to oppose, in one way or another, the acceleration of gravity. Most of the furniture in an Earth-surface—or sub-surface—house is stator machines intended to oppose gravity. All tables, chairs, beds, couches, clothing racks, shelves, drawers, et cetera, have that as their one purpose. All other furniture and equipment have it as a secondary purpose which strongly conditions design and strength.

The lack of need for the rugged strength necessary to all terrestrial equipment resulted in a fairylike grace in much of the equipment in Waldo's house. Stored supplies, massive in themselves, could be retained in convenient order by compartmentation of eggshell-thin transparent plastic. Ponderous machinery, which on Earth would necessarily be heavily cased and supported, was here either open to the air or covered by gossamerlike envelopes and held stationary by light elastic lines.

Everywhere were pairs of waldoes, large, small and life-size, with vision pickups to match. It was evident that Waldo could make use of the compartments through which they were passing without stirring out of his easy chair—if he used an easy chair. The ubiquitous waldoes, the insubstantial quality of the furniture, and the casual use of all walls as work or storage surfaces, gave the place a madly fantastic air. Stevens felt as if he were caught in a Disney.

So far the rooms were not living quarters. Stevens wondered what Waldo's private apartments could be like and tried to visualize what equipment would be appropriate. No chairs, no rugs, no bed. Pictures, perhaps. Something pretty clever in the way of indirect lighting, since the eyes might be turned in any direction. Communication instruments might be much the same. But what could a washstand be like? Or a water tumbler? A trap bottle for the last—or would any container be necessary at all? He could not decide and realized that even a competent engineer may be confused in the face of mechanical conditions strange to him.

What constitutes a good ash tray when there is no gravity to hold the debris in place? Did Waldo smoke? Suppose he played solitaire; how did he handle the cards? Magnetized cards, perhaps, and a magnetized playing surface.

"In through here, Jim." Grimes steadied himself with one hand, gesturing with the other. Stevens slid through the manhole indicated. Before he had had time to look around he was startled by a menacing bass growl. He looked up; charging through the air straight at him was an enormous mastiff, lips drawn back, jaws slavering. Its front legs were spread out stiffly as if to balance in flight; its hind legs were drawn up under its lean belly. By voice and manner it announced clearly its intention of tearing the intruder into pieces, then swallowing the pieces.

"Baldur!" A voice cut through the air from some point beyond. The dog's ferocity wilted, but it could not check its lunge. A waldo snaked out a good thirty feet and grasped it by the collar. "I am sorry, sir," the voice added. "My friend was not expecting you."

Grimes said, "Howdy, Baldur. How's your conduct?" The dog looked at him, whined, and wagged his tail. Stevens looked for the source of the commanding voice, found it.

The room was huge and spherical; floating in its center was a fat man—Waldo.

He was dressed conventionally enough in shorts and singlet, except that his feet were bare. His hands and forearms were covered by metallic gauntlets—primary waldoes. He was softly fat, with double chin, dimples, smooth skin; he looked like a great, pink cherub, floating attendance on a saint. But the eyes were not cherubic, and the forehead and skull were those of a man. He looked at Stevens. "Permit me to introduce you to my pet," he said in a high, tired voice. "Give the paw, Baldur."

The dog offered a foreleg, Stevens shook it gravely. "Let him smell you, please."

The dog did so, as the waldo at his collar permitted him to come closer. Satisfied, the animal bestowed a wet kiss on Stevens's wrist. Stevens noted that the dog's eyes were surrounded by large circular patches of brown in contrast to his prevailing white, and mentally tagged it the Dog with Eyes as Large as Saucers, thinking of the tale of the soldier and the flint box. He made noises to it of "Good boy!" and "That's a nice old fellow!" while Waldo looked on with faint distaste.

"Heel, sir!" Waldo commanded when the ceremony was complete. The dog turned in midair, braced a foot against Stevens's thigh, and shoved, projecting himself in the direction of his master. Stevens was forced to steady himself by clutching at the handgrip. Grimes shoved himself away from the manhole and arrested his flight on a stanchion near their host. Stevens followed him.

Waldo looked him over slowly. His manner was not overtly rude, but was somehow, to Stevens, faintly annoying. He felt a slow flush spreading out from his neck; to inhibit it he gave his attention to the room around him. The space was commodious, yet gave the impression of being cluttered because of the assemblage of, well, *junk* which surrounded Waldo. There were half a dozen vision receptors of various sizes around him at different angles, all normal to his line of sight. Three of them had pickups to match. There were control panels of several sorts, some of which seemed obvious enough in their purpose—one for lighting, which was quite complicated, with little ruby telltales for each circuit, one which was the keyboard of a voder, a multiplex television control panel, a board which seemed to be power relays, although its design was unusual. But there were at least half a dozen which stumped Stevens completely.

There were several pairs of waldoes growing out of a steel ring which surrounded the working space. Two pairs, mere monkey fists in size, were equipped with extensors. It had been one of these which had shot out to grab Baldur by his collar. There were waldoes rigged near the spherical wall, too, including one pair so huge that Stevens could not conceive of a use for it. Extended, each hand spread quite six feet from little finger tip to thumb tip.

There were books in plenty on the wall, but no bookshelves. They seemed to grow from the wall like so many cabbages. It puzzled Stevens momentarily, but he inferred—correctly it turned out later—that a small magnet fastened to the binding did the trick.

The arrangement of lighting was novel, complex, automatic, and convenient for Waldo. But it was not so convenient for anyone else in the room. The lighting was of course, indirect; but, furthermore, it was subtly controlled, so that none of the lighting came from the direction in which Waldo's head was turned. There was no glare—for Waldo. Since the lights behind his head burned brightly in order to provide more illumination for whatever he happened to be looking at, there was glare aplenty for anyone else. An electric eye circuit, obviously.

Stevens found himself wondering just how simple such a circuit could be made.

Grimes complained about it. "Damn it, Waldo; get those lights under control. You'll give us headaches."

"Sorry, Uncle Gus." He withdrew his right hand from its guantlet and placed his fingers over one of the control panels. The glare stopped. Light now came from whatever direction none of them happened to be looking, and much more brightly, since the area source of illumination was much reduced. Lights rippled across the walls in pleasant patterns. Stevens tried to follow the ripples, a difficult matter, since the setup was made *not* to be seen. He found that he could do so by rolling his eyes without moving his head. It was movement of the head which controlled the lights; movement of an eyeball was a little too much for it.

"Well, Mr. Stevens, do you find my house interesting?" Waldo was smiling at him with faint superciliousness.

"Oh—quite! Quite! I believe that it is the most remarkable place I have ever been in."

"And what do you find remarkable about it?"

"Well—the lack of definite orientation, I believe. That and the remarkable mechanical novelties. I suppose I am a bit of a groundlubber, but I keep expecting a floor underfoot and a ceiling overhead."

"Mere matters of functional design, Mr. Stevens; the conditions under which I live are unique; therefore, my house is unique. The novelty you speak of consists mainly in the elimination of unnecessary parts and the addition of new conveniences."

"To tell the truth, the most interesting thing I have seen yet is not a part of the house at all."

"Really? What is it, pray?"

"Your dog, Baldur." The dog looked around at the mention of his name. "I've never before met a dog who could handle himself in free flight."

Waldo smiled; for the first time his smile seemed gentle and warm. "Yes, Baldur is quite an acrobat. He's been at it since he was a puppy." He reached out and roughed the dog's ears, showing momentarily his extreme weakness, for the gesture had none of the strength appropriate to the size of the brute. The finger motions were flaccid, barely sufficient to disturb the coarse fur and to displace the great ears. But he seemed unaware, or unconcerned, by the disclosure. Turning back to Stevens, he added, "But if Baldur amuses you, you must see Ariel."

"Ariel?"

Instead of replying, Waldo touched the keyboard of the voder, producing a musical whistling pattern of three notes. There was a rustling near the wall of the room "above" them; a tiny yellow shape shot toward them—a canary. It sailed through the air with wings folded, bullet fashion. A foot or so away from Waldo it spread its wings, cupping the air, beat them a few times with tail down and spread, and came to a dead stop, hovering in the air with folded wings. Not quite a dead stop, perhaps, for it drifted slowly, came within an inch of Waldo's shoulder, let down its landing gear, and dug its claws into his singlet.

Waldo reached up and stoked it with a finger-tip. It preened. "No earth-hatched bird can learn to fly in that fashion," he stated. "I know. I lost half a dozen before I was sure that they were incapable of making the readjustment. Too much thalamus."

"What happened to them?"

"In a man you would call it acute anxiety psychosis. They try to fly; their own prime skill leads them to disaster. Naturally, everything they do is wrong and they don't understand it. Presently they quit trying; a little later they die. Of a broken heart, one might say, poetically." He smiled thinly. "But Ariel is a genius among birds. He came here as an egg; he invented, unassisted, a whole new school of flying." He reached up a finger, offering the bird a new perch, which it accepted. "That's enough, Ariel. Fly away home."

The bird started the "Bell Song" from *Lakmé*.

He shook it gently. "No, Ariel. Go to bed."

The canary lifted its feet clear of the finger, floated for an instant, then beat its wings savagely for a second or two to set course and pick up speed, and bulleted away whence he had come, wings folded, feet streamlined under.

"Jimmie's got something he wants to talk with you about," Grimes commenced.

"Delighted," Waldo answered lazily, "but shan't we dine first? Have you an appetite, sir?"

Waldo full, Stevens decided, might be easier to cope with than Waldo empty. Besides, his own mid-section informed him that wrestling with a calorie or two might be pleasant. "Yes, I have."

"Excellent." They were served.

Stevens was never able to decide whether Waldo had prepared the meal by means of his many namesakes, or whether servants somewhere out of sight had done the actual work. Modern food-preparation methods being what they were, Waldo could have done it alone; he,

Stevens, batched it with no difficulty, and so did Gus. But he made a mental note to ask Doc Grimes at the first opportunity what resident staff, if any, Waldo employed. He never remembered to do so.

The dinner arrived in a small food chest, propelled to their midst at the end of a long, telescoping, pneumatic tube. It stopped with a soft sigh and held its position. Stevens paid little attention to the food itself—it was adequate and tasty, he knew—for his attention was held by the dishes and serving methods. Waldo let his own steak float in front of him, cut bites from it with curved surgical shears, and conveyed them to his mouth by means of dainty tongs. He made hard work of chewing.

"You can't get good steaks any more," he remarked. "This one is tough. God knows I pay enough—and complain enough."

Stevens did not answer. He thought his own steak had been tenderized too much; it almost fell apart. He was managing it with knife and fork, but the knife was superfluous. It appeared that Waldo did not expect his guests to make use of his own admittedly superior methods and utensils. Stevens ate from a platter clamped to his thighs, making a lap for it after Grimes's example by squatting in mid air. The platter itself had been thoughtfully provided with sharp little prongs on its service side.

Liquids were served in small flexible skins, equipped with nipples. Think of a baby's plastic nursing bottle.

The food chest took the utensils away with a dolorous insufflation. "Will you smoke, sir?"

"Thank you." He saw what a weight-free ash tray necessarily should be: a long tube with a bell-shaped receptacle on its end. A slight suction in the tube, and ashes knocked into the bell were swept away, out of sight and mind.

"About the matter—" Grimes commenced again. "Jimmie here is Chief Engineer for North American Power-Air."

"*What?*" Waldo straightened himself, became rigid; his chest rose and fell. He ignored Stevens entirely. "Uncle Gus, do you mean to say that you have introduced an officer of *that* company into my—home?"

"Don't get your dander up. Relax. Damn it, I've warned you not to do anything to raise your blood pressure." Grimes propelled himself closer to his host and took him by the wrist in the age-old fashion of a physician counting pulse. "Breathe slower. Whatcha trying to do? Go on an oxygen jag?"

Waldo tried to shake himself loose. It was a rather pitiful gesture; the old man had ten times his strength. "Uncle Gus, you—"

"Shut up!"

The three maintained a silence for several minutes, uncomfortable for at least two of them. Grimes did not seem to mind it.

"There," he said at last. "That's better. Now keep your shirt on and listen to me. Jimmie is a nice kid, and he has never done anything to you. And he has behaved himself while he's been here. You've got no right to be rude to him, no mater who he works for. Matter of fact, you owe him an apology."

"Oh, really now, Doc," Stevens protested. "I'm afraid I *have* been here somewhat under false colors. I'm sorry, Mr. Jones. I didn't intend it to be that way. I tried to explain when we arrived."

Waldo's face was hard to read. He was evidently trying hard to control himself. "Not at all, Mr. Stevens. I am sorry that I showed temper. It is perfectly true that I should not transfer to you any animus I feel for your employers . . . though God knows I bear no love for them."

"I know it. Nevertheless, I am sorry to hear you say it."

"I was cheated, do you understand? *Cheated*—by as rotten a piece of quasi-legal chicanery as has ever——"

"Easy, Waldo!"

"Sorry, Uncle Gus." He continued, his voice less shrill. "You know of the so-called Hathaway patents?"

"Yes, of course."

"'So-called' is putting it mildly. The man was a mere machinist. Those patents are mine."

Waldo's version, as he proceeded to give it, was reasonably factual, Stevens felt, but quite biased and unreasonable. Perhaps Hathaway had been working, as Waldo alleged, simply as a servant—a hired artisan, but there was nothing to prove it, no contract, no papers of any sort. The man had filed certain patents, the only ones he had ever filed and admittedly Waldo-ish in their cleverness. Hathaway had then promptly died, and his heirs, through their attorneys, had sold the patents to a firm which had been dickering with Hathaway.

Waldo alleged that this firm had put Hathaway up to stealing from him, had caused him to hire himself out to Waldo for that purpose. But the firm was defunct; its assets had been sold to North American Power-Air. NAPA had offered a settlement; Waldo had chosen to sue. The suit went against him.

Even if Waldo were right, Stevens could not see any means by which the directors of NAPA could, legally, grant him any relief. The officers of a corporation are trustees for other people's money; if the directors of NAPA should attempt to give away property which had been adjudicated as belonging to the corporation, any stockholder could enjoin them before the act or recover from them personally after the act.

At least so Stevens thought. But he was no lawyer, he admitted to himself. The important point was that he needed Waldo's services, whereas Waldo held a bitter grudge against the firm he worked for.

He was forced to admit that it did not look as if Doc Grimes's presence was enough to turn the trick. "All that happened before my time," he began, "and naturally I know very little about it. I'm awfully sorry it happened. It's pretty uncomfortable for me, for right now I find myself in a position where I need your services very badly indeed."

Waldo did not seem displeased with the idea. "So? How does this come about?"

Stevens explained to him in some detail the trouble they had been having with the deKalb receptors. Waldo listened attentively. When Stevens had concluded he said, "Yes, that is much the same story your Mr. Gleason had to tell. Of course, as a technical man you have given a much more coherent picture than that money manipulator was capable of giving. But why do you come to me? I do not specialize in radiation engineering, nor do I have any degrees from fancy institutions."

"I come to you," Stevens said seriously, "for the same reason everybody else comes to you when they are really stuck with an engineering problem. So far as I know, you have an unbroken record of solving any problem you cared to tackle. Your record reminds me of another man——"

"Who?" Waldo's tone was suddenly sharp.

"Edison. He did not bother with degrees either, but solved all the hard problems of his day."

"Oh, Edison——I thought you were speaking of a contemporary. No doubt he was all right in his day," he added with overt generosity.

"I was not comparing him to you. I was simply recalling that Edison was reputed to prefer hard problems to easy ones. I've heard the same about you; I had hopes that this problem might be hard enough to interest you."

"It is mildly interesting," Waldo conceded. "A little out of my line, but interesting. I must say, however, that I am surprised to hear you, an executive of North American Power-Air, express such a high opinion of my talents. One would think that, if the opinion were sincere, it would not have been difficult to convince your firm of my indisputable handiwork in the matter of the so-called Hathaway patents."

Really, thought Stevens, the man is impossible. A mind like a weasel. Aloud, he said, "I suppose the matter was handled by the business management and the law staff. They would hardly be equipped to distinguish between routine engineering and inspired design."

The answer seemed to mollify Waldo. He asked, "What does your own research staff say about the problem?"

Stevens looked wry. "Nothing helpful. Dr. Rambeau does not really seem to believe the data I bring him. He says it's impossible, but it makes him unhappy. I really believe that he has been living on aspirin and Nembutal for a good many weeks."

"Rambeau," Waldo said slowly. "I recall the man. A mediocre mind. All memory and no intuition. I don't think I would feel discouraged simply because Rambeau is puzzled."

"You really feel that there is some hope?"

"It should not be too difficult. I had already given the matter some thought, after Mr. Gleason's phone call. You have given me additional data, and I think I see at least two new lines of approach which may prove fruitful. In any case, there is always some approach—the correct one."

"Does that mean you will accept?" Stevens demanded, nervous with relief.

"Accept?" Waldo's eyebrows climbed up. "My dear sir, what in the world are you talking about? We were simply indulging in social conversation. I would not help your company under any circumstances whatsoever. I hope to see your firm destroyed utterly, bankrupt and ruined. This may well be the occasion."

Stevens fought to keep control of himself. Tricked! The fat slob had simply been playing with him, leading him on. There was no decency in him. In careful tones he continued, "I do not ask that you have any mercy on North American, Mr. Jones, but I appeal to your sense of duty. There is public interest involved. Millions of people are vitally dependent on the service we provide. Don't you see that the service *must* continue, regardless of you or me?"

Waldo pursed his lips. "No," he said, "I'm afraid that does not affect me. The welfare of those nameless swarms of Earth crawlers is, I fear, not my concern. I have done more for them already than there was any need to do. They hardly deserve help. Left to their own devices, most of them would sink back to caves and stone axes. Did you ever see a performing ape, Mr. Stevens, dressed in a man's clothes and cutting capers on roller skates? Let me leave you with this thought: I am not a roller-skate mechanic for apes."

If I stick around here much longer, Stevens advised himself, there will be hell to pay. Aloud, he said, "I take it that is your last word?"

"You may so take it. Good day, sir. I enjoyed your visit. Thank you."

"Good-by. Thanks for the dinner."

"Not at all."

As Stevens turned away and prepared to shove himself toward the exit, Grimes called after him, "Jimmie, wait for me in the reception room."

As soon as Stevens was out of earshot, Grimes turned to Waldo and looked him up and down. "Waldo," he said slowly, "I always did know that you were on of the meanest, orneriest men alive, but—"

"Your compliments don't faze me, Uncle Gus."

"Shut up and listen to me. As I was saying, I knew you were too rotten selfish to live with, but this is the first time I ever knew you to be a four-flusher to boot."

"What do you mean by that? Explain yourself."

"Shucks! You haven't any more idea of how to crack the problem that boy is up against than I have. You traded on your reputation as a miracle man just to make him unhappy. Why, you cheap tinhorn bluffer, if you—"

*"Stop it!"*

"Go ahead," Grimes said quietly. "Run up your blood pressure. I won't interfere with you. The sooner you blow a gasket the better."

Waldo calmed down. "Uncle Gus—what makes you think I was bluffing?"

"Because I know you. If you had felt able to deliver the goods, you would have looked the situation over and worked out a plan to get NAPA by the short hair, through having something they had to have. That way you would have *proved* your revenge."

Waldo shook his head. "You underestimate the intensity of my feeling in the matter."

"I do like hell! I hadn't finished. About that sweet little talk you gave him concerning your responsibility to the race. You've got a head on you. You know damned well, and so do I, that of all people you can least afford to have anything serious happen to the setup down on Earth. That means you don't see any way to prevent it."

"Why, what do you mean? I have no interest in such troubles; I'm independent of such things. You know me better than that."

"Independent, eh? Who mined the steel in these walls? Who raised that steer you dined on tonight? You're as independent as a queen bee, and about as helpless."

Waldo looked startled. He recovered himself and answered, "Oh no, Uncle Gus. I really am independent. Why, I have supplies here for years."

*"How many years?"*

"Why . . . uh, five, about."

"And then what? You may live another *fifty—if* you have regular supply service. How do you prefer to die—starvation or thirst?"

"Water is no problem," Waldo said thoughtfully; "as for supplies, I suppose I could use hydroponics a little more and stock up with some meat animals—"

Grimes cut him short with a nasty laugh. "Proved my point. You don't *know* how to avert it, so you are figuring some way to save your own skin. I know you. You wouldn't talk about starting a truck garden if you knew the answers."

Waldo looked at him thoughtfully. "That's not entirely true. I don't know the solution, but I do have some ideas about it. I'll bet you a half interest in hell that I can crack it. Now that you have called my attention to it, I must admit I am rather tied in with the economic system down below, and"—he smiled faintly—"I was never one to neglect my own interests. Just a moment—I'll call your friend."

"Not so fast. I came along for another reason, besides introducing Jimmie to you. It can't be just any solution; it's got to be a particular solution."

"What do you mean?"

"It's got to be a solution that will do away with the need for filling up the air with radiant energy."

"Oh, *that*. See here, Uncle Gus, I know how interested you are in theory, and I've never disputed the possibility that you might be right, but you can't expect me to mix that into another and very difficult problem."

"Take another look. You're in this for self-interest. Suppose everybody was in the shape you are in."

"You mean my *physical condition*?"

"I mean just that. I know you don't like to talk about it, but we blamed well need to. If everybody was as weak as you are—presto! No coffee and cakes for Waldo. And that's just what I see coming. You're the only man I know of who can appreciate what it means."

"It seems fantastic."

"It is. But the signs are there for anybody to read who wants to. Epidemic *myasthenia*, not necessarily acute, but enough to raise hell with our mechanical civilization. Enough to play hob with your supply lines. I've been collating my data since I saw you last and drawing some curves. You should see 'em."

"Did you bring them?"

"No, but I'll send 'em up. In the meantime, you can take my word for it." He waited. "Well, how about it?"

"I'll accept it as a tentative working hypothesis," Waldo said slowly, "until I see your figures. I shall probably want you to conduct some further research for me, on the ground—if your data is what you say it is."

"Fair enough. G'by." Grimes kicked the air a couple of times as he absent-mindedly tried to walk.

STEVENS'S FRAME OF MIND AS he waited for Grimes is better left undescribed. The mildest thought that passed through his mind was a plaintive one about the things a man had to put up with to hold down what seemed like a simple job of engineering. Well, he wouldn't have the job very long. But he decided not to resign—he'd wait until they fired him; he wouldn't run out.

But he would damn well get that vacation before he looked for another job.

He spent several minutes wishing that Waldo were strong enough for him to be able to take a poke at him. Or kick him in the belly—that would be more fun!

He was startled when the dummy suddenly came to life and called him by name. "Oh, Mr. Stevens."

"Huh? Yes?"

"I have decided to accept the commission. My attorneys will arrange the details with your business office."

He was too surprised to answer for a couple of seconds; when he did so the dummy had already gone dead. He waited impatiently for Grimes to show up.

"Doc!" he said, when the old man swam into view. "What got into him. How did you do it?"

"He thought it over and reconsidered," Grimes said succinctly. "Let's get going."

Stevens dropped Dr. Augustus Grimes at the doctor's home, then proceeded to his office. He had no more than parked his car and entered the tunnel leading toward the zone plant when he ran into his assistant. McLeod seemed a little out of breath. "Gee, chief," he said, "I hoped that was you. I've had 'em watching for you. I need to see you."

"What's busted now?" Stevens demanded apprehensively. "One of the cities?"

"No. What made you think so?"

"Go ahead with your story."

"So far as I know ground power is humming sweet as can be. No trouble with the cities. What I had on my mind is this: *I fixed my heap*."

"Huh? You mean you fixed the ship you crashed in?"

"It wasn't exactly a crash. I had plenty of power in the reserve banks; when reception cut off, I switched to emergency and landed her."

"But you fixed it? Was it the deKalbs? Or something else?"

"It was the deKalbs all right. And they're fixed. But I didn't exactly do it myself. I got it done. You see——"

"What was the matter with them?"

"I don't know exactly. You see I decided that there was no point in hiring another skycar and maybe having another forced landing on the way home. Besides, it was my own crate I was flying, and I didn't want to dismantle her just to get the deKalbs out and have her spread out all over the countryside. So I hired a crawler, with the idea of taking her back all in one piece. I struck a deal with a guy who had a twelve-ton semitractor combination, and we——"

"For criminy's sake, make it march! What happened?"

"I'm trying to tell you. We pushed on into Pennsylvania and we were making pretty fair time when the crawler broke down. The right lead wheel, ahead of the treads. Honest to goodness, Jim, those roads are something fierce."

"Never mind that. Why waste taxes on roads when 90 per cent of the traffic is in the air? You messed up a wheel. So then what?"

"Just the same, those roads are a disgrace," McLeod maintained stubbornly. "I was brought up in that part of the country. When I was a kid the road we were on was six lanes wide and smooth as a baby's fanny. They ought to be kept up; we might need 'em someday." Seeing the look in his senior's eye, he went on hastily: "The driver mugged in with his home office, and they promised to send a repair car out from the next town. All told, it would take three, four hours—maybe more. Well, we were laid up in the county I grew up in. I says to myself, 'McLeod, this is a wonderful chance to return to the scenes of your childhood and the room where the sun came peeping in the morn.' Figuratively speaking, of course. Matter of fact, our house didn't have any windows."

"I don't care if you were raised in a barrel!"

"Temper . . . temper——" McLeod said imperturbably. "I'm telling you this so you will understand what happened. But you aren't going to like it."

"I don't like it now."

"You'll like it less. I climbed down out of the cab and took a look around. We were about five miles from my home town—too far for me to want to walk it. But I thought I recognized a clump of trees on the brow of a little rise maybe a quarter of a mile off the road, so I walked over to see. I was right; just over the rise was the cabin where Gramps Schneider used to live."

"Gramps Snyder?"

"Not Snyder—*Sch*neider. Old boy we kids used to be friendly with. Ninety years older than anybody. I figured he was dead, but it wouldn't hurt any to walk down and see. He wasn't. 'Hello, Gramps,' I said. 'Come in, Hugh Donald,' he said. 'Wipe the feet on the mat.'

"I came in and sat down. He was fussing with something simmering in a stewpan on his baseburner. I asked him what it was. 'For morning aches,' he said. Gramps isn't exactly a hex doctor."

"Huh?"

"I mean he doesn't make a living by it. He raises a few chickens and garden truck, and some of the Plain People—House Amish, mostly—give him pies and things. But he knows a lot about herbs and such.

"Presently he stopped and cut me a slice of shoofly pie. I told him *danke*. He said, 'You've been upgrowing, Hugh Donald,' and asked me how I was doing in school. I told him I was doing pretty well. He looked at me again and said, 'But you have trouble fretting you.' It wasn't a question; it was a statement. While I finished the pie I found myself trying to tell him what kind of troubles I had.

"It wasn't easy. I don't suppose Gramps has ever been off the ground in his life. And modern radiation theory isn't something you can explain in words of one syllable. I was getting more and more tangled up when he stood up, put on his hat and said, 'We will see this car you speak about.'

"We walked over to the highway. The repair gang had arrived, but the crawler wasn't ready yet. I helped Gramps up onto the platform and we got into my bus. I showed him the deKalbs and tried to explain what they did—or rather what they were supposed to do. Mind you, I was just killing time.

"He pointed to the sheaf of antennae and asked, 'These fingers—they reach out for the power?' It was as good an explanation as any, so I let it ride. He said, 'I understand,' and pulled a piece of chalk out of his trousers, and began drawing lines on each antenna, from front to back. I walked up front to see how the repair crew were doing. After a bit Gramps joined me. 'Hugh Donald,' he says, 'the fingers—now they will make.'

"I didn't want to hurt his feelings, so I thanked him plenty. The crawler was ready to go; we said good-by, and he walked back toward his shack. I went back to my car, and took a look in, just in case. I didn't think he could hurt anything, but I wanted to be sure. Just for the ducks of it. I tried out the receptors. They worked!"

"What!" put in Stevens. "You don't mean to stand there and tell me an old witch doctor fixed your deKalbs?"

"Not witch doctor—*hex* doctor. But you get the idea."

Stevens shook his head. "It's simply a coincidence. Sometimes they come back into order as spontaneously as they go out."

"That's what you think. Not this one. I've just been preparing you for the shock you're going to get. *Come take a look.*"

"What do you mean? Where?"

"In the inner hangar." While they walked to where McLeod had left his broomstick, he continued, "I wrote out a credit for the crawler pilot and flew back. I haven't spoken to anyone else about it. I've been biting my nails down to my elbows waiting for you to show up."

The skycar seemed quite ordinary. Stevens examined the deKalbs and saw some faint chalk marks on their metal sides—nothing else unusual. "Watch while I cut in reception," McLeod told him.

Stevens waited, heard the faint hum as the circuits became activized, and looked.

The antennae of the deKalbs, each a rigid pencil of metal, were bending, flexing, writhing like a cluster of worms. They were *reaching out*, like fingers.

Stevens remained squatting down by the deKalbs, watching their outrageous motion. McLeod left the control saddle, came back, and joined him. "Well, chief," he demanded, "tell me about it. Whaduh yuh make of it?"

"Got a cigarette?"

"What are those things sticking out of your pocket?"

"Oh! Yeah—sure." Stevens took one out, lighted it, and burned it halfway down, unevenly, with two long drags.

"Go on," McLeod urged. "Give us a tell. What makes it do that?"

"Well," Stevens said slowly, "I can think of three things to do next——"

"Yeah?"

"The first is to fire Dr. Rambeau and give his job to Gramps Schneider."

"That's a good idea in any case."

"The second is to just wait here quietly until the boys with the straitjackets show up to take us home."

"And what's the third?"

"The third," Stevens said savagely, "is to take this damned heap out and sink it in the deepest part of the Atlantic Ocean and pretend like it never happened!"

A mechanic stuck his head in the door of the car. "Oh, Dr. Stevens——"

"Get out of here!"

The head hastily withdrew; the voice picked up in aggrieved tones. "Message from the head office."

Stevens got up, went to the operator's saddle, cleared the board, then assured himself that the antennae had ceased their disturbing movements. They had; in fact, they appeared so beautifully straight and rigid that he was again tempted to doubt the correctness of his own senses. He climbed out to the floor of the hangar, McLeod behind him. "Sorry to have blasted at you, Whitey," he said to the workman in placating tones. "What is the message?"

"Mr. Gleason would like for you to come into his office as soon as you can."

"I will at once. And, Whitey, I've a job for you."

"Yeah?"

"This heap here—seal up its doors and don't let anybody monkey with it. Then have it dragged, dragged, mind you; don't try to start it—have it dragged over into the main lab."

"O.K."

Stevens started away; McLeod stopped him. "What do I go home in?"

"Oh yes, it's your personal property, isn't it? Tell you what, Mac—the company needs it. Make out a purchase order and I'll sign it."

"Weeeell, now—I don't rightly know as I want to sell it. It might be the only job in the country working properly before long."

"Don't be silly. If the others play out, it won't do you any good to have the only one in working order. Power will be shut down."

"I suppose there's that," McLeod conceded. "Still," he said, brightening visibly, "a crate like that, with its special talents, ought to be worth a good deal more than list. You couldn't just go out and buy one."

"Mac," said Stevens, "you've got avarice in your heart and thievery in your finger tips. How much do you want for it?"

"Suppose we say twice the list price, new. That's letting you off easy."

"I happen to know you bought that job at a discount. But go ahead. Either the company can stand it, or it won't make much difference in the bankruptcy."

GLEASON LOOKED UP AS STEVENS came in. "Oh, there you are, Jim. You seemed to have pulled a miracle with our friend Waldo the Great. Nice work."

"How much did he stick us for?"

"Just his usual contract. Of course his usual contract is a bit like robbery with violence. But it will be worth it if he is successful. And it's on a straight contingent basis. He must feel pretty sure of himself. They say he's never lost a contingent fee in his life. Tell me—what is he like? Did you really get into his house?"

"I did. And I'll tell you about it—sometime. Right now another matter has come up which has me talking to myself. You ought to hear about it at once."

"So? Go ahead."

Stevens opened his mouth, closed it again, and realized that it had to be seen to be believed. "Say, could you come with me to the main lab? I've got something to show you."

"Certainly."

Gleason was not as perturbed by the squirming metal rods as Stevens had been. He was surprised, but not upset. The truth of the matter is that he lacked the necessary technical background to receive the full emotional impact of the inescapable implications of the phenomenon. "That's pretty unusual, isn't it?" he said quietly.

"Unusual! Look, chief, if the sun rose in the west, what would you think?"

"I think I would call the observatory and ask them why."

"Well, all I can say is that I would a whole lot rather that the sun rose in the west than to have this happen."

"I admit it is pretty disconcerting," Gleason agreed. "I can't say that I've ever seen anything like it. What is Dr. Rambeau's opinion?"

"He hasn't seen it."

"Then perhaps we had better send for him. He may not have gone home for the night as yet."

"Why not show it to Waldo instead?"

"We will. But Dr. Rambeau is entitled to see it first. After all, it's his bailiwick, and I'm afraid the poor fellow's nose is pretty well out of joint as it is. I don't want to go over his head."

Stevens felt a sudden flood of intuition. "Just a second, chief. You're right, but if it's all the same to you I would rather that you showed it to him than for me to do it."

"Why so, Jimmie? You can explain it to him."

"I can't explain a damn thing to him I haven't already told you. And for the next few hours I'm going to be very, very busy indeed."

Gleason looked him over, shrugged his shoulders, and said mildly, "Very well, Jim, if you prefer it that way."

WALDO WAS QUITE BUSY, AND therefore happy. He would never have admitted—he did not admit even to himself, that there were certain drawbacks to his self-imposed withdrawal from the world and that chief among these was boredom. He had never had much opportunity to enjoy the time-consuming delights of social intercourse; he honestly believed that the smooth apes had nothing to offer him in the way of companionship. Nevertheless, the pleasure of the solitary intellectual life can pall.

He repeatedly urged Uncle Gus to make his permanent home in Freehold, but he told himself that it was a desire to take care of the old man which motivated him. True—he enjoyed arguing with Grimes, but he was not aware how much those arguments meant to him. The truth of the matter was that Grimes was the only one of the human race who treated him entirely as another human and an equal—and Waldo wallowed in it, completely unconscious that the pleasure he felt in the old man's company was the commonest and most precious of all human pleasures.

But at present he was happy in the only way he knew how to be happy—working.

There were two problems: that of Stevens and that of Grimes. Required: a single solution which would satisfy each of them. There were three stages to each problem; first, to satisfy himself that the problems really did exist, that the situations were in fact as they had been reported to him verbally; second, to undertake such research as the preliminary data suggested; and third, when he felt that his data was complete, to invent a solution.

"Invent," not "find." Dr. Rambeau might have said "find," or "search for." To Rambeau the universe was inexorably ordered cosmos, ruled by unvarying law. To Waldo the universe was the enemy, which he strove to force to submit to his will. They might have been speaking of the same thing, but their approaches were different.

There was much to be done. Stevens had supplied him with a mass of data, both on the theoretical nature of the radiated power system and the deKalb receptors which were the keystone of the system, and also on the various cases of erratic performance of which they had lately been guilty. Waldo had not given serious attention to power radiation up to this time, simply because he had not needed to. He found it interesting but comparatively simple. Several improvements suggested themselves to his mind. That standing wave, for example, which was the main factor in the coaxial beam—the efficiency of reception could be increased considerably by sending a message back over it which would automatically correct the aiming of the beam. Power delivery to moving vehicles could be made nearly as efficient as the power reception to stationary receivers.

Not that such an idea was important at present. Later, when he had solved the problem at hand, he intended to make NAPA pay through the nose for the idea; or perhaps it would be more amusing to compete with them. He wondered when their basic patents ran out—must look it up.

Despite inefficiencies the deKalb receptors should work every time, all the time, without failure. He went happily about finding out why they did not.

He had suspected some obvious—obvious to *him*—defect in manufacture. But the inoperative deKalbs which Stevens had delivered to him refused to give up their secret. He X-rayed them, measured them with micrometer and interferometer, subjected them to all the usual tests and some that were quite unusual and peculiarly Waldoish. They would not perform.

He built a deKalb in his shop, using one of the inoperative ones as a model and using the reworked metal of another of the same design, also inoperative, as the raw material. He used his finest scanners to see with and his smallest waldoes—tiny pixy hands, an inch across—for manipulation in the final stages. He created a deKalb which was as nearly identical with its model as technology and incredible skill could produce.

It worked beautifully.

Its elder twin still refused to work. He was not discouraged by this. On the contrary, he was elated. He had proved, proved with certainty, that the failure of the deKalbs was not a failure of workmanship, but a basic failure in theory. The problem was real.

Stevens had reported to him the scandalous performance of the deKalbs in McLeod's skycar, but he had not yet given his attention to the matter. Presently, in proper order, when he got around to it, he would look into the matter. In the meantime he tabled the matter. The smooth apes were an hysterical lot; there was probably nothing to the story. Writhing like Medusa's locks, indeed!

He gave fully half his time to Grimes's problem.

He was forced to admit that the biological sciences—if you could call them science!—were more fascinating than he had thought. He had shunned them, more or less; the failure of expensive "experts" to do anything for his condition when he was a child had made him contemptuous of such studies. Old wives' nostrums dressed up in fancy terminology! Grimes he liked and even respected, but Grimes was a special case.

Grimes's data had convinced Waldo that the old man had a case. Why, this was serious! The figures were incomplete, but nevertheless convincing. The curve of the third decrement, extrapolated not too unreasonably, indicated that in twenty years there would not be a man left with strength enough to work in heavy industries. Button pushing would be all they would be good for.

It did not occur to him that all he was good for was button pushing; he regarded weakness in the smooth apes as an old-style farmer might regard weakness in a draft animal. The farmer did not expect to pull the plow—that was the horse's job.

Grimes's medical colleagues must be utter fools.

Nevertheless, he sent for the best physiologists, neurologists, brain surgeons, and anatomists he could locate, ordering them as one might order goods from a catalogue. He must understand this matter.

He was considerably annoyed when he found that he could not make arrangements, by any means, to perform vivisection on human beings. He was convinced by this time that the damage done by ultra short-wave radiation was damage to the neurological system, and that the whole matter should be treated from the standpoint of electromagnetic theory. He wanted to perform certain delicate manipulations in which human beings would be hooked up directly to apparatus of his own design to find out in what manner nerve impulses differed from electrical current. He felt that if he could disconnect portions of a man's nervous circuit, replace it in part with electrical hookups, and examine the whole matter *in situ*, he might make illuminating discoveries. True, the man might not be much use to himself afterward.

But the authorities were stuffy about it; he was forced to content himself with cadavers and with animals.

Nevertheless, he made progress. Extreme short-wave radiation had a definite effect on the nervous system—a double effect: it produced "ghost" pulsations in the neurons, insufficient to accomplish muscular motor response, but, he suspected, strong enough to keep the body in a continual state of inhibited nervous excitation; and, secondly, a living specimen which had been subjected to this process for any length of time showed a definite, small but measurable, lowering in the efficiency of its neural impulses. If it had been an electrical circuit, he would have described the second effect as a decrease in insulating efficiency.

The sum of these two effects on the subject individual was a condition of mild tiredness, somewhat similar to the malaise of the early stages of pulmonary tuberculosis. The victim did not feel sick; he simply lacked pep. Strenuous bodily activity was not impossible; it was simply distasteful; it required too much effort, too much will power.

But an orthodox pathologist would have been forced to report that the victim was in perfect health—a little run-down, perhaps, but nothing wrong with him. Too sedentary a life, probably. What he needed was fresh air, sunshine, and healthy exercise.

Doc Grimes alone had guessed that the present, general, marked preference for a sedentary life was the effect and not the cause of the prevailing lack of vigor. The change had been slow, at least as slow as the increase in radiation in the air. The individuals concerned had noticed it, if at all, simply as an indication that they were growing a little bit older, "slowing down, not so young as I used to be." And they were content to slow down; it was more comfortable than exertion.

Grimes had first begun to be concerned about it when he began to notice that *all* of his younger patients were "the bookish type." It was all very well for a kid to like to read books, he felt, but a normal boy ought to be out doing a little hell raising too. What had become of the sand-lot football games, the games of scrub, the clothes-tearing activity that had characterized his own boyhood?

Damn it, a kid ought not to spend *all* his time poring over a stamp collection.

Waldo was beginning to find the answer.

The nerve network of the body was not dissimilar to antennae. Like antennae, it could and did pick up electromagnetic waves. But the pickup was evidenced not as induced electrical current, but as nerve pulsation—impulses which were maddeningly similar to, but distinctly different from, electrical current. Electromotive force could be used in place of nerve impulses, to activate muscle tissue, but e.m.f. was *not* nerve impulse. For one thing they traveled at vastly different rates of speed. Electrical current travels at a speed approaching that of light; neural impulse is measured in feet per second.

Waldo felt that somewhere in this matter of speed lay the key to the problem.

He was not permitted to ignore the matter of McLeod's fantastic sky-car as long as he had intended to. Dr. Rambeau called him up. Waldo accepted the call, since it was routed from the laboratories of NAPA. "Who are you and what do you want?" he demanded of the image.

Rambeau looked around cautiously. *"Sssh!* Not so loud," he whispered. "They might be listening."

"Who might be? And who are you?"

" 'They' are the ones who are doing it. Lock your doors at night. I'm Dr. Rambeau."

"Dr. Rambeau? Oh yes. Well, Doctor, what is the meaning of this intrusion?"

The doctor leaned forward until he appeared about to fall out of the stereo picture. "I've learned how to do it," he said tensely.

"How to do what?"

"Make the deKalbs work. The dear, dear deKalbs." He suddenly thrust his hands at Waldo, while clutching frantically with his fingers. "They go like this: *Wiggle, wiggle, wiggle!"*

Waldo felt a normal impulse to cut the man off, but it was overruled by a fascination as to what he would say next. Rambeau continued. "Do you know why? Do you? Riddle me that."

"Why?"

Rambeau placed a finger beside his nose and smiled roguishly. "Wouldn't you like to know? Wouldn't you give a pretty to know? *But I'll tell you!"*

"Tell me, then."

Rambeau suddenly looked terrified. "Perhaps I shouldn't. Perhaps they are listening. But I will, I will! Listen carefully: Nothing is certain."

"Is that all?" inquired Waldo, now definitely amused by the man's antics.

" 'Is that all?' Isn't that enough? Hens will crow and cocks will lay. You are here and I am there. Or maybe not. Nothing is certain. Nothing, *nothing*, NOTHING is certain! Around and around the little ball goes, and where it stops nobody knows. Only I've learned how to do it."

"How to do what?"

"How to make the little ball stop where I want it to. Look." He whipped out a penknife. "When you cut yourself, you bleed, don't you? Or do you?" He sliced at the forefinger of his left hand. "See?" He held the finger close to the pickup; the cut, though deep, was barely discernible and it was bleeding not at all.

Capital! thought Waldo. Hysteric vascular control—a perfect clinical case. "Anybody can do that," he said aloud. "Show me a hard one."

"Anybody? Certainly anybody can—if they know how. Try this one." He jabbed the point of the penknife straight into the palm of his left hand, so that it stuck out the back of his hand. He wiggled the blade in the wound, withdrew it, and displayed the palm. No blood, and the incision was closing rapidly. "Do you know why? The knife is only probably there, *and I've found the improbability!*"

Amusing as it had been, Waldo was beginning to be bored by it. "Is that all?"

"There is no end to it," pronounced Rambeau, "for nothing is certain any more. Watch this." He held the knife flat on his palm, then turned his hand over.

The knife did not fall, but remained in contact with the underside of his hand.

Waldo was suddenly attentive. It might be a trick; it probably was a trick—but it impressed him more, much more, than Rambeau's failure to bleed when cut. One was common to certain types of psychosis; the other should not have happened. He cut in another viewphone circuit. "Get me Chief Engineer Stevens at North American Power-Air," he said sharply. "At once!"

Rambeau paid no attention, but continued to speak of the penknife. "It does not know which way is down," he crooned, "for nothing is certain any more. Maybe it will fall—maybe not. I think it will. There—it has. Would you like to see me walk on the ceiling?"

"You called me, Mr. Jones?" It was Stevens.

Waldo cut his audio circuit to Rambeau. "Yes. That jumping jack, Rambeau. Catch him and bring him to me at once. I want to see him."

"But Mr. Jo—"

"Move!" He cut Stevens off, and renewed the audio to Rambeau.

"—uncertainty. Chaos is King, and Magic is loose in the world!" Rambeau looked vaguely at Waldo, brightened, and added, "Good day, Mr. Jones. Thank you for calling."

The screen went dead.

Waldo waited impatiently. The whole thing had been a hoax, he told himself. Rambeau had played a gigantic practical joke. Waldo disliked practical jokes. He put in another call for Stevens and left it in.

When Stevens did call back his hair was mussed and his face was red. "We had a bad time of it," he said.

"Did you get him?"

"Rambeau? Yes, finally."

"Then bring him up."

"To Freehold? But that's impossible. You don't understand. He's blown his top; he's crazy. They've taken him away to a hospital."

"You assume too much," Waldo said icily. "I know he's crazy, but I meant what I said. Arrange it. Provide nurses. Sign affidavits. Use bribery. Bring him to me at once. It is necessary."

"You really mean that?"

"I'm not in the habit of jesting."

"Something to do with your investigations? He's in no shape to be useful to you, I can tell you that."

"That," pronounced Waldo, "is for me to decide."

"Well," said Stevens doubtfully, "I'll try."

"See that you succeed."

Stevens called back thirty minutes later. "I can't bring Rambeau."

"You clumsy incompetent."

Stevens turned red, but held his temper. "Never mind the personalities. He's gone. He never got to the hospital."

"What?"

"That's the crazy part about it. They took him away in a confining stretcher, laced up like a corset. I saw them fasten him in myself. But when they got there he was gone. And the attendants claim *the straps weren't even unbuckled.*"

Waldo started to say, "Preposterous," thought better of it. Stevens went on.

"But that's not the half of it. I'd sure like to talk to him myself. I've been looking around his lab. You know that set of deKalbs that went nuts—the ones that were hexed?"

"I know to what you refer."

"Rambeau's got a second set to doing the same thing!"

Waldo remained silent for several seconds, then said quietly, "Dr. Stevens—"

"Yes."

"I want to thank you for your efforts. And will you please have both sets of receptors, the two sets that are misbehaving, sent to Freehold at once?"

There was no doubt about it. Once he had seen them with his own eyes, watched the inexplicable squirming of the antennae, applied such tests as suggested themselves to his mind, Waldo was forced to conclude that he was faced with new phenomena, phenomena for which he did not know the rules.

If there were rules . . .

For he was honest with himself. If he saw what he thought he saw, then rules were being broken by the new phenomena, rules which he had considered valid, rules to which he had never previously encountered exceptions. He admitted to himself that the original failures of the deKalbs should have been considered just as overwhelmingly upsetting to physical law as the unique behavior of these two; the difference lay in that one alien phenomenon was spectacular, the other was not.

Quite evidently Dr. Rambeau had found it so; he had been informed that the doctor had been increasingly neurotic from the first instance of erratic performance of the deKalb receptors.

He regretted the loss of Dr. Rambeau. Waldo was more impressed by Rambeau crazy than he had ever been by Rambeau sane. Apparently the man had had some modicum of ability after all; he had found out *something*—more, Waldo admitted, than he himself had been able to find out so far, even though it had driven Rambeau insane.

Waldo had no fear that Rambeau's experience, whatever it had been, could unhinge his own reason. His own self-confidence was, perhaps, fully justified. His own mild paranoid tendency was just sufficient to give him defenses against an unfriendly world. For him it was healthy, a necessary adjustment to an otherwise intolerable situation, no more pathological than a callus, or an acquired immunity.

Otherwise he was probably more able to face disturbing facts with equanimity than 99 per cent of his contemporaries. He had *been* born to disaster; he had met it and had overcome it, time and again. The very house which surrounded him was testimony to the calm and fearless fashion in which he had defeated a world to which he was not adapted.

He exhausted, temporarily, the obvious lines of direct research concerning the strangely twisting metal rods. Rambeau was not available for questioning. Very well, there remained one other man who knew more about it than Waldo did. He would seek him out. He called Stevens again.

"Has there been any word of Dr. Rambeau?"

"No word, and no sign. I'm beginning to think the poor old fellow is dead."

"Perhaps. That witch doctor friend of your assistant—was Schneider his name?"

"Gramps Schneider."

"Yes indeed. Will you please arrange for him to speak with me."

"By phone, or do you want to see him in person?"

"I would prefer for him to come here, but I understand that he is old and feeble; it may not be feasible for him to leave the ground. If he is knotted up with spacesickness, he will be no use to me."

"I'll see what can be done."

"Very good. Please expedite the matter. And, Dr. Stevens—"

"Well?"

"If it should prove necessary to use the phone, arrange to have a portable full stereo taken to his home. I want the circumstances to be as favorable as possible."

"O.K."

"Imagine that," Stevens added to McLeod when the circuit had been broken. "The Great-I-Am's showing consideration for somebody else's convenience."

"The fat boy must be sick," McLeod decided.

"Seems likely. This chore is more yours than mine, Mac. Come along with me; we'll take a run over into Pennsylvania."

"How about the plant?"

"Tell Carruthers he's 'It.' If anything blows, we couldn't help it anyway."

Stevens mugged back later in the day. "Mr. Jones—"

"Yes, Doctor?"

"What you suggest can't be arranged."

"You mean that Schneider can't come to Freehold?"

"I mean that and I mean that you can't talk with him on the viewphone."

"I presume that you mean he is dead."

"No, I do not. I mean that he will not talk over the viewphone under any circumstances whatsoever, to you or to anyone. He says that he is sorry not to accommodate you, but that he is opposed to everything of that nature—cameras, cinécams, television, and so forth. He considers them dangerous. I am afraid he is set in his superstition."

"As an ambassador, Dr. Stevens, you leave much to be desired."

Stevens counted up to ten, then said, "I assure you that I have done everything in my power to comply with your wishes. If you are dissatisfied with the quality of my co-operation, I suggest that you speak to Mr. Gleason." He cleared the circuit.

"How would you like to kick him in the teeth?" McLeod said dreamily.

"Mac, you're a mind reader."

Waldo tried again through his own agents, received the same answer. The situation was, to him, almost intolerable; it had been years since he had encountered a man whom he could not buy, bully, nor—in extremity—persuade. Buying had failed; he had realized instinctively that Schneider would be unlikely to be motivated by greed. And how can one bully, or wheedle, a man who cannot be seen to be talked with?

It was a dead end—no way out. Forget it.

Except, of course, for a means classed as a Fate-Worse-Than-Death.

No. No, not that. Don't think about it. Better to drop the whole matter, admit that it had him licked, and tell Gleason so. It had been seventeen years since he had been at Earth surface; nothing could induce him to subject his body to the intolerable demands of that terrible field. Nothing!

It might even kill him. He might choke to death, suffocate. No.

He sailed gracefully across his shop, an overpadded Cupid. Give up this freedom, even for a time, for that torturous bondage? Ridiculous! It was not worth it.

Better to ask an acrophobe to climb Half Dome, or demand that a claustrophobe interview a man in the world's deepest mine.

"UNCLE GUS?"

"Oh, hello, Waldo. Glad you called."

"Would it be safe for me to come down to Earth?"

"Eh? How's that? Speak up, man. I didn't understand you."

"I said would it hurt me to make a trip down to Earth."

"This hookup," said Grimes, "is terrible. It sounded just like you were saying you wanted to come down to Earth."

"That's what I did say."

"What's the matter, Waldo? Do you feel all right?"

"I feel fine, but I have to see a man at Earth surface. There isn't any other way for me to talk to him, and I've got to talk to him. Would the trip do me any harm?"

"Ought not to, if you're careful. After all, you were born there. Be careful of yourself, though. You've laid a lot of fat around your heart."

"Oh dear. Do you think it's *dangerous*?"

"No. You're sound enough. Just don't overstrain yourself. And be careful to keep your temper."

"I will. I most certainly will. Uncle Gus?"

"Yes?"

"Will you come along with me and help me see it through?"

"Oh, I don't think that's necessary."

"Please, Uncle Gus. I don't trust anybody else."

"Time you grew up, Waldo. However, I will, this once."

"NOW REMEMBER," WALDO TOLD THE pilot, "the absolute acceleration must never exceed one and one tenth gs, *even in landing*. I'll be watching the accelograph the whole time."

"I've been driving ambulances," said the pilot, "for twelve years, and I've never given a patient a rough ride yet."

"That's no answer. Understand me? One and one tenth; and it should not even approach that figure until we are under the stratosphere. Quiet, Baldur! Quit snuffling."

"I get you."

"Be sure that you do. Your bonuses depend on it."

"Maybe you'd like to herd it yourself."

"I don't like your attitude, my man. If I should die in the tank, you would never get another job."

The pilot muttered something.

"What was that?" Waldo demanded sharply.

"Well, I said it might be worth it."

Waldo started to turn red, opened his mouth.

Grimes cut in, "Easy, Waldo! Remember your heart."

"Yes, Uncle Gus."

Grimes snaked his way forward, indicated to the pilot that he wanted him to join him there.

"Don't pay any attention to anything he says," he advised the man quietly, "except what he said about acceleration. He really can't stand much acceleration. He *might* die in the tank."

"I still don't think it would be any loss. But I'll be careful."

"Good."

"I'm ready to enter the tank," Waldo called out. "Will you help me with the straps, Uncle Gus?"

The tank was not a standard deceleration type, but a modification built for this one trip. The tank was roughly the shape of an oversized coffin and was swung in gimbals to keep it always normal to the axis of absolute acceleration. Waldo floated in water—the specific gravity of his fat hulk was low—from which he was separated by the usual flexible, gasketed tarpaulin. Supporting his head and shoulders was a pad shaped to his contour. A mechanical artificial resuscitator was built into the tank, the back pads being under water, the breast pads out of the water but retracted out of the way.

Grimes stood by with neoadrenalin; a saddle had been provided for him on the left side of the tank. Baldur was strapped to a shelf on the right side of the tank; he acted as a counterweight to Grimes.

Grimes assured himself that all was in readiness, then called out to the pilot, "Start when you're ready."

"O.K." He sealed the access port; the entry tube folded itself back against the threshold flat of Freehold, freeing the ship. Gently they got under way.

Waldo closed his eyes; a look of seraphic suffering came over his face.

"Uncle Gus, suppose the deKalbs fail?"

"No matter. Ambulances store six times the normal reserve."

"You're *sure*?"

When Baldur began to feel weight, he started to whimper. Grimes spoke to him; he quieted down. But presently—days later, it seemed to Waldo—as the ship sank farther down into the Earth's gravitational field, the absolute acceleration necessarily increased, although the speed of the ship had not changed materially. The dog felt the weary heaviness creeping over his body. He did not understand it and he liked it even less; it terrified him. He began to howl.

Waldo opened his eyes. "Merciful heavens!" he moaned. "Can't you do something about that? He must be dying."

"I'll see." Grimes undid his safety belt and swung himself across the tank. The shift in weight changed the balance of the load in the gimbals; Waldo was rocked against the side of the tank.

"Oh!" he panted. "Be careful."

"Take it easy." Grimes caressed the dog's head and spoke to him. When he had calmed down, Grimes grabbed a handful of hide between the dog's shoulders, measured his spot, and jabbed in a hypo. He rubbed the area. "There, old fellow! That will make you feel better."

Getting back caused Waldo to be rocked again, but he bore it in martyred silence.

The ambulance made just one jerky maneuver after it entered the atmosphere. Both Waldo and the dog yelped. "Private ship," the pilot yelled back. "Didn't heed my right-of-way lights." He muttered something about women drivers.

"It wasn't his fault," Grimes told Waldo. "I saw it."

The pilot set them down with exquisite gentleness in a clearing which had been prepared between the highway and Schneider's house. A party of men was waiting for them there; under Grimes's supervision they unslung the tank and carried Waldo out into the open air. The evolution was performed slowly and carefully, but necessarily involved some degree of bumping and uneven movement. Waldo stood it with silent fortitude, but tears leaked out from under his lowered lids.

Once outside he opened his eyes and asked, "Where is Baldur?"

"I unstrapped him," Grimes informed him, "but he did not follow us out."

Waldo called out huskily, "Here, Baldur! Come to me, boy."

Inside the car the dog heard his boss's voice, raised his head, and gave a low bark. He still felt that terrifying sickness, but he inched forward on his belly, attempting to comply. Grimes reached the door in time to see what happened.

The dog reached the edge of his shelf and made a grotesque attempt to launch himself in the direction from which he had heard Waldo's voice. He tried the only method of propulsion he knew; no doubt he expected to sail through the door and arrest his flight against the tank on the ground. Instead he fell several feet to the inner floor plates, giving one agonized yelp as he did so, and breaking his fall most clumsily with stiffened forelegs.

He lay sprawled where he had landed, making no noise, but not attempting to move. He was trembling violently.

Grimes came up to him and examined him superficially, enough to assure him that the beast was not really hurt, then returned to the outside. "Baldur's had a little accident," he told Waldo; "he's not hurt, but the poor devil doesn't know how to walk. You had best leave him in the ship."

Waldo shook his head slightly. "I want him with me. Arrange a litter."

Grimes got a couple of men to help him, obtained a stretcher from the pilot of the ambulance, and undertook to move the dog. One of the men said, "I don't know as I care for this job. That dog looks vicious. Look't those eyes."

"He's not," Grimes assured him. "He's just scared out of his wits. Here, I'll take his head."

"What's the matter with him? Same thing as the fat guy?"

"No, he's perfectly well and strong; he's just never learned to walk. This is his first trip to Earth."

"Well, I'll be a cross-eyed owl!"

"I knew a case like it," volunteered the other. "Dog raised in Lunopolis—first week he was on Earth he wouldn't move—just squatted down, and howled, and made messes on the floor."

"So has this one," the first said darkly.

They placed Baldur alongside Waldo's tub. With great effort Waldo raised himself on one elbow, reached out a hand, and placed it on the creature's head. The dog licked it; his trembling almost ceased. "There! There!' Waldo whispered. "It's pretty bad, isn't it? Easy, old friend, take it easy."

Baldur thumped his tail.

It took four men to carry Waldo and two more to handle Baldur. Gramps Schneider was waiting for them at the door of his house. He said nothing as they approached, but indicated that they were to carry Waldo inside. The men with the dog hesitated. "Him, too," he said.

When the others had withdrawn—even Grimes returned to the neighborhood of the ship—Schneider spoke again. "Welcome, Mr. Waldo Jones."

"I thank you for your welcome, Grandfather Schneider."

The old man nodded graciously without speaking. He went to the side of Baldur's litter. Waldo felt impelled to warn him that the beast was dangerous with strangers, but some odd restraint—perhaps the effect of that enervating gravitational field—kept him from speaking in time. Then he saw that he need not bother.

Baldur had ceased his low whimpering, had raised his head, and was licking Gramps Schneider's chin. His tail thumped cheerfully. Waldo felt a sudden tug of jealousy; the dog had never been known to accept a stranger without Waldo's specific injunction. This was disloyalty—treason! But he suppressed the twinge and coolly assessed the incident as a tactical advantage to him.

Schneider pushed the dog's face out of the way and went over him thoroughly, prodding, thumping, extending his limbs. He grasped Baldur's muzzle, pushed back his lips, and eyed his gums. He peeled back the dog's eyelids. He then dropped the matter and came to Waldo's side. "The dog is not sick," he said; "his mind confuses. What made it?"

Waldo told him about Baldur's unusual background. Schneider nodded acceptance of the matter—Waldo could not tell whether he had understood or not—and turned his attention to Waldo. "It is not good for a sprottly lad to lie abed. The weakness—how long has it had you?"

"All my life, Grandfather."

"That is not good." Schneider went over him as he had gone over Baldur. Waldo, whose feeling for personal privacy was much more intense than that of an ordinarily sensitive man, endured it for pragmatic reasons. It was going to be necessary, he felt, to wheedle and cajole this strange old creature. It would not do to antagonize him.

To divert his own attention from the indignity he chose to submit to, and to gain further knowledge of the old quack, Waldo let his eyes rove the room. The room where they were seemed to be a combination kitchen-living room. It was quite crowded, rather narrow, but fairly long. A fireplace dominated the kitchen end, but it had been bricked up, and a hole for the flue pipe of the baseburner had been let into the chimney. The fireplace was lopsided, as an oven had been included in its left side. The corresponding space at the right was occupied by a short counter which supported a tiny sink. The sink was supplied with water by a small hand pump which grew out of the counter.

Schneider, Waldo decided, was either older than he looked, which seemed incredible, or he had acquired his house from someone now long dead.

The living room end was littered and crowded in the fashion which is simply unavoidable in constricted quarters. Books filled several cases, were piled on the floor, hung precariously on chairs. An ancient wooden desk, crowded with papers and supporting a long-obsolete mechanical typewriter, filled one corner. Over it, suspended from the wall, was an ornate clock, carved somewhat like a house. Above its face were two little doors; while Waldo looked at it, a tiny wooden bird painted bright red popped out of the lefthand door, whistled "*Th-wu th-woo*!" four times, and popped frantically back into its hole. Immediately thereafter a little gray bird came out of the righthand door, said "*Cuckoo*" three times in a leisurely manner, and returned to its hole. Waldo decided that he would like to own such a clock; of course its pendulum-and-weight movement would not function in Freehold, but he could easily devise a one-g certrifuge frame to inclose it, wherein it would have a pseudo Earth-surface environment.

It did not occur to him to fake a pendulum movement by means of a concealed power source; he liked things to work properly.

To the left of the clock was an old-fashioned static calendar of paper. The date was obscured, but the letters above the calendar proper were large and legible: New York World's Fair—Souvenir of the World of Tomorrow. Waldo's eyes widened a little and went back to something he had noticed before, sticking into a pincushion on the edge of the desk. It was a round plastic button mounted on a pin whereby it could be affixed to the clothing. It was not far from Waldo's eyes; he could read the lettering on it:

FREE SILVER
SIXTEEN TO ONE

Schneider must be—*old*!

There was a narrow archway, which led into another room. Waldo could not see into it very well; the arch as draped with a fringed curtain of long strings of large ornamental beads.

The room was rich with odors, many of them old and musty, but not dirty.

Schneider straightened up and looked down at Waldo. "There is nought wrong with your body. Up get yourself and walk."

Waldo shook his head feebly. "I am sorry, Grandfather, I cannot."

"You must reach for the power and make it serve you. Try."

"I am sorry. I do not know how."

"That is the only trouble. All matters are doubtful, unless one knows. You send your force into the Other World. You must reach into the Other World and claim it."

"Where is this 'Other World,' Grandfather?"

Schneider seemed a little in doubt as to how to answer this. "The Other World," he said presently, "is the world you do not see. It is here and it is there and it is everywhere. But it is especially *here*." He touched his forehead. "The mind sits in it and sends its messages through it to the body. Wait." He shuffled away to a little cupboard, from which he removed a small jar. It contained a salve, or unguent, which he rubbed on his hands.

He returned to Waldo and knelt down beside him. Grasping one of Waldo's hands in both of his, he began to knead it very gently. "Let the mind be quiet," he directed. "Feel for the power. The Other World is close and full of power. Feel it."

The massage was very pleasant to Waldo's tired muscles. The salve, or the touch of the old man's hand, produced a warm, relaxing tingle. If he were younger, thought Waldo, I would hire him as a masseur. He has a magnetic touch.

Schneider straightened up again and said, "There—that betters you? Now you rest while I some coffee make."

Waldo settled back contentedly. He was very tired. Not only was the trip itself a nervous strain, but he was still in the grip of this damnable, thick gravitational field, like a fly trapped in honey. Gramps Schneider's ministrations had left him relaxed and sleepy.

He must have dozed, for the last thing he remembered was seeing Schneider drop an eggshell into the coffeepot. Then the old man was standing before him, holding the pot in one hand and a steaming cup in the other. He set them down, got three pillows, which he placed at Waldo's back, then offered him the coffee. Waldo laboriously reached out both hands to take it.

Schneider held it back. "No," he reproved, "one hand makes plenty. Do as I showed. Reach into the Other World for the strength." He took Waldo's right hand and placed it on the handle of the cup, steadying Waldo's hand with his own. With his other hand he stroked Waldo's right arm gently, from shoulder to finger tips. Again the warm tingle.

Waldo was surprised to find himself holding the cup alone. It was a pleasant triumph; at the time he left Earth, seventeen years before, it had been his invariable habit never to attempt to grasp anything with only one hand. In Freehold, of course, he frequently handled small objects one-handed, without the use of waldoes. The years of practice must have improved his control. Excellent!

So, feeling rather cocky, he drank the cupful with one hand, using extreme care not to slop it on himself. It was good coffee, too, he was bound to admit—quite as good as the sort he himself made from the most expensive syrup extract—better, perhaps.

When Schneider offered him coffeecake, brown with sugar and cinnamon and freshly rewarmed, he swaggeringly accepted it with his left hand, without asking to be relieved of the cup. He continued to eat and drink, between bites and sips resting and steadying his forearms on the edges of the tank.

The conclusion of the *Kaffeeklatsch* seemed a good time to broach the matter of the deKalbs. Schneider admitted knowing McLeod and recalled, somewhat vaguely it seemed, the incident in which he had restored to service McLeod's broomstick. "Hugh Donald is a good boy," he said. "Machines I do not like, but it pleasures me to fix things for boys."

"Grandfather," asked Waldo, "will you tell me how you fixed Hugh Donald McLeod's ship?"

"Have you such a ship you wish me to fix?"

"I have many such ships which I have agreed to fix, but I must tell you that I have been unable to do so. I have come to you to find out the right way."

Schneider considered this. "That is difficult. I could show you, but it is not so much what you do as how you think about it. That makes only with practice."

Waldo must have looked puzzled, for the old man looked at him and added, "It is said that there are two ways of looking at everything. That is true and less than true, for there are many ways. Some of them are good ways and some are bad. One of the ancients said that everything either *is*, or *is not*. That is less than true, for a thing can both *be* and *not be*. With practice one can see it both ways. Sometimes a thing which *is* for this world is a thing which *is not* for the Other World. Which is important, since we live in the Other World."

"We live in the Other World?"

"How else could we live? The mind—not the brain, but the mind—is in the Other World, and reaches this world through the body. That is one true way of looking at it, though there are others."

"Is there more than one way of looking at deKalb receptors?"

"Certainly."

"If I had a set which is not working right brought in here, would you show me how to look at it?"

"It is not needful," said Schneider, "and I do not like for machines to be in my house. I will draw you a picture."

Waldo felt impelled to insist, but he squelched his feeling. "You have come here in humility," he told himself, "asking for instruction. Do not tell the teacher how to teach."

Schneider produced a pencil and a piece of paper, on which he made a careful and very neat sketch of the antennae sheaf and main axis of a skycar. The sketch was reasonably accurate as well, although it lacked several essential minor details.

"These fingers," Schneider said, "reach deep into the Other World to draw their strength. In turn it passes down this pillar"—he indicated the axis—"to where it is used to move the car."

A fair allegorical explanation, thought Waldo. By considering the "Other World" simply a term for the hypothetical ether, it could be considered correct if not complete. But told him nothing. "Hugh Donald," Schneider went on, "was tired and fretting. He found one of the bad truths."

"Do you mean," Waldo said slowly, "that McLeod's ship failed because he was worried about it?"

"How else?"

Waldo was not prepared to answer that one. It had become evident that the old man had some quaint superstitions; nevertheless, he might still be able to show Waldo *what* to do, even though Schneider did not know *why*. "And what did you do to change it?"

"I made no change; I looked for the other truth."

"But how? We found some chalk marks——"

"Those? They were but to aid me in concentrating my attention in the proper direction. I drew them down *so*"—he illustrated with pencil on the sketch—"and thought how the fingers reached out for power. And so they did."

"That is all? Nothing more?"

"That is enough."

Either, Waldo considered, the old man did not know how he had accomplished the repair, or he had had nothing to do with it—sheer and amazing coincidence.

He had been resting the empty cup on the rim of his tank, the weight supported by the metal while his fingers merely steadied it. His preoccupation caused him to pay too little heed to it; it slipped from his tired fingers, clattered and crashed to the floor.

He was much chagrined. "Oh, I'm *sorry*, Grandfather. I'll send you another."

"No matter. I will mend." Schneider carefully gathered up the pieces and placed them on the desk. "You have tired," he added. "That is not good. It makes you lose what you have gained. Go back now to your house, and when you have rested, you can practice reaching for the strength by yourself."

It seemed a good idea to Waldo; he was growing very tired, and it was evident that he was to learn nothing specific from the pleasant old fraud. He promised, emphatically and quite insincerely, to practice "reaching for strength," and asked Schneider to do him the favor of summoning his bearers.

The trip back was uneventful. Waldo did not even have the spirit to bicker with the pilot.

Stalemate. Machines that did not work but should, and machines that did work but in an impossible manner. And no one to turn to but one foggy-headed old man. Waldo worked lackadaisically for several days, repeating, for the most part, investigations he had already made rather than admit to himself that he was stuck, that he did not know what to do, that he was, in fact, whipped and might as well call Gleason and admit it.

The two "bewitched" sets of deKalbs continued to work whenever activated, with the same strange and incredible flexing of each antenna. Other deKalbs which had failed in operation and had been sent to him for investigation still refused to function. Still others, which had not yet failed, performed beautifully without the preposterous fidgeting.

For the umpteenth time he took out the little sketch Schneider had made and examined it. There was, he thought, just one more possibility: to return again to Earth and insist that Schneider actually *do*, in his presence, whatever it was he had done which caused the deKalbs to work. He knew now that he should have insisted on it in the first place, but he had been so utterly played out by having to fight that devilish thick field that he had not had the will to persist.

Perhaps he could have Stevens do it and have the process sterophotoed for later examination. No, the old man had a superstitious prejudice against artificial images.

He floated gently over to the vicinity of one of the inoperative deKalbs. What Schneider had claimed to have done was preposterously simple. He had drawn chalk marks down each antenna *so*, for the purpose of fixing his attention. Then he had gazed down them and thought about them "reaching out for power," reaching into the Other World, stretching—

Baldur began to bark frantically.

"Shut up, you fool!" Waldo snapped, without taking his eyes off the antennae.

*Each separate pencil of metal was wiggling, stretching. There was the low, smooth hum of perfect operation.*

Waldo was still thinking about it when the televisor demanded his attention. He had never been in any danger of cracking up mentally as Rambeau had done; nevertheless, he had thought about the matter in a fashion which made his head ache. He was still considerably bemused when he cut in his end of the sound-vision. "Yes?"

It was Stevens. "Hello, Mr. Jones. Uh, we wondered . . . that is——"

"Speak up man!"

Well, how close are you to a solution?" Stevens blurted out. "Matters are getting pretty urgent."

"In what way?"

"There was a partial breakdown in Great New York last night. Fortunately it was not at peak load and the ground crew were able to install spares before the reserves were exhausted, but you can imagine what it would have been like during the rush hour. In my own department the crashes have doubled in the past few weeks, and our underwriters have given notice. We need results pretty quick."

"You'll get your results," Waldo said loftily. "I'm in the final stages of the research." He was actually not that confident, but Stevens irritated him even more than most of the smooth apes.

Doubt and reassurance mingled in Stevens's face. "I don't suppose you could care to give us a hint of the general nature of the solution?"

No, Waldo could not. Still—it would be fun to pull Stevens's leg. "Come close to the pickup, Dr. Stevens. I'll tell you." He leaned forward himself, until they were almost nose to nose—in effect. "Magic is loose in the world!"

He cut the circuit at once.

Down in the underground labyrinth of North America's home plant, Stevens stared at the blank screen. "What's the trouble, chief?" McLeod inquired.

"I don't know. I don't rightly know. But I *think* that Fatty has slipped his cams, just the way Rambeau did."

McLeod grinned delightedly. "How sweet! I always did think he was a hoot owl."

Stevens looked very sober. "You had better pray that he *hasn't* gone nuts. We're depending on him. Now let me see those operation reports."

MAGIC LOOSE IN THE WORLD. It was as good an explanation as any, Waldo mused. Causation gone haywire; sacrosanct physical laws no longer operative. Magic. As Gramps Schneider had put it, it seemed to depend on the way one looked at it.

Apparently Schneider had known what he was talking about, although he naturally had no real grasp of the physical theory involved in the deKalbs.

Wait a minute now! Wait a minute. He had been going at this problem wrongly perhaps. He had approached it with a certain point of view himself, a point of view which had made him critical of the old man's statements—an assumption that he, Waldo, knew more about the whole matter than Schneider did. To be sure he had gone to see Schneider, but he had thought of him as a back-country hex doctor, a man who might possess one piece of information useful to Waldo, but who was basically ignorant and superstitious.

Suppose he were to review the situation from a different viewpoint. Let it be assumed that everything Schneider had to say was coldly factual and enlightened, rather than allegorical and superstitious—

He settled himself to do a few hours of hard thinking.

In the first place Schneider had used the phrase "the Other World" time and again. What did it mean, literally? A "world" was a space-time-energy continuum; an "Other World" was, therefore, such a continuum, but a different one from the one in which he found himself. Physical theory found nothing repugnant in such a notion; the possibility of infinite numbers of continua was a familiar, orthodox speculation. It was even convenient in certain operations to make such an assumption.

Had Gramps Schneider meant that? A literal physical "Other World"? On reflection, Waldo was convinced that he must have meant just that, even though he had not used conventional scientific phraseology. "Other World" sounds poetical, but to say an "additional continuum" implies physical meaning. The terms had led him astray.

Schneider had said that the Other World was all around, here, there, and everywhere. Well, was not that a fair description of a space superposed and in one-to-one correspondence? Such a space might be so close to this one that the interval between them was an infinitesimal, yet unnoticed and unreachable, just as two planes may be considered as coextensive and separated by an unimaginably short interval, yet be perfectly discrete, one from the other.

The Other Space was not entirely unreachable; Schneider had spoken of reaching into it. The idea was fantastic, yet he must accept it for the purposes of this investigation. Schneider had implied—no—*stated* that it was a matter of mental outlook.

Was that really so fantastic? If a continuum were an unmeasurably short distance away, yet completely beyond one's physical grasp, would it be strange to find that it was most easily reached through some subtle and probably subconscious operation of the brain? The whole matter was subtle—and Heaven knew that no one had any real idea of *how* the brain works. No idea at all. It was laughably insufficient to try to explain the writing of a symphony in terms of the mechanics of colloids. No, nobody knew how the brain worked; one more inexplicable ability in the brain was not too much to swallow.

Come to think of it, the whole notion of consciousness and thought was fantastically improbable.

All right, so McLeod disabled his skycar himself by thinking bad thoughts; Schneider fixed it by thinking the correct thoughts. Then what?

He reached a preliminary conclusion almost at once; by extension, the other deKalb failures were probably on the part of the operators. The operators were probably run-down, tired out, worried about something, and in some fashion still not clear they infected, or affected, the deKalbs with their own troubles. For convenience let us say that the deKalbs were short-circuited into the Other World. Poor terminology, but it helped him to form a picture.

Grimes's hypothesis! "Run-down, tired out, worried about something!" Not proved yet, but he felt sure of it. The epidemic of crashes though material was simply an aspect of the general *myasthenia* caused by short-wave radiation.

If that were true—

He cut in a sight-sound circuit to Earth and demanded to talk with Stevens.

"Dr. Stevens," he began at once, "there is a preliminary precautionary measure which should be undertaken right away."

"Yes?"

"First, let me ask you this: Have you had many failures of deKalbs in private ships? What is the ratio?"

"I can't give you exact figures at the moment," Stevens answered, somewhat mystified, "but there have been practically none. It's the commercial lines which have suffered."

"Just as I suspected. A private pilot won't fly unless he feels up to it, but a man with a job goes ahead no matter how he feels. Make arrangements for special physical and psycho examinations for all commercial pilots flying deKalb-type ships. Ground any who are not feeling in tiptop shape. Call Dr. Grimes. He'll tell you what to look for."

"That's a pretty tall order, Mr. Jones. After all, most of those pilots, practically all of them, aren't our employees. We don't have much control over them."

"That's your problem," Waldo shrugged. "I'm trying to tell you how to reduce crashes in the interim before my complete solution."

"But—"

Waldo heard no more of the remark; he had cut off when he himself was through. He was already calling over a permanently energized, leased circuit which kept him in touch with his terrestrial business office—with his "trained seals." He gave them some very odd instructions—orders for books, old books, rare books. Books dealing with magic.

Stevens consulted with Gleason before attempting to do anything about Waldo's difficult request. Gleason was dubious. "He offered no reason for the advice?"

"None. He told me to look up Dr. Grimes and get his advice as to what specifically to look for."

"Dr. Grimes?"

"The M.D. who introduced me to Waldo—mutual friend."

"I recall. Mm-m-m . . . it will be difficult to go about grounding men who don't work for us. Still, I suppose several of our larger customers would co-operate if we asked them to and gave them some sort of a reason. What are you looking so odd about?"

Stevens told him of Waldo's last, inexplicable statement. "Do you suppose it could be affecting him the way it did Dr. Rambeau?"

"Mm-m-m. Could be, I suppose. In which case it would not be well to follow his advice. Have you anything else to suggest?"

"No—frankly."

"Then I see no alternative but to follow his advice. He's our last hope. A forlorn one, perhaps but our only one."

Stevens brightened a little. "I could talk to Doc Grimes about it. He knows more about Waldo than anyone else."

"You have to consult him anyway, don't you? Very well—do so."

Grimes listened to the story without comment. When Stevens had concluded he said, "Waldo must be referring to the symptoms I have observed with respect to shortwave exposure. That's easy; you can have the proofs of the monograph I've been preparing. It'll tell you all about it."

The information did not reassure Stevens; it helped to confirm his suspicion that Waldo had lost his grip. But he said nothing. Grimes continued, "As for the other, Jim, I can't visualize Waldo losing his mind that way."

"He never did seem very stable to me."

"I know what you mean. But his paranoid streak is no more like what Rambeau succumbed to than chicken pox is like mumps. Matter of fact, one psychosis protects against the other. But I'll go see."

"You will? Good!"

"Can't go today. Got a broken leg and some children's colds that'll bear watching. Been some polio around. Ought to be able to make it the end of the week though."

"Doc, why don't you give up G.P. work! It must be deadly."

"Used to think so when I was younger. But about forty years ago I quit treating diseases and started treating people. Since then I've enjoyed it."

Waldo indulged in an orgy of reading, gulping the treatises on magic and related subjects as fast as he could. He had never been interested in such subjects before; now, in reading about them with the point of view that there might be—and even probably was—something to be learned, he found them intensely interesting.

There were frequent references to another world; sometimes it was called the Other World, sometimes the Little World. Read with the conviction that the term referred to an actual, material, different continuum, he could see that many of the practitioners of the forbidden arts had held the same literal viewpoint. They gave directions for using this other world; sometimes the directions were fanciful, sometimes they were baldly practical.

It was fairly evident that at least 90 per cent of all magic, probably more, was balderdash and sheer mystification. The mystification extended even to the practitioners, he felt; they lacked the scientific method; they employed a single-valued logic as faulty as the two-valued logic of the obsolete Spencer determinism; there was no suggestion of modern extensional, many-valued logic.

Nevertheless, the laws of contiguity, of sympathy, and of homeopathy had a sort of twisted rightness to them when considered in relation to the concept of another, different, but accessible, world. A man who had some access to a different space might well believe in a logic in which a thing could *be, not be,* or *be anything* with equal ease.

Despite the nonsense and confusion which characterized the treatments of magic which dated back to the period when the art was in common practice, the record of accomplishment of the art was impressive. There was curare and digitalis, and quinine, hypnotism, and telepathy. There was the hydraulic engineering of the Egyptian priests. Chemistry itself was derived from alchemy; for that matter, most modern science owed its origins to the magicians. Science had stripped off the surplusage, run it through the wringer of two-valued logic, and placed the knowledge in a form in which anyone could use it.

Unfortunately, that part of magic which refused to conform to the neat categories of the nineteenth-century methodologists was lopped off and left out of the body of science. It fell into disrepute, was forgotten save as fable and superstistion.

Waldo began to think of the arcane arts as aborted sciences, abandoned before they had been clarified.

And yet the manifestations of the sort of uncertainty which had characterized some aspects of magic and which he now attributed to hypothetical additional continua had occurred frequently, even in modern times. The evidence was overwhelming to anyone who approached it with an *open mind: Poltergeisten*, stones falling from the sky, apportation, "bewitched" persons—or, as he thought of them, persons who for some undetermined reason were loci of uncertainty—"haunted" houses, strange fires of the sort that would have once been attributed to salamanders. There were hundreds of such cases, carefully recorded and well vouched for, but ignored by orthodox science as being impossible. They *were* impossible, by known law, but considered from the standpoint of a coextensive additional continuum, they became entirely credible.

He cautioned himself not to consider his tentative hypothesis of the Other World as proved; nevertheless, it was an adequate hypothesis even if it should develop that it did not apply to some of the cases of strange events.

The Other Space might have different physical laws—no reason why it should not. Nevertheless, he decided to proceed on the assumption that it was much like the space he knew.

The Other World might even be inhabited. That was an intriguing thought! In which case anything could happen through "magic." Anything!

Time to stop speculating and get down to a little solid research. He had previously regretfully given up trying to apply the formulas of the medieval magicians. It appeared that they never wrote down *all* of a procedure; some essential—so the reports ran and so his experience confirmed—was handed down verbally from master to student. His experience with Schneider confirmed this; there were things, *attitudes*, which must needs be taught directly.

He regretfully set out to learn what he must unassisted.

"Gosh, Uncle Gus, I'm glad to see you!"

"Decided I'd better look in on you. You haven't phoned me in weeks."

"That's true, but I've been working awfully hard, Uncle Gus."

"Too hard, maybe. Mustn't overdo it. Lemme see your tongue."

"I'm O.K." But Waldo stuck out his tongue just the same; Grimes looked at it and felt his pulse.

"You seem to be ticking all right. Learning anything?"

"Quite a lot. I've about got the matter of the deKalbs whipped."

"That's good. The message you sent Stevens seemed to indicate that you had found some hookup that could be used on my pet problem too."

"In a way, yes; but around from the other end. It begins to seem as if it was your problem which created Stevens's problem."

'Huh?"

"I mean it. The symptoms caused by ultra short-wave radiation may have had a lot to do with the erratic behavior of the deKalbs."

"How?"

"I don't know myself. But I've rigged up a working hypothesis and I'm checking it."

"Hm-m-m. Want to talk about it?"

"Certainly—to you." Waldo launched into an account of his interview with Schneider, concerning which he had not previously spoken to Grimes, even though Grimes had made the trip with him. He never, as Grimes knew, discussed anything until he was ready to.

The story of the third set of deKalbs to be infected with the incredible writhings caused Grimes to raise his eyebrows. "Mean to say you caught on to how to do *that*?"

"Yes indeed. Not *'how'*, maybe, but I can do it. I've done it more than once. I'll show you." He drifted away toward one side of the great room where several sets of deKalbs, large and small, were mounted, with their controls, on temporary guys. "This fellow over on the end, it just came in today. Broke down. I'll give it Gramps Schneider's hocus-pocus and fix it. Wait a minute. I forgot to turn on the power."

He returned to the central ring which constituted his usual locus and switched on the beam-caster. Since the ship itself effectively shielded anything in the room from outer radiation, he had installed a small power plant and caster similar in type to NAPA's giant ones; without it he would have had no way to test the reception of the deKalbs.

He rejoined Grimes and passed down the line of deKalbs, switching on the activizing circuits. All save two began to display the uncouth motions he had begun to think of as the Schneider flex. "That one on the far end," he remarked, "is in operation but doesn't flex. It has never broken down, so it's never been treated. It's my control; but this one"—he touched the one in front of him—"needs fixing. Watch me."

"What are you going to do?"

"To tell the truth, I don't quite know. But I'll do it." He did not know. All he knew was that it was necessary to gaze down the antennae, think about them reaching into the Other World, think of them reaching for power, reaching—

The antennae began to squirm.

"That's all there is to it—strictly between ourselves. I learned it from Schneider." They had returned to the center of the sphere, at Grimes's suggestion, on the pretext of wanting to get a cigarette. The squirming deKalbs made him nervous, but he did not want to say so.

"How do you explain it?"

"I regard it as an imperfectly understood phenomenon of the Other Space. I know less about it than Franklin knew about lightning. But I will know—I will! I could give Stevens a solution right now for his worries if I knew some way to get around your problem too."

"I don't see the connection."

"There ought to be some way to do the whole thing through the Other Space. Start out by radiating power into the Other Space and pick up it up from there. Then the radiation could not harm human beings. It would never get at them; it would duck around them. I've been working on my caster, but with no luck so far. I'll crack it in time."

"I hope you do. Speaking of that, isn't the radiation from your own caster loose in this room?"

"Yes."

"Then I'll put on my shield coat. It's not good for you either."

"Never mind. I'll turn it off." As he turned to do so there was the sound of a sweet, chirruping whistle. Baldur barked. Grimes turned to see what caused it.

"What," he demanded, "have you got there?"

"Huh? Oh, that's my cuckoo clock. Fun, isn't it?" Grimes agreed that it was, although he could not see much use for it. Waldo had mounted it on the edge of a light metal hoop which spun with a speed just sufficient to produce a centrifugal force of one g.

"I rigged it up," Waldo continued, "while I was bogged down in this problem of the Other Space. Gave me something to do."

"This 'Other Space' business—I still don't get it."

"Think of another continuum much like our own and superposed on it the way you might lay one sheet of paper on another. The two spaces aren't identical, but they are separated from each other by the smallest interval you can imagine—coextensive but not touching—usually. There is an absolute one-to-one, point-for-point correspondence, as I conceive it, between the two spaces, but they are not necessarily the same size or shape."

"Hey? Come again—they would *have* to be."

"Not at all. Which has the larger number of points in it? A line an inch long, or a line a mile long?"

"A mile long, of course."

"No. They have exactly they same number of points. Want me to prove it?"

"I'll take your word for it. But I never studied that sort of math."

"All right. Take my word for it then. Neither size nor shape is any impediment to setting up a full, point-for-point correspondence between two spaces. Neither of the words is really appropriate. 'Size' has to do with a space's own inner structure, its dimensions in terms of its own unique constants. 'Shape' is a matter which happens inside itself—or at least not inside *our* space—and has to do with how it is curved, open or closed, expanding or contracting."

Grimes shrugged. "It all sounds like gibberish to me." He returned to watching the cuckoo clock swing round and round its wheel.

"Sure it does," Waldo assented cheerfully. "We are limited by our experience. Do you know how I think of the Other World?" The question was purely rhetorical. "I think of it as about the size and shape of an ostrich egg, but nevertheless a whole universe, existing side by side with our own, from here to the farthest star. I know that it's a false picture, but it helps me to think about it that way."

"I wouldn't know," said Grimes, and turned himself around in the air. The compound motion of the clock's pendulum was making him a little dizzy. "Say! I thought you turned off the caster?"

"I did," Waldo agreed, and looked where Grimes was looking. The deKalbs were still squirming. "I thought I did," he said doubtfully, and turned to the caster's control board. His eyes then opened wider. "But I *did*. It *is* turned off."

"Then what the devil—"

"Shut up!" He had to think—think hard. Was the caster actually out of operation? He floated himself over to it, inspected it. Yes, it was dead, dead as the dinosaurs. Just to make sure he went back, assumed his primary waldoes, cut in the necessary circuits, and partially disassembled it. But the deKalbs still squirmed.

The one deKalb set which had not been subjected to the Schneider treatment was dead; it gave out no power hum. But the others were working frantically, gathering power from—*where*?

He wondered whether or not McLeod had said anything to Gramps Schneider about the casters from which the deKalbs were intended to pick up their power. Certainly he himself had not. It simply had not come into the conversation. But Schneider had said something. "The Other World is close by and full of power!"

In spite of his own intention of taking the old man literally he had ignored that statement. The Other World is full of power. "I am sorry I snapped at you, Uncle Gus," he said.

"'S all right."

"But what do you make of that?"

"Looks like you've invented perpetual motion, son."

"In a way, perhaps. Or maybe we've repealed the law of conservation of energy. Those deKalbs are drawing energy that was never before in this world!"

"Hm-m-m!"

To check his belief he returned to the control ring, donned his waldoes, cut in a mobile scanner, and proceeded to search the space around the deKalbs with the most sensitive pickup for the radio power band he had available. The needles never jumped; the room was dead in the wave lengths to which the deKalbs were sensitive. The power came from Other Space.

The power came from Other Space. Not from his own beamcaster, not from NAPA's shiny stations, but from Other Space. In that case he was not even close to solving the problem of the defective deKalbs; he might never solve it. Wait, now—just what had he contracted to do? He tried to recall the exact words of the contract.

There just might be a way around it. Maybe. Yes, and this newest cockeyed trick of Gramps Schneider's little pets could have some very tricky aspects. He began to see some possibilities, but he needed to think about it.

"Uncle Gus—"

"Yes, Waldo?"

"You can go back and tell Stevens that I'll be ready with the answers. We'll get his problem licked, and yours too. In the meantime I've got to do some really heavy thinking, so I want to be by myself, please."

"GREETINGS, MR. GLEASON. *QUIET, BALDUR!* Come in. Be comfortable. How do you do, Dr. Stevens."

"How do you do, Mr. Jones."

"This," said Gleason, indicating a figure trailing him, "is Mr. Harkness, head of our legal staff."

"Ah, yes indeed. There will be matters of contract to be discussed. Welcome to Freehold, Mr. Harkness."

"Thank you," Harkness said coldly. "Will your attorneys be present?"

"They are present." Waldo indicated a stereo screen. Two figures showed in it; they bowed and murmured polite forms.

"This is most irregular," Harkness complained. "Witnesses should be present in person. Things seen and heard by television are not evidence."

Waldo drew his lips back. "Do you wish to make an issue of it?"

"Not at all," Gleason said hastily. "Never mind, Charles." Harkness subsided.

"I won't waste your time, gentlemen," Waldo began. "We are here in order that I may fulfill my contract with you. The terms are known—we will pass over them." He inserted his arms into his primary waldoes. "Lined up along the far wall you will see a number of radiant power receptors, commonly called deKalbs. Dr. Stevens may, if he wishes, check their serial numbers——"

"No need to."

"Very well. I shall start my local beamcaster, in order that we may check the efficiency of their operation." His waldoes were busy as he spoke. "Then I shall activate the receptors, one at a time." His hands pawed the air; a little pair of secondaries switched on the proper switches on the control board of the last set in line. "This is an ordinary type, supplied to me by Dr. Stevens, which has never failed in operation. You may assure yourself that it is now operating in the normal manner, if you wish, Doctor."

"I can see that it is."

"We will call such a receptor a 'deKalb' and its operation 'normal.'" The small waldoes were busy again. "Here we have a receptor which I choose to term a 'Schneider-deKalb' because of certain treatment it has received"—the antennae began to move—"and its operation 'Schneider-type' operation. Will you check it, Doctor?"

"O.K."

"You fetched with you a receptor set which has failed?"

"As you can see."

"Have you been able to make it function?"

"No, I have not."

"Are you sure? Have you examined it carefully?"

"Quite carefully," Stevens acknowledged sourly. He was beginning to be tired of Waldo's pompous flubdubbery.

"Very well. I will now proceed to make it operative." Waldo left his control ring, shoved himself over to the vicinity of the defective deKalb, and placed himself so that his body covered his exact actions from the sight of the others. He returned to the ring and, using waldoes, switched on the activating circuit of the deKalb.

It immediately exhibited Schneider-type activity.

"That is my case, gentlemen," he announced. "I have found out how to repair deKalbs which become spontaneously inoperative. I will undertake to apply the Schneider treatment to any receptors which you may bring to me. That is included in my fee. I will undertake to train others in how to apply the Schneider treatment. That is included in my fee, but I cannot guarantee that any particular man will profit by my instruction. Without going into technical details I may say that the treatment is very difficult, much harder than it looks. I think that Dr. Stevens will confirm that." He smiled thinly. "I believe that completes my agreement with you."

"Just a moment, Mr. Jones," put in Gleason. "Is a deKalb foolproof, once it has received the Schneider treatment?"

"Quite. I guarantee it."

They went into a huddle while Waldo waited. At last Gleason spoke for them. "These are not quite the results we had expected, Mr. Jones, but we agree that you have fulfilled your commission—with the understanding that you will Schneider-treat any receptors brought to you and instruct others, according to their ability to learn."

"That is correct."

"Your fee will be deposited to your account at once."

"Good. That is fully understood and agreed? I have completely and successfully performed your commission?"

"Correct."

"Very well then. I have one more thing too show you. If you will be patient——" A section of the wall folded back; gigantic waldoes reached into the room beyond and drew forth a large apparatus, which resembled somewhat in general form an ordinary set of deKalbs, but which was considerably more complicated. Most of the complications were sheer decoration, but it would have taken a skilled engineer a long time to prove the fact.

The machine did contain one novel feature: a built-in meter of a novel type, whereby it could be set to operate for a predetermined time and then destroy itself, and a radio control whereby the time limit could be varied. Furthermore, the meter would destroy itself and the receptors if tampered with by any person not familiar with its design. It was Waldo's tentative answer to the problem of selling free and unlimited power.

But of these matters he said nothing. Small waldoes had been busy attaching guys to the apparatus; when they were through he said, "This gentlemen, is an instrument which I choose to call a Jones-Schneider-deKalb. And it is the reason why you will not be in the business of selling power much longer."

"So?" said Gleason. "May I ask why?"

"Because," he was told, "I can sell it more cheaply and conveniently and under circumstances you cannot hope to match."

"That is a strong statement."

"I will demonstrate. Dr. Stevens, you have noted that the other receptors are operating. I will turn them off." The waldoes did so. "I will now stop the beamcast and I will ask you to assure yourself, by means of your own instruments, that there is *no* radiant power, other than ordinary visible light in this room."

Somewhat sullenly Stevens did so. "The place is dead," he announced some minutes later.

"Good. Keep your instruments in place, that you may be sure it remains dead. I will now activate my receptor." Little mechanical hands closed the switches. "Observe it, Doctor. Go over it thoroughly."

Stevens did so. He did not trust the readings shown by its instrument board; he attached his own meters in parallel. "How about it, James?" Gleason whispered.

Stevens looked disgusted. "The damn thing draws power from nowhere?"

They all looked at Waldo. "Take plenty of time, gentlemen," he said grandly. "Talk it over."

They withdrew as far away as the room permitted and whispered. Waldo could see that Harkness and Gleason were arguing, that Stevens was noncommittal. That suited him. He was hoping that Stevens would not decide to take another look at the fancy gadget he had termed a Jones-Schneider-deKalb. Stevens must not learn too much about it—yet. He had been careful to say nothing but the truth about it, but perhaps he had not said all of the truth; he had not mentioned that *all* Schneider-treated deKalbs were sources of free power.

Rather embarrassing if Stevens should discover that!

The meter-and-destruction device Waldo had purposely made mysterious and complex, but it was not useless. Later he would be able to point out, quite correctly, that without such a device NAPA simply could not remain in business.

Waldo was not easy. The whole business was a risky gamble; he would have much preferred to know more about the phenomena he was trying to peddle, but—he shrugged mentally while preserving a smile of smug confidence—the business had dragged on several months already, and the power situation really was critical. This solution would do—if he could get their names on the dotted line quickly enough.

For he had no intention of trying to compete with NAPA.

Gleason pulled himself away from Stevens and Harkness, came to Waldo. "Mr. Jones, can't we arrange this amicably?"

"What have you to suggest?"

IT WAS QUITE AN HOUR later that Waldo, with a sigh of relief, watched his guests' ship depart from the threshold flat. A fine caper, he thought, and it had worked; he had gotten away with it. He had magnanimously allowed himself to be persuaded to consolidate, provided—he had allowed himself to be quite temperamental about this—the contract was concluded at once, no fussing around and fencing between lawyers. Now or never—put up or shut up. The proposed contract, he had pointed out virtuously, gave him nothing at all unless his allegations about the Jones-Schneider-deKalb were correct.

Gleason considered this point and had decided to sign, had signed.

Even then Harkness had attempted to claim that Waldo had been an employee of NAPA. Waldo had written the contract himself—a specific commission for a contingent fee. Harkness did not have a leg to stand on; even Gleason had agreed to that.

In exchange for all rights to the Jones-Schneider-deKalb, for which he agreed to supply drawings—wait till Stevens saw, and understood, those sketches!—for that he had received the promise of senior stock in NAPA, non-voting, but fully paid up and nonassessable. The lack of active participation in the company had been his own idea. There were going to be more headaches in the power business, headaches aplenty. He could see them coming—bootleg designs, means of outwitting the metering, lots of things. Free power had come, and efforts to stop it would in the long run, he believed, be fruitless.

Waldo laughed so hard that he frightened Baldur, who set up an excited barking.

He could afford to forget Hathaway now.

His revenge on NAPA contained one potential flaw; he had assured

Gleason that the Schneider-treated deKalbs would continue to operate, would not come unstuck. He believed that to be true simply because he had faith in Gramps Schneider. But he was not prepared to prove it. He knew himself that he did not know enough about the phenomena associated with the Other World to be sure that something would, or would not, happen. It was still going to be necessary to do some hard, extensive research.

But the Other World was a devilishly difficult place to investigate!

Suppose, he speculated, that the human race were blind, had never developed eyes. No matter how civilized, enlightened, and scientific the race might have become, it is difficult to see how such a race could ever have developed the concepts of astronomy. They might know of the Sun as a cyclic source of energy having a changing, directional character, for the Sun is so overpowering that it may be "seen" with the skin. They would notice it and invent instruments to trap it and examine it.

But the pale stars, would they ever notice them? It seemed most unlikely. The very notion of the celestial universe, its silent depths and starlit grandeur, would be beyond them. Even if one of their scientists should have the concept forced on him in such a manner that he was obliged to accept the fantastic, incredible thesis as fact, how then would he go about investigating its details?

Waldo tried to imagine an astronomical phototelescope, conceived and designed by a blind man, intended to be operated by a blind man, and capable of collecting data which could be interpreted by a blind man. He gave it up; there were too many hazards. It would take a subtlety of genius far beyond his own to deal with the inescapably tortuous concatenations of inferential reasoning necessary to the solution of such a problem. It would strain him to invent such instruments *for* a blind man; he did not see how a blind man could ever overcome the difficulties unassisted.

In a way that was what Schneider had done for him; alone, he would have bogged down.

But even with Schneider's hints the problem of investigating the Other World was still much like the dilemma of the blind astronomer. He could not *see* the Other World; only through the Schneider treatment had he been able to contact it. Damnation! How could he design instruments to study it?

He suspected that he would eventually have to go back to Schneider for further instruction, but that was an expedient so distasteful that he refused to think much about it. Furthermore, Gramps Schneider might not be able to teach him much; they did not speak the same language.

This much he did know: the Other Space was there and it could be reached sometimes by proper orientation of the mind, deliberately as Schneider had taught him, or subconsciously as had happened to McLeod and others.

He found the idea distasteful. That thought and thought alone should be able to influence physical phenomena was contrary to the whole materialistic philosophy in which he had grown up. He had a prejudice in favor of order and invariable natural laws. His cultural predecessors, the experimental philosphers who had built up the world of science and its concomitant technology, Galileo, Newton, Edison, Einstein, Steinmetz, Jeans, and their myriad colleagues—these men had thought of the physical universe as a mechanism proceeding by inexorable necessity. Any apparent failure to proceed thus was regarded as an error in observation, an insufficient formulation of hypothesis, or an insufficiency of datum.

Even the short reign of the Heisenberg uncertainty principle had not changed the fundamental orientation toward Order and Cosmos; the Heisenberg uncertainty was one they were certain of! It could be formulated, expressed, and a rigorous statistical mechanics could be built from it. In 1958 Horowitz's reformulation of wave mechanics had eliminated the concept. Order and causation were restored.

But this damned business! One might as well pray for rain, wish on the Moon, go to faith healers, surrender whole hog to Bishop Berkely's sweetly cerebral world-in-your-head. "—the tree's not a tree, when there's no one about the quad!"

WALDO WAS NOT EMOTIONALLY WEDDED to Absolute Order as Rambeau had been; he was in no danger of becoming mentally unbalanced through a failure of his basic conceptions; nevertheless, consarn it, it was convenient for things to work the way one expected them to. On order and natural law was based predictability; without predictability it was impossible to live. Clocks should run evenly; water should boil when heat is applied to it; food should nourish, not poison; deKalb receptors should *work*, work the way they were designed to; Chaos was insupportable—it could not be lived with.

Suppose Chaos *were* king and the order we thought we detected in the world about us a mere phantasm of the imagination; where would that lead us? In that case, Waldo decided, it was entirely possible that a ten-pound weight *did* fall ten times as fast as a one-pound weight until the day the audacious Galileo decided in his mind that it was not so. Perhaps the whole meticulous science of ballistics derived from the convictions of a few firm-minded individuals who had sold the notion to the world. Perhaps the very stars were held firm in their courses by the unvarying faith of the astronomers. Orderly Cosmos, created out of Chaos—by Mind!

The world was flat before geographers decided to think of it otherwise. The world was flat, and the Sun, tub size, rose in the east and set in the west. The stars were little lights, studding a pellucid dome which barely cleared the tallest mountains. Storms were the wrath of gods and had nothing to do with the calculus of air masses. A Mind-created animism dominated the world then.

More recently it had been different. A prevalent convention of materialistic and invariable causation had ruled the world; on it was based the whole involved technology of a machine-served civilization. The machines *worked*, the way they were designed to work, because everybody believed in them.

Until a few pilots, somewhat debilitated by overmuch exposure to radiation, had lost their confidence and infected their machines with uncertainty—and thereby let magic loose in the world.

He was beginning, he thought, to understand what had happened to magic. Magic was the erratic law of an animistic world; it had been steadily pushed back by the advancing philosophy of invariant causation. It was gone now—until this new outbreak—and its world with it, except for backwaters of "superstition." Naturally an experimental scientist reported failure when investigating haunted houses, apportations, and the like; his convictions prevented the phenomena from happening.

The deep jungles of Africa might be very different places—when there was no white man around to see! The strangely slippery laws of magic might still obtain.

Perhaps these speculations were too extreme; nevertheless, they had one advantage which orthodox concepts had not: they included Gramps Schneider's hexing of the deKalbs. Any working hypothesis which failed to account for Schneider's—and his own—ability to *think* a set of deKalbs into operation was not worth a continental. This one did, and it conformed to Gramps's own statements: "All matters are doubtful" and "A thing can both *be, not be*, and *be anything*. There are many true ways of looking at the same thing. Some ways are good, some are bad."

Very well. Accept it. Act on it. The world varied according to the way one looked at it. In that case, thought Waldo, he knew how he wanted to look at it. He cast his vote for order and predictability!

He would *set* the style. He would impress his *own* concept of the Other World on the Cosmos!

It had been a good start to assure Gleason that the Schneider-treated deKalbs were foolproof. They would never get out of order.

He proceeded to formulate and clarify his own concept of the Other World in his mind. He would think of it as orderly and basically similar to this space. The connection between the two spaces lay in the neurological system; the cortex, the thalamus, the spinal cord, and the appended nerve system were closely connected with both spaces. Such a picture was consistent with what Schneider had told him and did not conflict with phenomena as he knew them.

Wait. If the neurological system lay in both spaces, then that might account for the relatively slow propagation of nerve impulses as compared with electromagnetic progression. Yes! If the other space had a *c* constant relatively smaller than that of this space, such would follow.

He began to feel a calm assurance that it was *so*.

Was he merely speculating—or creating a universe?

Perhaps he would have to abandon his mental picture of the Other Space as being the size and shape of an ostrich egg, since a space with a slower propagation of light is not smaller, but larger, than the space he was used to. No . . . no, wait a second, the *size* of a space did not depend on its *c* constant, but on its radius of curvature in terms of its *c* constant. Since *c* was a velocity, size was dependent on the notion of time—in this case time as entropy rate. Therein lay a characteristic which could be compared between the two spaces: they exchanged energy; they affected each other's entropy. The one which degenerated the more rapidly toward a state of level entropy was the "smaller."

He need not abandon his picture of the ostrich egg—good old egg! The Other World was a closed space, with a slow *c*, a high entropy rate, a short radius, and an entropy state near level—a perfect reservoir of power at every point, ready to spill over into this space wherever he might close the interval. To its inhabitants, if any, it might seem to be hundreds of millions of light years around; to him it was an ostrich egg, turgid to bursting with power.

He was already beginning to think of ways of checking his hypothesis. If, using a Schneider-deKalb, he were to draw energy at the highest rate he could manage, would he affect the local potential? Would it establish an entropy gradient? Could he reverse the process by finding a way to pump power into the Other World? Could he establish different levels at different points and thereby check for degeneration toward level, maximum entropy?

Did the speed of nerve impulse propagation furnish a clue to the *c* of the Other Space? Could such a clue be combined with the entropy and potential investigations to give a mathematical picture of the Other Space, in terms of its constants and its age?

He set about it. His untrammeled, wild speculations had produced some definite good: he'd tied down at least one line of attack on that Other Space; he'd devised a working principle for his blind man's telescope mechanism. Whatever the truth of the thing was, it was more than *a* truth; it was a complete series of new truths. It was the very complexity of that series of new truths—the truths, the characteristic laws, that were inherent properties of the Other Space, plus the new truth laws resultant from the interaction of the characteristics of the Other Space with Normal Space. No wonder Rambeau had said anything could happen! Almost anything could, in all probability, by a proper application and combination of the three sets of laws: the laws of Our Space, the laws of Other Space, and the co-ordinate laws of Both Spaces.

But before theoreticians could begin work, new data were most desperately needed. Waldo was no theoretician, a fact he admitted left-handedly in thinking of theory as impractical and unnecessary, time waste for him as a consulting engineer. Let the smooth apes work it out.

But the consulting engineer had to find out one thing: would the Schneider-deKalbs continue to function uninterruptedly as guaranteed? If not, what must be done to assure continuous function?

The most difficult and the most interesting aspect of the investigation had to do with the neurological system in relation to Other Space. Neither electromagnetic instruments nor neural surgery was refined enough to do accurate work on the levels he wished to investigate.

But he had waldoes.

The smallest waldoes he had used up to this time were approximately half an inch across their palms—with micro-scanners to match, of course. They were much too gross for his purpose. He wished to manipulate living nerve tissue, examine its insulation and its performance *in situ*.

He used the tiny waldoes to create tinier ones.

The last stage was tiny metal blossoms hardly an eighth of an inch across. The helices on their stems, or forearms, which served them as pseudo muscles, could hardly be seen by the naked eye—but, then, he used scanners.

His final team of waldoes used for nerve and brain surgery varied in succeeding stages from mechanical hands nearly life-size down to these fairy digits which could manipulate things much too small for the eye to see. They were mounted in bank to work in the same locus. Waldo controlled them all from the same primaries; he could switch from one size to another without removing his gauntlets. The same change in circuits which brought another size of waldoes under control automatically accomplished the change in sweep of scanning to increase or decrease the magnification so that Waldo always saw before him in his stereo receiver a "life-size" image of his other hands.

Each level of waldoes had its own surgical instruments, its own electrical equipment.

Such surgery had never been seen before, but Waldo gave that aspect little thought; no one had told him that such surgery was unheard-of.

He established, to his own satisfaction, the mechanism whereby short-wave radiation had produced a deterioration in human physical performance. The synapses between dendrites acted as if they were points of leakage. Never impulses would sometimes fail to make the jump, would leak off—to where? To Other Space, he was sure. Such leakage seemed to establish a preferred path, a canalization, whereby the condition of the victim became steadily worse. Motor action was not lost entirely, as both paths were still available, but efficiency was lost. It reminded him of a metallic electrical circuit with a partial ground.

An unfortunate cat, which had become dead undergoing the experimentation, had supplied him with much of his data. The kitten had been born and raised free from exposure to power radiation. He subjected it to heavy exposure and saw it acquire a *myasthenia* nearly as complete as his own—while studying in minute detail what actually went on in its nerve tissues.

He felt quite sentimental about it when it died.

YET, IF GRAMPS SCHNEIDER WERE right, human beings need not be damaged by radiation. If they had the wit to look at it with the proper orientation, the radiation would not affect them; they might even draw power out of the Other World.

That was what Gramps Schneider had told him to do.

That was what Gramps Schneider had told *him* to do!

Gramps Schneider had told him he need not be weak!

That he could be strong—

Strong!

STRONG!

He had never thought of it. Schneider's friendly ministrations to him, his advice about overcoming the weakness, he had ignored, had thrown off as inconsequential. His own weakness, his own peculiarity which made him different from the smooth apes, he had regarded as a basic implicit fact. He had accepted it as established when he was a small child, a final unquestioned factor.

Naturally he had paid no attention to Schneider's words in so far as they referred to him.

To be strong!

To stand alone—to work, to *run*!

Why, he . . . he could, he could go down to Earth surface without fear. He wouldn't mind the field. They *said* they didn't mind it; they even *carried* things—great, heavy things. Everybody did. They *threw* things.

He made a sudden convulsive movement in his primary waldoes, quite unlike his normal, beautifully economical rhythm. The secondaries were oversize, as he was making a new setup. The guys tore loose, a brace plate banged against the wall. Baldur was snoozing nearby; he pricked up his ears, looked around, then turned his face to Waldo, questioning him.

Waldo glared at him and the dog whined. "Shut up!"

The dog quieted and apologized with his eyes.

Automatically he looked over the damage—not much, but he would have to fix it. Strength. Why, if he were strong, he could do anything—anything! No. 6 extension waldoes and some new guys——Strong! Absent-mindedly he shifted to the No. 6 waldoes.

Strength!

He could even meet women—be stronger than they were!

HE COULD SWIM. HE COULD ride. He could fly a ship—run, jump. He could handle things with this bare hands. He could even learn to dance!

Strong!

He would have muscles! He could break things.

He could——He could——

He switched to the great waldoes with hands the size of a man's body. Strong—they were strong! With one giant waldo he hauled from the stock pile a quarter-inch steel plate, held it up, and shook it. A booming rumble. He shook it again. Strong!

He took it on both waldoes, bent it double. The metal buckled unevenly. Convulsively he crumpled it like wastepaper between the two huge palms. The grinding racket raised hackles on Baldur; he himself had not been aware of it.

He relaxed for a moment, gasping. There was sweat on his forehead; blood throbbed in his ears. But he was not spent; he wanted something heavier, *stronger*. Cutting to the adjoining storeroom he selected an L-beam twelve feet long, shoved it through to where the giant hands could reach it, and cut back to them.

The beam was askew in the port; he wrenched it loose, knocking a big dent in the port frame. He didn't notice it.

The beam made a fine club in the gross fist. He brandished it. Baldur backed away, placing the control ring between himself and the great hands.

Power! Strength! Smashing, unbeatable strength——

With a spastic jerk he checked his swing just before the beam touched the wall. No——But he grabbed the other end of the club with the left waldo and tried to bend it. The big waldoes were built for heavy work, but the beam was built to resist. He strained inside the primaries, strove to force the great fists to do his will. A warning light flashed on his control board. Blindly he kicked in the emergency overload and persisted.

The hum of the waldoes and the rasp of his own breath were drowned out by the harsh scrape of metal on metal as the beam began to give way. Exulting, he bore down harder in the primaries. The beam was bending double when the waldoes blew out. The right-hand tractors let go first; the fist flung open. The left fist, relieved of the strain, threw the steel from it.

It tore its way through the thin bulkhead, making a ragged hole, crashed and clanged in the room beyond.

But the giant waldoes were inanimate junk.

He drew his soft pink hands from the waldoes and looked at them. His shoulders heaved, and racking sobs pushed up out of him. He covered his face with his hands; the tears leaked out between his fingers. Baldur whimpered and edged closer.

On the control board a bell rang persistently.

THE WRECKAGE HAD BEEN CLEARED away and an adequate, neat patch covered the place where the L-beam had made its own exit. But the giant waldoes had not yet been replaced; their frame was uninhabited. Waldo was busy rigging a strength tester.

It had been years since he had paid any attention to the exact strength of his body. He had had so little use for strength; he had concentrated on dexterity, particularly on the exact and discriminating control of his namesakes. In the selective, efficient, and accurate use of his muscles he was second to none; he had control—he *had* to have. But he had had no need for strength.

With the mechanical equipment at hand it was not difficult to jerry-rig a device which would register strength of grip as pounds-force on a dial. A spring-loaded scale and a yoke to act on it sufficed. He paused and looked at the contrivance.

He need only take off the primary waldoes, place his bare hand on the grip, bear down—and he would know. Still he hesitated.

It felt strange to handle anything so large with his bare hand. Now. Reach into the Other World for power. He closed his eyes and pressed. He opened them. Fourteen pounds—less than he used to have.

But he had not really tried yet. He tried to imagine Gramps Schneider's hands on his arm, that warm tingle. Power. Reach out and claim it.

Fourteen pounds, fifteen—seventeen, eighteen, twenty, twenty-one! He was winning! He was winning!

Both his strength and his courage failed him, in what order he could not say. The needle spun back to zero; he had to rest.

Had he really shown exceptional strength—or was twenty-one pounds of grip simply normal for him at his present age and weight? A normally strong and active man, he knew, should have a grip on the order of one hundred and fifty pounds.

Nevertheless, twenty-one pounds of grip was six pounds higher than he had ever before managed on test.

Try, again. Ten, eleven—twelve. Thirteen. The needle hesitated. Why, he had just started—this was ridiculous. Fourteen.

There it stopped. No mater how he strained and concentrated his driving will he could not pass that point. Slowly, he dropped back from it.

SIXTEEN POUNDS WAS THE HIGHEST he managed in the following days. Twenty-one pounds seemed to have been merely a fluke, a good first effort. He ate bitterness.

But he had not reached his present position of wealth and prominence by easy surrender. He persisted, recalling carefully just what Schneider had said to him, and trying to *feel* the touch of Schneider's hands. He told himself now that he really had been stronger under Schneider's touch. But that he had failed to realize it because of the Earth's heavy field. He continued to try.

In the back of his mind he knew that he must eventually seek out Gramps Schneider and ask his help, if he did not find the trick alone. But he was extremely reluctant to do so, not because of the terrible trip it entailed—though that would ordinarily have been more than enough reason—but because if he did so and Schneider was not able to help him, then there would be no hope, no hope at all.

It was better to live with the disappointment and frustration than to live without hope. He continued to postpone it.

WALDO PAID LITTLE ATTENTION TO Earth time; he ate and slept when he pleased. He might catch a cat nap at any time; however, at fairly regular intervals he slept for longer periods. Not in a bed, of course. A man who floats in air has no need for a bed. But he did make it a habit to guy himself into place before undertaking eight hours of solid sleep, as it prevented him from casual drifting in random air currents which might carry him, unconscious, against controls or switches.

Since the obsession to become strong had possessed him he had frequently found it necessary to resort to soporifics to ensure sleep.

Dr. Rambeau had returned and was looking for him. Rambeau—crazy and filled with hate. Rambeau, blaming his troubles on Waldo. He was not safe, even in Freehold, as the crazy physicist had found out how to pass from one space to another. There he was now! Just his head, poked through from the Other World. "I'm going to get you, Waldo!" He was gone—no, there he was behind him! Reaching, reaching out with hands that were writhing antennae. "You, Waldo!" But Waldo's own hands were the giant waldoes; he snatched at Rambeau.

The big waldoes went limp.

Rambeau was at him, was on him; he had him around the throat.

Gramps Schneider said in his ear, in a voice that was calm and strong, "Reach out for the power, my son. Feel it in your fingers." Waldo grabbed at the throttling fingers, strained, tried.

They were coming loose. He was winning. He would stuff Rambeau back into the Other World and keep him there. There! He had one hand free. Baldur was barking frantically; he tried to tell him to shut up, to bite Rambeau, to help—

The dog continued to bark.

HE WAS IN HIS OWN home, in his own great room. Baldur let out one more yipe. "Quiet!" He looked himself over.

When he had gone to sleep he had been held in place by four light guys, opposed like the axes of a tetrahedron. Two of them were still fastened to his belt; he swung loosely against the control ring. Of the other two, one had snapped off at his belt; its end floated a few feet away. The fourth had broken in two places, near his belt and again several feet out; the severed piece was looped loosely around his neck.

He looked the situation over. Study as he might, he could conceive no way in which the guys could have been broken save by his own struggles in the nightmare. The dog could not have done it; he had no way to get a purchase. He had done it himself. The lines were light, being intended merely as stays. Still——

It took him a few minutes to rig a testing apparatus which would test pull instead of grip; the yoke had to be reversed. When it was done he cut in a medium waldo pair, fastened the severed pieces of line to the tester, and, using the waldo, pulled.

The line parted at two hundred and twelve pounds.

Hastily, but losing time because of nervous clumsiness, he rerigged the tester for grip. He paused, whispered softly, "Now is the time, Gramps!" and bore down on the grip.

Twenty pounds—twenty-one. Twenty-five!

Up past thirty. He was not even sweating! Thirty-five—forty, -one, -two, -three. Forty-five! And -six! And a half. Forty-seven pounds!

With a great sigh he let his hand relax. He was strong. Strong.

When he had somewhat regained his composure, he considered what to do next. His first impulse was to call Grimes, but he suppressed it. Soon enough when he was sure of himself.

He went back to the tester and tried his left hand. Not as strong as his right, but almost—nearly forty-five pounds. Funny thing, he didn't feel any different. Just normal, healthy. No sensation.

He wanted to try all of his muscles. It would take too long to rig testers for kick, and shove, and back lift, and, oh, a dozen others. He needed a field, that was it, a one-g field. Well, there was the reception room; it could be centrifuged.

But its controls were in the ring and it was long corridors away. There was a nearer one, the centrifuge for the cuckoo clock. He had rigged the wheel with a speed control as an easy way to regulate the clock. He moved back to the control ring and stopped the turning of the big wheel; the clockwork was disturbed by the sudden change; the little red bird popped out, said, "*Th-wu th-woo*" once, hopefully, and subsided.

Carrying in his hand a small control panel radio hooked to the motor which impelled the centrifuge wheel, he propelled himself to the wheel and placed himself inside, planting his feet on the inner surface of the rim and grasping one of the spokes, so that he would be in a standing position with respect to the centrifugal force, once it was impressed. He started the wheel slowly.

Its first motion surprised him and he almost fell off. But he recovered himself and gave it a little more power. All right so far. He speeded it up gradually, triumph spreading through him as he felt the pull of the pseudo gravitational field, felt his legs grow heavy, *but still strong*.

He let it out, one full g. He could take it. He could, indeed! To be sure, the force did not affect the upper part of his body so strongly as the lower, as his head was only a foot or so from the point of rotation.

He could fix that; he squatted down slowly, hanging on tight to the spoke. It was all right.

But the wheel swayed and the motor complained. His unbalanced weight, that far out from the center of rotation, was putting too much of a strain on a framework intended to support a cuckoo clock and its counterweight only. He straightened up with equal caution, feeling the fine *shove* of his thigh muscles and calves. He stopped the wheel.

Baldur had been much perturbed by the whole business. He had almost twisted his neck off trying to follow the motions of Waldo.

He still postponed calling Grimes. He wanted to arrange for some selective local controls on the centrifuging of the reception room, in order to have a proper place in which to practice standing up. Then he had to get the hang of this walking business; it looked easy, but he didn't know. Might be quite a trick to learn it.

Thereafter he planned to teach Baldur to walk. He tried to get Baldur into the cuckoo-clock wheel, but the dog objected. He wiggled free and retreated to the farthest part of the room. No matter—when he had the beast in the reception room he would damn well have to learn to walk. Should have seen to it long ago. A big brute like that, and couldn't walk!

He visualized a framework into which the dog could be placed which would force him to stand erect. It was roughly equivalent to a baby's toddler, but Waldo did not know that. He had never seen a baby's toddler.

"UNCLE GUS—"

"Oh, hello, Waldo. How have you been?"

"Fine. Look, Uncle Gus, could you come up to Freehold—right away?"

Grimes shook his head. "Sorry. My bus is in the shop."

"Your bus is too slow anyhow. Take a taxi, or get somebody to drive you."

"And have you insult 'em when we get there? Huh-uh."

"I'll be sweet as sugar."

"Well, Jimmie Stevens said something yesterday about wanting to see you."

Waldo grinned. "Get him. I'd like to see him."

"I'll try."

"Call me back. Make it soon."

Waldo met them in the reception room, which he had left uncentrifuged. As soon as they came in he started his act. "My, I'm glad you're here. Dr. Stevens—could you fly me down to Earth right away? Something's come up."

"Why—I suppose so."

"Let's go."

"Wait a minute, Waldo. Jimmie's not prepared to handle you the way you have to be handled."

"I'll have to chance it, Uncle Gus. This is urgent."

"But—"

"No 'buts.' Let's leave at once."

They hustled Baldur into the ship and tied him down. Grimes saw to it that Waldo's chair was tilted back in the best approximation of a deceleration rig. Waldo settled himself into it and closed his eyes to discourage questions. He sneaked a look and found Grimes grimly silent.

Stevens made very nearly a record trip, but set them down quite gently on the parking flat over Grimes's home. Grimes touched Waldo's arm. "How do you feel? I'll get someone and we'll get you inside. I want to get you to bed."

"Can't do that, Uncle Gus. Things to do. Give me your arm, will you?"

"Huh?" But Waldo reached for the support requested and drew himself up.

"I'll be all right now, I guess." He let go the physician's arm and started for the door. "Will you untie Baldur?"

"*Waldo!*"

He turned around, grinning happily. "Yes, Uncle Gus, it's true. I'm not weak any more. *I can walk.*"

Grimes took hold of the back of one of the seats and said shakily, "Waldo, I'm an old man. You ought not to do things like this to me." He wiped at his eyes.

"Yes," agreed Stevens, "it's a damn dirty trick."

Waldo looked blankly from one face to the other. "I'm sorry," he said humbly. "I just wanted to surprise you."

"It's all right. Let's go downside and have a drink. You can tell us about it then."

"All right. Come on, Baldur." The dog got up and followed after his master. He had a very curious gait; Waldo's trainer gadget had taught him to pace instead of trot.

WALDO STAYED WITH GRIMES FOR days, gaining strength, gaining new reflex patterns, building up his flabby muscles. He had no setbacks; the *myasthenia* was gone. All he required was conditioning.

Grimes had forgiven him at once for his unnecessarily abrupt and spectacular revelation of his cure, but Grimes had insisted that he take it easy and become fully readjusted before he undertook to venture out unescorted. It was a wise precaution. Even simple things were hazards to him. Stairs, for example. He could walk on the level, but going downstairs had to be learned. Going up was not so difficult.

Stevens showed up one day, let himself in, and found Waldo alone in the living room, listening to a stereo show. "Hello, Mr. Jones."

"Oh—hello, Dr. Stevens." Waldo reached down hastily, fumbled for his shoes, zipped them on. "Uncle Gus says I should wear them all the time," he explained. "Everybody does. But you caught me unawares."

"Oh, that's no matter. You don't have to wear them in the house. Where's Doc?"

"Gone for the day. Don't you, really? Seems to me my nurses always wore shoes."

"Oh yes, everybody does—but there's no law to make you."

"Then I'll wear them. But I can't say that I like them. They feel dead, like a pair of disconnected waldoes. But I want to learn how."

"How to wear shoes?"

"How to act like people act. It's really quite difficult," he said seriously.

Stevens felt a sudden insight, a welling of sympathy for this man with no background and no friends. It must be odd and strange to him. He felt an impulse to confess something which had been on his mind with respect to Waldo. "You really are strong now, aren't you?"

Waldo grinned happily. "Getting stronger every day. I gripped two hundred pounds this morning. And see how much fat I've worked off."

"You're looking fit, all right. Here's a funny thing. Ever since I first met you I've wished to high heaven that you were as strong as an ordinary man."

"You really did? Why?"

"Well . . . I think you will admit that you used some pretty poisonous language to me, one time and another. You had me riled up all the time. I wanted you to get strong so that I could just beat the hell out of you."

Waldo had been walking up and down, getting used to his shoes. He stopped and faced Stevens. He seemed considerably startled. "You mean you wanted to fist-fight me?"

"Exactly. You used language to me that a man ought not to use unless he is prepared to back it up with his fists. If you had not been an invalid I would have pasted you one, oh, any number of times."

Waldo seemed to be struggling with a new concept. "I think I see," he said slowly. "Well—all right." On the last word he delivered a roundhouse swipe with plenty of power behind it. Stevens was not in the least expecting it; it happened to catch him on the button. He went down, out cold.

When he came to he found himself in a chair. Waldo was shaking him. "Wasn't that right?" he said anxiously.

"What did you hit me with?"

"My hand. Wasn't that right? Wasn't that what you wanted?"

"Wasn't that what I——" He still had little bright lights floating in front of his eyes, but the situation began to tickle him. "Look here—is that your idea of the proper way to start a fight?"

"Isn't it?"

Stevens tried to explain to him the etiquette of fisticuffs, contemporary American. Waldo seemed puzzled, but finally he nodded. "I get it. You have to give the other man warning. All right—get up, and we'll do it over."

"Easy, easy! Wait a minute. You never did give me a chance to finish what I was saying. I *was* sore at you, but I'm not any more. That is what I was trying to tell you. Oh, you were utterly poisonous; there is no doubt about that. But you couldn't help being."

"I don't mean to be poisonous," Waldo said seriously.

"I know you don't, and you're not. I rather like you now—now that you're strong."

"Do you really?"

"Yes, I do. But don't practice any more of those punches on me."

"I won't. But I didn't understand. But, do you know, Dr. Stevens, it's——"

"Call me Jim."

"Jim. It's a very hard thing to know just what people do expect. There is so little pattern to it. Take belching; I didn't know it was forbidden to burp when other people are around. It seems obviously necessary to me. But Uncle Gus says not."

Stevens tried to clear up the matter for him—not too well, as he found that Waldo was almost totally lacking in any notion, even theoretical, of social conduct. Not even from fiction had he derived a concept of the intricacies of *mores*, as he had read almost no fiction. He had ceased reading stories in his early boyhood, because he lacked the background of experience necessary to appreciate fiction.

He was rich, powerful, and a mechanical genius, but he still needed to go to kindergarten.

Waldo had a proposition to make. "Jim, you've been very helpful. You explain these things better than Uncle Gus does. I'll hire you to teach me."

Stevens suppressed a slight feeling of pique. "Sorry. I've got a job that keeps me busy."

"Oh, that's all right. I'll pay you better than they do. You can name your own salary. It's a deal."

Stevens took a deep breath and sighed. "You don't understand. I'm an engineer and I don't hire out for personal service. You can't hire me. Oh, I'll help you all I can, but I won't take money for it."

"What's wrong with taking money?"

The question, Stevens thought, was stated wrongly. As it stood it could not be answered. He launched into a long, involved discussion of professional and business conduct. He was really not fitted for it; Waldo soon bogged down. "I'm afraid I don't get it. But see here—could you teach me how to behave with girls? Uncle Gus says he doesn't dare take me out in company."

"Well, I'll try. I'll certainly try. But, Waldo, I came over to see you about some of the problems we're running into at the plant. About this theory of the two spaces that you were telling me about——"

"It's not theory; it's fact."

"All right. What I want to know is this: When do you expect to go back to Freehold and resume research? We need some help."

"Go back to Freehold? I haven't any idea. I don't intend to resume research."

"You don't? But, my heavens, you haven't finished half the investigations you outlined to me."

"You fellows can do 'em. I'll help out with suggestions, of course."

"Well—maybe we could interest Gramps Schneider," Stevens said doubtfully.

"I would not advise it," Waldo answered. "Let me show you a letter he sent me." He left and fetched it back. "Here."

Steven glanced through it. "—your generous offer of your share in the new power project I appreciate, but, truthfully, I have no interest in such things and would find the responsibility a burden. As for the news of your new strength I am happy, but not surprised. The power of the Other World is his who would claim it—" There was more to it. It was written in a precise Spencerian hand, a trifle shaky; the rhetoric showed none of the colloquialisms with which Schneider spoke.

"Hm-m-m—I think I see what you mean."

"I believe," Waldo said seriously, "that he regards our manipulations with gadgets as rather childish."

"I suppose. Tell me, what do *you* intend to do with yourself?"

"Me? I don't know exactly. But I can tell you this: I'm going to have fun. I'm going to have lots of fun. I'm just beginning to find out how much fun it is to be a man!"

HIS DRESSER TACKLED THE OTHER slipper. "To tell you just why I took up dancing would be a long story," he continued.

"I want details."

"Hospital calling," someone in the dressing room said.

"Tell 'em I'll be right there, fast. Suppose you come in tomorrow afternoon?" he added to the woman reporter. "Can you?"

"Right."

A man was shouldering his way through a little knot around him. Waldo caught his eye. "Hello, Stanley. Glad to see you."

"Hello, Waldo." Gleason pulled some papers out from under his cape and dropped them in the dancer's lap. "Brought these over myself as I wanted to see your act again."

"Like it?"

"Swell!"

Waldo grinned and picked up the papers. "Where is the dotted line?"

"Better read them first," Gleason cautioned him.

"Oh shucks, no. If it suits you, it suits me. Can I borrow your stylus?"

A worried little man worked his way up to them. "About that recording, Waldo—"

"We've discussed that," Waldo said flatly. "I only perform before audiences."

"We've combined it with the Warm Springs benefit."

"That's different. O.K."

"While you're about it, take a look at this layout." It was a reduction, for a twenty-four sheet:

THE GREAT WALDO
AND HIS TROUPE

with the opening date and theater left blank, but with a picture of Waldo, as Harlequin, poised high in the air.

"Fine, Sam, fine!" Waldo nodded happily.

"Hospital calling again!"

"I'm ready now," Waldo answered, and stood up. His dresser draped his street cape over his lean shoulders. Waldo whistled sharply. "Here, Baldur! Come along." At the door he stopped an instant, and waved. "Good night, fellows!"

"Good night, Waldo."

They were all such grand guys.

# The Unpleasant Profession of Jonathan Hoag

*—the end it is not well.*
*From too much love of living.*
*From hope and fear set free.*
*We thank with brief thanksgiving*
*Whatever gods may be*
*That no life lives forever:*
*That dead men rise up never:*
*That even the weariest river*
*Winds somewhere safe to sea.*

—Swinburne

"It is blood, doctor?" Jonathan Hoag moistened his lips with his tongue and leaned forward in the chair, trying to see what was written on the slip of paper the medico held.

Dr. Potbury brought the slip of paper closer to his vest and looked at Hoag over his spectacles. "Any particular reason," he asked, "why you should find blood under your fingernails?"

"No. That is to say— Well, no—there isn't. But it *is* blood—isn't it?"

"No," Potbury said heavily. "No, it isn't blood."

Hoag knew that he should have felt relieved. But he was not. He knew in that moment that he had clung to the notion that the brown grime under his fingernails was dry blood rather than let himself dwell on other, less tolerable, ideas.

He felt sick at his stomach. But he had to know—

"What is it, doctor? Tell me."

Potbury looked him up and down. "You asked me a specific question. I've answered it. You did not ask me what the substance was; you asked me to find out whether or not it was blood. It is not."

"But— You are playing with me. Show me the analysis." Hoag half rose from his chair and reached for the slip of paper.

The doctor held it away from him, then tore it carefully in two. Placing the two pieces together he tore them again, and again.

"Why, you!"

"Take your practice elsewhere," Potbury answered. "Never mind the fee. Get out. And don't come back."

Hoag found himself on the street, walking toward the elevated station. He was still much shaken by the doctor's rudeness. He was afraid of rudeness as some persons are of snakes, or great heights, or small rooms. Bad manners, even when not directed at him personally but simply displayed to others in his presence, left him sick and helpless and overcome with shame.

If he himself were the butt of boorishness he had no defense save flight.

He set one foot on the bottom step of the stairs leading up to the elevated station and hesitated. A trip by elevated was a trying thing at best, what with the pushing and the jostling and the grimy dirt and the ever-present chance of uncouth behavior; he knew that he was not up to it at the moment. If he had to listen to the cars screaming around the curve as they turned north toward the Loop, he suspected that he would scream, too.

He turned away suddenly and was forced to check himself abruptly, for he was chest to chest with a man who himself was entering the stairway. He shied away. "Watch your step, buddy," the man said, and brushed on past him.

"Sorry," Hoag muttered, but the man was already on by.

The man's tone had been brisk rather than unkind; the incident should not have troubled Hoag, but it did. The man's dress and appearance, his very odor, upset Hoag. Hoag knew that there was no harm in well-worn dungarees and leather windbreaker, no lack of virtue in a face made a trifle greasy by sweat dried in place in the course of labor. Pinned to the bill of the man's cap was an oval badge, with a serial number and some lettering. Hoag guessed that he was a truck driver, a mechanic, a rigger, any one of the competent, muscular crafts which keep the wheels turning over. Probably a family man as well, a fond father and a good provider, whose greatest lapse from virtue might be an extra glass of beer and a tendency to up it a nickel on two pairs.

It was sheer childishness for Hoag to permit himself to be put off by such appearance and to prefer a white shirt, a decent topcoat, and gloves. Yet if the man had smelled of shaving lotion rather than sweat the encounter would not have been distasteful.

He told himself so and told himself that he was silly and weak.

Still— could such a coarse and brutal face really be the outward mark of warmth and sensitivity? The shapeless blob of nose, those piggish eyes?

Never mind, he would go home in a taxi, not looking at anyone. There was a stand just ahead, in front of the delicatessen.

"Where to?" The door of the cab was open; the hackman's voice was impersonally insistent.

Hoag caught his eye, hesitated and changed his mind. That brutishness again—eyes with no depth to them and a skin marred by blackheads and enlarged pores.

"Unnh . . . excuse me. I forgot something." He turned away quickly and stopped abruptly, as something caught him around the waist. It was a small boy on skates who had bumped into him. Hoag steadied himself and assumed the look of paternal kindliness which he used to deal with children. "Whoa, there, young fellow!" He took the boy by the shoulder and gently dislodged him.

*"Maurice!"* The voice screamed near his ear, shrill and senseless. It came from a large woman, smugly fat, who had projected herself out of the door of the delicatessen. She grabbed the boy's other arm, jerking him away and aiming a swipe at his ear with her free hand as she did so. Hoag started to plead on the boy's behalf when he saw that the woman was glaring at him. The youngster, seeing or sensing his mother's attitude, kicked at Hoag.

The skate clipped him in the shin. It hurt. He hurried away with no other purpose than to get out of sight. He turned down the first side street, his shin causing him to limp a little, and his ears and the back of his neck burning quite as if he had indeed been caught mistreating the brat. The side street was not much better than the street he had left. It was not lined with shops nor dominated by the harsh steel tunnel of the elevated's tracks, but it was solid with apartment houses, four stories high and crowded, little better than tenements.

Poets have sung of the beauty and innocence of childhood. But it could not have been this street, seen through Hoag's eyes, that they had in mind. The small boys seemed rat-faced to him, sharp beyond their years, sharp and shallow and snide. The little girls were no better in his eyes. Those of eight or nine, the shapeless stringy age, seemed to him to have tattletale written in their pinched faces—mean souls, born for troublemaking and cruel gossip. Their slightly older sisters, gutterwise too young, seemed entirely concerned with advertising their arrogant new sex—not for Hoag's benefit, but for their pimply counterparts loafing around the drugstore.

Even the brats in baby carriages—Hoag fancied that he liked babies, enjoyed himself in the role of honorary uncle. Not these. Snotty-nosed and sour-smelling, squalid and squalling—

The little hotel was like a thousand others, definitely third rate without pretension, a single bit of neon reading: "Hotel Manchester, Transient & Permanent," a lobby only a half lot wide, long and narrow and a little dark. You do not see such if you are not looking for them. They are stopped at by drummers careful of their expense accounts and are lived in by bachelors who can't afford better. The single elevator is an iron-grille cage, somewhat disguised with bronze paint. The lobby floor is tile, the cuspidors are brass. In addition to the clerk's desk there are two discouraged potted palms and eight leather armchairs. Unattached old men, who seem never to have had a past, sit in these chairs, live in the rooms above, and every now and then one is found hanging in his room, necktie to light fixture.

HOAG BACKED INTO THE DOOR of the Manchester to avoid being caught in a surge of children charging along the sidewalk. Some sort of game, apparently—he caught the tail end of a shrill chant, "—give him a slap to shut his trap; the last one home's a dirty Jap!"

"Looking for someone, sir? Or did you wish a room?"

He turned quickly around, a little surprised. A room? What he wanted was his own snug apartment but at the moment a room, any room at all, in which he could be alone with a locked door between himself and the world seemed the most desirable thing possible. "Yes, I do want a room."

The clerk turned the register around. "With or without? Five fifty with, three and a half without."

"With."

The clerk watched him sign, but did not reach for the key until Hoag counted out five ones and a half. "Glad to have you with us. Bill! Show Mr. Hoag up to 412."

The lone bellman ushered him into the cage, looked him up and down with one eye, noting the expensive cut of his topcoat and the absence of baggage. Once in 412 he raised the window a trifle, switched on the bathroom light, and stood by the door.

"Looking for someone?" he suggested. "Need any help?"

Hoag tipped him. "Get out," he said hoarsely.

The bellman wiped off the smirk. "Suit yourself," he shrugged.

The room contained one double bed, one chest of drawers with mirror, one straight chair and one armchair. Over the bed was a framed print titled "The Colosseum by Moonlight." But the door was lockable and equipped with a bolt as well and the window faced the alley, away from the street. Hoag sat down in the armchair. It had a broken spring, but he did not mind.

He took off his gloves and stared at his nails. They were quite clean. Could the whole thing have been hallucination? Had he ever gone to consult Dr. Potbury? A man who has had amnesia may have it again, he supposed, and hallucinations as well.

Even so, it could not all be hallucination; he remembered the incident too vividly. Or could it be? He strained to recall exactly what had happened.

TODAY WAS WEDNESDAY, HIS CUSTOMARY day off. Yesterday he had returned home from work as usual. He had been getting ready to dress for dinner—somewhat absentmindedly, he recalled, as he had actually been thinking about where he would dine, whether to try a new Italian place recommended by his friends, the Robertsons, or whether it would be more pleasing to return again for the undoubtedly sound goulash prepared by the chief at the Buda-Pesth.

He had about decided in favor of the safer course when the telephone had rung. He had almost missed it, as the tap was running in the washbasin. He had thought that he heard something and had turned off the tap. Surely enough, the phone rang again.

It was Mrs. Pomeroy Jameson, one of his favorite hostesses—not only a charming woman for herself but possessed of a cook who could make clear soups that were not dishwater. And sauces. She had offered a solution to his problem. "I've been suddenly left in the lurch at the last moment and I've just got to have another man for dinner. Are you free? Could you help me? You could? Dear Mr. Hoag!"

It had been a very pleasant thought and he had not in the least resented being asked to fill in at the last minute. After all, one can't expect to be invited to every small dinner. He had been delighted to oblige Edith Pomeroy. She served an unpretentious but sound dry white wine with fish and she never committed the vulgarism of serving champagne at any time. A good hostess and he was glad she felt free to ask him for help. It was a tribute to him that she felt that he would fit in, unplanned.

He had had such thoughts on his mind, he remembered, as he dressed. Probably, in his preoccupation, what with the interruption of the phone call breaking his routine, he had neglected to scrub his nails.

It must have been that. Certainly there had been no opportunity to dirty his nails so atrociously on the way to the Pomeroys'. After all, one wore gloves.

It had been Mrs. Pomeroy's sister-in-law—a woman he preferred to avoid!—who had called his attention to his nails. She had been insisting with the positiveness called "modern" that every man's occupation was written on his person. "Take my husband—what could he be but a lawyer? Look at him. And you, Dr. Fitts—the bedside manner!"

"Not at dinner, I hope."

"You can't shake it."

"But you haven't proved your point. You *knew* what we are."

Whereupon that impossible woman had looked around the table and nailed him with her eye. "Mr. Hoag can test me. I don't know what he does. No one does."

"Really, Julia." Mrs. Pomeroy had tried hopelessly to intervene, then had turned to the man on her left with a smile. "Julia has been studying psychology this season."

The man on her left, Sudkins, or Snuggins—Stubbins, that was his name. Stubbins had said, "What does Mr. Hoag do?"

"It's a minor mystery. He never talks shop."

"It's not that," Hoag had offered. "I do not consider—"

"Don't tell me!" that woman had commanded. "I'll have it in a moment. Some profession. I can see you with a brief case." He had not intended to tell her. Some subjects were dinner conversation; some were not. But she had gone on.

"You might be in finance. You might be an art dealer or a book fancier. Or you might be a writer. Let me see your hands."

He was mildly put off by the demand, but he had placed his hands on the table without trepidation. That woman had pounced on him. "Got you! You are a chemist."

EVERYONE LOOKED WHERE SHE POINTED. Everyone saw the dark mourning under his nails. Her husband had broken the brief silence by saying, "Nonsense, Julia. There are dozens of things that will stain nails. Hoag may dabble in photography, or do a spot of engraving. Your inference wouldn't stand in court."

"That's a lawyer for you! I know I'm right. Aren't I, Mr. Hoag?"

He himself had been staring unbrokenly at his hands. To be caught at a dinner party with untidy manicure would have been distressing enough—*if* he had been able to understand it.

But he had no slightest idea how his nails had become dirtied. At his work? Obviously—but what did he *do* in the daytime?

He did not know.

"Tell us, Mr. Hoag. I was right, was I not?"

He pulled his eyes away from those horrid fingernails and said faintly, "I must ask to be excused." With that he had fled from the table. He had found his way to the lavatory where, conquering an irrational revulsion, he had cleaned out the gummy reddish-brown filth with the blade of his penknife. The stuff stuck to the blade; he wiped it on cleansing tissue, wadded it up, and stuck it into the pocket of his waistcoat. Then he had scrubbed his nails, over and over again.

He could not recall when he had become convinced that the stuff was blood, was human blood.

He had managed to find his bowler, his coat, gloves, and stick without recourse to the maid. He let himself out and got away from there as fast as he could.

Thinking it over in the quiet of the dingy hotel room he was convinced that his first fear had been an instinctive revulsion at the sight of that dark-red tar under his nails. It was only on second thought that he had realized that he did not remember where he had dirtied his nails because he had no recollection of where he had been that day, nor the day before, nor any of the days before that. He did not know what his profession was.

It was preposterous, but it was terribly frightening.

He skipped dinner entirely rather than leave the dingy quiet of the hotel room; about ten o'clock he drew a tub of water just as hot as he could get it and let himself soak. It relaxed him somewhat and his twisted thoughts quieted down. In any case, he consoled himself, if he could not remember his occupation, then he certainly could not return to it. No chance again of finding that grisly horror under his fingernails.

He dried himself off and crawled under the covers. In spite of the strange bed he managed to get to sleep.

A nightmare jerked him awake, although he did not realize it at first, as the tawdry surroundings seemed to fit the nightmare. When he did recall where he was and why he was there the nightmare seemed preferable, but by that time it was gone, washed out of his mind. His watch told him that it was his usual getting-up time; he rang for the bellman and arranged for a breakfast tray to be fetched from around the corner.

By the time it arrived he was dressed in the only clothes he had with him and was becoming anxious to get home. He drank two cups of indifferent coffee standing up, fiddled with the food, then left the hotel.

After letting himself into his apartment he hung up his coat and hat, took off his gloves, and went as usual straight to his dressing room. He had carefully scrubbed the nails of his left hand and was just commencing on his right when he noticed what he was doing.

The nails of his left hand were white and clean; those of the right were dark and dirty. Carefully holding himself in check he straightened up, stepped over and examined his watch where he had laid it on his dresser, then compared the time with that shown by the electric clock in his bedroom. It was ten minutes past six P.M.—his usual time for returning home in the *evening*.

He might not recall his profession; his profession had certainly not forgotten him.

## II

The firm of Randall & Craig, Confidential Investigation, maintained its night phone in a double apartment. This was convenient, as Randall had married Craig early in their association. The junior partner had just put the supper dishes to soak and was trying to find out whether or not she wanted to keep the book-of-the-month when the telephone rang. She reached out, took the receiver, and said, "Yes?" in noncommittal tones.

To this she added, "Yes."

The senior partner stopped what he was doing—he was engaged in a ticklish piece of scientific research, involving deadly weapons, ballistics and some esoteric aspects of aerodynamics; specifically he was trying to perfect his overhand throw with darts, using a rotogravure likeness of café society's latest glamour girl thumbtacked to the bread board as a target. One dart had nailed her left eye; he was trying to match it in the right.

"Yes," his wife said again.

"Try saying 'No,'" he suggested.

She cupped the mouthpiece. "Shut up and hand me a pencil." She made a long arm across the breakfast-nook table and obtained a stenographer's pad from a hook there. "Yes, go ahead." Accepting the pencil she made several lines of the hooks and scrawls that stenographers use in place of writing. "It seems most unlikely," she said at last. "Mr. Randall is not usually in at this hour. He much prefers to see clients during office hours. Mr. Craig? No, I'm sure Mr. Craig couldn't help you. Positive. So? Hold the line and I'll find out."

Randall made one more try at the lovely lady; the dart stuck in the leg of the radio-record player. "Well?"

"There is a character on the other end of this who wants to see you very badly tonight. Name of Hoag, Jonathan Hoag. Claims that it is a physical impossibility for him to come to see you in the daytime. Didn't want to state his business and got all mixed up when he tried to."

"Gentleman or lug?"

"Gentleman."

"Money?"

"Sounds like it. Didn't seem worried about it. Better take it, Teddy. April 15th is coming up."

"O.K. Pass it over."

She waved him back and spoke again into the phone. "I've managed to locate Mr. Randall. I think he will be able to speak with you in a moment or two. Will you hold the line, please?" Still holding the phone away from her husband she consulted her watch, carefully counted off thirty seconds, then said, "Ready with Mr. Randall. Go ahead, Mr. Hoag," and slipped the instrument to her husband.

"Edward Randall speaking. What is it, Mr. Hoag?

"Oh, really now, Mr. Hoag, I think you had better come in in the morning. We are all human and we like our rest—I do, anyhow.

"I must warn you, Mr. Hoag, my prices go up when the sun goes down.

"Well, now, let me see—I was just leaving for home. Matter of fact, I just talked with my wife so she's expecting me. You know how women are. But if you could stop by my home in twenty minutes, at . . . uh . . . seventeen minutes past eight, we could talk for a few minutes. All right—got a pencil handy? Here is the address—" He cradled the phone.

"What am I this time? Wife, partner, or secretary?"

"What do you think? You talked to him."

"'Wife,' I'd guess. His voice sounded prissy."

"O.K."

"I'll change to a dinner gown. And you had better get your toys off the floor, Brain."

"Oh, I don't know. It gives a nice touch of eccentricity."

"Maybe you'd like some shag tobacco in a carpet slipper. Or some Regie cigarettes." She moved around the room, switching off the overhead lights and arranging table and floor lamps so that the chair a visitor would naturally sit in would be well lighted.

Without answering he gathered up his darts and the bread board, stopping as he did so to moisten his finger and rub the spot where he had marred the radio, then dumped the whole collection into the kitchen and closed the door. In the subdued light, with the kitchen and breakfast nook no longer visible, the room looked serenely opulent.

"HOW DO YOU DO, SIR? Mr. Hoag, my dear. Mr. Hoag . . . Mrs. Randall."

"How do you do, madame."

Randall helped him off with his coat, assuring himself in the process that Mr. Hoag was not armed, or—if he was—he had found somewhere other than shoulder or hip to carry a gun. Randall was not suspicious, but he was pragmatically pessimistic.

"Sit down, Mr. Hoag. Cigarette?"

"No. No, thank you."

Randall said nothing in reply. He sat and stared, not rudely but mildly, nevertheless thoroughly. The suit might be English or it might be Brooks Brothers. It was certainly not Hart, Schaffner & Marx. A tie of that quality had to be termed a cravat, although it was modest as a nun. He upped his fee mentally. The little man was nervous—he wouldn't relax in his chair. Woman's presence, probably. Good—let him come to a slow simmer, then move him off the fire.

"You need not mind the presence of Mrs. Randall," he said presently. "Anything that I may hear, she may hear also."

"Oh . . . oh, yes. Yes, indeed." He bowed from the waist without getting up. "I am very happy to have Mrs. Randall present." But he did not go on to say what his business was.

"Well, Mr. Hoag," Randall added presently, "you wished to consult me about something, did you not?"

"Uh, yes."

"Then perhaps you had better tell me about it."

"Yes, surely. It— That is to say—Mr. Randall, the whole business is preposterous."

"Most businesses are. But go ahead. Woman trouble? Or has someone been sending you threatening letters?"

"Oh, no! Nothing as simple as that. But I'm afraid."

"Of what?"

"I don't know," Hoag answered quickly with a little intake of breath. "I want you to find out."

"Wait a minute, Mr. Hoag," Randall said. "This seems to be getting more confused rather than less. You say you are afraid and you want me to find out what you are afraid of. Now I'm not a psychoanalyst; I'm a detective. What is there about this business that a detective can do?"

Hoag looked unhappy, then blurted out, "I want you to find out what I do in the daytime."

Randall looked him over, then said slowly, "You want *me* to find out what *you* do in the daytime?"

"Yes. Yes, that's it."

"Mm-m-m. Wouldn't it be easier for you to *tell* me what you do?"

"Oh, I couldn't tell you!"

"Why not?"

"I don't know."

Randall was becoming somewhat annoyed. "Mr. Hoag," he said, "I usually charge double for playing guessing games. If you won't tell me what you do in the daytime, it seems to me to indicate a lack of confidence in me which will make it very difficult indeed to assist you. Now come clean with me—what is it you do in the daytime and what has it to do with the case? What *is* the case?"

Mr. Hoag stood up. "I might have known I couldn't explain it," he said unhappily, more to himself than to Randall. "I'm sorry I disturbed you. I—"

"Just a minute, Mr. Hoag." Cynthia Craig Randall spoke for the first time. "I think perhaps you two have misunderstood each other. You mean, do you not, that you really and literally do not *know* what you do in the daytime?"

"Yes," he said gratefully. "Yes, that is exactly it."

"And you want us to find out what you do? Shadow you, find out where you go, and tell you what you have been doing?"

Hoag nodded emphatically. "That is what I have been trying to say."

Randall glanced from Hoag to his wife and back to Hoag. "Let's get this straight," he said slowly. "You really don't know what you do in the daytime and you want me to find out. How long has this been going on?"

"I . . . I don't know."

"Well—what *do* you know?"

HOAG MANAGED TO TELL HIS story, with prompting. His recollection of any sort ran back about five years, to the St. George Rest Home in Dubuque. Incurable amnesia—it no longer worried him and he had regarded himself as completely rehabilitated. They—the hospital authorities—had found a job for him when he was discharged.

"What sort of job?"

He did not know that. Presumably it was the same job he now held, his present occupation. He had been strongly advised, when he left the rest home, never to worry about his work, never to take his work home with him, even in his thoughts. "You see," Hoag explained, "they work on the theory that amnesia is brought on by overwork and worry. I remember Dr. Rennault telling me emphatically that I must never talk shop, never let my mind dwell on the day's work. When I got home at night I was to forget such things and occupy myself with pleasant subjects. So I tried to do that."

"Hm-m-m. You certainly seem to have been successful, almost too successful for belief. See here—did they use hypnosis on you in treating you?"

"Why, I really don't know."

"Must have. How about it, Cyn? Does it fit?"

His wife nodded, "It fits. Posthypnosis. After five years of it he couldn't possibly think about his work after hours no matter how he tried. Seems like a very odd therapy, however."

Randall was satisfied. She handled matters psychological. Whether she got her answers from her rather extensive formal study, or straight out of her subconscious, he neither knew nor gave a hang. They seemed to work. "Something still bothers me," he added. "You go along for five years, apparently never knowing where or how you work. Why this sudden yearning to know?"

He told them the story of the dinner-table discussion, the strange substance under his nails, and the non-co-operative doctor. "I'm frightened," he said miserably. "I thought it was blood. And now I know it's something—worse."

Randall looked at him. "Why?"

Hoag moistened his lips. "Because—" He paused and looked helpless. "You'll help me, won't you?"

Randall straightened up. "This isn't in my line," he said. "You need help all right, but you need help from a psychiatrist. Amnesia isn't in my line. I'm a detective."

"But I *want* a detective. I want you to watch me and find out what I do."

Randall started to refuse; his wife interrupted. "I'm sure we can help you, Mr. Hoag. Perhaps you should see a psychiatrist—"

"Oh, no!"

"—but if you wish to be shadowed, it will be done."

"I don't like it," said Randall. "He doesn't need us."

Hoag laid his gloves on the side table and reached into his breast pocket. "I'll make it worth your while." He started counting out bills. "I brought only five hundred," he said anxiously. "Is it enough?"

"It will do," she told him.

"As a retainer," Randall added. He accepted the money and stuffed it into his side pocket. "By the way," he added, "if you don't know what you do during business hours and you have no more background than a hospital, where do you get the money?" He made his voice casual.

"Oh, I get paid every Sunday. Two hundred dollars, in bills."

When he had gone Randall handed the cash over to his wife. "Pretty little tickets," she said, smoothing them out and folding them neatly. "Teddy, why did you try to queer the pitch?"

"Me? I didn't—I was just running up the price. The old 'get-away-closer.'"

"That's what I thought. But you almost overdid it."

"Not at all. I knew I could depend on you. *You* wouldn't let him out of the house with a nickel left on him."

She smiled happily. "You're a nice man, Teddy. And we have so much in common. We both like money. How much of his story did you believe?"

"Not a damned word of it."

"Neither did I. He's rather a horrid little beast—I wonder what he's up to."

"I don't know, but I mean to find out."

"You aren't going to shadow him yourself, are you?"

"Why not? Why pay ten dollars a day to some ex-flattie to muff it?"

"Teddy, I don't like the set-up. Why should he be willing to pay this much"—she gestured with the bills—"to lead you around by the nose?"

"That is what I'm going to find out."

"You be careful. You remember 'The Red-headed League.'"

"The 'Red-headed—' Oh, Sherlock Holmes again. Be your age, Cyn."

"I am. You be yours. That little man is *evil.*"

She left the room and cached the money. When she returned he was down on his knees by the chair in which Hoag had sat, busy with an insufflator. He looked around as she came in.

"Cyn—"

"Yes, Brain."

"You haven't touched this chair?"

"Of course not. I polished the arms as usual before he showed up."

"That's not what I mean. I meant since he left. Did he ever take off his gloves?"

"What a minute. Yes, I'm sure he did. I looked at his nails when he told his yarn about them."

"So did I, but I wanted to make sure I wasn't nuts. Take a look at that surface."

She examined the polished chair arms, now covered with a thin film of gray dust. The surface was unbroken—no fingerprints. "He must never have touched them— But he *did.* I *saw* him. When he said, 'I'm frightened,' he gripped both arms. I remember noticing how blue his knuckles looked."

"Collodion, maybe?"

"Don't be silly. There isn't even a smear. You shook hands with him. Did he have collodion on his hands?"

"I don't think so. I think I would have noticed it. The Man with No Fingerprints. Let's call him a ghost and forget it."

"Ghosts don't pay out hard cash to be watched."

"No, they don't. Not that I ever heard of." He stood up and marched out into the breakfast nook, grabbed the phone and dialed long distance. "I want the Medical Exchange in Dubuque, uh—" He cupped the phone and called to his wife. "Say, honey, what the hell state *is* Dubuque in?"

Forty-five minutes and several calls later he slammed the instrument back into its cradle. "That tears it," he announced. "There is no St. George Rest Home in Dubuque. There never was and probably never will be. And no Dr. Rennault."

## III

"There he is!" Cynthia Craig Randall nudged her husband.

He continued to hold the *Tribune* in front of his face as if reading it. "I see him," he said quietly. "Control yourself. Yuh'd think you had never tailed a man before. Easy does it."

"Teddy, do be careful."

"I will be." He glanced over the top of the paper and watched Jonathan Hoag come down the steps of the swank Gotham Apartments in which he made his home. When he left the shelter of the canopy he turned to the left. The time was exactly seven minutes before nine in the morning.

Randall stood up, folded his paper with care, and laid it down on the bus-station bench on which he had been waiting. He then turned toward the drugstore behind him, dropped a penny in the slot of a gum-vending machine in the shop's recessed doorway. In the mirror on the face of the machine he watched Hoag's unhurried progress down the far side of the street. With equal lack of rush he started after him, without crossing the street.

Cynthia waited on the bench until Randall had had time enough to get a half block ahead of her, then got up and followed him.

Hoag climbed on a bus at the second corner. Randall took advantage of a traffic-light change which held the bus at the corner, crossed against the lights, and managed to reach the bus just as it was pulling out. Hoag had gone up to the open deck; Randall seated himself down below.

Cynthia was too late to catch the bus, but not too late to note its number. She yoohooed at the first cruising taxi that came by, told the driver the number of the bus, and set out. They covered twelve blocks before the bus came in sight; three blocks later a red light enabled the driver to pull up alongside the bus. She spotted her husband inside; it was all she needed to know. She occupied the time for the rest of the ride in keeping the exact amount shown by the meter plus a quarter tip counted out in her hand.

When she saw them get out of the bus she told the driver to pull up. He did so, a few yards beyond the bus stop. Unfortunately they were headed in her direction; she did not wish to get out at once. She paid the driver the exact amount of the tariff while keeping one eye—the one in the back of her head—on the two men. The driver looked at her curiously.

"Do you chase after women?" she said suddenly.

"No, lady. I gotta family."

"*My* husband does," she said bitterly and untruthfully. "Here." She handed him the quarter.

Hoag and Randall were some yards past by now. She got out, headed for the shop just across the walk, and waited. To her surprise she saw Hoag turn and speak to her husband. She was too far away to hear what was said.

She hesitated to join them. The picture was wrong; it made her apprehensive—yet her husband seemed unconcerned. He listened quietly to what Hoag had to say, then the two of them entered the office building in front of which they had been standing.

She closed in at once. The lobby of the office building was as crowded as one might expect at such an hour in the morning. Six elevators, in bank, were doing rushing business. No. 2 had just slammed its doors, No. 3 had just started to load. They were not in No. 3; she posted herself near the cigar stand and quickly cased the place.

There were not in the lobby. Nor were they, she quickly made sure, in the barber shop which opened off the lobby. They had probably been the last passengers to catch Elevator No. 2 on its last trip. She had been watching the indicator for No. 2 without learning anything useful from it; the car had stopped at nearly every floor.

No. 2 was back down by now; she made herself one of its passengers, not the first nor the last, but one of the crowd. She did not name a floor, but waited until the last of the others had gotten off.

The elevator boy raised his eyebrows at her. "Floor, please!" he commanded.

She displayed a dollar bill. "I want to talk to you."

He closed the gates, accomplishing an intimate privacy. "Make it snappy," he said, glancing at the signals on his board.

"Two men got on together your last trip." She described them, quickly and vividly. "I want to know what floor they got off at."

He shook his head. "I wouldn't know. This is the rush hour."

She added another bill. "Think. They were probably the last two to get aboard. Maybe they had to step out to let others off. The shorter one probably called out the floor."

He shook his head again. "Even if you made it a fin I couldn't tell you. During the rush Lady Godiva *and* her horse could ride this cage and I wouldn't know it. Now—do you want to get out or go down?"

"Down." She handed him one of the bills. "Thanks for trying."

He looked at it, shrugged, and pocketed it.

THERE WAS NOTHING TO DO but to take up her post in the lobby. She did, fuming. Done in, she thought, done in by the oldest trick known for shaking a tail. Call yourself a dick and get taken in by the office-building trick! They were probably out of the building and gone by now, with Teddy wondering where she was and maybe needing her to back up his play.

She ought to take up tatting! Damn!

She bought a bottle of Pepsi-Cola at the cigar stand and drank it slowly, standing up. She was just wondering whether or not she could stand another, in the interest of protective coloration, when Randall appeared.

It took the flood of relief that swept over her to make her realize how much she had been afraid. Nevertheless, she did not break character. She turned her head away, knowing that her husband would see her and recognize the back of her neck quite as well as her face.

He did not come up and speak to her, therefore she took position on him again. Hoag she could not see anywhere; had she missed him herself, or what?

Randall walked down to the corner, glanced speculatively at a stand of taxis, then swung aboard a bus which had just drawn up to its stop. She followed him, allowing several others to mount it before her. The bus pulled away. Hoag had certainly not gotten aboard; she concluded that it was safe to break the routine.

He looked up as she sat down beside him. "Cyn! I thought we had lost you."

"You darn near did," she admitted. "Tell me—what's cookin'?"

"Wait till we get to the office."

She did not wish to wait, but she subsided. The bus they had entered took them directly to their office, a mere half-dozen blocks away. When they were there he unlocked the door of the tiny suite and went at once to the telephone. Their listed office phone was connected through PBX of a secretarial service.

"Any calls?" he asked, then listened for a moment. "O.K. Send up the slips. No hurry."

He put the phone down and turned to his wife. "Well, babe, that's just about the easiest five hundred we ever promoted."

"You found out what he does with himself?"

"Of course."

"What does he do?"

"Guess."

She eyed him. "How would you like a paste in the snoot?"

"Keep your pants on. You wouldn't guess it, though it's simple enough. He works for a commercial jeweler—polishes gems. You know that stuff he found under his fingernails, that got him so upset?"

"Yes?"

"Nothing to it. Jeweler's rouge. With the aid of a diseased imagination he jumps to the conclusion it's dried blood. So we make half a grand."

"Mn-m-m. And that seems to be that. This place he works is somewhere in the Acme Building, I suppose."

"Room 1310. Or rather Suite 1310. Why didn't you tag along?"

SHE HESITATED A LITTLE IN replying. She did not want to admit how clumsy she had been, but the habit of complete honesty with each other was strong upon her. "I let myself get misled when Hoag spoke to you outside the Acme Building. I missed you at the elevator."

"I see, Well, I— Say! What did you say? Did you say Hoag *spoke* to me?"

"Yes, certainly."

"But he didn't speak to me. He never laid eyes on me. What are you talking about?"

"What am *I* talking about? What are *you* talking about! Just before the two of you went into the Acme Building, Hoag stopped, turned around and spoke to you. The two of you stood there chinning, which threw me off stride. Then you went into the lobby together, practically arm in arm."

He sat there, saying nothing, looking at her for a long moment. At last she said, "Don't sit there staring like a goon! That's what happened."

He said, "Cyn, listen to my story. I got off the bus after he did and followed him into the lobby. I used the old heel-and-toe getting into the elevator and swung behind him when he faced the front of the car. When he got out, I hung back, then fiddled around, half in and half out, asking the operator simpleton questions, and giving him long enough to get clear. When I turned the corner he was just disappearing into 1310. He never spoke to me. He never saw my face. I'm sure of that."

She was looking white, but all she said was, "Go on."

"When you go in this place there is a long glass partition on your right, with benches built up against it. You can look through the glass and see the jewelers, or jewelsmiths, or whatever you call 'em at work. Clever—good salesmanship. Hoag ducked right on in and by the time I passed down the aisle he was already on the other side, his coat off and a smock on, and one of those magnifying dinguses screwed into his eye. I went on past him to the desk—he never looked up—and asked for the manager. Presently a little birdlike guy shows up and I ask him if they have a man named Jonathan Hoag in their employ. He says yes and asks if I want to speak to him. I told him no, that I was an investigator for an insurance company. He wants to know if there is anything wrong and I told him that it was simply a routine investigation of what he had said on his application for a life policy, and how long had he worked there? Five years, he told me. He said that Hoag was one of the most reliable and skillful employees. I said fine, and asked if he thought Mr. Hoag could afford to carry as much as ten thousand. He says certainly and that they were always glad to see their employees invest in life insurance. Which was what I had figured when I gave him the stall.

"As I went out I stopped in front of Hoag's bench and looked at him through the glass. Presently he looked up and stared at me, then looked down again. I'm sure I would have spotted it if he had recognized me. A case of complete skeezo, sheezo . . . how do you pronounce it?"

"Schizophrenia. Completely split personalities. But look, Teddy—"

"Yeah?"

"You *did* talk with him. I saw you."

"Now slow down, puss. You may think you did, but you must have been looking at two other guys. How far away were you?"

"Not *that* far. I was standing in front of Beecham's Bootery. Then comes *Chez Louis*, and then the entrance to the Acme Building. You had your back to the newspaper stand at the curb and were practically facing me. Hoag had his back to me, but I couldn't have been mistaken, as I had him in full profile when the two of you turned and went into the building together."

Randall looked exasperated. "I didn't speak with him. And I didn't go in with him; I followed him in."

"Edward Randall, don't give me that! I admit I lost the two of you, but that's no reason to rub it in by trying to make a fool of me."

Randall had been married too long and too comfortably not to respect danger signals. He got up, went to her, and put an arm around her. "Look, kid," he said, seriously and gently, "I'm not pulling your leg. We've got our wires crossed somehow, but I'm giving it to you just as straight as I can, the way I remember it."

She searched his eyes, then kissed him suddenly, and pulled away. "All right. We're both right and it's impossible. Come on."

"'Come on' where?"

"To the scene of the crime. If I don't get this straightened out I'll never sleep again."

THE ACME BUILDING WAS JUST where they had left it. The Bootery was where it belonged, likewise *Chez Louis,* and the newsstand. He stood where she had stood and agreed that she could not have been mistaken in her identification unless blind drunk. But he was equally positive as to what he had done.

"You didn't pick up a snifter or two on the way, did you?" he suggested hopefully.

"Certainly not."

"What do we do now?"

"I don't know. Yes, I do, too! We're all finished with Hoag, aren't we? You've traced him down and that's that."

"Yes . . . why?"

"Take me up to where he works. I want to ask his daytime personality whether or not he spoke to you getting off the bus."

He shrugged. "O.K., kid. It's your party."

They went inside and entered the first free elevator. The starter clicked his castanets, the operator slammed his doors and said, "Floors, please."

Six, three, and nine. Randall waited until those had been served before announcing, "Thirteen."

The operator looked around. "I can give you twelve and fourteen, buddy, and you can split 'em."

"Huh?"

"There ain't no thirteenth floor. If there was, nobody would rent on it."

"You must be mistaken. I was on it this morning."

The operator gave him a look of marked restraint. "See for yourself." He shot the car upward and halted it. "Twelve." He raised the car slowly, the figure 12 slid out of sight and was quickly replaced by another. "Fourteen. Which way will you have it?"

"I'm sorry," Randall admitted. "I've made a silly mistake. I really was in here this morning and I thought I had noted the floor."

Might ha' been eighteen," suggested the operator. "Sometimes an eight will look like a three. Who you lookin' for?"

"Detheridge & Co. They're manufacturing jewelers."

The operator shook his head. "Not in this building. No jewelers, and no Detheridge."

"You're sure?"

Instead of answering, the operator dropped his car back to the tenth floor. "Try 1001. It's the office of the building."

No, they had no Detheridge. No, no jewelers, manufacturing or otherwise. Could it be the Apex Building the gentleman wanted, rather than the Acme? Randall thanked them and left, considerably shaken.

CYNTHIA HAD MAINTAINED COMPLETE SILENCE during the proceedings. Now she said, "Darling—"

"Yeah. What is it?"

"We could go up to the top floor, and work down."

"Why bother? If they were here, the building office would know about it."

"So they would, but they might not be telling. There is something fishy about this whole business. Come to think about it, you could hide a whole floor of an office building by making its door look like a blank wall."

"No, that's silly. I'm just losing my mind, that's all. You better take me to a doctor."

"It's not silly and you're not losing your grip. How do you count height in an elevator? By floors. If you didn't see a floor, you would never realize an extra one was tucked in. We may be on the trail of something big." She did not really believe her own arguments, but she knew that he needed something to do.

He started to agree, then checked himself. "How about the stairways? You're bound to notice a floor from a staircase."

"Maybe there is some hanky-panky with the staircases, too. If so, we'll be looking for it. Come on."

But there was not. There was exactly the same number of steps—eighteen—between floors twelve and fourteen as there were between any other pair of adjacent floors. They worked down from the top floor and examined the lettering on each frosted-glass door. This took them rather long, as Cynthia would not listen to Randall's suggestion that they split up and take half a floor apiece. She wanted him in her sight.

No thirteenth floor and nowhere a door which announced the tenancy of a firm of manufacturing jewelers, neither Detheridge & Co. nor any other name. There was not time to do more than read the firm names on the doors; to have entered each office, on one pretext or another, would have taken much more than a day.

Randall stared thoughtfully at a door labeled: "Pride, Greenway, Hamilton, Steinbolt, Carter & Greenway, Attorneys at Law." "By this time," he mused, "they could have changed the lettering on the door."

"Not on *that* one," she pointed out. "Anyhow, if it was a set-up, they could have cleaned out the whole joint, too. Changed it so you wouldn't recognize it." Nevertheless she stared at the innocent-seeming letters thoughtfully. An office building was a terribly remote and secret place. Soundproof walls, Venetian blinds—and a meaningless firm name. Anything could go on in such a place—anything. Nobody would know. Nobody would care. No one would ever notice. No policeman on his beat, neighbors as remote as the moon, not even scrub service if the tenant did not wish it. As long as the rent was paid on time, the management would leave a tenant alone. Any crime you fancied and park the bodies in the closet.

She shivered. "Come on, Teddy. Let's hurry."

They covered the remaining floors as quickly as possible and came out at last in the lobby. Cynthia felt warmed by the sight of faces and sunlight, even though they had not found the missing firm. Randall stopped on the steps and looked around. "Do you suppose we *could* have been in a different building?" he said doubtfully.

"Not a chance. See that cigar stand? I practically lived there. I know every flyspeck on the counter."

"Then what's the answer?"

"Lunch is the answer. Come on."

"O.K. But I'm going to drink mine."

She managed to persuade him to encompass a plate of corned-beef hash after the third whiskey sour. That and two cups of coffee left him entirely sober, but unhappy. "Cyn—"

"Yes, Teddy."

"What happened to me?"

She answered slowly. "I think you were made the victim of an amazing piece of hypnosis."

"So do I—now. Either that, or I've finally cracked up. So call it hypnosis. I want to know why."

She made doodles with her fork. "I'm not sure that I want to know. You know what I would like to do, Teddy?"

"What?"

"I would like to send Mr. Hoag's five hundred dollars back to him with a message that we can't help him, so we are returning his money."

He stared at her. "Send the money back? Good heavens!"

Her face looked as if she had been caught making an indecent suggestion, but she went on stubbornly. "I know. Just the same, that's what I would like to do. We can make enough on divorce cases and skip-tracing to eat on. We don't have to monkey with a thing like this."

"You talk like five hundred was something you'd use to tip a waiter."

"No, I don't. I just don't think it's enough to risk your neck—or your sanity—for. Look, Teddy, somebody is trying to get us in the nine hole; before we go any further, I want to know *why.*"

"And I want to know why, too. Which is why I'm not willing to drop the matter. Damn it, I don't like having shenanigans put over on me."

"What are you going to tell Mr. Hoag?"

He ran a hand through his hair, which did not matter as it was already mussed. "I don't know. Suppose you talk to him. Give him a stall."

"That's a *fine* idea. That's a *swell* idea. I'll tell him you've broken your leg but you'll be all right tomorrow."

"Don't be like that, Cyn. You know you can handle him."

"All right. But you've got to promise me this, Teddy."

"Promise what?"

"As long as we're on this case we do everything together."

"Don't we always?"

"I mean really together. I don't want you out of my sight *any* of the time."

"But see here, Cyn, that may not be practical."

"Promise."

"O.K., O.K. I promise."

"That's better." She relaxed and looked almost happy. "Hadn't we better get back to the office?"

"The hell with it. Let's go out and take in a triple feature."

O.K., Brain." She gathered up her gloves and purse.

THE MOVIES FAILED TO AMUSE him, although they had selected an all-Western bill, a fare of which he was inordinately fond. But the hero seemed as villainous as the foreman, and the mysterious masked riders, for once, appeared really sinister. And he kept seeing the thirteenth floor of the Acme Building, the long glass partition behind which the crafstmen labored, and the little dried-up manager of Detheridge & Co. Damn it—could a man be hypnotized into believing that he had seen anything as detailed as that?

Cynthia hardly noticed the pictures. She was preoccupied with the people around them. She found herself studying their faces guardedly whenever the lights went up. If they looked like this when they were amusing themselves, what were they like when they were unhappy? With rare exceptions the faces looked, at the best, stolidly uncomplaining. Discontent, the grim marks of physical pain, lonely unhappiness, frustration, and stupid meanness she found in numbers, but rarely a merry face. Even Teddy, whose habitual debonair gaity was one of his chief virtues, was looking dour—with reason, she conceded. She wondered what were the reasons for those other unhappy masks.

She recalled once having seen a painting entitled "Subway." It showed a crowd pouring out the door of an underground train while another crowd attempted to force its way in. Getting on or getting off, they were plainly in a hurry, yet it seemed to give them no pleasure. The picture had no beauty in itself; it was plain that the artist's single purpose had been to make a bitter criticism of a way of living.

She was glad when the show was over and they could escape to the comparative freedom of the street. Randall flagged a taxi and they started home.

"Teddy—"

"Uh?"

"Did you notice the faces of the people in the theater?"

"No, not especially. Why?"

"Not a one of them looked as if they got any fun out of life."

"Maybe they don't."

"But why don't they? Look—we have fun, don't we?"

"You bet."

"We always have fun. Even when we were broke and trying to get the business started we had fun. We went to bed smiling and got up happy. We still do. What's the answer?"

He smiled for the first time since the search for the thirteenth floor and pinched her. "It's fun living with you, kid."

"Thanks. And right back at you. You know, when I was a little girl, I had a funny idea."

"Spill it."

"I was happy myself, but as I grew up I could see that my mother wasn't. And my father wasn't. My teachers weren't—most of the adults around me weren't happy. I got an idea in my head that when you grew up you found out something that kept you from ever being happy again. You know how a kid is treated: 'You're not old enough to understand, dear,' and 'Wait till you grow up, darling, and then you'll understand.' I used to wonder what the secret was they were keeping from me and I'd listen behind doors to try and see if I couldn't find out."

"Born to be a detective!"

"*Slush.* But I could see that, whatever it was, it didn't make the grown-ups happy; it made 'em sad. Then I used to pray never to find out." She gave a little shrug. "I guess I never did."

He chuckled. "Me neither. A professional Peter Pan, that's me. Just as happy as if I had good sense."

She placed a small gloved hand on his arm. "Don't laugh, Teddy. That's what scares me about this Hoag case. I'm afraid that if we go ahead with it we really will find out what it is the grown-ups know. And then we'll never laugh again."

He started to laugh, then looked at her hard. "Why, you're really serious, aren't you?" He chucked her under the chin. "Be your age, kid. What you need is dinner—and a drink."

## IV

After dinner, Cynthia was just composing in her mind what she would say to Mr. Hoag on telephoning him when the house buzzer rang. She went to the entrance of their apartment and took up the house phone. "Yes?"

Almost immediately she turned to her husband and voicelessly shaped the words, "It's Mr. Hoag." He raised his brows, put a cautioning finger to his lips, and with an exaggerated tiptoe started for the bedroom. She nodded.

"Just a moment, please. There—that's better. We seem to have had a bad connection. Now who is it, please?"

"Oh . . . Mr. Hoag. Come up, Mr. Hoag." She punched the button controlling the electrical outer lock.

He came in bobbing nervously. "I trust this is not an intrusion, but I have been so upset that I felt I couldn't wait for a report."

She did not invite him to sit down. "I am sorry," she said sweetly, "to have to disappoint you. Mr. Randall has not yet come home."

"Oh." He seemed pathetically disappointed, so much so that she felt a sudden sympathy. Then she remembered what her husband had been put through that morning and froze up again.

"Do you know," he continued, "when he will be home?"

"That I couldn't say. Wives of detectives, Mr. Hoag, learn not to wait up."

"Yes, I suppose so. Well, I presume I should not impose on you further. But I *am* anxious to speak with him."

"I'll tell him so. Was there anything in particular you had to say to him? Some new data, perhaps?"

"No—" he said slowly. "No, I suppose . . . it all seems so silly!"

"What does, Mr. Hoag?"

He searched her face. "I wonder—Mrs. Randall, do you believe in possession?"

"Possession?"

"Possession of human souls—by devils."

"I can't say that I've thought much about it," she answered cautiously. She wondered if Teddy were listening, if he could reach her quickly if she screamed.

Hoag was fumbling strangely at his shirt front; he got a button opened; she whiffed an acrid, unclean smell, then he was holding out something in his hand, something fastened by a string around his neck under his shirt.

She forced herself to look at it and with intense relief recognized it for what it was—a cluster of fresh cloves of garlic, worn as a necklace. "Why do you wear it?" she asked.

"It does seem silly, doesn't it?" he admitted. "Giving way to superstition like that—but it comforts me. I've had the most frightening feeling of being watched—"

"Naturally. We've been— Mr. Randall has been watching you, by your instructions."

"Not that. A man in a mirror—" He hesitated.

"A man in a mirror?"

"Your reflection in a mirror watches you, but you expect it; it doesn't worry you. This is something new, as if someone were trying to get at me, waiting for a chance. Do you think I'm crazy?" he concluded suddenly.

Her attention was only half on his words, for she had noticed something when he held out the garlic which had held her attention. His fingertips were ridged and grooved in whorls and loops and arches like anyone else's—and they were certainly not coated with collodion tonight. She decided to get a set of prints for Teddy. "No, I don't think you're crazy," she said soothingly, "but I think you've let yourself worry too much. You should relax. Wouldn't you like a drink?"

"I would be grateful for a glass of water."

WATER OR LIQUOR, IT WAS the glass she was interested in. She excused herself and went out to the kitchen where she selected a tall glass with smooth, undecorated sides. She polished it carefully, added ice and water with equal care not to wet the sides. She carried it in, holding it near the bottom.

Intentionally or unintentionally, he had outmaneuvered her. He was standing in front of the mirror near the door, where he had evidently been straightening his tie and tidying himself after returning the garlic to its hide-away. When he turned around at her approach she saw that he had put his gloves back on.

She invited him to sit down, thinking that if he did so he would remove his gloves. But he said, "I've imposed on you too long as it is." He drank half the glass of water, thanked her, and left silently.

Randall came in. "He's gone?"

She turned quickly. "Yes, he's gone. Teddy, I wish you would do your own dirty work. He makes me nervous. I wanted to scream for you to come in."

"Steady, old girl."

"That's all very well, but I wish we had never laid eyes on him." She went to a window and opened it wide.

"Too late for Herpicide. We're in it now." His eye rested on the glass. "Say—did you get his prints?"

"No such luck. I think he read my mind."

"Too bad."

"Teddy, what do you intend to do about him now?"

"I've got an idea, but let me work it out first. What was this song and dance he was giving you about devils and a man in a mirror watching him?"

"That wasn't what he said."

"Maybe I was the man in the mirror. I watched him in one this morning."

"Huh-uh. He was just using a metaphor. He's got the jumps." She turned suddenly, thinking that she had seen something move over her shoulder. But there was nothing there but the furniture and the wall.

Probably just a reflection in the glass, she decided, and said nothing about it. "I've got 'em, too," she added. "As for devils, he's all the devil I want. You know what I'd like?"

"What?"

"A big, stiff drink and early to bed."

"Good idea." He wandered out into the kitchen and started mixing the prescription. "Want a sandwich, too?"

RANDALL FOUND HIMSELF STANDING IN his pajamas in the living room of their apartment, facing the mirror that hung near the outer door. His reflection—no, not his reflection, for the image was properly dressed in conservative clothes appropriate to a solid man of business—the image spoke to him.

"Edward Randall."

"Huh?"

"Edward Randall, you are summoned. Here—take my hand. Pull up a chair and you will find you can climb through easily."

It seemed a perfectly natural thing to do, in fact the only reasonable thing to do. He placed a straight chair under the mirror, took the hand offered him, and scrambled through. There was a washstand under the mirror on the far side, which gave him a leg down. He and his companion were standing in a small, white-tiled washroom such as one finds in office suites.

"Hurry," said his companion. "The others are all assembled."

"Who are you?"

"The name is Phipps," the other said, with a slight bow. "This way, please."

He opened the door of the washroom and gave Randall a gentle shove. He found himself in a room that was obviously a board room—with a meeting in session, for the long table was surrounded by about a dozen men. They all had their eyes on him.

"Up you go, Mr. Randall."

Another shove, not quite so gentle and he was sitting in the middle of the polished table. Its hard top felt cold through the thin cotton of his pajama trousers.

He drew the jacket around him tightly and shivered. "Cut it out," he said. "Let me down from here. I'm not dressed." He tried to get up, but he seemed unable to accomplish that simple movement.

Somebody behind him chuckled. A voice said, "He's not very fat." Someone answered, "That doesn't matter, for this job."

He was beginning to recognize the situation—the last time it had been Michigan Boulevard without his trousers. More than once it had found him back in school again, not only undressed, but lessons unprepared, and late in the bargain. Well, he knew how to beat it—close your eyes and reach down for the covers, then wake up safe in bed.

He closed his eyes.

"No use to hide, Mr. Randall. We can see you and you are simply wasting time."

He opened his eyes. "What's the idea?" he said savagely. "Where am I? Why'dju bring me here? What's going on?"

FACING HIM AT THE HEAD of the table was a large man. Standing, he must have measured six feet two at least, and he was broad-shouldered and heavy-boned in proportion. Fat was laid over his huge frame liberally. But his hands were slender and well shaped and beautifully manicured; his features were not large and seemed smaller, being framed in fat jowls and extra chins. His eyes were small and merry; his mouth smiled a good deal and he had a trick of compressing his lips and shoving them out.

"One thing at a time, Mr. Randall," he answered jovially. "As to where you are, this is the thirteenth floor of the Acme Building—you remember." He chuckled, as if they shared a private joke. "As to what goes on, this is a meeting of the board of Detheridge & Co. I" —he managed to bow sitting down, over the broad expanse of his belly—"am R. Jefferson Stoles, chairman of the board, at your service, sir."

"But—"

"Please, Mr. Randall—introductions first. On my right. Mr. Townsend."

"How do you do, Mr. Randall."

"How do you do," Randall answered mechanically. "Look here, this has gone far—"

"Then Mr. Gravesby, Mr. Wells, Mr. Yoakum, Mr. Printemps, Mr. Jones. Mr. Phipps you have met. He is our secretary. Beyond him is seated Mr. Reifsnider and Mr. Snyder—no relation. And finally Mr. Parker and Mr. Crewes. Mr. Potiphar, I am sorry to say, could not attend, but we have a quorum."

Randall tried to get up again, but the table top seemed unbelievably slippery. "I don't care," he said bitterly, "whether you have a quorum or a gang fight. Let me out of here."

"*Tut,* Mr. Randall. *Tut.* Don't you want your questions answered?"

"Not that bad. Damn it, let me—"

"But they really must be answered. This is a business session and you are the business at hand."

"Me?"

"Yes, you. You are, shall we say, a minor item on the agenda, but one which must be cleared up. We do not like your activity, Mr. Randall. You really must cease it."

Before Randall could answer, Stoles shoved a palm in his direction. "Don't be hasty, Mr. Randall. Let me explain. Not all your activities. We do not care how many blondes you plant in hotel rooms to act as complacent correspondents in divorce cases, nor how many wires you tap, nor letters you open. There is only one activity of yours we are concerned with. I refer to Mr. Hoag." He spat out the last word.

Randall could feel a stir of uneasiness run through the room.

"What about Mr. Hoag?" he demanded. There was the stir again. Stoles' face no longer even pretended to smile.

"Let us refer to him hereafter," he said, "as 'your client.' It comes to this, Mr. Randall. We have other plans for Mr. . . . for your client. You must leave him alone. You must forget him, you must never see him again."

Randall stared back, uncowed. "I've never welshed on a client yet. I'll see you in hell first."

"That," admitted Stoles, shoving out his lips, "is a distinct possibility, I grant you, but one that neither you nor I would care to contemplate, save as a bombastic metaphor. Let us be reasonable. You *are* a reasonable man, I know, and my confreres and I, we are reasonable creatures, too. Instead of trying to coerce or cajole you I want to tell you a story, so that you may understand why."

"I don't care to listen to any stories. I'm leaving."

"Are you really? I think not. And you will listen!"

He pointed a finger at Randall; Randall attempted to reply, found that he could not. "This," he thought, "is the damnedest no-pants dream I ever had. Shouldn't eat before going to bed—knew better."

"IN THE BEGINNING," STOLES STATED, "there was the Bird." He suddenly covered his face with his hands; all the others gathered around the table did likewise.

The Bird—Randall felt a sudden vision of what those two simple words meant when mouthed by this repulsive fat man; no soft and downy chick, but a bird of prey, strong-winged and rapacious—unwinking eyes, whey-colored and staring—purple wattles—but most especially he saw its feet, bird feet, covered with yellow scales, fleshless and taloned and foul from use. Obscene and terrible—

Stoles uncovered his face. "The Bird was alone. Its great wings beat the empty depths of space where there was none to see. But deep within It was the Power and the Power was Life. It looked to the north when there was no north; It looked to the south when there was no south; east and west It looked, and up and down. Then out of the nothingness and out of Its Will It wove the nest.

"The nest was broad and deep and strong. In the nest It laid one hundred eggs. It stayed on the nest and brooded the eggs, thinking Its thoughts, for ten thousand thousand years. When the time was ripe It left the nest and hung it about with lights that the fledglings might see. It watched and waited.

"From each of the hundred eggs a hundred Sons of the Bird were hatched—ten thousand strong. Yet so wide and deep was the nest there was room and to spare for each of them—a kingdom apiece and each was a king—king over the things that creep and crawl and swim and fly and go on all fours, things that had been born from the crevices of the nest, out of the warmth and the waiting.

"Wise and cruel was the Bird, and wise and cruel were the Sons of the Bird. For twice ten thousand thousand years they fought and ruled and the Bird was pleased. Then there were some who decided that they were as wise and strong as the Bird Itself. Out of the stuff of the nest they created creatures like unto themselves and breathed in their nostrils, that they might have sons to serve them and fight for them. But the sons of the Sons were not wise and strong and cruel, but weak and soft and stupid. The Bird was not pleased.

"Down It cast Its Own Sons and let them be chained by the softly stupid— Stop fidgeting, Mr. Randall! I know this is difficult for your little mind, but for once you really must think about something longer than your nose and wider than your mouth, believe me!

"The stupid and the weak could not hold the Sons of the Bird; therefore, the Bird placed among them, here and there, others more powerful, more cruel, and more shrewd, who by craft and cruelty and deceit could circumvent the attempts of the Sons to break free. Then the Bird sat back, well content, and waited for the game to play itself out.

"The game is being played. Therefore, we cannot permit you to interfere with your client, nor to assist him in any way. You see that, don't you?"

"I don't see," shouted Randall, suddenly able to speak, "a damn thing! To hell with the bunch of you! This joke has gone far enough."

"Silly and weak and stupid," Stoles sighed. "Show him, Mr. Phipps."

Phipps got up, placed a briefcase on the table, opened it, and drew something from it, which he shoved under Randall's nose—a mirror.

"Please look this way, Mr. Randall," he said politely.

Randall looked at himself in the mirror.

"What are you thinking of, Mr. Randall?"

The image faded, he found himself staring into his own bedroom, as if from a slight height. The room was dark, but he could plainly see his wife's head on her pillow. His own pillow was vacant.

She stirred, and half turned over, sighing softly. Her lips were parted a trifle and smiling faintly, as if what she dreamed were pleasant.

"See, Mr. Randall?" said Stoles. "You wouldn't want anything to happen to her, now, would you?"

"Why, you dirty, low-down—"

"Softly, Mr. Randall, softly. And that will be enough from you. Remember your own interests—and *hers.*" Stoles turned away from him. "Remove him, Mr. Phipps."

"Come, Mr. Randall." He felt again that undignified shove from behind, then he was flying through the air with the scene tumbling to pieces around him.

He was wide-awake in his own bed, flat on his back and covered with cold sweat.

Cynthia sat up. "What's the matter, Teddy?" she said sleepily. "I heard you cry out."

"Nothing. Bad dream, I guess. Sorry I woke you."

"'S all right. Stomach upset?"

"A little, maybe."

"Take some bicarb."

"I will." He got up, went to the kitchen and fixed himself a small dose. His mouth was a little sour, he realized, now that he was awake; the soda helped matters.

Cynthia was already asleep when he got back; he slid into bed quietly. She snuggled up to him without waking, her body warming his. Quickly he was asleep, too.

"'NEVER MIND TROUBLE! FIDDLE-DE-DEE!'" He broke off singing suddenly, turned the shower down sufficiently to permit ordinary conversation, and said, "Good morning, beautiful!"

Cynthia was standing in the door of the bathroom, rubbing one eye and looking blearily at him with the other. "People who sing before breakfast—good morning."

"Why shouldn't I sing? It's a beautiful day and I've had a beautiful sleep. I've got a new shower song. Listen."

"Don't bother."

"This is a song," he continued, unperturbed, "dedicated to a Young Man Who Has Announced His Intention of Going Out into the Garden to Eat Worms."

"Teddy, you're nasty."

"No, I'm not. Listen." He turned the shower on more fully. "You have to have the water running to get the full effect," he explained. "First verse:

> *"I don't think I'll go out in the garden;*
> *I'll make the worms come in to me!*
> *If I have to be miser'ble,*
> *I might as well be so comfort'bly!"*

He paused for effect. "Chorus," he announced.

> *"Never mind trouble! Fiddle-de-dee!*
> *Eat your worms with Vitamin B!*
> *Follow this rule and you will be*
> *Still eating worms at a hundred 'n' three!"*

He paused again. "Second verse," he stated. "Only I haven't thought up a second verse yet. Shall I repeat the first verse?"

"No, thanks. Just duck out of that shower and give me a chance at it."

"You don't like it," he accused her.

"I didn't say I didn't."

"Art is rarely appreciated," he mourned. But he got out.

He had the coffee and the orange juice waiting by the time she appeared in the kitchen. He handed her a glass of the fruit juice. "Teddy, you're a darling. What do you want in exchange for all this coddling?"

"You. But not now. I'm not only sweet, I'm brainy."

"So?"

"Uh-huh. Look— I've figured out what to do with friend Hoag."

"Hoag? Oh, dear!"

"Look out—you'll spill it!" He took the glass from her and set it down. "Don't be silly, babe. What's gotten into you?"

"I don't know, Teddy. I just feel as if we were tackling the kingpin of Cicero with a pea shooter."

"I shouldn't have talked business before breakfast. Have your coffee—you'll feel better."

"All right. No toast for me, Teddy. What's your brilliant idea?"

"It's this," he explained, while crunching toast. "Yesterday we tried to keep out of his sight in order not to shake him back into his nighttime personality. Right?"

"Uh-huh."

"Well, today we don't have to. We can stick to him like a leech, both of us, practically arm in arm. If it interferes with the daytime half of his personality, it doesn't matter, because we can lead him to the Acme Building. Once there, habit will take him where he usually goes. Am I right?"

"I don't know, Teddy. Maybe. Amnesia personalities are funny things. He might just drift into a confused state."

"You don't think it will work?"

"Maybe it will, maybe it won't. But as long as you plan for us to stay close together, I'm willing to try it—if you won't give up the whole matter."

He ignored the condition she placed on it. "Fine. I'll give the old buzzard a ring and tell him to wait for us at his apartment." He reached across the breakfast table and grabbed the phone, dialed it and talked briefly with Hoag. "He's certainly a June bug, that one," he said as he put the phone down. "At first he couldn't place me at all. Then all of a sudden he seemed to click and everything was all right. Ready to go, Cyn?"

"Half a sec."

"O. K." He got up and went into the living room, whistling softly.

THE WHISTLING BROKE OFF; HE came quickly back into the kitchen. "Cyn—"

"What's the matter, Teddy?"

"Come into the living room—please!"

She hurried to do so, suddenly apprehensive at the sight of his face. He pointed to a straight chair which had been pulled over to a point directly under the mirror near the outer door. "Cyn—how did that get where it is?"

"That chair? Why, I pulled a chair over there to straighten the mirror just before I went to bed. I must have left it there."

"Mm-m-m— I suppose you must have. Funny I didn't notice it when I turned out the light."

"Why does it worry you? Think somebody might have gotten into the apartment last night?"

"Yeah. Yeah, sure—that's what I was thinking." But his brow was still wrinkled.

Cynthia looked at him, then went back into the bedroom. There she gathered up her purse, went through it rapidly, then opened a small, concealed drawer in her dressing table. "If anyone *did* manage to get in, they didn't get much. Got your wallet? Everything in it? How about your watch?"

He made a quick check and reported, "They're all right. You must have left the chair there and I just didn't notice it. Ready to go?"

"Be right with you."

He said no more about it. Privately he was thinking what an involved mess a few subconscious memories and a club sandwich just before turning in could make. He must have noticed the chair just before turning out the light—hence its appearance in the nightmare. He dismissed the matter.

## V

Hoag was waiting for them. "Come in," he said. "Come in. Welcome, madame, to my little hide-away. Will you sit down? Have we time for a cup of tea? I'm afraid," he added apologetically, "that I haven't coffee in the house."

"I guess we have," agreed Randall. "Yesterday you left the house at eight fifty-three and it's only eight thirty-five now. I think we ought to leave at the same time."

"Good." Hoag bustled away, to return at once with a tea service on a tray, which he placed on a table at Cynthia's knees. "Will you pour, Mrs. Randall? It's Chinese tea," he added. "My own blend."

"I'd be pleased." He did not look at all sinister this morning, she was forced to admit. He was just a fussy little bachelor with worry lines around his eyes—and a most exquisite apartment. His pictures were good, just how good she had not the training to tell, but they looked like originals. There were not too many of them, either, she noticed with approval. Arty little bachelors were usually worse than old maids for crowding a room full of too much.

Not Mr. Hoag's flat. It had an airy perfection to it as pleasing, in its way, as a Brahms waltz. She wanted to ask him where he had gotten his drapes.

He accepted a cup of tea from her, cradled it in his hand and sniffed the aroma before sipping from it. He then turned to Randall. "I am afraid, sir, that we are off on a wild-goose chase this morning."

"Perhaps. Why do you think so?"

"Well, you see, I really am at a loss as to what to do next. Your telephone call—I was preparing my morning tea—I don't keep a servant—as usual, when you called, I suppose I am more or less in a brown fog in the early mornings—absent-minded, you know, just doing the things one does when one gets up, making one's toilet and all that with one's thoughts elsewhere. When you telephoned I was quite bemused and it took me a moment to recall who you were and what business we had with each other. In a way the conversation cleared my head, made me consciously aware of myself, that it is to say, but now—" He shrugged helplessly. "Now I haven't the slightest idea of what I am to do next."

Randall nodded. "I had that possibility in mind when I phoned you. I don't claim to be a psychologist but it seemed possible that your transition from your nighttime self to your daytime self took place as you left your apartment and that any interruption in your routine might throw you off."

"Then why—"

"It won't matter. You see, we shadowed you yesterday; we know where you go."

"You *do*? Tell me, sir! Tell me."

"Not so fast. We lost track of you at the last minute. What I had in mind is this: We could guide you along the same track, right up to the point where we lost track of you yesterday. At that point I am hoping that your habitual routine will carry you on through—and we will be right at your heels."

"You say 'we.' Does Mrs. Randall assist you in this?"

RANDALL HESITATED, REALIZING THAT HE had been caught out in a slight prevarication. Cynthia moved in and took over the ball.

"Not ordinarily, Mr. Hoag, but this seemed like an exceptional case. We felt that you would not enjoy having your private affairs looked into by the ordinary run of hired operator, so Mr. Randall has undertaken to attend to your case personally, with my help when necessary."

"Oh, I say, that's awfully kind of you!"

"Not at all."

"But it is—it is. But, uh, in that case—I wonder if I have paid you enough. Do not the services of the head of the firm come a little higher?"

Hoag was looking at Cynthia; Randall signaled to her an emphatic "Yes"—which she chose to ignore. "What you have already paid, Mr. Hoag, seems sufficient. If additional involvements come up later, we can discuss them then."

"I suppose so." He paused and pulled at his lower lip. "I do appreciate your thoughtfulness in keeping my affairs to yourselves. I shouldn't like—" He turned suddenly to Randall. "Tell me—what would your attitude be if it should develop that my daytime life is—scandalous?" The word seemed to hurt him.

"I can keep scandal to myself."

"Suppose it were worse than that. Suppose it were—criminal. Beastly."

Randall stopped to choose his words. "I am licensed by the State of Illinois. Under that license I am obliged to regard myself as a special police officer in a limited sense. I certainly could not cover up any major felony. But it's not my business to turn clients in for any ordinary peccadillo. I can assure you that it would have to be something pretty serious for me to be willing to turn over a client to the police."

"But you can't assure me that you would *not* do so?"

"No," he said flatly.

Hoag sighed. "I suppose I'll just have to trust to your good judgment." He held up his right hand and looked at his nails. "No. No, I can't risk it. Mr. Randall, suppose you did find something you did not approve of—couldn't you just call me up and tell me that you were dropping the case?"

"No."

He covered his eyes and did not answer at once. When he did his voice was barely audible. "You've found nothing—yet?" Randall shook his head. "Then perhaps it is wiser to drop the matter now. Some things are better never known."

His evident distress and helplessness, combined with the favorable impression his apartment had made on her, aroused in Cynthia a sympathy which she would have thought impossible the evening before. She leaned toward him. "Why should you be so distressed, Mr. Hoag? You have no reason to think that you have done anything to be afraid of—have you?"

"No. No, nothing really. Nothing but an overpowering apprehension."

"But why?"

"Mrs. Randall, have you ever heard a noise behind you and been afraid to look around? Have you ever awakened in the night and kept your eyes tightly shut rather than find out what it was that had startled you? Some evils reach their full effect only when acknowledged and faced.

"I don't dare face this one," he added. "I thought that I did, but I was mistaken."

"Come now," she said kindly, "facts are never as bad as our fears—"

"Why do you say so? Why shouldn't they be much worse?"

"Why, because they just aren't." She stopped, suddenly conscious that her Pollyanna saying had no truth in it, that it was the sort of thing adults use to pacify children. She thought of her own mother, who had gone to the hospital, fearing an appendectomy—which her friends and loving family privately diagnosed as hypochondria—there to *die,* of cancer.

No, the facts were frequently worse than our most nervous fears.

Still, she could not agree with him. "Suppose we look at it in the worst possible light," she suggested. "Suppose you *have* been doing something criminal, while in your memory lapses. No court in the State would hold you legally responsible for your actions."

He looked at her wildly. "No. No, perhaps they would not. But you know what they would do? You do, don't you? Have you any idea what they do with the criminally insane?"

"I certainly do," she answered positively. "They receive the same treatment as any other psycho patient. They aren't discriminated against. I know; I've done field work at the State Hospital."

"Suppose you have—you looked at it from the *outside.* Have you any idea what it feels like from the inside? Have you ever been placed in a wet pack? Have you ever had a guard put you to bed? Or force you to eat? Do you know what it's like to have a key turned in a lock every time you make a move? Never to have *any* privacy no matter how much you need it?"

He got up and began to pace. "But that isn't the worst of it. It's the other patients. Do you imagine that a man, simply because his own mind is playing him tricks, doesn't recognize insanity in others? Some of them drool and some of them have habits too beastly to tell of. And they talk, they talk, they *talk.* Can you imagine lying in a bed, with the sheet bound down, and a *thing* in the next bed that keeps repeating, 'The little bird flew up and then flew away; the little bird flew up and then flew away; the little bird flew up, and then flew away—'"

"Mr. Hoag!" Randall stood up and took him by the arm. "Mr. Hoag—control yourself! That's no way to behave."

Hoag stopped, looking bewildered. He looked from one face to the other and an expression of shame came over him. "I . . . I'm sorry, Mrs. Randall," he said. "I quite forgot myself. I'm not myself today. All this worry—"

"It's all right, Mr. Hoag," she said stiffly. But her earlier revulsion had returned.

"It's not entirely all right," Randall amended. "I think the time has come to get a number of things cleared up. There has been entirely too much going on that I don't understand and I think it is up to you, Mr. Hoag, to give me a few plain answers."

The little man seemed honestly at a loss. "I surely will, Mr. Randall, if there is anything I can answer. Do you feel that I have not been frank with you?"

"I certainly do. First—when were you in a hospital for the criminally insane?"

"Why, I never was. At least, I don't *think* I ever was. I don't remember being in one."

"Then why all this hysterical balderdash you have been spouting the past five minutes? Were you just making it up?"

"Oh, no! That . . . that was . . . that referred to St. George Rest Home. It had nothing to do with a . . . with such a hospital."

"St. George Rest Home, eh? We'll come back to that. Mr. Hoag, tell me what happened yesterday."

"Yesterday? During the day? But Mr. Randall, you *know* I can't tell you what happened during the day."

"*I* think you can. There has been some damnable skulduggery going on and you're the center of it. When you stopped me in front of the Acme Building—*what did you say to me?*"

"The Acme Building? I know nothing of the Acme Building. Was I there?"

"You're damned right you were there and you pulled some sort of a shenanigan on me, drugged me or doped me, or something. *Why?*"

Hoag looked from Randall's implacable face to that of his wife. But her face was impassive; she was having none of it. He turned hopelessly back to Randall. "Mr. Randall, believe me—I don't know what you are talking about. I may have been at the Acme Building. If I were and if I did anything to you, I know nothing of it."

His words were so grave, so solemnly sincere in their sound that Randall was unsettled in his own conviction. And yet—damn it, *somebody* had led him up an alley. He shifted his approach. "Mr. Hoag, if you have been as sincere with me as you claim to be, you won't mind what I'm going to do next." He drew from the inner pocket of his coat a silver cigarette case, opened it, and polished the mirrorlike inner surface of the cover with his handkerchief. "Now, Mr. Hoag, if you please."

"What do you want?"

"I want your fingerprints."

Hoag looked startled, swallowed a couple of times, and said in a low voice, "Why should you want my fingerprints?"

"Why not? If you haven't done anything, it can't do any harm, can it?"

"You're going to turn me over to the police!"

"I haven't any reason to. I haven't anything on you. Let's have your prints."

"No!"

Randall got up, stepped toward Hoag and stood over him. "How would you like both your arms broken?" he said savagely.

Hoag looked at him and cringed, but he did not offer his hands for prints. He huddled himself together, face averted and his hands drawn in tight to his chest.

Randall felt a touch on his arm. "That's enough, Teddy. Let's get out of here."

Hoag looked up. "Yes," he said huskily. "Get out. Don't come back."

"Come on, Teddy."

"I will in a moment. I'm not quite through. Mr. Hoag!"

Hoag met his eye as if it were a major effort.

"Mr. Hoag, you've mentioned St. George Rest Home twice as being your old *alma mater.* I just wanted you to know that *I* know that there is no such place!"

Again Hoag looked genuinely startled. "But there is," he insisted. "Wasn't I there for— At least they told me that was its name," he added doubtfully.

"Humph!" Randall turned toward the door. "Come on, Cynthia."

ONCE THEY WERE ALONE IN the elevator she turned to him. "How did you happen to play it that way, Teddy?"

"Because," he said bitterly, "while I don't mind opposition, it makes me sore when my own client crosses me up. He dished us a bunch of lies, and obstructed us, and pulled some kind of sleight of hand on me in that Acme Building deal. I don't like for a client to pull stunts like that; I don't need their money that bad."

"Well," she sighed, "I, for one, will be very happy to give it back to him. I'm glad it's over."

"What do you mean, 'give it back to him'? I'm not going to give it back to him; I'm going to earn it."

The car arrived at the ground floor by now, but she did not touch the gate. "Teddy! What do you mean?"

"He hired me to find out what he does. Well, damn it, I'm going to *find* out—with or without his co-operation."

He waited for her to answer, but she did not. "Well," he said defensively, "you don't have to have anything to do with it."

"If you are going on with it, I certainly am. Remember what you promised me?"

"What did I promise?" he asked, with a manner of complete innocence.

"*You* know."

"But look here, Cyn—all I'm going to do is to hang around until he comes out, and then tail him. It may take all day. He may decide not to come out."

"All right. I'll wait with you."

"Somebody has to look out for the office."

"You look out for the office," she suggested. "I'll shadow Hoag."

"Now that's ridiculous. You—" The car started to move upward. "Woops! Somebody wants to use it." He jabbed the button marked "Stop," then pushed the one which returned the car to the ground floor. This time they did not wait inside; he immediately opened the gate and the door.

Adjacent to the entrance of the apartment house was a little lounge or waiting room. He guided her into it. "Now let's get this settled," he commenced.

"It *is* settled."

"O.K., you win. Let's get ourselves staked out."

"How about right here? We can sit down and he can't possibly get out without us seeing him."

"O.K."

The elevator had gone up immediately after they had quitted it; soon they heard the typical clanging grunt which announced its return to the ground floor. "On your toes, kid."

She nodded and drew back into the shadows of the lounge. He placed himself so that he could see the elevator door by reflection in an ornamental mirror hanging in the lounge. "Is it Hoag?" she whispered.

"No," he answered in a low voice, "it's a bigger man. It looks like—" He shut up suddenly and grabbed her wrist.

Past the open door of the lounge she saw the hurrying form of Jonathan Hoag go by. The figure did not turn its eyes in their direction but went directly through the outer door. When it swung closed Randall relaxed the hold on her wrist. "I darn near muffed that one," he admitted.

"What happened?"

"Don't know. Bum glass in the mirror. Distortion. Tallyho, kid."

They reached the door as their quarry got to the sidewalk and, as on the day before, turned to the left.

Randall paused uncertainly. "I think we'll take a chance on him seeing us. I don't want to lose him."

"Couldn't we follow him just as effectively in a cab? If he gets on a bus where he did before, we'll be better off than we would be trying to get on it with him." She did not admit, even to herself, that she was trying to keep them away from Hoag.

"No, he might not take a bus. Come on."

THEY HAD NO DIFFICULTY IN following him; he was heading down the street at a brisk, but not a difficult, pace. When he came to the bus stop where he had gotten on the day before, he purchased a paper and sat down on the bench. Randall and Cynthia passed behind him and took shelter in a shop entrance.

When the bus came he went up to the second deck as before; they got on and remained on the lower level. "Looks like he was going right where he went yesterday," Randall commented. "We'll get him today, kid."

She did not answer.

When the bus approached the stop near the Acme Building they were ready and waiting—but Hoag failed to come down the steps. The bus started up again with a jerk; they sat back down. "What do you suppose he is up to?" Randall fretted. "Do you suppose he saw us?"

"Maybe he gave us the slip," Cynthia suggested hopefully.

"How? By jumping off the top of the bus? Hm-m-m!"

"Not quite, but you're close. If another bus pulled alongside us at a stop light, he could have done it by stepping across, over the railing. I saw a man do that once. If you do it toward the rear, you stand a good chance of getting away with it entirely."

He considered the matter. "I'm pretty sure no bus has pulled up by us. Still, he could do it to the top of a truck, too, though Lord knows how he would get off again." He fidgeted. "Tell you what—I'm gong back to the stairs and sneak a look."

"And meet him coming down? Be your age, Brain."

He subsided; the bus went on a few blocks. "Coming to our own corner," he remarked.

She nodded, naturally having noticed as soon as he did that they were approaching the corner nearest the building in which their own office was located. She took out her compact and powdered her nose, a routine she had followed eight times since getting on the bus. The little mirror made a handy periscope whereby to watch the passengers getting off the rear of the bus. "There he is, Teddy!"

Randall was up out of his seat at once and hurrying down the aisle, waving at the conductor. The conductor looked annoyed but signaled the driver not to start. "Why don't you watch the streets?" he asked.

"Sorry, buddy. I'm a stranger here myself. Come on, Cyn."

Their man was just turning into the door of the building housing their own office. Randall stopped. "Something screwy about this, kid."

"What do we do?"

"Follow him," he decided.

They hurried on; he was not in the lobby. The Midway-Copton is not a large building, nor swank—else they could not have rented there. It has but two elevators. One was down and empty; the other, by the indicator, had just started up.

Randall stepped up to the open car, but did not enter. "Jimmie," he said, "how many passengers in that other car?"

"Two," the elevator pilot answered.

"Sure?"

"Yeah. I was breezin' with Bert when he closed the door. Mr. Harrison and another bird. Why?"

Randall passed him a quarter. "Never mind," he said, his eyes on the slowly turning arrow of the indicator. "What floor does Mr. Harrison go to?"

"Seven." The arrow had just stopped at seven.

"Swell." The arrow started up again, moved slowly past eight and nine, stopped at ten. Randall hustled Cynthia into the car. "Our floor, Jimmie," he snapped, "and step on it!"

An "up" signal flashed from the fourth floor; Jimmie reached for his controls; Randall grabbed his arm. "Skip it this time, Jim."

The operator shrugged and complied with the request.

The corridor facing the elevators on the tenth floor was empty. Randall saw this at once and turned to Cynthia. "Give a quick gander down the other wing, Cyn," he said, and headed to the right, in the direction of their office.

CYNTHIA DID SO, WITH NO particular apprehension. She was sure in her own mind that, having come this far, Hoag was certainly heading for their office. But she was in the habit of taking direction from Teddy when they were actually doing something; if he wanted the other corridor looked at, she would obey, of course.

The floor plan was in the shape of a capital H, with the elevators located centrally on the cross bar. She turned to the left to reach the other wing, then glanced to the left—no one in that alley. She turned around and faced the other way—no one down there. It occurred to her that just possibly Hoag could have stepped out on the fire escape; as a matter of fact the fire escape was in the direction she had first looked, toward the rear of the building—but habit played a trick on her; she was used to the other wing in which their office was located, in which, naturally, everything was swapped right for left from the way in which it was laid out in this wing.

She had taken three or four steps toward the end of the corridor facing the street when she realized her mistake—the open window certainly had no fire escape beyond it. With a little exclamation of impatience at her own stupidity she turned back.

Hoag was standing just behind her.

She gave a most unprofessional squeak.

Hoag smiled with his lips. "Ah, Mrs. Randall!"

She said nothing—she could think of nothing to say. There was a .32 pistol in her handbag; she felt a wild desire to snatch it out and fire. On two occasions, at a time when she was working as a decoy for the narcotics squad, she had been commended officially for her calm courage in a dangerous pinch—she felt no such calm now.

He took a step toward her. "You wanted to see me, did you not?"

She gave way a step. "No," she said breathlessly. "No!"

"Ah, but you did. You expected to find me at your office, but I chose to meet you—here!"

The corridor was deserted; she could not even hear a sound of typing or conversation from any of the offices around them. The glazed doors stared sightlessly; the only sounds, other than their own sparse words, were the street noises ten stories below, muted, remote and unhelpful.

He came closer. "You wanted to take my fingerprints, didn't you? You wanted to check them—find out things about me. You and your meddlesome husband."

"Get away from me!"

He continued to smile. "Come, now. You wanted my fingerprints—you shall have them." He raised his arms toward her and spread his fingers, reaching. She backed away from the clutching hands. He no longer seemed small; he seemed taller, and broader—bigger than Teddy. His eyes stared down at her.

Her heel struck something behind her; she knew that she had backed to the very end of the passage—dead end.

His hands came closer. "Teddy!" she screamed. "Oh, Teddy!"

TEDDY WAS BENDING OVER HER, slapping her face. "Stop that," she said indignantly. "It hurts!"

He gave a sigh of relief. "Gee, honey," he said tenderly. "You sure gave me a turn. You've been out for minutes."

"Unnnh!"

"Do you know where I found you? There!" He pointed to the spot just under the open window. "If you hadn't fallen just right, you would have been hamburger by now. What happened? Lean out and get dizzy?"

"Didn't you catch him?"

He looked at her admiringly. "Always the professional! No, but I damn near did. I saw him, from down the corridor. I watched a moment to see what he was up to. If you hadn't screamed, I would have had him."

"If I *hadn't* screamed?"

"Sure. He was in front of our office door, apparently trying to pick the lock, when—"

"*Who* was?"

He looked at her in surprise. "Why, Hoag, of course—*Baby!* Snap out of it! You aren't going to faint again, are you?"

She took a deep breath. "I'm all right," she said grimly, "—now. Just as long as you're here. Take me to the office."

"Shall I carry you?"

"No, just give me your hand." He helped her up and brushed at her dress. "Never mind that now." But she did stop to moisten, ineffectively, a long run in what had been until that moment brand-new stockings.

He let them into the office and sat her carefully in an armchair, then fetched a wet towel with which he bathed her face. "Feel better?"

"I'm all right—physically. But I want to get something straight. You say you saw Hoag trying to get into this office?"

"Yeah. Damned good thing we've special locks."

"This was going on when I screamed?"

"Yeah, sure."

She drummed on the arms of the chair.

"'S matter, Cyn?"

"Nothing. Nothing at all—only this: The reason I screamed was because Hoag was trying to choke me!"

It took him some time even to say, "Hunh?"

She replied. "Yes, I know, darling. That's how it is and it's nuts. Somehow or other, he's done it to us again. But I swear to you that he was about to choke me. Or I thought he was." She rehearsed her experience, in detail. "What does it add up to?"

"I wish I knew," he told her, rubbing his face. "I wish I did. If it hadn't been for that business in the Acme Building, I would say that you were sick and had fainted and when you came to you were still kinda lightheaded. But now I don't know which one of us is batty. I surely thought I saw him."

"Maybe we're both crazy. It might be a good idea if we both went to see a good psychiatrist."

"Both of us? Can two people go crazy the same way? Wouldn't it be one or the other of us?"

"Not necessarily. It's rare, but it does happen. *Folie à deux.*"

"Folee adooh?"

"Contagious insanity. Their weak points match up and they make each other crazier." She thought of the cases she had studied and recalled that usually one was dominant and the other subordinate, but she decided not to bring it up, as she had her own opinion as to who was dominant in their family, an opinion kept private for reasons of policy.

"MAYBE," RANDALL SAID THOUGHTFULLY, "WHAT we need is a nice, long rest. Down on the Gulf, maybe, where we could lie around in the sunshine."

"*That,*" she said, "is a good idea in any case. Why in the world anyone chooses to live in a dismal, dirty, ugly spot like Chicago is beyond me."

"How much money have we?"

"About eight hundred dollars, after the bills and taxes are paid. And there's the five hundred from Hoag, if you want to count that."

"I think we've earned it," he said grimly. "Say! *Do* we have that money? Maybe that was a hoax, too."

"You mean maybe there never was any Mr. Hoag and pretty soon the nurse will be in to bring us our nice supper."

"Mm-m-m—that's the general idea. Have you got it?"

"I *think* I have. Wait a minute." She opened her purse, in turn opened a zippered compartment, and felt in it. "Yes, it's here. Pretty green bills. Let's take that vacation, Teddy. I don't know why we stay in Chicago, anyway."

"Because the business is here," he said practically. "Coffee and cakes. Which reminds me, slaphappy or not, I'd better see what calls have come in." He reached across her desk for the phone; his eye fell on a sheet of paper in her typewriter. He was silent for a moment, then said in a strained voice, "Come here, Cyn. Take a took at this."

She got up at once, came around and looked over his shoulder. What she saw was one of their letterheads, rolled into the typewriter; on it was a single line of typing:

She said nothing at all and tried to control the quivering at the pit of her stomach.

Randall asked, "Cyn, did you write that?"

"No."

"Positive?"

"Yes." She reached out to take it out of the machine; he checked her.

"Don't touch it. Fingerprints."

"All right. But I have a notion," she said, "that you won't find any fingerprints on *that.*"

"Maybe not."

Nevertheless, he took his outfit out of the lower drawer of his desk and dusted the paper and the machine—with negative results on each. There were not even prints of Cynthia to confuse the matter; she had a business-college neatness in her office habits and made a practice of brushing and wiping her typewriter at the end of each day.

While watching him work she remarked, "Looks as if you saw him getting *out* rather than *in.*"

"Huh? How?"

"Picked the lock, I suppose."

"Not that lock. You forget, baby, that that lock is one of Mr. Yale's proudest achievements. You could break it, maybe, but you couldn't pick it."

She made no answer—she could think of none. He stared moodily at the typewriter as if it should tell him what had happened, then straightened up, gathered up his gear, and returned it to its proper drawer. "The whole thing stinks," he said, and commenced to pace the room.

Cynthia took a rag from her own desk and wiped the print powder from the machine, then sat down and watched him. She held her tongue while he fretted with the matter. Her expression was troubled but she was not worried for herself—nor was it entirely maternal. Rather was she worried for them.

"Cyn," he said suddenly, "this has got to stop!"

"All right," she agreed. "Let's stop it."

"How?"

"Let's take that vacation."

He shook his head. "I can't run away from it. I've got to know."

She sighed. "I'd rather not know. What's wrong with running away from something too big for us to fight?"

He stopped and looked at her. "What's come over you, Cyn? You never went chicken before."

"No," she answered slowly, "I never did. But I never had reason to. Look at me, Teddy—you know I'm not a *female* female. I don't expect you to pick fights in restaurants when some lug tries to pick me up. I don't scream at the sight of blood and I don't expect you to clean up your language to fit my ladylike ears. As for the job, did I ever let you down on a case? Through timidity, I mean. Did I ever?"

"Hell, no. I didn't say you did."

"But this is a different case. I had a gun in my bag a few minutes ago, but I couldn't use it. Don't ask me why. I *couldn't*."

He swore, with emphasis and considerable detail. "I wish I had seen him then. I would have used mine!"

"Would you have, Teddy?" Seeing his expression, she jumped up and kissed him suddenly, on the end of his nose. "I don't mean you would have been afraid. You know I didn't mean that. You're brave and you're strong and *I* think you're brainy. But look, dear—yesterday he led you around by the nose and made you believe you were seeing things that weren't there. Why didn't you use your gun then?"

"I didn't see any occasion to use it."

"That's exactly what I mean. You saw what was intended for you to see. How can you fight when you can't believe your own eyes?"

"But, damn it, he can't do this to us—"

"*Can't* he? Here's what he *can* do." She ticked them off on her fingers. "He can be two places at once. He can make you see one thing and me another, at the same time—outside the Acme Building, remember? He can make you think you went to an office suite that doesn't exist on a floor that doesn't exist. He can pass through a locked door to use a typewriter on the other side. And he doesn't leave fingerprints. What does that add up to?"

He made an impatient gesture. "To nonsense. or to magic. And I don't believe in magic."

"Neither do I."

"Then," he said, "we've both gone bats." He laughed, but it was not merry.

"Maybe. If it's magic, we had best see a priest—"

"I told you I don't believe in magic."

"Skip it. If it's the other, it won't do us any good to try to tail Mr. Hoag. A man with the D.T.'s can't catch the snakes he thinks he sees and take them to a zoo. He needs a doctor—and maybe we do, too."

Randall was suddenly alert. "Say!"

"Say what?"

"You've just reminded me of an angle that I had forgotten—Hoag's doctor. We never checked on *him.*"

"Yes, you did, too. Don't you remember? There wasn't any such doctor."

"I don't mean Dr. Rennault; I mean Dr. Potbury—the one he went to see about the stuff under his fingernails."

"Do you think he really did that? I thought it was just part of the string of lies he told us."

"So do I. But we ought to check up on it."

"I'll bet you there isn't any such doctor."

"You're probably right, but we ought to *know.* Gimme the phone book." She handed it to him; he thumbed through it, searching for the P's. "Potbury—Potbury. There's half a column of them. But no M.D.'s though," he announced presently. "Let's have the yellow section; sometimes doctors don't list their home addresses." She got it for him and he opened it. "'Physical Culture Studios'—'Physicians & Surgeons.' What a slog of 'em! More doctors than saloons—half the town must be sick most of the time. Here we are: 'Potbury, P.Y., M.D.'"

"That *could* be the one," she admitted.

"What are we waiting for? Let's go find out."

"Teddy!"

"Why not?" he said defensively. "Potbury isn't Hoag—"

"I wonder."

"Huh? What do you mean? Do you mean that Potbury might be mixed up in this huggermugger, too?"

"I don't know. I'd just like to forget all about our Mr. Hoag."

"But there's no harm in this, bright eyes. I'll just pop into the car, slide down there, ask the worthy doctor a few pertinent questions, and be back for you in time for lunch."

"The car is laid up for a valve grind; you know that."

"O.K., I'll take the el. Quicker, anyway."

"If you insist on going, we'll both take the el. We stick together, Teddy."

He pulled at his lip. "Maybe you're right. We don't know where Hoag is. If you prefer it—"

"I certainly do. I got separated from you for just three minutes a little while ago and look what happened."

"Yeah, I guess so. I sure wouldn't want anything to happen to you, kid."

She brushed it away. "It's not me; it's *us.* If anything happens to us, I want it to be the same thing."

"All right," he said seriously. "From now on, we stick together. I'll handcuff us together, if you'd rather."

"You won't need to. I'm going to hang on."

# VI

Potbury's office was to the south, beyond the university. The tracks of the elevated ran between familiar miles of apartment houses. There were sights which one ordinarily sees without any impression registering on the brain; today she looked at them and saw them, through her own brown mood.

Four- and five-story walk-up apartment houses, with their backs to the tracks, at least ten families to a building, more usually twenty or more, and the buildings crushed together almost wall to wall. Wood-construction back porches which proclaimed the fire-trap nature of the warrens despite the outer brick shells, family wash hung out to dry on those porches, garbage cans, and trash bins. Mile after mile of undignified and unbeautiful squalor, seen from the rear.

And over everything a film of black grime, old and inescapable, like the dirt on the window sill beside her.

She thought of that vacation, clean air and clear sunshine. Why stay in Chicago; what did the town have to justify its existence? One decent boulevard, one decent suburb to the north, priced for the rich, two universities and a lake. As for the rest, endless miles of depressing, dirty streets. The town was one big stockyard.

The apartments gave to elevated-train yards; the train turned left and headed east. After a few minutes they got off at Stoney Island station; she was glad to be off it and free of that too-frank back view of everyday life, even though she exchanged it for the noise and seedy commercialism of Sixty-third Street.

Potbury's office faced on the street, with an excellent view of the elevated and the trains. It was the sort of location in which a G.P. could be sure of a busy practice and equally sure of never being bothered by riches nor fame. The stuffy little waiting room was crowded but the turnover was fast; they did not have long to wait.

Potbury looked them over as they came in. "Which one of you is the patient?" he asked. His manner was slightly testy.

They had planned to lead up to the subject of Hoag by using Cynthia's fainting spell as an excuse for consultation; Potbury's next remark queered the scheme, from Cynthia's viewpoint. "Whichever one it is, the other can wait outside. I don't like holding conventions."

"My wife—" Randall began. She clutched his arm.

"My wife and I," he went on smoothly, "want to ask you a couple of questions, doctor."

"Well? Speak up."

"You have a patient—a Mr. Hoag."

Potbury got up hastily, went to the reception-room door, and assured himself that it was closed tightly. He then stood and faced them, his back to the only exit. "What about—Hoag?" he said forebodingly.

Randall produced his credentials. "You can see for yourself that I am a proper inquiry agent," he said. "My wife is licensed, too."

"What do you have to do with—the man you mentioned?"

"We are conducting an investigation for him. Being a professional man yourself, you can appreciate that I prefer to be frank—"

"You *work* for him?"

"Yes and no. Specifically, we are trying to find out certain things about him, but he is aware that we are doing so; we aren't going around behind his back. If you like, you can phone him and find out for yourself." Randall made the suggestion because it seemed necessary to make it; he hoped that Potbury would disregard it.

Potbury did so, but not in any reassuring manner. "Talk with *him?* Not if I can help it! What did you want to know about him?"

"A few days ago," Randall said carefully, "Hoag brought to you a substance to be analyzed. I want to find out what that substance was."

"Hrrumph! You reminded me a moment ago that we were both professional men; I am surprised that you should make such a request."

"I appreciate your viewpoint, doctor, and I know that a doctor's knowledge of his patients is privileged. But in this case there is—"

"You wouldn't want to know!"

Randall considered this. "I've seen a good deal of the seamy side of life, doctor, and I don't think there is anything that can shock me any more. Do you hesitate to tell me in Mrs. Randall's presence?"

Potbury looked him over quizzically, then surveyed Mrs. Randall. "You look like decent enough people," he conceded. "I suppose you do think you are beyond being shocked. But let me give you some advice. Apparently you are connected in some way with this man. *Stay away from him!* Don't have anything to do with him. And don't ask me what he had under his fingernails."

CYNTHIA SUPPRESSED A START. SHE had been keeping out of the conversation but following it carefully. As she remembered it, Teddy had made no mention of fingernails.

"*Why,* doctor?" Randall continued insistently.

Potbury was beginning to be annoyed. "You are a rather stupid young man, sir. Let me tell you this: If you know no more of this person than you appear to know, then you have no conception of the depths of beastliness possible in this world. In that you are lucky. It is much, much better never to know."

Randall hesitated, aware that the debate was going against him. Then he said, "Supposing you are right, doctor—how is it, if he is so vicious, you have not turned Hoag over to the police?"

"How do you know I haven't? But I will answer that one, sir. No, I have not turned him over to the police, for the simple reason that it would do no good. The authorities have not had the wit nor the imagination to conceive of the possibility of the peculiar evil involved. No law can touch him—not in this day and age."

"What do you mean, 'not in this day and age'?"

"Nothing. Disregard it. The subject is closed. You said something about your wife when you came in; did she wish to consult me about something?"

"It was nothing," Cynthia said hastily. "Nothing of importance."

"Just a pretext, eh?" He smiled almost jovially. "What was it?"

"Nothing. I fainted earlier today. But I'm all right now."

"Hm-m-m. You're not expecting, are you? Your eyes don't look like it. You look sound enough. A little anemic, perhaps. Fresh air and sunshine wouldn't do you any harm." He moved away from them and opened a white cabinet on the far wall; he busied himself with bottles for a moment. Presently he returned with a medicine glass filled with amber-brown liquid. "Here—drink this."

"What is it?"

"A tonic. It contains just enough of What Made the Preacher Dance to make you enjoy it."

Still she hesitated, looking to her husband. Potbury noticed it and remarked, "Don't like to drink alone, eh? Well, one wouldn't do us any harm, either." He returned to the cabinet and came back with two more medicine glasses, one of which he handed to Randall. "Here's to forgetting all unpleasant matters," he said. "Drink up!" He lifted his own glass to his lips and tossed it off.

Randall drank, Cynthia followed suit. It was not bad stuff, she thought. Something a little bitter in it, but the whiskey—it *was* whiskey, she concluded—covered up the taste. A bottle of that tonic might not do you any real good but it would make you feel better.

Potbury ushered them out. "If you have another fainting spell, Mrs. Randall, come back to see me and we'll give you a thorough going over. In the meantime, don't worry about matters you can't help."

THEY TOOK THE LAST CAR of the train in returning and were able to pick a seat far away enough from other passengers for them to talk freely. "Whatja make of it?" he asked, as soon as they were seated.

She wrinkled her brow. "I don't know, quite. He certainly doesn't like Mr. Hoag, but he never said why."

"Um-m-m."

"What do you make of it, Teddy?"

"First, Potbury knows Hoag. Second, Potbury is very anxious that we know nothing about Hoag. Third, Potbury hates Hoag—and is afraid of him!"

"Huh? How do you figure that out?"

He smiled maddeningly. "Use the little gray cells, my sweet. I think I'm on to friend Potbury—and if he thinks he can scare me out of looking into what Hoag does with his spare time he's got another think coming!"

Wisely, she decided not to argue it with him just then—they had been married quite some time.

At her request they went home instead of back to the office. "I don't feel up to it, Teddy. If *he* wants to play with my typewriter, let him!"

"Still feeling rocky from the Brodie you pulled?" he asked anxiously.

"Kinda."

She napped most of the afternoon. The tonic, she reflected, that Dr. Potbury had given her did not seem to have done her any good—left her dizzy, if anything, and with a furry taste in her mouth.

Randall let her sleep. He fiddled around the apartment for a few minutes, set up his dart board and tried to develop an underhand shot, then desisted when it occurred to him that it might wake Cynthia. He looked in on her and found that she was resting peacefully. He decided that she might like a can of beer when she woke up—it was a good excuse to go out; he wanted a beer himself. Bit of a headache, nothing much, but he hadn't felt really chipper since he left the doctor's office. A couple of beers would fix it up.

THERE WAS A TAPROOM JUST this side of the nearest delicatessen. Randall decided to stop for one on draught before returning. Presently he found himself explaining to the proprietor just *why* the reform amalgamation would never turn out the city machine.

He recalled, as he left the place, his original intention. When he got back to their apartment, laden with beer and assorted cold cuts, Cynthia was up and making domestic noises in the kitchen. "Hi, babe!"

"Teddy!"

He kissed her before he put down the packages. "Were you scared when you woke up and found me gone?"

"Not really. But I would rather you had left a note. What have you got there?"

"Suds and cold cuts. Like?"

"Swell. I didn't want to go out for dinner and I was trying to see what I could stir up. But I hadn't any meat in the house." She took them from him.

"Anybody call?"

"Huh-uh. I called the exchange when I woke up. Nothing of interest. But the mirror came."

"Mirror?"

"Don't play innocent. It was a nice surprise, Teddy. Come see how it dresses up the bedroom."

"Let's get this straight," he said. "I don't know anything about a mirror."

She paused, puzzled. "I thought you bought it for me for a surprise. It came prepaid."

"Whom was it addressed to; you or me?"

"I didn't pay much attention; I was half asleep. I just signed something and they unpacked it and hung it for me."

It was a very handsome piece of glass, beveled plate, without a frame, and quite large. Randall conceded that it did things for her dressing table. "If you want a glass like that, honey, I'll get one for you. But this isn't ours. I suppose I'd better call up somebody and tell 'em to take it back. Where's the tag?"

"They took it off, I think. Anyhow it's after six o'clock."

He grinned at her indulgently. "You like it, don't you? Well, it looks like it's yours for tonight—and tomorrow I'll see about getting you another."

It *was* a beautiful mirror; the silvering was well-nigh perfect and the glass was air-clear. She felt as if she could push her hand through it.

He went to sleep, when they turned in, a little more readily than she did—the nap, no doubt. She rested on one elbow and looked at him for a long time after his breathing had become regular. Sweet Teddy! He was a good boy—good to her certainly. Tomorrow she would tell him not to bother about the other mirror—she didn't need it. All she really wanted was to be with him, for nothing ever to separate them. *Things* did not matter; just being together was the only thing that really mattered.

She glanced at the mirror. It certainly was handsome. So beautifully clear—like an open window. She felt as if she could climb through it, like Alice Through the Looking Glass.

HE AWOKE WHEN HIS NAME was called. "Up out of there, Randall! You're late!"

It wasn't Cynthia; that was sure. He rubbed the sleep out of his eyes and managed to focus them. "Wha's up?"

"You," said Phipps, leaning out through the beveled glass. "Get a move on! Don't keep us waiting."

Instinctively he looked toward the other pillow. Cynthia was gone.

Gone! Then he was up out of bed at once, wide awake, and trying frantically to search everywhere at once. Not in the bathroom. "Cyn!" Not in the living room, not in the kitchen-breakfast room. "Cyn! Cynthia! Where are you?" He pawed frantically in each of the closets. "Cyn!"

He returned to the bedroom and stood there, not knowing where to look next—a tragic, barefooted figure in rumpled pajamas and tousled hair.

Phipps put one hand on the lower edge of the mirror and vaulted easily into the room. "This room should have had a place to install a full-length mirror," he remarked curtly as he settled his coat and straightened his tie. "Every room should have a full-length mirror. Presently we will require it—I shall see to it."

Randall focused his eyes on him as if seeing him for the first time. "Where is she?" he demanded. "What have you done with her?" He stepped toward Phipps menacingly.

"None of your business," retorted Phipps. He inclined his head toward the mirror. "Climb through it."

"*Where is she?*" he screamed and attempted to grab Phipps by the throat.

Randall was never clear as to just what happened next. Phipps raised one hand—and he found himself tumbled against the side of the bed. He tried to struggle up again—fruitlessly. His efforts had a helpless, nightmare quality. "Mr. Crewes!" Phipps called out. "Mr. Reifsnider—I need your help."

Two more faces, vaguely familiar, appeared in the mirror. "On this side, Mr. Crewes, if you please," Phipps directed. Mr. Crewes climbed through. "Fine! We'll put him through feet first, I think."

RANDALL HAD NOTHING TO SAY about it; he tried to resist, but his muscles were water. Vague twitchings were all he could accomplish. He tried to bite a wrist that came his way and was rewarded with a faceful of hard knuckles—a stinging rap rather than a blow.

"I'll add to that later," Phipps promised him.

They poked him through and dumped him on a table—*the* table. It was the same room he had been in once before, the board room of Detheridge & Co. There were the same pleasant icy faces around the table, the same jovial, pig-eyed fat man at the head. There was one minor difference; on the long wall was a large mirror which did not reflect the room, but showed their bedroom, his and Cynthia's, as if seen in a mirror, with everything in it swapped left for right.

But he was not interested in such minor phenomena. He tried to sit up, found that he could not, and was forced to make do with simply raising his head. "Where did you put her?" he demanded of the huge chairman.

Stoles smiled at him sympathetically. "Ah, Mr. Randall! So you've come to see us again. You do get around, don't you? Entirely too much, in fact."

"Silly and weak and stupid," Stoles mused. "To think that my own brothers and I could create nothing better than you. Well, you shall pay for it. The Bird is cruel!"

At his last emphatic remark he covered his face briefly. The others present followed his motions; someone reached out and clapped a hand roughly over Randall's eyes, then took it away.

Stoles was speaking again; Randall tried to interrupt him—once again Stoles thrust a finger at him and said sternly, "Enough!" Randall found himself unable to talk; his throat choked up and nauseated him whenever he tried it.

"One would suppose," Stoles continued urbanely, "that even one of your poor sort would understand the warning you were given, and heed it." Stoles stopped for a moment and shoved out his lips, pressing them tightly together. "I sometimes think that my own weakness lies in not realizing the full depths of the weakness and stupidity of men. As a reasonable creature myself I seem to have an unfortunate tendency to expect others unlike myself to be reasonable."

He stopped and turned his attention away from Randall and toward one of his colleagues. "Don't raise up any false hopes, Mr. Parker," he said, smiling sweetly. "I do not underrate *you.* And if you should wish to wrestle for my right to sit where I sit, I shall oblige you—later. I wonder," he added thoughtfully, "what your blood tastes like."

Mr. Parker was equally courteous. "Much the same as yours, Mr.

Chairman, I imagine. It's a pleasant idea, but I am satisfied with the present arrangements."

"I'm sorry to hear it. I like you, Mr, Parker; I had hoped you were ambitious."

"I am patient—like our Ancestor."

"So? Well—back to business. Mr. Randall, I tried before to impress you with the necessity of having nothing to do with—your client. You know the client I mean. What do *you* think would impress you with the fact that the Sons of the Bird will tolerate no interference with their plans? Speak up—tell me."

Randall had heard little of what had taken place and had understood none of it. His whole being was engrossed with a single terrible thought. When he found he could speak again, it spilled forth. "Where is she?" he demanded in a hoarse whisper. "What have you done with her?"

Stoles gestured impatiently. "Sometimes," he said pettishly, "it is almost impossible to get into communication with one of them—almost no mind at all. Mr. Phipps!"

"Yes, sir."

"Will you please see that the other one is fetched in?"

"Certainly, Mr. Stoles." Phipps gathered up an assistant with his eye; the two left the room to return shortly with a burden which they dumped casually on the table beside Randall. It was Cynthia.

The surge of relief was almost more than he could stand. It roared through him, choking him, deafening him, blinding him with tears, and leaving him nothing with which to weigh the present danger of their situation. But gradually the throbbing of his being slowed down enough for him to see that something was wrong; she was quiet. Even if she had been asleep when they carried her in, the rough handling she had received should have been enough to waken her.

His alarm was almost as devastating as his joy had been. "What have you done to her?" he begged. "Is she—"

"No," Stoles answered in disgusted tones, "she is not dead. Control yourself, Mr. Randall." With a wave of his hand he directed his colleagues, "Wake her up."

One of them poked her in the ribs with a forefinger. "Don't bother to wrap it," he remarked; "I'll eat it on the way."

Stoles smiled. "Very witty, Mr. Printemps—but I said to wake her up. Don't keep me waiting."

"Certainly, Mr. Chairman." He slapped her stingingly across the face; Randall felt it on his own face—in his helpless condition it almost unhinged his reason. "In the Name of the Bird—wake up!"

He saw her chest heave under the silk of her nightgown; her eyes fluttered and she said one word, "Teddy?"

"Cyn! Here, darling, here!"

She turned her head toward him and exclaimed. "Teddy!" then added, "I had such a bad dream—*Oh!*" She had caught sight of them staring greedily at her. She looked slowly around her, wide-eyed and serious, then turned back to Randall. "Teddy—is this still a dream?"

"I'm afraid not, darling. Chin up."

She looked once more at the company, then back to him. "I'm not afraid," she said firmly. "Make your play, Teddy. I won't faint on you again." Thereafter she kept her eyes on his.

Randall stole a glance at the fat chairman; he was watching them, apparently amused by the sight, and showed no present disposition to interfere. "Cyn," Randall said in an urgent whisper, "they've done something to me so I can't move. I'm paralyzed. So don't count on me too much. If you get a chance to make a break for it, take it!"

"I can't move, either," she whispered back. "We'll have to wait." She saw his agonized expression and added, "'Chin up,' you said. But I wish I could touch you." The fingers of her right hand trembled slightly, found some traction on the polished table top, and began a slow and painful progress across the inches that separated them.

Randall found that he could move his own fingers a little; he started his left hand on its way to join hers, a half inch at a time, his arm a dead weight against the movement. At last they touched and her hand crept into his, pressing it faintly. She smiled.

Stoles rapped loudly on the table top. "This little scene is very touching," he said in sympathetic tones, "but there is business to attend to. We must decide the best thing to do with them."

"Hadn't we better eliminate them entirely?" suggested the one who had jabbed Cynthia in the ribs.

"That would be a pleasure," Stoles conceded, "but we must remember that these two are merely an incident in our plans for . . . for Mr. Randall's client. He is the one who must be destroyed!"

"I don't see—"

"Of course you don't see and that is why I am chairman. Our immediate purpose must be to immobilize these two in a fashion which will cause no suspicion on *his* part. The question is merely one of method and of the selection of the subject."

Mr. Parker spoke up. "It would be very amusing," he suggested, "to return them as they are. They would starve slowly, unable to answer the door, unable to answer the telephone, helpless."

"So it would be," Stoles said approvingly. "That is about the caliber of suggestion I expected from you. Suppose he attempted to see them, found them so. Do you think he would not understand their story? No, it must be something which seals their tongues. I intend to send them back with one of them—dead-alive!"

THE WHOLE BUSINESS WAS SO preposterous, so utterly unlikely, that Randall had been telling himself that it could not be real. He was in the clutches of a nightmare; if he could just manage to wake up, everything would be all right. The business of not being able to move—he had experienced that before in dreams. Presently you woke up from it and found that the covers had become wound around you, or you had been sleeping with both hands under your head. He tried biting his tongue so that the pain might wake him, but it did no good.

Stoles' last words brought his attention sharply to what was going on around him, not because he understood them—they meant very little to him, though they were fraught with horror—but because of the stir of approval and anticipation which went around the table.

The pressure of Cynthia's hand in his increased faintly. "What are they going to do, Teddy?" she whispered.

"I don't know, darling."

"The man, of course," Parker commented.

Stoles looked at him. Randall had a feeling that Stoles had intended the—whatever it was that was coming!—for the man, for him, until Parker had suggested it. But Stoles answered, "I'm always grateful for your advice. It makes it so easy to know just what one *should* do." Turning to the others he said, "Prepare the woman."

*"Now,"* thought Randall. "It's got to be *now.*" Summoning all the will he possessed he attempted to raise himself up from the table—rise up and fight!

He might just as well not have made the effort.

He let his head sink back, exhausted by the effort. "It's no use, kid," he said miserably.

Cynthia looked at him. If she felt any fear, it was masked by the concern she showed for him. "Chin up, Brain," she answered with the mere suggestion of increased pressure of her hand in his.

Printemps stood up and leaned over her. "This is properly Potiphar's job," he objected.

"He left a prepared bottle," Stoles answered. "You have it, Mr. Phipps?"

Phipps answered by reaching into his brief case and producing it. At a nod from Stoles he passed it over; Printemps accepted it. "The wax?" he added.

"Here you are," Phipps acknowledged, dipping into his brief case again.

"Thank you, sir. Now, if someone will get *that* out of the way"—indicating Randall as he spoke—"we seem to be ready." Half a dozen savagely willing hands manhandled Randall to the extreme far edge of the table; Printemps bent over Cynthia, bottle in hand.

"One moment," Stoles interrupted. "I want them both to understand what is happening and why. Mrs. Randall," he continued, bowing gallantly, "in our short interview earlier I believe I made you understand that the Sons of the Bird will brook no interference from such as you two. You understood that, did you not?"

"I understood you," she answered. But her eyes were defiant.

"Good. Be it understood that it is our wish that your husband have nothing more to do with . . . a certain party. In order to ensure that result we are about to split you into two parts. The part that keeps you going, that which you rather amusingly call the soul, we will squeeze into this bottle and keep. As for the rest, well, your husband may have that to keep with him, as a reminder that the Sons of the Bird have you in pawn. You understand me?"

She ignored the question. Randall tried to answer, found that his throat was misbehaving again.

"Listen to me, Mrs. Randall; if you are ever to see your husband again it is imperative that he obey us. He must not, on pain of your death, see his client again. Under the same penalty he must hold his tongue concerning us and all that has transpired. If he does not—well, we will make your death very interesting, I assure you."

Randall tried to cry out that he would promise anything they wanted to spare her, but his voice was still silenced—apparently Stoles wanted to hear from Cynthia first. She shook her head. "He'll do as he thinks wise."

Stoles smiled. "Fine," he said. "That was the answer I wanted. You, Mr. Randall—do you promise?"

He wanted to agree, he was about to agree—but Cynthia was saying, "No!" with her eyes. From her expression he knew that *her* speech was now being blocked. Inside his head, clear as speech, he seemed to hear her say, "It's a trick, Brain. Don't promise!"

He kept quiet.

Phipps dug a thumb into his eye. "Answer when you are spoken to!"

He had to squint the injured eye in order to see Cynthia, but her expression still approved; he kept his mouth shut.

Presently Stoles said, "Never mind. Get on with it, gentlemen."

Printemps stuck the bottle under Cynthia's nose, held it against her left nostril. "Now!" he directed. Another of them pressed down on her short ribs vigorously, so that her breath was expelled suddenly. She grunted.

"Teddy," she said, "they're pulling me apar—*Ugh!*"

The process had been repeated with the bottle at the other nostril. Randall felt the soft warm hand in his suddenly relax. Printemps held up the bottle with his thumb over its top. "Let's have the wax," he said briskly. Having sealed it he passed it over to Phipps.

Stoles jerked a thumb toward the big mirror. "Put them back," he directed.

Phipps superintended the passing of Cynthia back through the glass, then turned to Stoles. "Couldn't we give him something to make him remember us?" he inquired.

"Help yourselves," Stoles answered indifferently, as he stood up to go, "but try not to leave any permanent marks."

"Fine!" Phipps smiled, and hit Randall a backhanded swipe that loosened his teeth. "We'll be careful!"

He remained conscious through a considerable portion of it, though, naturally, he had no way of judging what proportion. He passed out once or twice, only to come to again under the stimulus of still greater pain. It was the novel way Phipps found of holding a man down without marking him which caused him to pass out for the last time.

He was in a small room, every side of which was a mirror—four walls, floor, and ceiling. Endlessly he was repeated in every direction and every image was himself—selves that hated him but from which there was no escape. "Hit him again!" they yelled—*he* yelled—and struck himself in the teeth with his closed fist. They—*he*—cackled.

They were closing in on him and he could not run fast enough. His muscles would not obey him, no matter how urgently he tried. It was because he was handcuffed—handcuffed to the treadmill they had put him on. He was blindfolded, too, and the handcuffs kept him from reaching his eyes. But he had to keep on—Cynthia was at the top of the climb; he had to reach her.

Only, of course, there is no top when you are on a treadmill.

He was terribly tired, but every time he slowed down the least little bit they hit him again. And he was required to count the steps, too, else he got no credit for it—ten thousand ninety-one, ten thousand ninety-two, ten thousand ninety-three, up and down, up and down—if he could only *see* where he was going.

He stumbled; they clipped him from behind and he fell forward on his face.

WHEN HE WOKE HIS FACE was pressed up against something hard and lumpy and cold. He shifted away from it and found that his whole body was stiff. His feet did not work as they should—he investigated by the uncertain light from the window and found that he had dragged the sheet half off the bed and had it tangled around his ankles.

The hard cold object was the steam radiator; he had been huddled in a heap against it. He was beginning to regain his orientation; he was in his own familiar bedroom. He must have walked in his sleep—he hadn't pulled that stunt since he was a kid! Walked in his sleep, tripped, and smashed his head into the radiator. Must 'a' knocked him silly, colder'n a coot—damn lucky he hadn't killed himself.

He was beginning to pull himself together, and to crawl painfully to his feet, when he noticed the one unfamiliar thing in the room—the new big mirror. It brought the rest of his dream back with a rush; he leaped toward the bed. "Cynthia!"

But she was there where she belonged, safe and unharmed. She had not awakened at his outcry, of which he was glad; he did not want to frighten her. He tiptoed away from the bed and let himself quietly into the bathroom, closing the door behind him before he turned on the light.

A pretty sight! he mused. His nose had been bloodied; it had long since stopped bleeding and the blood had congealed. It made a gory mess of the front of his pajama jacket. Besides that, he had apparently lain with the right side of his face in the stuff—it had dried on, messily, making him appear much more damaged than he was, as he discovered when he bathed his face.

Actually, he did not seem to be much damaged, except that—*Wow!*—the whole right side of his body was stiff and sore—probably banged it and wrenched it when he fell, then caught cold in it. He wondered how long he had been out.

He took off the jacket, decided that it would be too much effort to try to wash it out then, rolled it into a ball and chucked it behind the toilet seat. He didn't want Cyn to see it until he had had a chance to explain to her what had happened. "Why, Teddy, what in the world have you done to yourself?" "Nothing, kid, nothing at all—just ran into a radiator!"

*That* sounded worse than the old one about running into a door.

He was still groggy, groggier than he had thought—he had almost pitched on his head when he threw the jacket down, had been forced to steady himself by grabbing the top of the tank. And his head was pounding like a Salvation Army drum. He fiddled around in the medicine cabinet, located some aspirin and took three tablets, then looked thoughtfully at a prescription box of Amytal Cynthia had obtained some months before. He had never needed anything of the sort before; he slept soundly—but this was a special case. Nightmares two nights running and now sleepwalking and damn near breaking his silly neck.

He took one of the capsules, thinking as he did so that the kid had something when she thought they needed a vacation—he felt all shot.

Clean pajamas were too hard to find without turning on the bedroom light—he slipped into bed, waited a moment to see if Cyn would stir, then closed his eyes and tried to relax. Inside of a few minutes the drugs began to take hold, the throbbing in his head eased up, and soon he was sound asleep.

## VII

Sunlight in his face woke him up; he focused one eye on the clock on the dressing table and saw that it was past nine o'clock, whereupon he got out of bed hastily. It was, he found, not quite a bright thing to do—his right side gave him fits. Then he saw the brown stain under the radiator and recalled his accident.

Cautiously he turned his head and took a look at his wife. She was still sleeping quietly, showing no disposition to stir. That suited him; it would be better, he thought, to tell her what had happened *after* he had dosed her with orange juice. No point in scaring the kid.

He groped on his slippers, then hung his bathrobe around him, as his bare shoulders felt cold and the muscles were sore. His mouth tasted better after he had brushed his teeth; breakfast began to seem like a good idea.

His mind dwelt absent-mindedly on the past night, fingering his recollections rather than grasping them. These nightmares, he thought as he squeezed the oranges—not so good. Maybe not crazy, but definitely not so good, neurotic. Got to put a stop to 'em. Man couldn't work if he spent the night chasing butterflies, even if he didn't fall over his feet and break his neck. Man had to have sleep—definitely.

He drank his own glass of juice, then carried the other into the bedroom. "Come on, bright eyes—*reveille!*" When she did not stir at once he began to sing. "Up with the buttercup, come on, get up, get up! Here comes the sun!"

Still she did not budge. He set the glass down carefully on the bedside table, sat down on the edge of the bed, and took her by the shoulder. "Wake up, kid! They're movin' hell—two loads have gone by already!"

She did not move. Her shoulder was cold.

"Cyn!" he yelled. "Cyn! *Cyn!*" He shook her violently.

She flopped lifelessly. He shook her again. "Cyn darling—Oh, God!"

Presently the shock itself steadied him; he blew his fuses, so to speak, and was ready, with a sort of ashy dead calmness to do whatever might be necessary. He was convinced without knowing why, nor yet fully appreciating it, that she was dead. But he set about making sure by such means as he knew. He could not find her pulse—perhaps he was too clumsy, he told himself, or perhaps it was too weak; all the while a chorus in the back of his mind shouted, "She's dead . . . dead . . . dead—and you let her die!"

He placed an ear over her heart. It seemed that he could hear her heart beat, but he could not be sure; it might have been only the pounding of his own. He gave up presently and looked around for a small mirror.

He found what he wanted in Cynthia's handbag, a little make-up glass. He polished it carefully on the sleeve of his robe and held it to her half-opened mouth.

It fogged faintly.

He took it away in a bemused fashion, not letting himself hope, polished it again, and put it back to her mouth. Again it fogged, lightly but definitely.

She was alive—she was *alive!*

He wondered a moment later why he could not see her clearly and discovered that his face was wet. He wiped his eyes and went on with what he had to do. There was that needle business—if he could find a needle. He did find one in a pincushion on her dressing table. He brought it back to the bed, took a pinch of skin on her forearm, and said, "Excuse me, kid," in a whisper, and jabbed it in.

The puncture showed a drop of blood, then closed at once—alive. He wished for a fever thermometer, but they had none—they were both too healthy. But he did remember something he had read somewhere, something about the invention of the stethoscope. You rolled up a piece of paper—

He found one of suitable size and rolled it into a one-inch tube which he pushed against the bare skin just over her heart. He put his ear to the other end and listened.

*Lubadup—lubadup—lubadup—lubadup*—Faint, but steady and strong. No doubt about it this time; she was alive; her heart was beating.

He had to sit down for a moment.

RANDALL FORCED HIMSELF TO CONSIDER what to do next. Call a doctor, obviously. When people were sick, you called a doctor. He had not thought of it up to this time because Cyn and he just never did, never needed to. He could not recall that either one of them had had occasion to do so since they had been married.

Call the police and ask for an ambulance maybe? No, he'd get some police surgeon more used to crash cases and shootings than anything like this. He wanted the best.

But who? They didn't have a family physician. There was Smyles—a rum dum, no good. And Hartwick—hell, Hartwick specialized in very private operations for society people. He picked up the phone book.

Potbury! He didn't know anything about the old beezer, but, he looked competent. He looked up the number, misdialed three times, then got the operator to call it for him.

"Yes, this is Potbury. What do you want? Speak up, man."

"I said this is Randall. Randall. R-A-N-D-A-double L. My wife and I came to see you yesterday, remember? About—"

"Yes, I remember. What is it?"

"My wife is sick."

"What is the trouble? Did she faint again?"

"No . . . yes. That is, she's unconscious. She woke up unconscious—I mean she never did wake up. She's unconscious now; she looks like she's dead."

"Is she?"

"I don't think so—but she's awful bad off, doctor. I'm scared. Can you come over right away?"

There was a short silence, then Potbury said gruffly, "I'll be over."

"Oh, good! Look—what should I do before you get here?"

"Don't do anything. Don't touch her. I'll be right over." He hung up.

Randall put the phone down and hurried back to the bedroom. Cynthia was just the same. He started to touch her, recalled the doctor's instructions, and straightened up with a jerk. But his eye fell on the piece of paper from which he had improvised a stethoscope and he could not resist the temptation to check up on his earlier results.

The tube gave back a cheering *lubadup;* he took it away at once and put it down.

Ten minutes of standing and looking at her with nothing more constructive to do than biting his nails left him too nervous to continue the occupation. He went out to the kitchen and removed a bottle of rye from the top shelf from which he poured a generous three fingers into a water glass. He looked at the amber stuff for a moment, then poured it down the sink, and went back into the bedroom.

She was still the same.

It suddenly occurred to him that he had not given Potbury the address. He dashed into the kitchen and snatched the phone. Controlling himself, he managed to dial the number correctly. A girl answered the phone. "No, the doctor isn't in the office. Any message?"

"My name is Randall. I—"

"Oh—Mr. Randall. The doctor left for your home about fifteen minutes ago. He should be there any minute now."

"But he doesn't have my address!"

"What? Oh, I'm sure he has—if he didn't have he would have telephoned me by now."

He put the phone down. It was damned funny—well, he would give Potbury three more minutes, then try another one.

The house phone buzzed; he was up out of his chair like a punch-drunk welterweight. "Yes?"

"Potbury. That you, Randall?"

"Yes, yes—come on up!" He punched the door release as he spoke.

Randall was waiting with the door open when Potbury arrived. "Come in, doctor! Come in, come in!" Potbury nodded and brushed on by him.

"Where's the patient?"

"In here." Randall conducted him with nervous haste into the bedroom and leaned over the other side of the bed while Potbury took his first look at the unconscious woman. "How is she? Will she be all right? Tell me, doctor—"

Potbury straightened up a little, grunting as he did so, and said, "If you will kindly stand away from the bed and quit crowding me, perhaps we will find out."

"Oh, sorry!" Randall retreated to the doorway. Potbury took his stethoscope from his bag, listened for a while with an inscrutable expression on his face which Randall tried vainly to read, shifted the instrument around, and listened again. Presently he put the stethoscope back in the bag, and Randall stepped forward eagerly.

But Potbury ignored him. He peeled up an eyelid with his thumb and examined her pupil, lifted an arm so that it swung free over the side of the bed and tapped it near the elbow, then straightened himself up and just looked at her for several minutes.

Randall wanted to scream.

Potbury performed several more of the strange, almost ritualistic things physicians do, some of which Randall thought he understood, others which he definitely did not. At last he said suddenly, "What did she do yesterday—after you left my office?"

Randall told him; Potbury nodded sagely. "That's what I expected—it all dates back to the shock she had in the morning. All your fault, if I may say so!"

"My fault, doctor?"

"You were warned. Should never have let her get close to a man like that."

"But . . . but . . . you didn't warn me until *after* he had frightened her."

Potbury seemed a little vexed at this. "Perhaps not, perhaps not. Thought you told me someone had warned you before I did. Should know better, anyhow, with a creature like that."

Randall dropped the matter. "But how is she, doctor? Will she get well? She will, won't she?"

"You've got a very sick woman on your hands, Mr. Randall."

"Yes, I know she is—but what's the matter with her?"

"*Lethargic gravis,* brought on by psychic trauma."

"Is that—serious?"

"Quite serious enough. If you take proper care of her, I expect she will pull through."

"Anything, doctor, anything? Money's no object. What do we do now? Take her to a hospital?"

Potbury brushed the suggestion aside. "Worst thing in the world for her. If she wakes up in strange surroundings, she may go off again. Keep her here. Can you arrange your affairs so as to watch her yourself?"

"You bet I can."

"Then do so. Stay with her night and day. If she wakes up, the most favorable condition will be for her to find herself in her own bed with you awake and near her."

"Oughtn't she to have a nurse?"

"I wouldn't say so. There isn't much that can be done for her, except to keep her covered up warm. You might keep her feet a little higher than her head. Put a couple of books under each of the lower feet of the bed."

"Right away."

"If this condition persists for more than a week or so, we'll have to see about glucose injections, or something of the sort." Potbury stooped over, closed his bag and picked it up. "Telephone me if there is any change in her condition."

"I will. I—" Randall stopped suddenly; the doctor's last remark reminded him of something he had forgotten. "Doctor—how did you find your way over here?"

Potbury looked startled. "What do you mean? This place isn't hard to find."

"But I didn't give you the address."

"Eh? Nonsense."

"But I didn't. I remembered the oversight just a few minutes later and called your office back, but you had already left."

"I didn't say you gave it to me today," Potbury said testily; "you gave it to me yesterday."

Randall thought it over. He *had* offered Potbury his credentials the day before, but they contained only his business address. True, his home telephone was listed, but it was listed simply as a night business number, without address, both in his credentials and in the phone book. Perhaps Cynthia—

But he could not ask Cynthia and the thought of her drove minor considerations out of his mind. "Are you sure there is nothing else I should do, doctor?" he asked anxiously.

"Nothing. Stay here and watch her."

"I will. But I surely wish I were twins for a while," he added emphatically.

"Why?" Potbury inquired, as he gathered up his gloves and turned toward the door.

"That guy Hoag. I've got a score to settle with him. Never mind—I'll put somebody else on his tail until I have a chance to settle his hash myself."

Potbury had wheeled around and was looking at him ominously. "You'll do nothing of the sort. Your place is here."

"Sure, sure—but I want to keep him on ice. One of these days I'm going to take him apart to see what makes him tick!"

"Young man," Potbury said slowly, "I want you to promise me that you will have nothing to do *in any way* with . . . with this man you mentioned."

Randall glanced toward the bed. "In view of what has happened," he said savagely, "do you think I'm going to let him get away scot-free?"

"In the name of—Look. I'm older than you are and I've learned to expect silliness and stupidity. Still—how much does it take to teach you that some things are too dangerous to monkey with?" He gestured toward Cynthia. "How can you expect me to be responsible for her recovery if you insist on doing things that might bring on a catastrophe?"

"But—listen, Dr. Potbury, I told you that I intended to follow your instructions about *her.* But I'm not going to just forget what he has done. If she dies . . . if she dies, so help me, I'll take him apart with a rusty ax!"

Potbury did not answer at once. When he did all he said was, "And if she doesn't die?"

"If she doesn't die, my first business is here, taking care of her. But don't expect me to promise to forget Hoag. I won't—and that's final."

Potbury jammed his hat on his head. "We'll let it go at that—and trust she doesn't die. But let me tell you, young man, you're a fool." He stomped out of the apartment.

THE LIFT HE HAD GOTTEN from tangling wills with Potbury wore off in a few minutes after the doctor had gone, and a black depression settled down on him. There was nothing to do, nothing to distract his mind from the aching apprehension he felt over Cynthia. He did make the arrangements to raise the foot of the bed a little as suggested by Potbury, but it takes only a few minutes to perform such a trifling chore; when it was done he had nothing to occupy him.

In raising the foot of the bed he had been very cautious at first to avoid jarring the bed for fear of waking her; then he realized that waking her was just what he wanted most to do. Nevertheless he could not bring himself to be rough and noisy about it—she looked so helpless lying there.

He pulled a chair up close to the bed, where he could touch one of her hands and watch her closely for any change. By holding rigidly still he found that he could just perceive the rise and fall of her breast. It reassured him a little; he spent a long time watching for it—the slow, unnoticeable intake, the much quicker spilling of the breath.

Her face was pale and frighteningly deathlike, but beautiful. It wrung his heart to look at her. So fragile—she had trusted him so completely—and now there was nothing he could do for her. If he had listened to her, if he had only listened to what she had said, this would not have happened to her. She had been afraid, but she had done what he asked her to do.

Even the Sons of the Bird had not been able to frighten her—

What was he saying? Get a grip on yourself, Ed—*that* didn't happen; that was part of your nightmare. Still, if anything like that had happened, that was just what she would do—stick in there and back up his play, no matter how badly things were going.

He got a certain melancholy satisfaction out of the idea that, even in his dreams, he was sure of her, sure of her courage and her devotion to him. Guts—more than most men. There was the time she knocked the acid bottle out of the hands of that crazy old biddy he had caught out in the Midwell case. If she hadn't been quick and courageous then, he would probably be wearing smoked glasses now, with a dog to lead him around.

He displaced the covers a little and looked at the scar on her arm she had picked up that day. None of the acid had touched him, but some had touched her—it still showed, it always would show. But she didn't seem to care.

"Cynthia! Oh, Cyn, my darling!"

THERE CAME A TIME WHEN even he could not remain in one position any longer. Painfully—the cold he had caught in his muscles after the accident last night made his cramped legs ache like fury—he got himself up and prepared to cope with necessities. The thought of food was repugnant but he knew that he had to feed himself if he were to be strong enough to accomplish the watching and waiting that was going to be necessary.

Rummaging through the kitchen shelves and the icebox turned up some oddments of food, breakfast things, a few canned goods, staples, some tired lettuce. He had no stomach for involved cooking; a can of soup seemed as good a bet as anything. He opened a can of Scotch broth, dumped it into a saucepan and added water. When it had simmered for a few minutes he took it off the fire and ate it from the pan, standing up. It tasted like stewed cardboard.

He went back to the bedroom and sat down again to resume the endless watching. But it soon developed that his feelings with respect to food were sounder than his logic; he bolted hastily for the bathroom and was very sick for a few minutes. Then he washed his face, rinsed out his mouth, and came back to his chair, weak and pale, but feeling sound enough physically.

It began to grow dusky outside; he switched on the dressing-table lamp, shaded it so that it would not shine directly in her eyes, and again sat down. She was unchanged.

The telephone rang.

It startled him almost out of rational response. He and his sorrow had been sitting there watching for so long that he was hardly aware that there could be anything else in the world. But he pulled himself together and answered it.

"Hello? Yes, this is Randall, speaking."

"Mr. Randall, I've had time to think it over and I feel that I owe you an apology—and an explanation."

"Owe me what? Who is this speaking?"

"Why, this is Jonathan Hoag, Mr. Randall. When you—"

"Hoag! Did you say *'Hoag'?*"

"Yes, Mr. Randall. I want to apologize for my peremptory manner yesterday morning and to beg your indulgence. I trust that Mrs. Randall was not upset by my—"

By this time Randall was sufficiently recovered from his first surprise to express himself. He did so, juicily, using words and figures of speech picked up during years of association with the sort of characters that a private detective inevitably runs into. When he had finished there was a gasp from the other end of the line and then a dead silence.

He was not satisfied. He wanted Hoag to speak so that he could interrupt him and continue the tirade. "Are you there, Hoag?"

"Uh, yes."

"I wanted to add this: Maybe you think that it is a joke to catch a woman alone in a hallway and scare the daylights out of her. I don't! But I'm not going to turn you over to the police—no, indeed! Just as soon as Mrs. Randall gets well, I'm going to look you up myself and then—God help you, Hoag. You'll need it."

There followed such a long silence that Randall was sure that his victim had hung up. But it seemed that Hoag was merely collecting his wits. "Mr. Randall, this is terrible—"

"You bet it is!"

"Do you mean to tell me that I accosted Mrs. Randall and frightened her?"

"You should know!"

"But I don't know, truly I don't." He paused, and then continued in an unsteady voice. "This is the sort of thing I have been afraid of, Mr. Randall, afraid that I might discover that during my lapses of memory I might have been doing terrible things. But to have harmed Mrs. Randall—she was so good to me, so kind to me. This is horrible."

"You're telling me!"

Hoag sighed as if he were tired beyond endurance. "Mr. Randall?" Randall did not answer. "Mr. Randall—there is no use in my deluding myself; there is only one thing to be done. You've got to turn me over to the police."

"Huh?"

"I've known it ever since our last conversation; I thought about it all day yesterday, but I did not have the courage. I had hoped that I was through with my . . . my *other* personality, but today it happened again. The whole day is a blank and I just came to myself this evening, on getting home. Then I knew that I *had* to do something about it, so I called you to ask you to resume your investigations. But I never suspected that I could possibly have done anything to Mrs. Randall." He seemed most convincingly overcome by shock at the idea. "When did . . . did *this* happen, Mr. Randall?"

Randall found himself in a most bewildered state of mind. He was torn between the desire to climb through the phone and wring the neck of the man he held responsible for his wife's desperate condition and the necessity for remaining where he was to care for her. In addition to that he was bothered by the fact that Hoag refused to talk like a villain. While speaking with him, listening to his mild answers and his worried tones, it was difficult to maintain the conception of him as a horrid monster of the Jack-the-Ripper type—although he knew consciously that villains were often mild in manner.

Therefore his answer was merely factual. "Nine thirty in the morning, about."

"Where was I at nine thirty this morning?"

"Not *this* morning, you so-and-so; yesterday morning."

"Yesterday morning? But that's not possible. Don't you remember? I was at home yesterday morning."

"Of course I remember, and I saw you leave. Maybe you didn't know *that*." He was not being very logical; the other events of the previous morning had convinced him that Hoag knew that they were shadowing him—but he was in no state of mind to be logical.

"But you couldn't have seen me. Yesterday morning was the only morning, aside from my usual Wednesdays, on which I can be sure where I was. I was at home, in my apartment, I didn't leave it until nearly one o'clock when I went to my club."

"Why, that's a—"

"Wait a minute, Mr. Randall, please! I'm just as confused and upset about this as you are, but you've got to listen to me. You broke my routine—remember? And my other personality did not assert itself. After you left I remained my . . . my *proper* self. That's why I had had hopes that I was free at last."

"The hell you did. What makes you think you did?"

"I know my own testimony doesn't count for much," Hoag said meekly, "but I wasn't alone. The cleaning woman arrived just after you left and was here all morning."

"Damned funny I didn't see her go up."

"She works in the building," Hoag explained. "She's the wife of the janitor—her name is Mrs. Jenkins. Would you like to talk with her? I can probably locate her and get her on the line."

"But—" Randall was getting more and more confused and was beginning to realize that he was at a disadvantage. He should never have discussed matters with Hoag at all; he should have simply save him up until there was opportunity to take a crack at him. Potbury was right; Hoag was a slick and insidious character. Alibi indeed!

Furthermore he was becoming increasingly nervous and fretful over having stayed away from the bedroom as long as he had. Hoag must have had him on the phone at least ten minutes; it was not possible to see into the bedroom from where he sat at the breakfast table. "No, I don't want to talk to her," he said roughly. "You lie in circles!" He slammed the phone back into its cradle and hurried into the bedroom.

Cynthia was just as he had left her, looking merely asleep and heartbreakingly lovely. She was breathing, he quickly determined; her respiration was light but regular. His homemade stethoscope rewarded him with the sweet sound of her heartbeat.

He sat and watched her for a while, letting the misery of his situation soak into him like a warm and bitter wine. He did not want to forget his pain; he hugged it to him, learning what countless others had learned before him, that even the deepest pain concerning a beloved one is preferable to any surcease.

Later he stirred himself, realizing that he was indulging himself in a fashion that might work to her detriment. It was necessary to have food in the house for one thing, and to manage to eat some and keep it down. Tomorrow, he told himself, he would have to get busy on the telephone and see what he could do about keeping the business intact while he was away from it. The Night Watch Agency might do as a place to farm out any business that could not be put off; they were fairly reliable and he had done favors for them—but that could wait until tomorrow.

Just now— He called up the delicatessen on the street below and did some very desultory telephone shopping. He authorized the proprietor to throw in anything else that looked good and that would serve to keep a man going for a day or two. He then instructed him to find someone who would like to earn four bits by delivering the stuff to his apartment.

That done, he betook himself to the bathroom and shaved carefully, having a keen appreciation of the connection between a neat toilet and morale. He left the door open and kept one eye on the bed. He then took a rag, dampened it, and wiped up the stain under the radiator. The bloody pajama jacket he stuffed into the dirty-clothes hamper in the closet.

He sat down and waited for the order from the delicatessen to arrive. All the while he had been thinking over his conversation with Hoag. There was only one thing about Hoag that was clear, he concluded, and that was that everything about him was confusing. His original story had been wacky enough—imagine coming in and offering a high fee to have himself shadowed! But the events since made that incident seem downright reasonable. There was the matter of the thirteenth floor—damn it! He *had* seen that thirteenth floor, been on it, watched Hoag at work with a jeweler's glass screwed in his eye.

Yet he could not possibly have done so.

What did it add up to? Hypnotism, maybe? Randall was not naïve about such things; he knew that hypnotism existed, but he knew also that it was not nearly as potent as the Sunday-supplement feature writers would have one believe. As for hypnotizing a man in a split second on a crowded street so that he believed in and could recall clearly a sequence of events that had never taken place—well, he just didn't believe in it. If a thing like that were true, then the whole world might be just a fraud and an illusion.

Maybe it was.

Maybe the whole world held together only when you kept your attention centered on it and believed in it. If you let discrepancies creep in, you began to doubt and it began to go to pieces. Maybe this had happened to Cynthia because he had doubted her reality. If he just closed his eyes and *believed* in her alive and well, then she would be—

He tried it. He shut out the rest of the world and concentrated on Cynthia—Cynthia alive and well, with that little quirk to her mouth she had when she was laughing at something he had said—Cynthia, waking up in the morning, sleepy-eyed and beautiful—Cynthia in a tailored suit and a pert little hat, ready to start out with him anywhere. Cynthia—

He opened his eyes and looked at the bed. There she still lay, unchanged and deathly. He let himself go for a while, then blew his nose and went in to put some water on his face.

## VIII

The house buzzer sounded. Randall went to the hall door and jiggled the street-door release without using the apartment phone—he did not want to speak to anyone just then, certainly not to whoever it was that Joe had found to deliver the groceries.

After a reasonable interval there was a soft knock at the door. He opened it, saying, "Bring 'em in," then stopped suddenly.

Hoag stood just outside the door.

Neither of them spoke at first. Randall was astounded; Hoag seemed diffident and waiting for Randall to commence matters. At last he said shyly, "I *had* to come, Mr. Randall. May I . . . come in?"

Randall stared at him, really at loss for words. The brass of the man—the sheer gall!

"I came because I had to prove to you that I would not willingly harm Mrs. Randall," he said simply. "If I have done so unknowingly, I want to do what I can to make restitution."

"It's too late for restitution!"

"But, Mr. Randall—why do you think that *I* have done anything to your wife? I don't see how I could have—not yesterday morning." He stopped and looked hopelessly at Randall's stony face. "You wouldn't shoot a dog without a fair trial—would you?"

Randall chewed his lip in an agony of indecision. Listening to him, the man seemed so damned decent— He threw the door open wide "Come in," he said gruffly.

"Thank you, Mr. Randall." Hoag came in diffidently. Randall started to close the door.

"Your name Randall?" Another man, a stranger, stood in the door, loaded with bundles.

"Yes," Randall admitted, fishing in his pocket for change. "How did you get in?"

"Came in with *him,*" the man said, pointing at Hoag, "but I got off at the wrong floor. The beer is cold, chief," he added ingratiatingly. "Right off the ice."

"Thanks," Randall added a dime to the half dollar and closed the door on him. He picked the bundles up from the floor and started for the kitchen. He would have some of that beer now, he decided; there was never a time when he needed it more. After putting the packages down in the kitchen he took out one of the cans, fumbled in the drawer for an opener, and prepared to open it. A movement caught his eye—Hoag, shifting restlessly from one foot to the other. Randall had not invited him to sit down; he was still standing. "Sit down!"

"Thank you." Hoag sat down.

Randall turned back to his beer. But the incident had reminded him of the other's presence; he found himself caught in the habit of good manners; it was almost impossible for him to pour himself a beer and offer none to a guest, no matter how unwelcome.

He hesitated just a moment, then thought, Shucks, it can't hurt either Cynthia or me to let him have a can of beer. "Do you drink beer?"

"Yes, thank you." As a matter of fact Hoag rarely drank beer, preferring to reserve his palate for the subtleties of wines, but at the moment he would probably have said yes to synthetic gin, or ditch water, if Randall had offered it.

Randall brought in the glasses, put them down, then went into the bedroom, opening the door for the purpose just enough to let him slip in. Cynthia was just as he had come to expect her to be. He shifted her position a trifle, in the belief that any position grows tiring even to a person unconscious, then smoothed the coverlet. He looked at her and thought about Hoag and Potbury's warnings against Hoag. Was Hoag as dangerous as the doctor seemed to think? Was he, Randall, even now playing into his hands?

No, Hoag could not hurt him now. When the worst has happened any change is an improvement. The death of both of them—or even Cyn's death alone, for then he would simply follow her. That he had decided earlier in the day—and he didn't give a damn who called it cowardly!

No—if Hoag were responsible for this, at least he had shot his bolt. He went back into the living room.

Hoag's beer was still untouched. "Drink up," Randall invited, sitting down and reaching for his own glass. Hoag complied, having the good sense not to offer a toast nor even to raise his glass in the gesture of one. Randall looked him over with tired curiosity. "I don't understand you, Hoag."

"I don't understand myself, Mr. Randall."

"Why did you come here?"

Hoag spread his hands helplessly. "To inquire about Mrs. Randall. To find out what it is that I have done to her. To make up for it, if I can."

"You admit you did it?"

"No, Mr. Randall. No. I don't see how I could possibly have done anything to Mrs. Randall *yesterday* morning—"

"You forget that I saw you."

"But— What did I do?"

"You cornered Mrs. Randall in a corridor of the Midway-Copton Building and tried to choke her."

"Oh, dear! But—you *saw* me do this?"

"No, not exactly. I was—" Randall stopped, realizing how it was going to sound to tell Hoag that he had not seen him in one part of the building because he was busy watching Hoag in another part of the building.

"Go on, Mr. Randall, please."

Randall got nervously to his feet. "It's no use," he snapped. "I don't know what you did. I don't know that you did anything! All I know is this: Since the first day you walked in that door, odd things have been happening to my wife and me—*evil* things—and now she's lying in there as if she were dead. She's—" He stopped and covered his face with his hands.

He felt a gentle touch on his shoulder. "Mr. Randall . . . please, Mr. Randall. I'm sorry and I would like to help."

"I don't know how anyone can help—unless you know some way of waking up my wife. Do you, Mr. Hoag?"

Hoag shook his head slowly. "I'm afraid I don't. Tell me—what is the matter with her? I don't know yet."

"There isn't much to tell. She didn't wake up this morning. She acts as if she never would wake up."

"You're sure she's not . . . dead?"

"No, she's not dead."

"You had a doctor, of course. What did he say?"

"He told me not to move her and to watch her closely."

"Yes, but what did he say was the matter with her?"

"He called it *lethargica gravis.*"

"*Lethargica gravis?* Was that all he called it?"

"Yes—why?"

"But didn't he attempt to diagnose it?"

"That was his diagnosis—*lethargica gravis.*"

Hoag still seemed puzzled. "But, Mr. Randall, that isn't a diagnosis; it is just a pompous way of saying 'heavy sleep.' It really doesn't mean anything. It's like telling a man with skin trouble that he has *dermatitis,* or a man with stomach trouble that he has *gastritis.* What tests did he make?"

"Uh . . . I don't know. I—"

"Did he take a sample with a stomach pump?"

"No."

"X ray?"

"No, there wasn't any way to."

"Do you mean to tell me, Mr. Randall, that a doctor just walked in, took a look at her, and walked out again, without doing anything for her, or applying any tests, or bringing in a consulting opinion? Was he your family doctor?"

"No," Randall said miserably. "I'm afraid I don't know much about doctors. We never need one. But you ought to know whether he's any good or not—it was Potbury."

"Potbury? You mean the Dr. Potbury I consulted? How did you happen to pick him?"

"Well, we didn't *know* any doctors—and we had been to see him, checking up on your story. What have you got against Potbury?"

"Nothing, really. He was rude to me—or so I thought."

"Well, then, what's he got against you?"

"I don't see how he could have anything against me," Hoag answered in puzzled tones. "I only saw him once. Except, of course, the matter of the analysis. Though why he should—" He shrugged helplessly.

"You mean about the stuff under your nails? I thought that was just a song and dance."

"No."

"Anyhow it couldn't be just that. After all the things he said about you."

"What did he say about me?"

"He said—" Randall stopped, realizing that Potbury had not said anything specific against Hoag; it had been entirely what he did not say. "It wasn't so much what he said; it was how he felt about you. He hates you, Hoag—and he is afraid of you."

"Afraid of me?" Hoag smiled feebly, as if he were sure Randall must be joking.

"He didn't *say* so, but it was plain as daylight."

Hoag shook his head. "I don't understand it. I'm more used to being afraid of people than of having them afraid of me. Wait—did he tell *you* the results of the analysis he made for me?"

"No. Say, that reminds me of the queerest thing of all about you, Hoag." He broke off, thinking of the impossible adventure of the thirteenth floor. "Are you a hypnotist?"

"Gracious, no! Why do you ask?"

Randall told him the story of their first attempt to shadow him. Hoag kept quiet through the recital, his face intent and bewildered. "And that's the size of it," Randall concluded emphatically. "No thirteenth floor, no Detheridge & Co., no nothing! And yet I remember every detail of it as plainly as I see your face."

"That's all?"

"Isn't that enough? Still, there is one more thing I might add. It can't be of real importance, except in showing the effect the experience had on me."

"What is it?"

"Wait a minute."

Randall got up and went again into the bedroom. He was not quite so careful this time to open the door the bare minimum, although he did close it behind him. It made him nervous, in one way, not to be constantly at Cynthia's side; yet had he been able to answer honestly he would have been forced to admit that even Hoag's presence was company and some relief to his anxiety. Consciously, he excused his conduct as an attempt to get to the bottom of their troubles.

He listened for her heartbeats again. Satisfied that she still was in this world, he plumped her pillow and brushed vagrant hair up from her face. He leaned over and kissed her forehead lightly, then went quickly out of the room.

Hoag was waiting. "Yes?" he inquired.

Randall sat down heavily and rested his head on his hands. "Still the same." Hoag refrained from making a useless answer; presently Randall commenced in a tired voice to tell him of the nightmares he had experienced the last two nights. "Mind you, I don't say they are significant," he added, when he had done. "I'm not superstitious."

"I wonder," Hoag mused.

"What do you mean?"

"I don't mean anything supernatural, but isn't it possible that the dreams were not entirely accidental ones, brought on by your experiences? I mean to say, if there is someone who can make you dream the things you dreamed in the Acme Building in broad daylight, why couldn't they force you to dream at night as well?"

"Huh?"

"Is there anyone who hates you, Mr. Randall?"

"Why, not that I know of. Of course, in my business, you sometimes do things that don't exactly make friends, but you do it for somebody else. There's a crook or two who doesn't like me any too well, but—well, they couldn't do anything like this. It doesn't make sense. Anybody hate you? Besides Potbury?"

"Not that I know of. And I don't know why he should. Speaking of him, you're going to get some other medical advice, aren't you?"

"Yes. I guess I don't think very fast. I don't know just what to do, except to pick up the phone book and try another number."

"There's a better way. Call one of the big hospitals and ask for an ambulance."

"I'll do that!" Randall said, standing up.

"You might wait until morning. You wouldn't get any useful results until morning, anyway. In the meantime she *might* wake up."

"Well . . . yes, I guess so. I think I'll take another look at her."

"Mr. Randall?"

"Eh?"

"Uh, do you mind if— May I see her?"

Randall looked at him. His suspicions had been lulled more than he had realized by Hoag's manner and words, but the suggestion brought him up short, making him recall Potbury's warnings vividly. "I'd rather you didn't," he said stiffly.

Hoag showed his disappointment but tried to cover it. "Certainly. Certainly. I quite understand, sir."

When Randall returned he was standing near the door with his hat in his hand. "I think I had better go," he said. When Randall did not comment he added, "I would sit with you until morning if you wished it."

"No. Not necessary. Good night."

"Good night, Mr. Randall."

When Hoag had gone he wandered around aimlessly for several minutes, his beat ever returning him to the side of his wife. Hoag's comments about Potbury's methods had left him more uneasy than he cared to admit; in addition to that Hoag had, by partly allaying his suspicions of the man, taken from him his emotional whipping boy—which did him no good.

He ate a cold supper and washed it down with beer—and was pleased to find it remained in place. He then dragged a large chair into the bedroom, put a footstool in front of it, got a spare blanket, and prepared to spend the night. There was nothing to do and he did not feel like reading—he tried it and it didn't work. From time to time he got up and obtained a fresh can of beer from the icebox. When the beer was gone he took down the rye. The stuff seemed to quiet his nerves a little, but otherwise he could detect no effect from it. He did not want to become drunk.

HE WOKE WITH A TERRIFIED start, convinced for the moment that Phipps was at the mirror and about to kidnap Cynthia. The room was dark; his heart felt as if it would burst his ribs before he could find the switch and assure himself that it was not so, that his beloved, waxy pale, still lay on the bed.

He had to examine the big mirror and assure himself that it did reflect the room and not act as a window to some other, awful place before he was willing to snap off the light. By the dim reflected light of the city he poured himself a bracer for his shaken nerves.

He thought that he caught a movement in the mirror, whirled around, and found that it was his own reflection. He sat down again and stretched himself out, resolving not to drop off to sleep again.

*What was that?*

He dashed into the kitchen in pursuit of it. Nothing—nothing that he could find. Another surge of panic swept him back into the bedroom—it could have been a ruse to get him away from her side.

They were laughing at him, goading him, trying to get him to make a false move. He *knew* it—they had been plotting against him for days, trying to shake his nerve. They watched him out of every mirror in the house, ducking back when he tried to catch them at it. The Sons of the Bird—

"The Bird is Cruel!"

Had he said that? Had someone shouted it at him? The Bird is Cruel. Panting for breath, he went to the open window of the bedroom and looked out. It was still dark, pitchdark. No one moved on the streets below. The direction of the lake was a lowering bank of mist. What time was it? Six o'clock in the morning by the clock on the table. Didn't it *ever* get light in this God-forsaken city?

The Sons of the Bird. He suddenly felt very sly; they thought they had him, but he would fool them—they couldn't do this to him and to Cynthia. He would smash every mirror in the place. He hurried out to the kitchen, where he kept a hammer in the catch-all drawer. He got it and came back to the bedroom. First, the big mirror—

He hesitated just as he was about to swing on it. Cynthia wouldn't like this—seven years bad luck! He wasn't superstitious himself, but—Cynthia wouldn't like it! He turned to the bed with the idea of explaining it to her; it seemed so obvious—just break the mirrors and then they would be safe from the Sons of the Bird.

But he was stumped by her still face.

He thought of a way around it. They had to use a mirror. What was a mirror? A piece of glass that reflects. Very well—fix 'em so they wouldn't reflect! Furthermore he knew how he could do it; in the same drawer with the hammer were three or four dime-store cans of enamel, and a small brush, leftovers from a splurge of furniture refinishing Cynthia had once indulged in.

He dumped them all into a small mixing bowl; together they constituted perhaps a pint of heavy pigment—enough, he thought, for his purpose. He attacked the big beveled glass first, slapping enamel over it in quick careless strokes. It ran down his wrists and dripped onto the dressing table; he did not care. Then the others—

There was enough, though barely enough, to finish the living room mirror. No matter—it was the last mirror in the house—except, of course, the tiny mirrors in Cynthia's bags and purses, and he had already decided that they did not count. Too small for a man to crawl through and packed away out of sight, anyhow.

The enamel had been mixed from a small amount of black and perhaps a can and a half, net, of red. It was all over his hands now; he looked like the central figure in an ax murder. No matter—he wiped it, or most of it, off on a towel and went back to his chair and his bottle.

Let 'em try now! Let 'em try dirty, filthy black magic! He had them stymied.

He prepared to wait for the dawn.

THE SOUND OF THE BUZZER brought him up out of his chair, much disorganized, but convinced that he had not closed his eyes. Cynthia was all right—that is to say, she was still asleep, which was the best he had expected. He rolled up his tube and reassured himself with the sound of her heart.

The buzzing continued—or resumed; he did not know which. Automatically he answered it.

"Potbury," came a voice. "What's the matter? You asleep? How's the patient?"

"No change, doctor," he answered, striving to control his voice.

"That so? Well, let me in."

Potbury brushed on by him when he opened the door and went directly to Cynthia. He leaned over her for a moment or two, then straightened up. "Seems about the same," he said. "Can't expect much change for a day or so. Crisis about Wednesday, maybe." He looked Randall over curiously. "What in the world have you been doing? You look like a four-day bender."

"Nothing," said Randall. "Why didn't you have me send her to a hospital, doctor?"

"Worst thing you could do for her."

"What do you know about it? You haven't really examined her. You don't know what's wrong with her. *Do you?*"

"Are you crazy? I told you yesterday."

Randall shook his head. "Just double talk. You're trying to kid me about her. And I want to know why."

Potbury took a step toward him. "You *are* crazy—and drunk, too." He looked curiously at the big mirror. "*I* want to know what's been going on here." He touched a finger to smeared enamel.

"Don't touch it!"

Potbury checked himself. "What's it for?"

Randall looked sly. "I foxed 'em."

"Who?"

"The Sons of the Bird. They come in through mirrors—but I stopped them."

Potbury stared at him. "I know them," Randall said. "They won't fool me again. The Bird is Cruel."

Potbury covered his face with his hands.

They both stood perfectly still for several seconds. It took that long for a new idea to percolate through Randall's abused and bemused mind. When it did he kicked Potbury in the crotch. The events of the next few seconds were rather confused. Potbury made no outcry, but fought back. Randall made no attempt to fight fair, but followed up his first panzer stroke with more dirty work.

When matters straightened out, Potbury was behind the bathroom door, whereas Randall was on the bedroom side with the key in his pocket. He was breathing hard but completely unaware of such minor damage as he had suffered.

Cynthia slept on.

"MR. RANDALL—LET ME OUT of here!"

Randall had returned to his chair and was trying to think his way out of his predicament. He was fully sobered by now and made no attempt to consult the bottle. He was trying to get it through his head that there really were "Sons of the Bird" and that he had one of them locked up in there right now.

In that case Cynthia was unconscious because—God help them!—the Sons had stolen her soul. Devils—they had fallen afoul of devils.

Potbury pounded on the door. "What's the meaning of this, Mr. Randall? Have you lost your mind? Let me out of here!"

"What'll you do if I do? Will you bring Cynthia back to life?"

"I'll do what a physician can for her. Why did you do it?"

"You know why. Why did you cover your face?"

"What do you mean? I started to sneeze and you kicked me."

"Maybe I should have said, '*Gesundheit!*' You're a devil, Potbury. You're a Son of the Bird!"

There was a short silence. "What nonsense is this?"

Randall thought about it. Maybe it was nonsense; maybe Potbury *had* been about to sneeze. No! This was the only explanation that made sense. Devils, devils and black magic. Stoles and Phipps and Potbury and the others.

Hoag? That would account for—wait a minute, now. Potbury hated Hoag. Stoles hated Hoag. All the Sons of the Bird hated Hoag. Very well, devil or whatever, he and Hoag were on the same side.

Potbury was pounding on the door again, no longer with his fists, but with a heavier, less frequent blow which meant the shoulder with the whole weight of the body behind it. The door was no stronger than interior house doors usually are; it was evident that it could take little of such treatment.

Randall pounded on his side. "Potbury! Potbury! Do you hear me?"

"Yes."

"Do you know what I'm going to do now? I'm going to call up Hoag and get him to come over here. Do you hear that, Potbury? He'll kill you, Potbury, he'll kill you!"

There was no answer, but presently the heavy pounding resumed. Randall got his gun. "Potbury!" No answer. "Potbury, cut that out or I'll shoot." The pounding did not even slacken.

Randall had a sudden inspiration. "Potbury—*in the Name of the Bird*—get away from that door!"

The noise stopped as if chopped off.

Randall listened and then pursued his advantage. "In the Name of the Bird, don't touch that door again. Hear me, Potbury?" There was no answer, but the quiet continued.

It was early; Hoag was still at his home. He quite evidently was confused by Randall's incoherent explanations, but he agreed to come over, at once, or a little quicker.

Randall went back into the bedroom and resumed his double vigil. He held his wife's still, cool hand with his left hand; in his right he carried his gun, ready in case the invocation failed to bind. But the pounding was not resumed; there was a deathly silence in both rooms for some minutes. Then Randall heard, or imagined he heard, a faint scraping sibilance from the bathroom—an unaccountable and ominous sound.

He could think of nothing to do about it, so he did nothing. It went on for several minutes and stopped. After that—nothing.

HOAG RECOILED AT THE SIGHT of the gun. "Mr. Randall!"

"Hoag," Randall demanded, "are you a devil?"

"I don't understand you."

"'The Bird is Cruel!'"

Hoag did not cover his face; he simply looked confused and a bit more apprehensive.

"O.K.," decided Randall. "You pass. If you *are* a devil, you're my kind of a devil. Come on—I've got Potbury locked up, and I want you to confront him."

"Me? Why?"

"Because he *is* a devil—a Son of the Bird. And they're afraid of you. Come on!" He urged Hoag into the bedroom, continuing with, "The mistake I made was in not being willing to believe in something when it happened to me. *Those weren't dreams.*" He pounded on the door with the muzzle of the gun. "Potbury! Hoag is here. Do what I want and you *may* get out of it alive."

"What do you want of him?" Hoag said nervously.

"*Her*—of course."

"Oh—"

Randall pounded again, then turned to Hoag and whispered, "If I open the door, will you confront him? I'll be right alongside you."

Hoag gulped, looked at Cynthia, and answered, "Of course."

"Here goes."

The bath was empty; it had no window, nor any other reasonable exit, but the means by which Potbury had escaped was evident. The surface of the mirror had been scraped free of enamel, with a razor blade.

They risked the seven years of bad luck and broke the mirror. Had he known how to do so, Randall would have swarmed through and tackled them all; lacking the knowledge it seemed wiser to close the leak.

After that there was nothing to do. They discussed it, over the silent form of Randall's wife, but there was nothing to do. They were not magicians. Hoag went into the living room presently, unwilling to disturb the privacy of Randall's despair but also unwilling to desert him entirely. He looked in on him from time to time. It was on one such occasion that he noticed a small black bag half under the bed and recognized it for what it was—a doctor's kit. He went in and picked it up. "Ed," he asked, "have you looked at this?"

"At what?" Randall looked up with dull eyes, and read the inscription, embossed in well-worn gold letters on the flap:

POTIPHAR T. POTBURY, M.D.

"Huh?"

"He must have left it behind."

"He didn't have a chance to take it." Randall took it from Hoag and opened it—a stethoscope, head forceps, clamps, needles, an assortment of vials in a case, the usual props of a G.P.'s work. There was one prescription bottle as well; Randall took it out and read the prescription. "Hoag, look at this."

**POISON!**

This Prescription Can Not Be Refilled
MRS. RANDALL—TAKE AS PRESCRIBED
BONTON CUTRATE PHARMACY

"Was he trying to poison her?" Hoag suggested.

"I don't think so—that's the usual narcotic warning. But I want to see what it is." He shook it. It seemed empty. He started to break the seal.

"Careful!" Hoag warned.

"I will be." He held it well back from his face to open it, then sniffed it very cautiously. It gave up a fragrance, subtle and infinitely sweet.

"Teddy?" He whirled around, dropping the bottle. It was indeed Cynthia, eyelids fluttering. "Don't promise them anything, Teddy!" She sighed and her eyes closed again.

"'The Bird is Cruel!'" she whispered.

# IX

"Your memory lapses are the key to the whole thing," Randall was insisting. "If we knew what you do in the daytime, if we knew your profession, we would know why the Sons of the Bird are out to get you. More than that, we would know how to fight them—for they are obviously afraid of you."

Hoag turned to Cynthia. "What do you think, Mrs. Randall?"

"I think Teddy is right. If I knew enough about hypnotism, we would try that—but I don't, so scopolamine is the next best bet. Are you willing to try it?"

"If you say so, yes."

"Get the kit, Teddy." She jumped down from where she had been perched, on the edge of his desk. He put out a hand to catch her.

"You ought to take it easy, baby," he complained.

"Nonsense, I'm all right—now."

They had adjourned to their business office almost as soon as Cynthia woke up. To put it plainly, they were scared—scared stiff, but not scared silly. The apartment seemed an unhealthy place to be. The office did not seem much better. Randall and Cynthia had decided to *get out of town*—the stop at the office was a penultimate stop, for a conference of war.

Hoag did not know what to do.

"Just forget you ever saw this kit," Randall warned him, as he prepared the hypodermic. "Not being a doctor, nor an anaesthetist, I shouldn't have it. But it's convenient, sometimes." He scrubbed a spot of Hoag's forearm with an alcohol swab. "Steady now—there!" He shoved in the needle.

They waited for the drug to take hold. "What do you expect to get," Randall whispered to Cynthia.

"I don't know. If we're lucky, his two personalities will knit. Then we may find out a lot of things."

A little later Hoag's head sagged forward; he breathed heavily. She stepped forward and shook his shoulder. "Mr. Hoag—do you hear me?"

"Yes."

"What is your name?"

"Jonathan . . . Hoag."

"Where do you live?"

"Six-oh-two—Gotham Apartments."

"What do you do?"

"I . . . don't know."

"Try to remember. What is your profession?"

No answer. She tried again. "Are you a hypnotist?"

"No."

"Are you a—magician?"

The answer was delayed a little, but finally came. "No."

*"What are you, Jonathan Hoag?"*

He opened his mouth, seemed about to answer—then sat up suddenly, his manner brisk and completely free of the lassitude normal to the drug. "I'm sorry, my dear, but this will have to stop—for the present."

He stood up, walked over to the window, and looked out. "Bad," he said, glancing up and down the street. "How distressingly bad." He seemed to be talking to himself rather than to them. Cynthia and Randall looked at him, then to each other for help.

"What is bad, Mr. Hoag?" Cynthia asked, rather diffidently. She did not have the impression analyzed, but he seemed like another person—younger, more vibrant.

"Eh? Oh, I'm sorry. I owe you an explanation. I was forced to, uh, dispense with the drug."

"Dispense with it?"

"Throw it off, ignore it, make it as nothing. You see, my dear, while you were talking I recalled my profession." He looked at them cheerily, but offered no further explanation.

Randall was the first to recover. "What *is* your profession?"

Hoag smiled at him, almost tenderly. "It wouldn't do to tell you," he said. "Not now, at least." He turned to Cynthia. "My dear, could I trouble you for a pencil and a sheet of paper?"

"Uh—why, certainly." She got them for him; he accepted them graciously and, seating himself, began to write.

When he said nothing to explain his conduct Randall spoke up. "Say, Hoag, look here—" Hoag turned a serene face to him; Randall started to speak, seemed puzzled by what he saw in Hoag's face, and concluded lamely, "Er . . . Mr. Hoag, what's this all about?"

"Are you not willing to trust me?"

Randall chewed his lip for a moment and looked at him; Hoag was patient and serene. "Yes . . . I suppose I am," he said at last.

"Good. I am making a list of some things I want you to buy for me. I shall be quite busy for the next two hours or so."

"You are leaving us?"

"You are worried about the Sons of the Bird, aren't you? Forget them. They will not harm you. I promise it." He resumed writing. Some minutes later he handed the list to Randall. "I've noted at the bottom the place where you are to meet me—a filling station outside Waukegan."

"Waukegan? Why Waukegan?"

"No very important reason. I want to do once more something I am very fond of doing and don't expect to be able to do again. You'll help me, won't you? Some of the things I've asked you to buy may be hard to get, but you will try?"

"I suppose so."

"Good." He left at once.

Randall looked from the closing door back to the list in his hand. "Well, I'll be a— Cyn, what do you suppose he wants us to get for him?—groceries!"

"Groceries? Let me see that list."

# X

They were driving north in the outskirts of the city, with Randall at the wheel. Somewhere up ahead lay the place where they were to meet Hoag; behind them in the trunk of the car were the purchases he had directed them to make.

"Teddy?"

"Yeah, kid."

"Can you make a U-turn here?"

"Sure—if you don't get caught. Why?"

"Because that's just what I'd like to do. Let me finish," she went on hurriedly. "We've got the car; we've got all the money we have in the world with us; there isn't anything to stop us from heading south if we want to."

"Still thinking of that vacation? But we're going on it—just as soon as we deliver this stuff to Hoag."

"I don't mean a vacation. I mean go away and never come back—*now!*"

"With eighty dollars' worth of fancy groceries that Hoag ordered and hasn't paid for yet? No soap."

"We could eat them ourselves."

"Humph! Caviar and humming-bird wings. We can't afford it, kid. We're the hamburger type. Anyhow, even if we could, I want to see Hoag again. Some plain talk—and explanations."

She sighed. "That's just what I thought, Teddy, and that's why I want to cut and run. I don't want explanations; I'm satisfied with the world the way it is. Just you and me—and no complications. I don't *want* to know anything about Mr. Hoag's profession—or the Sons of the Bird—or anything like that."

He fumbled for a cigarette, then scratched a match under the instrument board, while looking at her quizzically out of the corner of his eye. Fortunately the traffic was light. "I think I feel the same way you do about it, kid, but I've got a different angle on it. If we drop it now, I'll be jumpy about the Sons of the Bird the rest of my life, and scared to shave, for fear of looking in a mirror. But there is a rational explanation for the whole thing—bound to be—and I'm going to get it. Then we can sleep."

She made herself small and did not answer.

"Look at it this way," Randall went on, somewhat irritated. "Everything that has happened could have been done in the ordinary way, without recourse to supernatural agencies. As for supernatural agencies—well, out here in the sunlight and the traffic it's a little too much to swallow. Sons of the Bird—rats!"

She did not answer. He went on, "The first significant point is that Hoag is a consummate actor. Instead of being a prissy little Milquetoast, he's a dominant personality of the first water. Look at the way I shut up and said, 'Yes, sir,' when he pretended to throw off the drug and ordered us to buy all those groceries."

"Pretended?"

"Sure. Somebody substituted colored water for my sleepy juice—probably done the same time the phony warning was stuck in the typewriter. But to get back to the point—he's a naturally strong character and almost certainly a clever hypnotist. Pulling that illusion about the thirteenth floor and Detheridge & Co. shows how skillful he is—or somebody is. Probably used drugs on me as well, just as they did on you."

"On me?"

"Sure. Remember that stuff you drank in Potbury's office? Some sort of a delayed-action Mickey Finn."

"But you drank it, too!"

"Not necessarily the *same* stuff. Potbury and Hoag were in cahoots, which is how they created the atmosphere that made the whole thing possible. Everything else was little stuff, insignificant when taken alone."

Cynthia had her own ideas about that, but she kept them to herself. However, one point bothered her. "How did Potbury get out of the bathroom? You told me he was locked in."

"I've thought about that. He picked the lock while I was phoning Hoag, hid in the closet and just waited his chance to walk out."

"Hm-m-m—" She let it go at that for several minutes.

Randall stopped talking, being busy with the traffic in Waukegan. He turned left and headed out of town.

"Teddy—if you are sure that the whole thing was just a hoax and there are no such things as the Sons, then why can't we drop it and head south? We don't need to keep this appointment."

"I'm sure of my explanation all right," he said, skillfully avoiding a suicide-bent boy on a bicycle, "in its broad outlines, but I'm *not* sure of the motivation—and *that's* why I have to see Hoag. Funny thing, though," he continued thoughtfully, "I don't think Hoag has anything against us; I think he had some reasons of his own and paid us five hundred berries to put up with some discomfort while he carried out his plans. But we'll see. Anyhow, it's too late to turn back; there's the filling station he mentioned—and there's Hoag!"

Hoag climbed in with no more than a nod and a smile; Randall felt again the compulsion to do as he was told which had first hit him some two hours before. Hoag told him where to go.

The way lay out in the country and, presently, off the pavement. In due course they came to a farm gate leading into pasture land, which Hoag instructed Randall to open and drive through. "The owner does not mind," he said. "I've been here many times, on my Wednesdays. A beautiful spot."

It *was* a beautiful spot. The road, a wagon track now, led up a gradual rise to a tree-topped crest. Hoag had him park under a tree, and they got out. Cynthia stood for a moment, drinking it in, and savoring deep breaths of the clean air. To the south Chicago could be seen and beyond it and east of it a silver gleam of the lake. "Teddy, isn't it gorgeous?"

"It is," he admitted, but turned to Hoag. "What I want to know is—why are we here?"

"Picnic," said Hoag. "I chose this spot for my finale."

"Finale?"

"Food first," said Hoag. "Then, if you must, we'll talk."

It was a very odd menu for a picnic; in place of hearty foods there were some dozens of gourmets' specialties—preserved cumquats, guava jelly, little potted meats, tea—made by Hoag over a spirit lamp—delicate wafers with a famous name on the package. In spite of this both Randall and Cynthia found themselves eating heartily. Hoag tried everything, never passing up a dish—but Cynthia noticed that he actually ate very little, tasting rather than dining.

In due course Randall got his courage up to brace Hoag; it was beginning to appear that Hoag had no intention of broaching the matter himself. "Hoag?"

"Yes, Ed?"

"Isn't it about time you took off the false face and quit kidding us?"

"I have not kidded you, my friend."

"You know what I mean—this whole rat race that has been going on the past few days. You're mixed up in it and know more about it than we do—that's evident. Mind you, not that I'm accusing you of anything," he added hastily. "But I want to know what it means."

"Ask yourself what it means."

"O.K.," Randall accepted the challenge, "I will." He launched into the explanation which he had sketched out to Cynthia. Hoag encouraged him to continue it fully, but, when he was through, said nothing.

"Well," Randall said nervously, "that's how it happened—wasn't it?"

"It seems like a good explanation."

"I thought so. But you've still got to clear some things up. Why did you do it?"

Hoag shook his head thoughtfully. "I'm sorry, Ed, I cannot possibly explain my motives to you."

"But, damn it, that's not fair! The least you could—"

"When did you ever find fairness, Edward?"

"Well—I expected you to play fair with us. You encouraged us to treat you as a friend. You owe us explanations."

"I promised you explanations. But consider, Ed—do you want explanations? I assure you that you will have no more trouble, no more visitations from the Sons."

Cynthia touched his arm. "Don't ask for them, Teddy!"

He brushed her off, not unkindly but decisively. "I've got to *know.* Let's have the explanation."

"You won't like it."

"I'll chance it."

"Very well." Hoag settled back. "Will you serve the wine, my dear? Thank you. I shall have to tell you a little story first. It will be partly allegorical, as there are not the . . . the words, the concepts. Once there was a race, quite unlike the human race—quite. I have no way of describing to you what they looked like or how they lived, but they had one characteristic you can understand: they were creative. The creating and enjoying of works of art was their occupation and their reason for being. I say 'art' advisedly, for art is undefined, undefinable, and without limits. I can use the word without fear of misusing it, for it has no exact meaning. There are as many meanings as there are artists. But remember that these artists are not human and their art is not human.

"Think of one of this race, in your terms—young. He creates a work of art, under the eye and the guidance of his teacher. He has talent, this one, and his creation has many curious and amusing features. The teacher encourages him to go on with it and prepare it for the judging. Mind you, I am speaking in metaphorical terms, as if this were a human artist, preparing his canvases to be judged in the annual showing."

He stopped and said suddenly to Randall, "Are you a religious man? Did it ever occur to you that all this"—he included the whole quietly beautiful countryside in the sweep of his arm—"might have had a Creator? *Must* have had a Creator?"

Randall stared and turned red. "I'm not exactly a church-going man," he blurted, "but— Yes, I suppose I do believe it."

"And you, Cynthia?"

She nodded, tense and speechless.

"The Artist created this world, after His Own fashion and using postulates which seemed well to Him. His teacher approved on the whole, but—"

"Wait a minute," Randall said insistently. "Are you trying to describe the creation of the world—the Universe?"

"What else?"

"But—damn it, this is preposterous! I asked for an explanation of the things that have just happened to *us.*"

"I told you that you would not like the explanation." He waited for a moment, then continued, "The Sons of the Bird were the dominant feature of the world, at first."

Randall listened to him, feeling that his head would burst. He knew, with sick horror, that the rationalization he had made up on the way to the rendezvous had been sheerest moonshine, thrown together to still the fears that had overcome him. The Sons of the Bird—real, real and horrible—and potent. He felt that he knew now the sort of race of which Hoag spoke. From Cynthia's tense and horrified face she *knew,* also—and there would never again be peace for either of them. "In the Beginning there was the Bird—"

Hoag looked at him with eyes free of malice but without pity. "No," he said serenely, "there was never the Bird. They who call themselves Sons of the Bird there are. But they are stupid and arrogant. Their sacred story is so much superstition. But in their way and by the rules of this world they are powerful. The things, Edward, that you thought you saw you did see."

"You mean that—"

"Wait, let me finish. I must hasten. You saw what you thought you saw, with one exception. Until today you have seen *me* only in your apartment, or mine. The creatures you shadowed, the creature that frightened Cynthia—Sons of the Bird, all of them. Stoles and his friends.

"The teacher did not approve of the Sons of the Bird and suggested certain improvements in the creation. But the Artist was hasty or careless; instead of removing them entirely He merely—painted over them, made them appear to be some of the new creations with which He peopled His world.

"All of which might not have mattered if the work had not been selected for judging. Inevitably the critics noticed them; they were—bad art, and they disfigured the final work. There was some doubt in their minds as to whether or not the creation was worth preserving. That is why I am here."

He stopped, as if there were no more to say. Cynthia looked at him fearfully. "Are you . . . are you—"

He smiled at her. "No, Cynthia, I am not the Creator of your world. You asked me my profession once.

"I am an art critic."

Randall would like to have disbelieved. It was impossible for him to do so; the truth rang in his ears and would not be denied. Hoag continued, "I said to you that I would have to speak to you in terms you use. You must know that to judge a creation such as this, your world, is not like walking up to a painting and looking at it. This world is peopled with *men;* it must be looked at through the eyes of men. I am a man."

Cynthia looked still more troubled. "I don't understand. You act through the body of a man?"

"I *am* a man. Scattered around the human race are the Critics—men. Each is the projection of a Critic, but each is a man—in every way a man, not knowing that he is also a Critic."

Randall seized on the discrepancy as if his reason depended on it—which, perhaps, it did. "But *you* know—or say you do. It's a contradiction."

Hoag nodded, undisturbed. "Until today, when Cynthia's questioning made it inconvenient to continue as I was—and for other reasons—this *persona*"— he tapped his chest—"had no idea of why he was here. He was a man, and no more. Even now, I have extended my present *persona* only as far as is necessary for my purpose. There are questions which I could not answer—as Jonathan Hoag.

"Jonathan Hoag came into being, as a man, for the purpose of examining, *savoring,* certain of the artistic aspects of this world. In the course of that it became convenient to use him to smell out some of the activities of those discarded and painted-over creatures that call themselves the Sons of the Bird. You two happened to be drawn into the activity—innocent and unknowing, like the pigeons used by armies. But it so happened that I observed something else of artistic worth while in contact with you, which is why we are taking the trouble for these explanations."

"What do you mean?"

"Let me speak first of the matters I observed as a critic. Your world has several pleasures. There is eating." He reached out and pulled off from its bunch a muscat grape, fat and sugar-sweet, and ate it appreciatively. "An odd one, that. And very remarkable. No one ever before thought of making an art of the simple business of obtaining the necessary energy. Your Artist has very real talent.

"And there is sleeping. A strange reflexive business in which the Artist's own creations are allowed to create more worlds of their own. You see now, don't you," he said, smiling, "why the critic must be a *man* in truth—else he could not dream as a man does?

"There is drinking—which mixes both eating and dreaming.

"There is the exquisite pleasure of conversing together, friend with friend, as we are doing. That is not new, but it goes to the credit of the Artist that He included it.

"And there is sex. Sex is ridiculous. As a critic I would have disregarded it entirely had not you, my friends, let me see something which had not come to the attention of Jonathan Hoag, something which, in my own artistic creations, I had never had the wit to invent. As I said, your Artist has talent." He looked at them almost tenderly. "Tell me, Cynthia, what do you love in this world and what is it that you hate and fear?"

She made no attempt to answer him, but crept closer to her husband. Randall put a protecting arm around her. Hoag spoke then to Randall. "And you, Edward? Is there something in this world for which you'd surrender your life and your soul, if need be? You need not answer—I saw in your face and in your heart, last night, as you bent over the bed. Good art, good art—both of you. I have found several sorts of good and original art in this world, enough to justify encouraging your Artist to try again. But there was so much that was bad, poorly drawn and amateurish, that I could not find it in me to approve the work as a whole until I encountered and savored this, the tragedy of human love."

Cynthia looked at him wildly. "Tragedy? You say 'tragedy'?"

He looked at her with eyes that were not pitying, but serenely appreciative. "What else could it be, my dear?"

She stared at him, then turned and buried her face on the lapel of her husband's coat. Randall patted her head. "Stop it, Hoag!" he said savagely. "You've frightened her again."

"I did not wish to."

"You have. And I can tell you what I think of your story. It's got holes in it you can throw a cat through. You made it up."

"You do not believe that."

It was true; Randall did not. But he went on bravely, his hand still soothing his wife. "The stuff under your nails—how about that? I notice you left that out. And your fingerprints."

"The stuff under my nails has little to do with the story. It served its purpose, which was to make fearful the Sons of the Bird. They knew what it was."

"But what was it?"

"The ichor of the Sons—planted there by my other *persona*. But what is this about fingerprints? Jonathan Hoag was honestly fearful of having them taken; Jonathan Hoag is a man, Edward. You must remember that."

Randall told him; Hoag nodded. "I see. Truthfully I do not recall it, even today, although my full *persona* knows of it. Jonathan Hoag had a nervous habit of polishing things with his handkerchief; perhaps he polished the arm of your chair."

"I don't remember it."

"Nor do I."

Randall took up the fight again. "That isn't all and that isn't half of it. What about the rest home you said you were in? And who pays you? Where do you get your money? Why was Cynthia always so darned scared of you?"

Hoag looked out toward the city; a fog was rolling in from the lake. "There is little time for these things," he said, "and it does not matter, even to you, whether you believe or not. But you do believe—you cannot help it. But you have brought up another matter. Here." He pulled a thick roll of bills from his pocket and handed them to Randall. "You might as well take them with you; I shall have no more use for them. I shall be leaving you in a few minutes."

"Where are you going?"

"Back to myself. After I leave, you must do this: Get into your car and drive at once, south, through the city. *Under no circumstances* open a window of your car until you are miles away from the city."

"Why? I don't like this."

"Nevertheless, do it. There will be certain—changes, readjustments going on."

"What do you mean?"

"I told you, did I not, that the Sons of the Bird are being dealt with? They, and all their works."

"How?"

Hoag did not answer, but stared again at the fog. It was creeping up on the city. "I think I must go now. Do as I have told you to do." He started to turn away. Cynthia lifted up her face and spoke to him.

"Don't go! Not yet."

"Yes, my dear?"

"You must tell me one thing: *Will Teddy and I be together?*"

He looked into her eyes and said, "I see what you mean. I don't know."

"But you *must* know!"

"I do not know. If you are both creatures of this world, then your patterns may run alike. But there are the Critics, you know."

"The Critics? What have *they* to do with *us?*"

"One, or the other, or both of you may *be* Critics. I would not know. Remember, the Critics are men—here. I did not even know myself as one until today." He looked at Randall meditatively. "*He* may be one. I suspected it once today."

"Am—I?"

"I have no way of knowing. It is most unlikely. You see, we can't know each other, for it would spoil our artistic judgment."

"But . . . but . . . if we *are* not the same, then—"

"That is all." He said it, not emphatically, but with such a sound of finality that they were both startled. He bent over the remains of the feast and selected one more grape, ate it, and closed his eyes.

He did not open them. Presently Randall said, "Mr. Hoag?" No answer. "Mr. Hoag!" Still no answer. He separated himself from Cynthia, stood up, and went around to where the quiet figure sat. He shook him. "Mr. Hoag!"

"But we can't just leave him there!" Randall insisted, some minutes later.

"Teddy, he knew what he was doing. The thing for us to do is to follow his instructions."

"Well—we can stop in Waukegan and notify the police."

"Tell them we left a dead man back there on a hillside? Do you think they would say, 'Fine,' and let us drive on? No, Teddy—just what he told us to do."

"Honey—you don't believe all that stuff he was telling us, do you?"

She looked him in the eyes, her own eyes welling with tears, and said, "Do you? Be honest with me, Teddy."

He met her gaze for a moment, then dropped his eyes and said, "Oh, never mind! We'll do what he said. Get in the car."

The fog which appeared to have engulfed the city was not visible when they got down the hill and had started back toward Waukegan, nor did they see it again after they had turned south and drove toward the city. The day was bright and sunny, as it had started to be that morning, with just enough nip in the air to make Hoag's injunction about keeping the windows rolled up tight seem like good sense.

They took the lake route south, skipping the Loop thereby, with the intention of continuing due south until well out of the city. The traffic had thickened somewhat over what it had been when they started out in the middle of the morning; Randall was forced to give his attention to the wheel. Neither of them felt like talking and it gave an excuse not to.

They had left the Loop area behind them when Randall spoke up, "Cynthia—"

"Yes."

"We ought to tell somebody. I'm going to ask the next cop we see to call the Waukegan station."

"Teddy!"

"Don't worry. I'll give him some stall that will make them investigate without making them suspicious of us. The old run-around—you know."

She knew his powers of invention were fertile enough to do such a job; she protested no more. A few blocks later Randall saw a patrolman standing on the sidewalk, warming himself in the sun, and watching some boys playing sand-lot football. He pulled up to the curb beside him. "Run down the window, Cyn."

She complied, then gave a sharp intake of breath and swallowed a scream. He did not scream, but he wanted to.

Outside the open window was no sunlight, no cops, no kids—nothing. Nothing but a gray and formless mist, pulsing slowly as if with inchoate life. They could see nothing of the city through it, not because it was too dense but because it was—empty. No sound came out of it; no movement showed in it.

It merged with the frame of the window and began to drift inside. Randall shouted, "Roll up the window!" She tried to obey, but her hands were nerveless; he reached across her and cranked it up himself, jamming it hard into its seat.

The sunny scene was restored; through the glass they saw the patrolman, the boisterous game, the sidewalk, and the city beyond. Cynthia put a hand on his arm. "Drive on, Teddy!"

"Wait a minute," he said tensely, and turned to the window beside him. Very cautiously he rolled it down—just a crack, less than an inch.

It was enough. The formless gray flux was out there, too; through the glass the city traffic and sunny street were plain, through the opening—nothing.

"Drive on, Teddy—*please!*"

She need not have urged him; he was already gunning the car ahead with a jerk.

THEIR HOUSE IS NOT EXACTLY on the Gulf, but the water can be seen from the hilltop near it. The village where they do their shopping has only eight hundred people in it, but it seems to be enough for them. They do not care much for company, anyway, except their own. They get a lot of that. When he goes out to the vegetable patch, or to the fields, she goes along, taking with her such woman's work as she can carry and do in her lap. If they go to town, they go together, hand in hand—always.

He wears a beard, but it is not so much a peculiarity as a necessity, for there is not a mirror in the entire house. They do have one peculiarity which would mark them as odd in any community, if anyone knew about it, but it is of such a nature that no one else *would* know.

When they go to bed at night, before he turns out the light, he handcuffs one of his wrists to one of hers.

# Our Fair City

*Pete Perkins turned into the* All-Nite parking lot and called out, "Hi, Pappy!"

The old parking lot attendant looked up and answered, "Be with you in a moment, Pete." He was tearing a Sunday comic sheet in narrow strips. A little whirlwind waltzed near him, picking up pieces of old newspaper and bits of dirt and flinging them in the faces of passing pedestrians. The old man held out to it a long streamer of the brightly colored funny-paper. "Here, Kitten," he coaxed. "Come, Kitten—"

The whirlwind hesitated, then drew itself up until it was quite tall, jumped two parked cars, and landed *sur le point* near him.

It seemed to sniff at the offering.

"Take it, Kitten," the old man called softly and let the gay streamer slip from his fingers. The whirlwind whipped it up and wound it around its middle. He tore off another and yet another; the whirlwind wound them in a corkscrew through the loose mass of dirty paper and trash that constituted its visible body. Renewed by cold gusts that poured down the canyon of tall buildings, it swirled faster and ever taller, while it lifted the colored paper ribbons in a fantastic upswept hairdo. The old man turned, smiling. "Kitten does like new clothes."

"Take it easy, Pappy, or you'll have me believing in it."

"Eh? You don't have to believe in Kitten—you can *see* her."

"Yeah, sure—but you act as if she—I mean 'it'—could understand what you say."

"You still don't think so?" His voice was gently tolerant.

"Now, Pappy!"

"Hmmm . . . lend me your hat." Pappy reached up and took it.

"Here, Kitten," he called. "Come back, Kitten!" The whirlwind was playing around over their heads, several stories high. It dipped down.

"Hey! Where you going with that chapeau?" demanded Perkins.

"Just a moment— Here, Kitten!" The whirlwind sat down suddenly, spilling its load. The old man handed it the hat. The whirlwind snatched it and started it up a fast, long spiral.

"Hey!" yelped Perkins. "What do you think you're doing? That's not funny—that hat cost me six bucks only three years ago."

"Don't worry," the old man soothed. "Kitten will bring it back."

"She will, huh? More likely she'll dump it in the river."

"Oh, no! Kitten never drops anything she doesn't want to drop. Watch." The old man looked up to where the hat was dancing near the penthouse of the hotel across the street. "Kitten! Oh, Kitten! Bring it back."

The whirlwind hesitated, the hat fell a couple of stories. It swooped, caught it, and juggled it reluctantly. "Bring it *here*, Kitten."

The hat commenced a downward spiral, finishing in a long curving swoop. It hit Perkins full in the face. "She was trying to put it on your head," the attendant explained. "Usually she's more accurate."

"She is, eh?" Perkins picked up his hat and stood looking at the whirlwind, mouth open.

"Convinced?" asked the old man.

"'Convinced?' Oh, sho' sho'." He looked back at his hat, then again at the whirlwind. "Pappy, this calls for a drink."

They went inside the lot's little shelter shack; Pappy found glasses; Perkins produced a pint, nearly full, and poured two generous slugs. He tossed his down, poured another, and sat down. "The first was in honor of Kitten," he announced. "This one is to fortify me for the Mayor's banquet."

Pappy cluck-clucked sympathetically. "You have to cover that?"

"Have to write a column about *something*, Pappy. 'Last night Hizzoner the Mayor, surrounded by a glittering galaxy of highbinders, grifters, sycophants, and ballot thieves, was the recipient of a testimonial dinner celebrating—' Got to write something, Pappy; the cash customers expect it. Why don't I brace up like a man and go on relief?"

"Today's column was good, Pete," the old man comforted him. He picked up a copy of the *Daily Forum*; Perkins took it from him and ran his eye down his own column.

"OUR FAIR CITY, by Peter Perkins," he read, and below that "What, No Horsecars? It is the tradition of our civic paradise that what was good enough for the founding fathers is good enough for us. We stumble over the very chuckhole in which Great-uncle Tozier broke his leg in '09. It is good to know that the bath water, running out, is not gone forever, but will return through the kitchen faucet, thicker and disguised with chlorine, but the same. (Memo—Hizzoner uses bottled spring water. Must look into this.)

"But I must report a dismaying change. Someone has done away with the horsecars!

"You may not believe this. Our public conveyances run so seldom and slowly that you may not have noticed it; nevertheless I swear that I saw one wobbling down Grand Avenue with no horses of any sort. It seemed to be propelled by some new-fangled electrical device.

"Even in the atomic age some changes are too much. I urge all citizens—" Perkins gave a snort of disgust. "It's tackling a pillbox with a beanshooter, Pappy. This town is corrupt; it'll stay corrupt. Why should I beat out my brains on such piffle? Hand me the bottle."

"Don't be discouraged, Pete. The tyrant fears the laugh more than the assassin's bullet."

"Where'd you pick that up? Okay, so I'm not funny. I've tried laughing them out of office and it hasn't worked. My efforts are as pointless as the activities of your friend the whirling dervish."

The windows rattled under a gusty impact. "Don't talk that way about Kitten," the old man cautioned. "She's sensitive."

"I apologize." He stood up and bowed toward the door. "Kitten, I apologize. Your activities are *more* useful than mine." He turned to his host. "Let's go out and talk to her, Pappy. I'd rather do that than go to the Mayor's banquet, if I had my druthers."

They went outside, Perkins bearing with him the remains of the colored comic sheet. He began tearing off streamers. "Here, Kitty! Here, Kitty! Soup's on!"

The whirlwind bent down and accepted the strips as fast as he tore them. "She's still got the ones you gave her."

"Certainly," agreed Pappy. "Kitten is a pack rat. When she likes something she'll keep it indefinitely."

"Doesn't she ever get tired? There must be some calm days."

"It's never really calm here. It's the arrangement of the buildings and the way Third Street leads up from the river. But I think she hides her pet playthings on tops of buildings."

The newspaperman peered into the swirling trash. "I'll bet she's got newspapers from months back. Say, Pappy, I see a column in this, one about our trash collection service and how we don't clean our streets.

I'll dig up some papers a couple of years old and claim that they have been blowing around town since publication."

"Why fake it?" answered Pappy, "Let's see what Kitten has." He whistled softly. "Come, baby—let Pappy see your playthings." The whirlwind bulged out; its contents moved less rapidly. The attendant plucked a piece of old newspaper from it in passing. "Here's one three months old."

"We'll have to do better than that."

"I'll try again." He reached out and snatched another. "Last June."

"That's better."

A car honked for service and the old man hurried away. When he returned Perkins was still watching the hovering column. "Any luck?" asked Pappy.

"She won't let me have them. Snatches them away."

"Naughty Kitten," the old man said. "Pete is a friend of ours. You be nice to him." The whirlwind fidgeted uncertainly.

"It's all right," said Perkins. "She didn't know. But look, Pappy—see that piece up there? A front page."

"You want it?"

"Yes. Look closely—the headline reads 'DEWEY' something. You don't suppose she's been hoarding it since the '48 campaign?"

"Could be. Kitten has been around here as long as I can remember. And she does hoard things. Wait a second." He called out softly. Shortly the paper was in his hands. "Now we'll see."

Perkins peered at it. "I'll be a short-term Senator! Can you top that, Pappy?"

The headline read: DEWEY CAPTURES MANILA: the date was "1898".

TWENTY MINUTES LATER THEY WERE still considering it over the last of Perkins' bottle. The newspaperman stared at the yellowed, filthy sheet. "Don't tell me this has been blowing around town for the last half century."

"Why not?"

"'Why not?' Well, I'll concede that the streets haven't been cleaned in that time, but this paper wouldn't last. Sun and rain and so forth."

"Kitten is very careful of her toys. She probably put it under cover during bad weather."

"For the love of Mike, Pappy, you don't really believe—But you do. Frankly, I don't care where she got it; the official theory is going to be that this particular piece of paper has been kicking around our dirty streets, unnoticed and uncollected, for the past fifty years. Boy, am I going to have fun!" He rolled the fragment carefully and started to put it in his pocket.

"Say, don't do that!" his host protested.

"Why not? I'm going to take it down and get a pic of it."

"You mustn't! It belongs to Kitten—I just borrowed it."

"Huh? Are you nuts?"

"She'll be upset if she doesn't get it back. Please, Pete—she'll let you look at it any time you want to."

The old man was so earnest that Perkins was stopped. "Suppose we never see it again? My story hangs on it."

"It's no good to *you—she* has to keep it, to make your story stand up. Don't worry—I'll tell her that she mustn't lose it under any circumstances."

"Well—okay." They stepped outside and Pappy talked earnestly to Kitten, then gave her the 1898 fragment. She promptly tucked it into the top of her column. Perkins said good-bye to Pappy, and started to leave the lot. He paused and turned around, looking a little befuddled. "Say, Pappy—"

"Yes, Pete?"

"You don't really think that whirlwind is alive, do you?"

"Why not?"

"'Why not?' Why not, the man says?"

"Well," said Pappy reasonably, "how do you know *you* are alive?"

"But . . . why, because I—well, now if you put it—" He stopped. "I don't know. You got me, pal."

Pappy smiled. "You see?"

"Uh, I guess so. G'night, Pappy. G'night, Kitten." He tipped his hat to the whirlwind. The column bowed.

THE MANAGING EDITOR SENT FOR Perkins.

"Look, Pete," he said, chucking a sheaf of grey copy paper at him, "whimsy is all right, but I'd like to see some copy that wasn't dashed off in a gin mill."

Perkins looked over the pages shoved at him. "OUR FAIR CITY by Peter Perkins. Whistle Up The Wind. Walking our streets always is a piquant, even adventurous, experience. We pick our way through the assorted trash, bits of old garbage, cigarette butts, and other less appetizing items that stud our sidewalks while our faces are assaulted by more buoyant souvenirs, the confetti of last Hallowe'en, shreds of dead leaves, and other items too weather-beaten to be identified. However, I had always assumed that a constant turnover in the riches of our streets caused them to renew themselves at least every seven years—" The column then told of the whirlwind that contained the fifty-year-old newspaper and challenged any other city in the country to match it.

"'Smatter with it?" demanded Perkins.

"Beating the drum about the filth in the streets is fine, Pete, but give it a factual approach."

Perkins leaned over the desk. "Boss, this *is* factual."

"Huh? Don't be silly, Pete."

"Silly, he says. Look—" Perkins gave him a circumstantial account of Kitten and the 1898 newspaper.

"Pete, you must have been drinking."

"Only Java and tomato juice. Cross my heart and hope to die."

"How about yesterday? I'll bet the whirlwind came right up to the bar with you."

"I was cold, stone—" Perkins stopped himself and stood on his dignity. "That's my story. Print it, or fire me."

"Don't be like that, Pete. I don't want your job; I just want a column with some meat. Dig up some facts on man-hours and costs for street cleaning, compared with other cities."

"Who'd read that junk? Come down the street with me. I'll *show* you the facts. Wait a moment—I'll pick up a photographer."

A few minutes later Perkins was introducing the managing editor and Clarence V. Weems to Pappy. Clarence unlimbered his camera. "Take a pic of him?"

"Not yet, Clarence. Pappy, can you get Kitten to give us back the museum piece?"

"Why, sure." The old man looked up and whistled. "Oh, Kitten! Come to Pappy." Above their heads a tiny gust took shape, picked up bits of paper and stray leaves, and settled on the lot. Perkins peered into it.

"She hasn't got it," he said in aggrieved tones.

"She'll get it." Pappy stepped forward until the whirlwind enfolded him. They could see his lips move, but the words did not reach them.

"Now?" said Clarence.

"Not yet." The whirlwind bounded up and leapt over an adjoining building. The managing editor opened his mouth, closed it again.

Kitten was soon back. She had dropped everything else and had just one piece of paper—*the* paper. "Now!" said Perkins. "Can you get a shot of that paper, Clarence—while it's in the air?"

"Natch," said Clarence, and raised his Speed Graphic. "Back a little, and hold it," he ordered, speaking to the whirlwind.

Kitten hesitated and seemed about to skitter away. "Bring it around slow and easy, Kitten," Pappy supplemented, "and turn it over—no, no! Not that way—the other edge up." The paper flattened out and sailed slowly past them, the headline showing.

"Did you get it?" Perkins demanded.

"Natch," said Clarence. "Is that all?" he asked the editor.

"Natc—I mean, 'that's all'."

"Okay," said Clarence, picked up his case, and left.

The editor sighed. "Gentlemen," he said, "let's have a drink."

Four drinks later Perkins and his boss were still arguing. Pappy had left. "Be reasonable, Boss," Pete was saying, "you can't print an item about a live whirlwind. They'd laugh you out of town."

Managing Editor Gaines straightened himself.

"It's the policy of the *Forum* to print all the news, and print it straight. This is news—we print it." He relaxed. "Hey! Waiter! More of the same—and not so much soda."

"But it's scientifically impossible."

"You saw it, didn't you?"

"Yes, but—"

Gaines stopped him. "We'll ask the Smithsonian Institution to investigate it."

"They'll laugh at you," Perkins insisted. "Ever hear of mass hypnotism?"

"Huh? No, that's no explanation—Clarence saw it, too."

"What does that prove?"

"Obvious—to be hypnotized you have to have a mind. *Ipso facto.*"

"You mean *Ipse dixit.*"

"Quit hiccuping. Perkins, you shouldn't drink in the daytime. Now start over and say it slowly."

"How do you know Clarence doesn't have a mind?"

"Prove it."

"Well, he's alive—he must have some sort of a mind, then."

"That's just what I was saying, The whirlwind is alive; therefore it has a mind. Perkins, if those longbeards from the Smithsonian are going to persist in their unscientific attitude, I for one will not stand for it. The *Forum* will not stand for it. You will not stand for it."

"Won't I?"

"Not for one minute. I want you to know the *Forum* is behind you, Pete. You go back to the parking lot and get an interview with that whirlwind."

"But I've got one. You wouldn't let me print it."

"Who wouldn't let you print it? I'll fire him! Come on, Pete. We're going to blow this town sky high. Stop the run. Hold the front page.

Get busy!" He put on Pete's hat and strode rapidly into the men's room.

PETE SETTLED HIMSELF AT HIS desk with a container of coffee, a can of tomato juice, and the Midnight Final (late afternoon) edition. Under a 4-col. cut of Kitten's toy was his column, boxed and moved to the front page. 18-point boldface ordered SEE EDITORIAL PAGE 12. On page 12 another black line enjoined him to SEE "OUR FAIR CITY" PAGE ONE. He ignored this and read: MR. MAYOR—RESIGN!!!!

Pete read it and chuckled. "An ill wind—" "—symbolic of the spiritual filth lurking in the dark corners of the city hall." "—will grow to cyclonic proportions and sweep a corrupt and shameless administration from office." The editorial pointed out that the contract for street cleaning and trash removal was held by the Mayor's brother-in-law, and then suggested that the whirlwind could give better service cheaper.

The telephone jingled. He picked it up and said, "Okay—you started it."

"Pete—is that you?" Pappy's voice demanded. "They got me down at the station house."

"What for?"

"They claim Kitten is a public nuisance."

"I'll be right over." He stopped by the Art Department, snagged Clarence, and left. Pappy was seated in the station lieutenant's office, looking stubborn. Perkins shoved his way in. "What's he here for?" he demanded, jerking a thumb at Pappy.

The lieutenant looked sour. "What are you butting in for, Perkins? You're not his lawyer."

"Now?" said Clarence.

"Not yet, Clarence. For news, Dumbrosky,—I work for a newspaper, remember? I repeat—what's he in for?"

"Obstructing an officer in the performance of his duty."

"That right, Pappy?"

The old man looked disgusted. "This character—" He indicated one of the policemen "—comes up to my lot and tries to snatch the Manila-Bay paper away from Kitten. I tell her to keep it up out of his way. Then he waves his stick at me and orders me to take it away from her. I tell him what he can do with his stick." He shrugged. "So here we are."

"I get it," Perkins told him, and turned to Dumbrosky. "You got a call from the city hall, didn't you? So you sent Dugan down to do the dirty work. What I don't get is why you sent Dugan. I hear he's so dumb you don't even let him collect the pay-off on his own beat."

"That's a lie!" put in Dugan. "I do so—"

"Shut up, Dugan!" his boss thundered. "Now, see here, Perkins—you clear out. There ain't no story here."

"'No story'?" Perkins said softly. "The police force tries to arrest a whirlwind and you say there's no story?"

"Now?" said Clarence.

"Nobody tried to arrest no whirlwind. Now scram."

"Then how come you're charging Pappy with obstructing an officer? What was Dugan doing—flying a kite?"

"He's not charged with obstructing an officer."

"He's not, eh? Just what have you booked him for?"

"He's not booked. We're holding him for questioning."

"So? Not booked, no warrant, no crime alleged, just pick up a citizen and roust him around, Gestapo style." Perkins turned to Pappy. "You're not under arrest. My advice is to get up and walk out that door."

Pappy started to get up. "Hey!" Lieutenant Dumbrosky bounded out of his chair, grabbed Pappy by the shoulder and pushed him down. "I'm giving the orders around here. You stay—"

"*Now!*" yelled Perkins. Clarence's flashbulb froze them. Then Dumbrosky started up again.

"Who let him in here? Dugan—get that camera."

"*Nyannh!*" said Clarence and held it away from the cop. They started doing a little Maypole dance, with Clarence as the Maypole.

"Hold it!" yelled Perkins. "Go ahead and grab the camera, Dugan—I'm just aching to write the story. Police Lieutenant Destroys Evidence of Police Brutality.'"

"What do you want I should do, Lieutenant?" pleaded Dugan.

Dumbrosky looked disgusted. "Siddown and close your face. Don't use that picture, Perkins—I'm warning you."

"Of what? Going to make me dance with Dugan? Come on, Pappy. Come on, Clarence." They left.

"OUR FAIR CITY" read the next day. "City Hall Starts Clean Up. While the city street cleaners were enjoying their usual siesta, Lieutenant Dumbrosky, acting on orders of Hizzoner's office, raided our Third Avenue whirlwind. It went sour, as Patrolman Dugan could not entice the whirlwind into the paddy wagon. Dauntless Dugan was undeterred; he took a citizen standing nearby, one James Metcalfe, parking lot attendant, into custody as an accomplice of the whirlwind. An accomplice in what, Dugan didn't say—everybody knows that an accomplice is something pretty awful. Lieutenant Dumbrosky questioned the accomplice. See cut. Lieutenant Dumbrosky weighs 215 pounds, without his shoes. The accomplice weighs 119.

"Moral: Don't get underfoot when the police department is playing games with the wind.

"P.S. As we go to press, the whirlwind is still holding the 1898 museum piece. Stop by Third and Main and take a look. Better hurry—Dumbrosky is expected to make an arrest momentarily."

Pete's column continued needling the administration the following day: "Those Missing Files. It is annoying to know that any document needed by the Grand Jury is sure to be mislaid before it can be introduced in evidence. We suggest that Kitten, our Third Avenue Whirlwind, be hired by the city as file clerk extraordinary and entrusted with any item which is likely to be needed later. She could take the special civil exam used to reward the faithful—the one nobody ever flunks.

"Indeed, why limit Kitten to a lowly clerical job? She is persistent—and she hangs on to what she gets. No one will argue that she is less qualified than some city officials we have had.

"Let's run Kitten for Mayor! She's an ideal candidate—she has the common touch, she doesn't mind hurly-burly, she runs around in circles, she knows how to throw dirt, and the opposition can't pin anything on her.

"As to the sort of Mayor she would make, there is an old story—Aesop told it—about King Log and King Stork. We're fed up with King Stork; King Log would be welcome relief.

"Memo to Hizzoner—what *did* become of those Grand Avenue paving bids?

"P.S. Kitten still has the 1898 newspaper on exhibit. Stop by and see it before our police department figures out some way to intimidate a whirlwind."

Pete snagged Clarence and drifted down to the parking lot. The lot was fenced now; a man at a gate handed them two tickets but waved away their money. Inside he found a large circle chained off for Kitten and Pappy inside it. They pushed their way through the crowd to the old man. "Looks like you're coining money, Pappy."

"Should be, but I'm not. They tried to close me up this morning, Pete. Wanted me to pay the $50-a-day circus-and-carnival fee and post a bond besides. So I quit charging for the tickets—but I'm keeping track of them. I'll sue 'em, by gee."

"You won't collect, not in this town. Never mind, we'll make 'em squirm till they let up."

"That's not all. They tried to capture Kitten this morning."

"Huh? Who? How?"

"The cops. They showed up with one of those blower machines used to ventilate manholes, rigged to run backwards and take a suction. The idea was to suck Kitten down into it, or anyhow to grab what she was carrying."

Pete whistled. "You should have called me."

"Wasn't necessary. I warned Kitten and she stashed the Spanish-War paper someplace, then came back. She loved it. She went through that machine about six times, like a merry-go-round. She'd zip through and come out more full of pep than ever. Last time through she took Sergeant Yancel's cap with her and it clogged the machine and ruined his cap. They got disgusted and left."

Pete chortled. "You still should have called me. Clarence should have gotten a picture of that."

"Got it," said Clarence.

"Huh? I didn't know you were here this morning, Clarence."

"You didn't ask me."

Pete looked at him. "Clarence, darling—the idea of a news picture is to print it, not to hide it in the art department."

"On your desk," said Clarence.

"Oh. Well, let's move on to a less confusing subject. Pappy, I'd like to put up a big sign here."

"Why not? What do you want to say?"

"Kitten-for-Mayor—Whirlwind Campaign Headquarters. Stick a 24-sheet across the corner of the lot, where they can see it both ways. It fits in with—oh, oh! Company, girls!" He jerked his head toward the entrance.

Sergeant Yancel was back. "All right, all right!" he was saying. "Move on! Clear out of here." He and three cohorts were urging the spectators out of the lot. Pete went to him.

"What goes on, Yancel?"

Yancel looked around. "Oh, it's you, huh? Well, you, too—we got to clear this place out. Emergency."

Pete looked back over his shoulder. "Better get Kitten out of the way, Pappy!" he called out. "*Now,* Clarence."

"Got it," said Clarence.

"Okay," Pete answered. "Now, Yancel, you might tell me what it is we just took a picture of, so we can title it properly."

"Smart guy. You and your stooge had better scram if you don't want your heads blown off. We're setting up a bazooka."

"You're setting up a *what?*" Pete looked toward the squad car, unbelievingly. Sure enough, two of the cops were unloading a bazooka. "Keep shooting, kid," he said to Clarence.

"Natch," said Clarence.

"And quit popping your bubble gum. Now, look, Yancel—I'm just a newsboy. What in the world is the idea?"

"Stick around and find out, wise guy." Yancel turned away. "Okay there! Start doing it—commence firing!"

One of the cops looked up. "At what, Sergeant?"

"I thought you used to be a marine—at the whirlwind, of course."

Pappy leaned over Pete's shoulder. "What are they doing?"

"I'm beginning to get a glimmering. Pappy, keep Kitten out of range—I think they mean to put a rocket shell through her gizzard. It might bust up her dynamic stability or something."

"Kitten's safe. I told her to hide. But this is crazy, Pete. They must be absolute, complete and teetotal nuts."

"Any law says a cop has to be sane to be on the force?"

"What whirlwind, Sergeant?" the bazooka man was asking. Yancel started to tell him, forcefully, then deflated when he realized that no whirlwind was available.

"You wait," he told him, and turned to Pappy. "You!" he yelled. "You chased away that whirlwind. Get it back here."

Pete took out his notebook. "This is interesting, Yancel. Is it your professional opinion that a whirlwind can be ordered around like a trained dog? Is that the official position of the police department?"

"I— No comment! You button up, or I'll run you in."

"By all means. But you have that Buck-Rogers cannon pointed so that, after the shell passes through the whirlwind, if any, it should end up just about at the city hall. Is this a plot to assassinate Hizzoner?"

Yancel looked around suddenly, then let his gaze travel an imaginary trajectory.

"Hey, you lugs!" he shouted. "Point that thing the other way. You want to knock off the Mayor?"

"That's better," Pete told the Sergeant. "Now they have it trained on the First National Bank. I can't wait."

Yancel looked over the situation again. "Point it where it won't hurt nobody," he ordered. "Do I have to do all your thinking?"

"But, Sergeant—"

"Well?"

"You *point* it. We'll fire it."

Pete watched them. "Clarence," he sighed, "you stick around and get a pic of them loading it back into the car. That will be in about five minutes. Pappy and I will be in the Happy Hour Bar-Grill. Get a nice picture, with Yancel's features."

"Natch," said Clarence.

The next installment of OUR FAIR CITY featured three cuts and was headed. "Police Declare War on Whirlwind." Pete took a copy and set out for the parking lot, intending to show it to Pappy.

Pappy wasn't there. Nor was Kitten. He looked around the neighborhood, poking his nose in lunchrooms and bars. No luck.

He headed back toward the *Forum* building, telling himself that Pappy might be shopping, or at a movie. He returned to his desk, made a couple of false starts on a column for the morrow, crumpled them up and went to the art department. "Hey! Clarence! Have you been down to the parking lot today?"

"Nah."

"Pappy's missing."

"So what?"

"Well, come along. We got to find him."

"Why?" But he came, lugging his camera.

The lot was still deserted, no Pappy, no Kitten—not even a stray breeze. Pete turned away. "Come on, Clarence—say, what are you shooting now?"

Clarence had his camera turned up toward the sky. "Not shooting," said Clarence. "Light is no good."

"What was it?"

"Whirlwind."

"Huh? Kitten?"

"Maybe."

"Here, Kitten—come, Kitten." The whirlwind came back near him, spun faster, and picked up a piece of cardboard it had dropped. It whipped it around, then let him have it in the face.

"That's not funny, Kitten," Pete complained. "Where's Pappy?"

The whirlwind sidled back toward him. He saw it reach again for the cardboard. "No, you don't!" he yelped and reached for it, too.

The whirlwind beat him to it. It carried it up some hundred feet and sailed it back. The card caught him edgewise on the bridge of the nose. "Kitten!" Pete yelled. "Quit the horsing around."

It was a printed notice, about six by eight inches. Evidently it had been tacked up; there were small tears at all four corners. It read: "THE RITZ-CLASSIC" and under that, "Room 2013, Single Occupancy $6.00, Double Occupancy $8.00." There followed a printed list of the house rules.

Pete stared at it and frowned. Suddenly he chucked it back at the whirlwind. Kitten immediately tossed it back in his face.

"Come on, Clarence," he said briskly. "We're going to the Ritz-Classic—room 2013."

"Natch," said Clarence.

The Ritz-Classic was a colossal fleabag, favored by the bookie-and-madame set, three blocks away. Pete avoided the desk by using the basement entrance. The elevator boy looked at Clarence's camera and said, "No, you don't, Doc. No divorce cases in this hotel."

"Relax," Pete told him. "That's not a real camera. We peddle marijuana—that's the hay mow."

"Whyn't you say so? You hadn't ought to carry it in a camera. You make people nervous. What floor?"

"Twenty-one."

The elevator operator took them up non-stop, ignoring other calls. "That'll be two bucks. Special service."

"What do you pay for the concession?" inquired Pete.

"You gotta nerve to beef—with your racket."

They went back down a floor by stair and looked up room 2013. Pete tried the knob cautiously; the door was locked. He knocked on it—no answer. He pressed an ear to it and thought he could hear movement inside. He stepped back, frowning.

Clarence said, "I just remember something," and trotted away. He returned quickly, with a red fire ax. "Now?" he asked Pete.

"A lovely thought, Clarence! Not yet." Pete pounded and yelled, "Pappy! Oh, Pappy!"

A large woman in a pink coolie coat opened the door behind them. "How do you expect a party to sleep?" she demanded.

Pete said, "Quiet, madame! We're on the air." He listened. This time there were sounds of struggling and then, "Pete! Pe—"

"*Now!*" said Pete. Clarence started swinging.

The lock gave up on the third swing. Pete poured in, with Clarence after him. He collided with someone coming out and sat down abruptly. When he got up he saw Pappy on a bed. The old man was busily trying to get rid of a towel tied around his mouth.

Pete snatched it away. "Get 'em!" yelled Pappy.

"Soon as I get you untied."

"I ain't tied. They took my pants. Boy, I thought you'd never come!"

"Took Kitten a while to make me understand."

"I got 'em," announced Clarence. "Both of 'em."

"Where?" demanded Pete.

"Here," said Clarence proudly, and patted his camera.

Pete restrained his answer and ran to the door. "They went that-away," said the large woman, pointing. He took out, skidded around the corner and saw an elevator door just closing.

Pete stopped, bewildered by the crowd just outside the hotel. He was looking uncertainly around when Pappy grabbed him. "There! That car!" The car Pappy pointed out was even then swinging out from the curb just beyond the rank of cabs in front of the hotel; with a deep growl it picked up speed, and headed away. Pete yanked open the door of the nearest cab.

"Follow that car!" he yelled. They all piled in.

"Why?" asked the hackie.

Clarence lifted the fire ax. "Now?" he asked.

The driver ducked. "Forget it," he said. "It was just a yak." He started after the car.

The hack driver's skill helped them in the downtown streets, but the driver of the other car swung right on Third and headed for the river. They streamed across it, fifty yards apart, with traffic snarled behind them, and then were on the no-speed-limit freeway. The cabbie turned his head. "Is the camera truck keeping up?"

"What camera truck?"

"Ain't this a movie?"

"Good grief, no! That car is filled with kidnappers. Faster!"

"A snatch? I don't want no part of it." He braked suddenly.

Pete took the ax and prodded the driver. "You catch 'em!"

The hack speeded up again but the driver protested, "Not in this wreck. They got more power than me."

Pappy grabbed Pete's arm. "There's Kitten!"

"Where? Oh, never mind that now!"

"Slow down!" yelled Pappy. "Kitten, oh, Kitten—over here!"

The whirlwind swooped down and kept pace with them. Pappy called to it. "Here, baby! Go get that car! Up ahead—*get it!*"

Kitten seemed confused, uncertain. Pappy repeated it and she took off—like a whirlwind. She dipped and gathered a load of paper and trash as she flew.

They saw her dip and strike the car ahead, throwing paper in the face of the driver. The car wobbled. She struck again. The car veered, climbed the curb, ricocheted against the crash rail, and fetched up against a lamp post.

FIVE MINUTES LATER PETE, HAVING left Kitten, Clarence, and the fire ax to hold the fort over two hoodlums suffering from abrasion, multiple contusions and shock, was feeding a dime into a pay phone at the nearest filling station. He dialed long distance. "Gimme the FBI's kidnap number," he demanded. "You know—the Washington, D.C., snatch number."

"My goodness," said the operator, "do you mind if I listen in?"

"Get me that number!"

"Right away!"

Presently a voice answered, "Federal Bureau of Investigation."

"Lemme talk to Hoover! Huh? Okay, okay—I'll talk to you. Listen this is a snatch case. I've got 'em on ice, for the moment, but unless you get one of your boys from your local office here pronto there won't be any snatch case—not if the city cops get here first. What?" Pete quieted down and explained who he was, where he was, and the more believable aspects of the events that had led up to the present situation. The government man cut in on him as he was urging speed and more speed and assured him that the local office was already being notified.

Pete got back to the wreck just as Lieutenant Dumbrosky climbed out of a squad car. Pete hurried up. "Don't do it, Dumbrosky," he yelled.

The big cop hesitated. "Don't do what?"

"Don't do anything. The FBI are on their way now—and you're already implicated. Don't make it any worse."

Pete pointed to the two hoodlums; Clarence was sitting on one and resting the spike of the ax against the back of the other. "These birds have already sung. This town is about to fall apart. If you hurry, you might be able to get a plane for Mexico."

Dumbrosky looked at him. "Wise guy," he said doubtfully.

"Ask them. They confessed."

One of the hoods raised his head. "We was threatened," he announced. "Take 'em in, lieutenant. They assaulted us."

"Go ahead," Pete said cheerfully. "Take us all in—together. Then you won't be able to lose that pair before the FBI can question them. Maybe you can cop a plea."

"Now?" asked Clarence.

Dumbrosky swung around. "Put that ax down!"

"Do as he says, Clarence. Get your camera ready to get a picture as the G-men arrive."

"You didn't send for no G-men."

"Look behind you!"

A dark blue sedan slid quietly to a stop and four lean, brisk men got out. The first of them said, "Is there someone here named Peter Perkins?"

"Me," said Pete. "Do you mind if I kiss you?"

It was after dark but the parking lot was crowded and noisy. A stand for the new Mayor and distinguished visitors had been erected on one side, opposite it was a bandstand; across the front was a large illuminated sign: HOME OF KITTEN—HONORARY CITIZEN OF OUR FAIR CITY.

In the fenced-off circle in the middle Kitten herself bounced and spun and swayed and danced. Pete stood on one side of the circle with Pappy opposite him; at four-foot intervals around it children were posted. "All set?" called out Pete.

"All set," answered Pappy. Together, Pete, Pappy and the kids started throwing serpentine into the ring. Kitten swooped, gathered the ribbons up and wrapped them around herself.

"Confetti!" yelled Pete. Each of the kids dumped a sackful toward the whirlwind—little of it reached the ground.

"Balloons!" yelled Pete. "Lights!" Each of the children started blowing up toy balloons; each had a dozen different colors. As fast as they were inflated they fed them to Kitten. Floodlights and searchlights came on; Kitten was transformed into a fountain of boiling, bubbling color, several stories high.

"Now?" said Clarence.

"Now!"

# The Man Who Traveled in Elephants

Rain *streamed across the bus's* window. John Watts peered out at wooded hills, content despite the weather. As long as he was rolling, moving, traveling, the ache of loneliness was somewhat quenched. He could close his eyes and imagine that Martha was seated beside him.

They had always traveled together; they had honeymooned covering his sales territory. In time they had covered the entire country—Route 66, with the Indians' booths by the highway, Route 1, up through the District, the Pennsylvania Turnpike, zipping in and out through the mountain tunnels, himself hunched over the wheel and Martha beside him, handling the maps and figuring the mileage to their next stop.

He recalled one of Martha's friends saying, "But, dear, don't you get tired of it?"

He could hear Martha's bubbly laugh. "With forty-eight wide and wonderful states to see, grow *tired?* Besides, there is always something new—fairs and expositions and things."

"But when you've seen one fair you've seen them all."

"You think there is no difference between the Santa Barbara Fiesta and the Fort Worth Fat Stock Show? Anyhow," Martha had gone on, "Johnny and I are country cousins; we like to stare at the tall buildings and get freckles on the roofs of our mouths."

"Do be sensible, Martha." The woman had turned to him. "John, isn't it time that you two were settling down and making something out of your lives?"

Such people tired him. "It's for the 'possums," he had told her solemnly. "They like to travel."

"The opossums? What in the world is he talking about, Martha?"

Martha had shot him a private glance, then dead-panned, "Oh, I'm sorry! You see, Johnny raises baby 'possums in his umbilicus."

"I'm equipped for it," he had confirmed, patting his round stomach.

That had settled her hash! He had never been able to stand people who gave advice "for your own good."

Martha had read somewhere that a litter of new-born opossums would no more than fill a teaspoon and that as many as six in a litter were often orphans through lack of facilities in mother 'possums pouch to take care of them all. They had immediately formed the Society for the Rescue and Sustenance of the Other Six 'Possums, and Johnny himself had been unanimously selected—by Martha—as the site of Father Johnny's 'Possum Town.

They had had other imaginary pets, too. Martha and he had hoped for children; when none came, their family had filled out with invisible little animals; Mr. Jenkins, the little grey burro who advised them about motels. Chipmink the chattering chipmunk, who lived in the glove compartment, *Mus Followalongus* the traveling mouse, who never said anything but who would bite unexpectedly, especially around Martha's knees.

They were all gone now; they had gradually faded away for lack of Martha's gay, infectious spirit to keep them in health. Even Bindlestiff, who was not invisible, was no longer with him. Bindlestiff was a dog they had picked up beside the road, far out in the desert, given water and succor and received in return his large and uncritical heart. Bindlestiff had traveled with them thereafter, until he, too, had been called away, shortly after Martha.

John Watts wondered about Bindlestiff. Did he roam free in the Dog Star, in a land lush with rabbits and uncovered garbage pails? More likely he was with Martha, sitting on her feet and getting in the way. Johnny hoped so.

He sighed and turned his attention to the passengers. A thin, very elderly woman leaned across the aisle and said, "Going to the Fair, young man?"

He started. It was twenty years since anyone had called him "young man." "Unh? Yes, certainly." They were *all* going to the Fair: the bus was special.

"You like going to fairs?"

"Very much." He knew that her inane remarks were formal gambits to start a conversation. He did not resent it; lonely old women have need of talk with strangers—and so did he. Besides, he liked perky old women. They seemed the very spirit of America to him, putting him in mind of church sociables and farm kitchens—and covered wagons.

"I like fairs, too," she went on. "I even used to exhibit—quince jelly and my Crossing-the-Jordan pattern."

"Blue ribbons, I'll bet."

"Some," she admitted, "but mostly I just liked to go to them. I'm Mrs. Alma Hill Evans. Mr. Evans was a great one for doings. Take the exposition when they opened the Panama Canal—but you wouldn't remember that."

John Watts admitted that he had not been there.

"It wasn't the best of the lot, anyway. The Fair of '93, there was a fair for you: There'll never be one that'll even be a patch on that one."

"Until this one, perhaps?"

"This one? Pish and tush! Size isn't everything." The All-American Exposition would certainly be the biggest thing yet—and the best. If only Martha were along, it would seem like heaven. The old lady changed the subject. "You're a traveling man, aren't you?"

He hesitated, then answered, "Yes."

"I can always tell. What line are you in, young man?"

He hesitated longer, then said flatly, "I travel in elephants."

She looked at him sharply and he wanted to explain, but loyalty to Martha kept his mouth shut. Martha had insisted that they treat their calling seriously, never explaining, never apologizing. They had taken it up when he had planned to retire; they had been talking of getting an acre of ground and doing something useful with radishes, or rabbits, or such. Then, during their final trip over his sales route, Martha had announced after a long silence, "John, you don't want to stop traveling."

"Eh? Don't I? You mean we should keep the territory?"

"No, that's done. But we won't settle down, either."

"What do you want to do? Just gypsy around?"

"Not exactly. I think we need some new line to travel in."

"Hardware? Shoes? Ladies' ready-to-wear?"

"No." She had stopped to think. "We ought to travel in *something*. It gives point to your movements. I think it ought to be something that doesn't turn over too fast, so that we could have a really large territory, say the whole United States."

"Battleships perhaps?"

"Battleships are out of date, but that's close." Then they had passed a barn with a tattered circus poster. "I've got it!" she had shouted. "Elephants! We'll travel in elephants."

"Elephants, eh? Rather hard to carry samples."

"We don't need to. Everybody knows what an elephant looks like. Isn't that right, Mr. Jenkins?" The invisible burro had agreed with Martha, as he always did; the matter was settled.

Martha had known just how to go about it. "First we make a survey. We'll have to comb the United States from corner to corner before we'll be ready to take orders."

For ten years they had conducted the survey. It was an excuse to visit every fair, zoo, exposition, stock show, circus, or punkin doings anywhere, for were they not all prospective customers? Even national parks and other natural wonders were included in the survey, for how was one to tell where a pressing need for an elephant might turn up? Martha had treated the matter with a straight face and had kept a dogeared notebook: "La Brea Tar Pits, Los Angeles—surplus of elephants, obsolete type, in these parts about 25,000 years ago." "Philadelphia—sell at least six to the Union League." "Brookfield Zoo, Chicago—African elephants, rare." "Gallup, New Mexico—stone elephants east of town, very beautiful." "Riverside, California, Elephant Barbershop—brace owner to buy mascot." "Portland, Oregon—query Douglas Fir Association. Recite *Road to Mandalay.* Same for Southern Pine group. N.B. this calls for trip to Gulf Coast as soon as we finish with rodeo in Laramie."

Ten years and they had enjoyed every mile of it. The survey was still unfinished when Martha had been taken. John wondered if she had buttonholed Saint Peter about the elephant situation in the Holy City. He'd bet a nickel she had.

But he could not admit to a stranger that traveling in elephants was just his wife's excuse for traveling around the country they loved.

The old woman did not press the matter. "I knew a man once who sold mongooses," she said cheerfully. "Or is it 'mongeese'? He had been in the exterminator business and—what does that driver think he is doing?"

The big bus had been rolling along easily despite the driving rain. Now it was swerving, skidding. It lurched sickeningly—and crashed.

John Watts banged his head against the seat in front. He was picking himself up, dazed, not too sure where he was, when Mrs. Evans' thin, confident soprano oriented him. "Nothing to get excited about, folks. I've been expecting this—and you can see it didn't hurt a bit."

John Watts admitted that he himself was unhurt. He peered nearsightedly around, then fumbled on the sloping floor for his glasses. He found them, broken. He shrugged and put them aside; once they arrived he could dig a spare pair out of his bags.

"Now let's see what has happened." Mrs. Evans went on. "Come along, young man." He followed obediently.

The right wheel of the bus leaned drunkenly against the curb of the approach to a bridge. The driver was standing in the rain, dabbing at a cut on his cheek. "I couldn't help it," he was saying. "A dog ran across the road and I tried to avoid it."

"You might have killed us!" a woman complained.

"Don't cry till you're hurt," advised Mrs. Evans. "Now let's get back into the bus while the driver phones for someone to pick us up."

John Watts hung back to peer over the side of the canyon spanned by the bridge. The ground dropped away steeply; almost under him were large, mean-looking rocks. He shivered and got back into the bus.

The relief car came along very promptly, or else he must have dozed. The latter, he decided, for the rain had stopped and the sun was breaking through the clouds. The relief driver thrust his head in the door and shouted, "Come on folks! Time's a-wastin'! Climb out and climb in." Hurrying, John stumbled as he got aboard. The new driver gave him a hand.

" 'Smatter, Pop? Get shaken up?"

"I'm all right, thanks."

"Sure you are. Never better."

He found a seat by Mrs. Evans, who smiled and said, "Isn't it a heavenly day?"

He agreed. It *was* a beautiful day, now that the storm had broken. Great fleecy clouds tumbling up into warm blue sky, a smell of clean wet pavement, drenched fields and green things growing—he lay back and savored it. While he was soaking it up a great double rainbow formed and blazed in the eastern sky. He looked at them and made two wishes, one for himself and one for Martha. The rainbows' colors seemed to be reflected in everything he saw. Even the other passengers seemed younger, happier, better dressed, now that the sun was out. He felt light-hearted, almost free from his aching loneliness.

They were there in jig time; the new driver more than made up the lost minutes. A great arch stretched across the road: THE ALL-AMERICAN CELEBRATION AND EXPOSITION OF ARTS and under it PEACE AND GOOD WILL TO ALL. They drove through and sighed to a stop.

Mrs. Evans hopped up. "Got a date—must run!" She trotted to the door, then called back, "See you on the midway, young man," and disappeared in the crowd.

John Watts got out last and turned to speak to the driver. "Oh, uh, about my baggage. I want to—"

The driver had started his engine again. "Don't worry about your baggage," he called out. "You'll be taken care of." The huge bus moved away.

"But—" John Watts stopped; the bus was gone. All very well—but what was he to do without his glasses?

But there were sounds of carnival behind him, that decided him. After all, he thought, tomorrow will do. If anything is too far away for me to see, I can always walk closer. He joined the queue at the gate and went in.

It was undeniably the greatest show ever assembled for the wonderment of mankind. It was twice as big as all outdoors, brighter than bright lights, newer than new, stupendous, magnificent, breathtaking, awe inspiring, supercolossal, incredible—and a lot of fun. Every community in America had sent its own best to this amazing show. The marvels of P.T. Barnum, of Ripley, and of all Tom Edison's godsons had been gathered in one spot. From up and down a broad continent the riches of a richly endowed land and the products of a clever and industrious people had been assembled, along with their folk festivals, their annual blow-outs, their celebrations, and their treasured carnival customs. The result was as American as strawberry shortcake and as gaudy as a Christmas tree, and it all lay there before him, noisy and full of life and crowded with happy, holiday people.

Johnny Watts took a deep breath and plunged into it.

He started with the Fort Worth Southwestern Exposition and Fat Stock Show and spent an hour admiring gentle, whitefaced steers, as wide and square as flat-topped desks, scrubbed and curried, with their hair parted neatly from skull to base of spine, then day-old little black lambs on rubbery stalks of legs, too new to know themselves, fat ewes, their broad backs paddled flatter and fatter by grave-eyed boys intent on blue ribbons. Next door he found the Pomona Fair with solid matronly Percherons and dainty Palominos from the Kellog Ranch.

And harness racing. Martha and he had always loved harness racing. He picked out a likely looking nag of the famous Dan Patch line, bet and won, then moved on, as there was so much more to see. Other county fairs were just beyond, apples from Yakima, the cherry festival from Beaumont and Banning, Georgia's peaches. Somewhere off beyond him a band was beating out, "Ioway, Ioway, that's where the tall corn grows!"

Directly in front of him was a pink cotton candy booth.

Martha had loved the stuff. Whether at Madison Square Garden or at Imperial County's fair grounds she had always headed first for the cotton candy booth. "The big size, honey?" he muttered to himself. He felt that if he were to look around he would see her nodding. "The large size, please," he said to the vendor.

The carnie was elderly, dressed in a frock coat and stiff shirt. He handled the pink gossamer with dignified grace. "Certainly, sir, there is no other size." He twirled the paper cornucopia and presented it. Johnny handed him a half dollar. The man flexed and opened his fingers; the coin disappeared. That appeared to end the matter.

"The candy is fifty cents?" Johnny asked diffidently.

"Not at all, sir." The old showman plucked the coin from Johnny's lapel and handed it back. "On the house—I see you are with it. After all, what is money?"

"Why, thank you, but, uh, I'm not really 'with it,' you know."

The old man shrugged. "If you wish to go incognito, who am I to dispute you? But your money is no good here."

"Uh, if you say so."

"You will see."

He felt something brush against his leg. It was a dog of the same breed, or lack of breed, as Bindlestiff had been. It looked amazingly like Bindlestiff. The dog looked up and waggled its whole body.

"Why, hello, old fellow!" He patted it—then his eyes blurred; it even felt like Bindlestiff. "Are you lost, boy? Well, so am I. Maybe we had better stick together, eh? Are you hungry?"

The dog licked his hand. He turned to the cotton candy man. "Where can I buy hot dogs?"

"Just across the way, sir."

He thanked him, whistled to the dog, and hurried across. "A half dozen hot dogs, please."

"Coming up! Just mustard, or everything on?"

"Oh, I'm sorry. I want them raw, they are for a dog."

"I getcha. Just a sec."

Presently he was handed six wienies, wrapped in paper. "How much are they?"

"Compliments of the house."

"I beg pardon?"

"Every dog has his day. This is his."

"Oh. Well, thank you." He became aware of increased noise and excitement behind him and looked around to see the first of the floats of the Priests of Pallas, from Kansas City, coming down the street. His friend the dog saw it, too, and began to bark.

"Quiet, old fellow." He started to unwrap the meat. Someone whistled across the way; the dog darted between the floats and was gone. Johnny tried to follow, but was told to wait until the parade had passed. Between floats he caught glimpses of the dog, leaping up on a lady across the way. What with the dazzling lights of the floats and his own lack of glasses he could not see her clearly, but it was plain that the dog knew her; he was greeting her with the all-out enthusiasm only a dog can achieve.

He held up the package and tried to shout to her; she waved back, but the band music and the noise of the crowd made it impossible to hear each other. He decided to enjoy the parade, then cross and find the pooch and its mistress as soon as the last float had passed.

It seemed to him the finest Priests of Pallas parade he had ever seen. Come to think about it, there hadn't been a Priests of Pallas parade in a good many years. Must have revived it just for this.

That was like Kansas City—a grand town. He didn't know of any he liked as well. Possibly Seattle. And New Orleans, of course.

And Duluth—Duluth was swell. And so was Memphis. He would like to own a bus someday that ran from Memphis to Saint Joe, from Natchez to Mobile, wherever the wide winds blow.

Mobile—there was a town.

The parade was past now, with a swarm of small boys tagging after it. He hurried across.

The lady was not there, neither she, nor the dog. He looked quite thoroughly. No dog. No lady with a dog.

He wandered off, his eyes alert for marvels, but his thoughts on the dog. It really had been a great deal like Bindlestiff . . . and he wanted to know the lady it belonged to—anyone who could love that sort of a dog must be a pretty good sort herself. Perhaps he could buy her ice cream, or persuade her to go to the midway with him. Martha would approve he was sure. Martha would know he wasn't up to anything.

Anyhow, no one ever took a little fat man seriously.

But there was too much going on to worry about it. He found himself at St. Paul's Winter Carnival, marvelously constructed in summer weather through the combined efforts of York and American. For fifty years it had been held in January, yet there it was, rubbing shoulders with the Pendleton Round-Up, the Fresno Raisin Festival, and Colonial Week in Annapolis. He got in at the tail end of the ice show, but in time for one of his favorite acts, the Old Smoothies, out of retirement for the occasion and gliding as perfectly as ever to the strains of *Shine On, Harvest Moon.*

His eyes blurred again and it was not his lack of glasses.

Coming out he passed a large sign: SADIE HAWKINS DAY—STARTING POINT FOR BACHELORS. He was tempted to take part; perhaps the lady with the dog might be among the spinsters. But he was a little tired by now; just ahead there was an outdoor carnival of the pony-ride-and-ferris-wheel sort; a moment later he was on the marry-go-round and was climbing gratefully into one of those swan gondolas so favored by parents. He found a young man already seated there, reading a book.

"Oh, excuse me," said Johnny. "Do you mind?"

"Not at all," the young man answered and put his book down. "Perhaps you are the man I'm looking for."

"You are looking for someone?"

"Yes. You see, I'm a detective. I've always wanted to be one and now I am."

"Indeed?"

"Quite. Everyone rides the merry-go-round eventually, so it saves trouble to wait here. Of course, I hang around Hollywood and Vine, or Times Square, or Canal Street, but here I can sit and read."

"How can you read while watching for someone?"

"Ah, I know what is in the book—" He held it up; it was *The Hunting of the Snark*. "—so that leaves my eyes free for watching."

Johnny began to like this young man. "Are there boojums about?"

"No, for we haven't softly and silently vanished away. But would we notice it if we did? I must think it over. Are you a detective, too?"

"No, I—uh—I travel in elephants."

"A fine profession. But not much for you here. We have giraffes—" He raised his voice above the music of the calliope and let his eyes rove around the carrousel. "—camels, two zebras, plenty of horses, but no elephants. Be sure to see the Big Parade; there will be elephants."

"Oh, I wouldn't miss it!"

"You mustn't. It will be the most amazing parade in all time, so long that it will never pass a given point and every mile choked with wonders more stupendous than the last. You're sure you're not the man I'm looking for?"

"I don't think so. But see here—how would you go about finding a lady with a dog in this crowd?"

"Well, if she comes here, I'll let you know. Better go down on Canal Street. Yes, I think if I were a lady with a dog I'd be down on Canal Street. Women love to mask; it means they can unmask."

Johnny stood up. "How do I get to Canal Street?"

"Straight through Central City past the opera house, then turn right at the Rose Bowl. Be careful then, for you pass through the Nebraska section with Ak-Sar-Ben in full sway. Anything could happen. After than, Calaveras County—Mind the frogs!—then Canal Street.

"Thank you so much." He followed the directions, keeping an eye out for a lady with a dog. Nevertheless he stared with wonder at the things he saw as he threaded through the gay crowds. He did see a dog, but it was a seeing-eye dog—and that was a great wonder, too, for the live clear eyes of the dog's master could and did see everything that was going on around him, yet the man and the dog traveled together with the man letting the dog direct their way, as if no other way of travel were conceivable, or desired, by either one.

He found himself in Canal Street presently and the illusion was so complete that it was hard to believe that he had not been transported to New Orleans. Carnival was at height; it was Fat Tuesday here; the crowds were masked. He got a mask from a street vendor and went on.

The hunt seemed hopeless. The street was choked by merrymakers watching the parade of the Krewe of Venus. It was hard to breathe, much harder to move and search. He eased into Bourbon Street—the entire French Quarter had been reproduced—when he saw the dog.

He was sure it was the dog. It was wearing a clown suit and a little peaked hat, but it looked like his dog. He corrected himself; it looked like Bindlestiff.

And it accepted one of the frankfurters gratefully. "Where is she, old fellow?" The dog woofed once, then darted away into the crowd. He tried to follow, but could not; he required more clearance. But he was not downhearted; he had found the dog once, he would find him again. Besides, it had been at a masked ball that he had first met Martha, she a graceful Pierrette, he a fat Pierrot. They had watched the dawn come up after the ball and before the sun had set again they had agreed to marry.

He watch the crowd for Pierrettes, sure somehow that the dog's mistress would costume so.

Everything about this fair made him think even more about Martha, if that were possible. How she had traveled his territory with him, how it had been their habit to start out, anywhere, whenever a vacation came along. Chuck the Duncan Hines guide and some bags in the car and be off. Martha . . . sitting beside him with the open highway a broad ribbon before them . . . singing their road song *America the Beautiful* and keeping him on key: "—thine alabaster cities gleam, undimmed by human tears—"

Once she had said to him, while they were bowling along through—where was it? The Black Hills? The Ozarks? The Poconos? No matter. She had said, 'Johnny, you'll never be President and I'll never be First Lady, but I'll bet we know more about the United States than any President ever has. Those busy, useful people never have time to *see* it, not really."

"It's a wonderful country, darling."

"It is, it is indeed. I could spend all eternity just traveling around in it—traveling in elephants, Johnny, with you."

He had reached over and patted her knee; he remembered how it felt.

The revellers in the mock French Quarter were thinning out; they had drifted away while he daydreamed. He stopped a red devil. "Where is everyone going?"

"To the parade, of course."

"The Big Parade?"

"Yes, it's forming now." The red devil moved on, he followed.

His own sleeve was plucked. "Did you find her?" It was Mrs. Evans, slightly disguised by a black domino and clinging to the arm of a tall elderly Uncle Sam.

"Eh? Why, hello, Mrs. Evans! What do you mean?"

"Don't be silly. Did you find her?"

"How did you know I was looking for anyone?"

"Of course you were. Well, keep looking. We must go now." They trailed after the mob.

The Big Parade was already passing by the time he reached its route. It did not matter, there was endlessly more to come. The Holly, Colorado, Boosters were passing; they were followed by the prize Shriner drill team. Then came the Veiled Prophet of Khorassan and his Queen of Love and Beauty, up from their cave in the bottom of the Mississippi . . . the Anniversary Day Parade from Brooklyn, with the school children carrying little American flags . . . the Rose Parade from Pasadena, miles of flower-covered floats . . . the Indian Powwow from Flagstaff, twenty-two nations represented and no buck in the march wearing less than a thousand dollars worth of hand-wrought jewelry. After the indigenous Americans rode Buffalo Bill, goatee jutting out and hat in hand, locks flowing in the breeze. Then was the delegation from Hawaii with King Kamehameha himself playing Alii, Lord of Carnival, with royal abandon, while his subjects in dew-fresh leis pranced behind him, giving aloha to all.

There was no end. Square dancers from Ojai and from upstate New York, dames and gentlemen from Annapolis, the Cuero, Texas, Turkey Trot, all the Krewes and marching clubs of old New Orleans, double flambeaux blazing, nobles throwing favors to the crowd—the King of Zulus and his smooth brown court, singing; "Everybody who was anybody doubted it—"

And the Mummers came, "taking a suit up the street" to *Oh Dem Golden Slippers*. Here was something older than the country celebrating it, the shuffling jig of the masquers, a step that was young when mankind was young and first celebrating the birth of spring. First the fancy clubs, whose captains wore capes worth a king's ransom—or a mortgage on a row house—with fifty pages to bear them. Then the Liberty Clowns and the other comics and lastly the ghostly, sweet string bands whose strains bring tears.

Johnny thought back to '44 when he had first seen them march, old men and young boys, because the proper "shooters" were away to war. And of something that should not be on Broad Street in Philadelphia on the first day of January, men riding in the parade because, merciful Heaven forgive us, they could not walk.

He looked and saw that there were indeed automobiles in the line of march—wounded of the last war, and one G.A.R., hat square, hands folded over the head of his cane. Johnny held his breath and waited. When each automobile approached the judges' stand, it stopped short of it, and everyone got out. Somehow, with each other's help, they hobbled or crawled past the judging line, under their own power—and each club's pride was kept intact.

There followed another wonder—they did not get back into the automobiles, but marched on up Broad Street.

Then it was Hollywood Boulevard, disguised as Santa Claus Lane, in a production more stupendous than movieland had ever attempted before. There were baby stars galore and presents and favors and candy for all the children and all the grown up children, too. When, at last, Santa Claus's own float arrived, it was almost too large to be seen, a veritable iceberg, almost the North Pole itself, with John Barrymore and Mickey Mouse riding one on each side of Saint Nicholas.

On the tail end of the great, icy float was a pathetic little figure. Johnny squinted and recognized Mr. Emmett Kelly, dean of all clowns, in his role as Weary Willie. Willie was not merry—oh, no, he was shivering. Johnny did not know whether to laugh or to cry. Mr. Kelly had always affected him that way.

And the elephants came.

Big elephants, little elephants, middle-sized elephants, from pint-sized Wrinkles to might Jumbo . . . and with them the bull men, Chester Conklin, P. T. Barnum, Wallie Beery, Mowgli. "This," Johnny said to himself, "must be Mulberry Street."

There was commotion on the other side of the column; one of the men was shooing something away. Then Johnny saw what it was—the dog. He whistled; the animal seemed confused, then it spotted him, scampered up, and jumped into Johnny's arms. "You stay with me," Johnny told him. "You might have gotten stepped on."

The dog licked his face. He had lost his clown suit, but the little peaked cap hung down under his neck. "What have you been up to?" asked Johnny. "And where is you mistress?"

The last of the elephants were approaching, three abreast, pulling a great carriage. A bugle sounded up front and the procession stopped. "Why are they stopping?" Johnny asked a neighbor.

"Wait a moment. You'll see."

The Grand Marshal of the march came trotting back down the line. He rode a black stallion and was himself brave in villain's boots, white pegged breeches, cutaway, and top hat. He glanced all around.

He stopped immediately in front of Johnny. Johnny held the dog more closely to him. The Grand Marshal dismounted and bowed. Johnny looked around to see who was behind him. The Marshal removed his tall silk hat and caught Johnny's eye. "You, sir, are the Man Who Travels in Elephants?" It was more a statement than a question.

"Uh? Yes."

"Greetings, Rex! Serene Majesty, your Queen and your court await you." The man turned slightly, as if to lead the way.

Johnny gulped and gathered Bindlestiff under one arm. The Marshal led him to the elephant-drawn carriage. The dog slipped out of his arms and bounded up into the carriage and into the lap of the lady. She patted it and looked proudly, happily, down at Johnny Watts. "Hello, Johnny! Welcome home, darling!"

"Martha!" he sobbed—and Rex stumbled and climbed into his carriage to embrace his queen.

The sweet voice of a bugle sounded up ahead, the parade started up again, wending its endless way—

# "—All You Zombies—"

*2217 Time Zone V (EST) 7 Nov 1970 NYC—"Pop's Place":* I was polishing a brandy snifter when the Unmarried Mother came in. I noted the time—10.17 P.M. zone five or eastern time November 7th, 1970. Temporal agents always notice time & date; we must.

The Unmarried Mother was a man twenty-five years old, no taller than I am, immature features and a touchy temper. I didn't like his looks—I never had—but he was a lad I was here to recruit, he was my boy. I gave him my best barkeep's smile.

Maybe I'm too critical. He wasn't swish; his nickname came from what he always said when some nosy type asked him his line: "I'm an unmarried mother." If he felt less than murderous he would add: "—at four cents a word. I write confession stories."

If he felt nasty, he would wait for somebody to make something of it. He had a lethal style of in-fighting, like a female cop—one reason I wanted him. Not the only one.

He had a load on and his face showed that he despised people more than usual. Silently I poured a double shot of Old Underwear and left the bottle. He drank, poured another.

I wiped the bar top. "How's the 'Unmarried Mother' racket?"

His fingers tightened on the glass and he seemed about to throw it at me; I felt for the sap under the bar. In temporal manipulation you try to figure everything, but there are so many factors that you never take needless risks.

I saw him relax that tiny amount they teach you to watch for in the Bureau's training school. "Sorry," I said. "Just asking, 'How's business?' Make it 'How's the weather?'"

He looked sour. "Business is okay. I write 'em, they print 'em, I eat."

I poured myself one, leaned toward him, "Matter of fact," I said, "you write a nice stick—I've sampled a few. You have an amazingly sure touch with the woman's angle."

It was a slip I had to risk; he never admitted what pennames he used. But he was boiled enough to pick up only the last. "'Woman's angle!'" he repeated with a snort. "Yeah, I know the woman's angle. I should."

"So?" I said doubtfully. "Sisters?"

"No. You wouldn't believe me if I told you."

"Now, now," I answered mildly, "bartenders and psychiatrists learn that nothing is stranger than the truth. Why, son, if you heard the stories I do—well, you'd make yourself rich. Incredible."

"You don't know what 'incredible' means!"

"So? Nothing astonishes me. I've always heard worse."

He snorted again. "Want to bet the rest of the bottle?"

"I'll bet a full bottle." I placed one on the bar.

"Well—" I signaled my other bartender to handle the trade. We were at the far end, a single-stool space that I kept private by loading the bar top by it with jars of pickled eggs and other clutter. A few were at the other end watching the fights and somebody was playing the juke box—private as a bed where we were. "Okay," he began, "to start with, I'm a bastard."

"No distinction around here," I said.

"I mean it," he snapped. "My parents weren't married."

"Still no distinction," I insisted. "Neither were mine."

"When—" He stopped, gave me the first warm look I ever saw on him. "You mean that?"

"I do. A one-hundred-percent bastard. In fact," I added, "No one in my family ever marries. All bastards."

"Don't try to top me—*you're* married." He pointed at my ring.

"Oh that." I showed it to him. "It just looks like a wedding ring; I wear it to keep women off." That ring is an antique I bought in 1985 from a fellow operative—he had fetched it from pre-Christian Crete. "The Worm Ouroboros . . . the World Snake that eats its own tail, forever without end. A symbol of the Great Paradox."

He barely glanced at it. "If you're really a bastard, you know how it feels. When I was a little girl—"

"Wups!" I said. "Did I hear you correctly?"

"Who's telling this story? When I was a little girl—Look, every hear of Christine Jorgenson? Or Roberta Cowell?"

"Uh, sex change cases. You're trying to tell me—"

"Don't interrupt or swelp me, I won't talk. I was a foundling, left at an orphanage in Cleveland in 1945 when I was a month old. When I was a little girl, I envied kids with parents. Then, when I learned about sex—and, believe me, Pop, you learn fast in an orphanage—"

"I know."

"—I made a solemn vow that any kid of mine would have both a pop and a mom. It kept me 'pure,' quite a feat in that vicinity—I had to learn to fight to manage it. Then I got older and realized I stood darned little chance of getting married—for the same reason I hadn't been adopted." He scowled. "I was horse-faced and buck-toothed, flat-chested and straight-haired."

"You don't look any worse than I do."

"Who cares how a barkeep looks? Or a writer? But people wanting to adopt pick little blue-eyed golden-haired morons. Later on, the boys want bulging breasts, a cute face, and an Oh-you-wonderful-male manner." He shrugged. "I couldn't compete. So I decided to join the W.E.N.C.H.E.S."

"Eh?"

"Women's Emergency National Corps, Hospitality & Entertainment Section, what they now call 'Space Angels'—Auxiliary Nursing Group, Extraterrestrial Legions."

I knew both terms, once I had them chronized. Although we now use still a third name; it's that elite military service corps; Women's Hospitality Order Refortifying & Encouraging Spacemen. Vocabulary shift is the worst hurdle in time-jumps—did you know that "service station" once meant a dispensary for petroleum fractions? Once on an assignment in the Churchill Era a woman said to me, "Meet me at the service station next door"—which is *not* what it sounds; a "service station" (then) wouldn't have a bed in it.

He went on: "It was when they first admitted you can't send men into space for months and years and not relieve the tension. You remember how the wowsers screamed?—that improved my chances, volunteers were scarce. A gal had to be respectable, preferably virgin (they liked to train them from scratch), above average mentally, and stable emotionally. But most volunteers were old hookers, or neurotics who would crack up ten days off Earth. So I didn't need looks; if they accepted me, they would fix my buck teeth, put a wave in my hair, teach me to walk and dance and how to listen to a man pleasingly, and everything else—plus training for the prime duties. They would even use plastic surgery if it would help—nothing too good for Our Boys.

"Best yet, they made sure you didn't get pregnant during your enlistment—and you were almost certain to marry at the end of your hitch. Same way today, A.N.G.E.L.S. marry spacers—they talk the language.

"When I was eighteen I was placed as a 'mother's helper.' This family simply wanted a cheap servant but I didn't mind as I couldn't enlist till I was twenty-one. I did housework and went to night school—pretending to continue my high school typing and shorthand but going to charm class instead, to better my chances for enlistment.

"Then I met this city slicker with his hundred dollar bills." He scowled. "The no-good actually did have a wad of hundred dollar bills. He showed me one night, told me to help myself.

"But I didn't. I liked him. He was the first man I ever met who was nice to me without trying to take my pants off. I quit night school to see him oftener. It was the happiest time of my life.

"Then one night in the park my pants did come off." He stopped. I said, "And then?"

"And then *nothing!* I never saw him again. He walked me home and told me he loved me—and kissed me good-night and never came back." He looked grim. "If I could find him, I'd kill him!"

"Well," I sympathized, "I know how you feel, but killing him—just for doing what comes naturally—hmm . . . Did you struggle?"

"Huh? What's that got to do with it?"

"Quite a bit. Maybe he deserves a couple of broken arms for running out on you, but—"

"He deserves worse than that! Wait till you hear. Somehow I kept anyone from suspecting and decided it was all for the best. I hadn't really loved him and probably would never love anybody—and I was more eager to join the W.E.N.C.H.E.S. than ever. I wasn't disqualified, they didn't insist on virgins. I cheered up.

"It wasn't until my skirts got tight that I realized."

"Pregnant?"

"The bastard had me higher 'n a kite! Those skinflints I lived with ignored it as long as I could work—then kicked me out and the orphanage wouldn't take me back. I landed in a charity ward surrounded by other big bellies and trotted bedpans until my time came.

"One night I found myself on an operating table, with a nurse saying, 'Relax. Now breathe deeply.'

"I woke up in bed, numb from the chest down. My surgeon came in. 'How do you feel?' he says cheerfully.

" 'Like a mummy.'

" 'Naturally. You're wrapped like one and full of dope to keep you numb. You'll get well—but a Caesarian isn't a hangnail.'

" ' "Caesarian?" ' I said. 'Doc—*did I lose the baby?*'

" 'Oh, no. Your baby's fine.'

" 'Oh. Boy or girl?'

" 'A healthy little girl. Five pounds, three ounces.'

"I relaxed. It's something, to have made a baby. I told myself I would go somewhere and tack 'Mrs.' on my name and let the kid think her papa was dead—no orphanage for *my* kid!

"But the surgeon was talking. 'Tell me, uh—' He avoided my name. '—did you ever think your glandular setup was odd?'

"I said, 'Huh? Of course not. What are you driving at?'

"He hesitated. 'I'll give you this in one dose, then a hypo to let you sleep off your jitters. You'll have 'em.'

" 'Why?' I demanded.

" 'Ever hear of that Scottish physician who was female until she was thirty-five?—then had surgery and became legally and medically a man? Got married. All okay.'

" 'What's that got to do with me?'

" 'That's what I'm saying. You're a man.'

"I tried to sit up. '*What?*'

" 'Take it easy. When I opened you, I found a mess. I sent for the Chief of Surgery while I got the baby out, then we held a consultation with you on the table—and worked for hours to salvage what we could. You had two full sets of organs, both immature, but with the female set well enough developed that you had a baby. They could never be any use to you again, so we took them out and rearranged things so that you can develop properly as a man.' He put a hand on me. 'Don't worry. You're young, your bones will readjust, we'll watch your glandular balance—and make a fine young man out of you.'

"I started to cry. 'What about my *baby?*'

" 'Well, you can't nurse her, you haven't milk enough for a kitten. If I were you, I wouldn't see her—put her up for adoption.'

" '*No!*'

"He shrugged. 'The choice is yours; you're her mother—well, her parent. But don't worry now; we'll get you well first.'

"Next day they let me see the kid and I saw her daily—trying to get used to her. I had never seen a brand-new baby and had no idea how awful they look—my daughter looked like an orange monkey. My feeling changed to cold determination to do right by her. But four weeks later that didn't mean anything."

"Eh?"

"She was snatched."

" 'Snatched?' "

The Unmarried Mother almost knocked over the bottle we had bet. "Kidnapped—stolen from the hospital nursery!" He breathed hard. "How's that for taking the last thing a man's got to live for?"

"A bad deal," I agreed. "Let's pour you another. No clues?"

"Nothing the police could trace. Somebody came to see her, claimed to be her uncle. While the nurse had her back turned, he walked out with her."

"Description?"

"Just a man, with a face-shaped face, like yours or mine." He frowned. "I think it was the baby's father. The nurse swore it was an older man but he probably used makeup. Who else would swipe my baby? Childless women pull such stunts—but whoever heard of a man doing it?"

"What happened to you then?"

"Eleven more months of that grim place and three operations. In four months I started to grow a beard; before I was out I was shaving regularly . . . and no longer doubted that I was male." He grinned wryly. "I was staring down nurses' necklines."

"Well," I said, "seems to me you came through okay. Here you are, a normal man, making good money, no real troubles. And the life of a female is not an easy one."

He glared at me. "A lot you know about it!"

"So?"

"Ever hear the expression 'a ruined woman'?"

"Mmm, years ago. Doesn't mean much today."

"I was as ruined as a woman can be; that bastard *really* ruined me—I was no longer a woman . . . and I didn't know *how* to be a man."

"Takes getting used to, I suppose."

"You have no idea. I don't mean learning how to dress, or not walking into the wrong rest room; I learned those in the hospital. But how could I *live?* What job could I get? Hell, I couldn't even drive a car. I didn't know a trade; I couldn't do manual labor—too much scar tissue, too tender.

"I hated him for having ruined me for the W.E.N.C.H.E.S., too, but I didn't know how much until I tried to join the Space Corps instead. One look at my belly and I was marked unfit for military service. The medical officer spent time on me just from curiosity; he had read about my case.

"So I changed my name and came to New York. I got by as a fry cook, then rented a typewriter and set myself up as a public stenographer—what a laugh! In four months I typed four letters and one manuscript. The manuscript was for *Real Life Tales* and a waste of paper, but the goof who wrote it, sold it. Which gave me an idea; I bought a stack of confession magazines and studied them." He looked cynical. "Now you know how I get the authentic woman's angle on an unmarried-mother story . . . through the only version I haven't sold—the true one. Do I win the bottle?"

I pushed it toward him. I was upset myself, but there was work to do. I said, "Son, you still want to lay hands on that so-and-so?"

His eyes lighted up—a feral gleam.

"Hold it!" I said. "You wouldn't kill him?"

He chuckled nastily. "Try me."

"Take it easy. I know more about it than you think I do. I can help you. I know where he is."

He reached across the bar. "*Where is he?*"

I said softly, "Let go my shirt, sonny—or you'll land in the alley and we'll tell the cops you fainted." I showed him the sap.

He let go. "Sorry, but where is he?" He looked at me. "And how do you know so much?"

"All in good time. There are records—hospital records, orphanage records, medical records. The matron of your orphanage was Mrs. Fetherage—right? She was followed by Mrs. Gruenstein—right? Your name, as a girl, was 'Jane'—right? And you didn't tell me any of this—right?"

I had him baffled and a bit scared. "What's this? You trying to make trouble for me?"

"No indeed. I've your welfare at heart. I can put this character in your lap. You do to him as you see fit—and I guarantee that you'll get away with it. But I don't think you'll kill him. You'd be nuts to—and you aren't nuts. Not quite."

He brushed it aside. "Cut the noise. *Where is he?*"

I poured him a short one; he was drunk but anger was offsetting it. "Not so fast, I do something for you—you do something for me."

"Uh . . . what?"

"You don't like your work. What would you say to high pay, steady work, unlimited expense account, your own boss on the job, and lots of variety and adventure?"

He stared. "I'd say, 'Get those goddam reindeer off my roof!' Shove it, Pop—there's no such job."

"Okay, put it this way: I hand him to you, you settle with him, then try my job. If it's not all I claim—well, I can't hold you."

He was wavering; the last drink did it. "When d'yuh d'liver 'im?" he said thickly.

"If it's a deal—*right now!*"

He shoved out his hand. "It's a deal!"

I nodded to my assistant to watch both ends, noted the time—2300—started to duck through the gate under the bar—when the juke box blared out: *"I'm My Own Granpaw!"* The service man had orders to load it with old Americana and classics because I couldn't stomach the "music" of 1970, but I hadn't known that tape was in it. I called out, "Shut that off! Give the customer his money back." I added, "Storeroom, back in a moment," and headed there with my Unmarried Mother following.

It was down the passage across from the johns, a steel door to which no one but my day manager and myself had a key; inside was a door to an inner room to which only I had a key. We went there.

He looked blearily around at windowless walls. "Where is 'e?"

"Right away." I opened a case, the only thing in the room; it was a U.S.F.F. Co-ordinates Transformer Field Kit, series 1992, Mod. II—a beauty, no moving parts, weight twenty-three kilos fully charged, and shaped to pass as a suitcase. I had adjusted it precisely earlier that day; all I had to do was to shake out the metal net which limits the transformation field.

Which I did. "Wha's that?" he demanded.

"Time machine," I said and tossed the net over us.

"Hey!" he yelled and stepped back. There is a technique to this; the net has to be thrown so that the subject will instinctively step back *onto* the metal mesh, then you close the net with both of you inside completely—else you might leave shoe soles behind or a piece of foot, or scoop up a slice of floor. But that's all the skill it takes. Some agents con a subject into the net; I tell the truth and use that instant of utter astonishment to flip the switch. Which I did.

***1030-V-3 April 1963-Cleveland, Ohio-Apex Bldg.:*** "Hey!" he repeated "Take this damn thing off!"

"Sorry," I apologized and did so, stuffed the net into the case, closed it. "You said you wanted to find him."

"But—You said that was a time machine!"

I pointed out a window. "Does that look like November? Or New York?" While he was gawking at new buds and spring weather, I reopened the case, took out a packet of hundred dollar bills, checked that the numbers and signatures were compatible with 1963. The Temporal Bureau doesn't care how much you spend (it costs nothing) but they don't like unnecessary anachronisms. Too many mistakes and a general court martial will exile you for a year in a nasty period, say 1974 with its strict rationing and forced labor. I never make such mistakes, the money was okay. He turned around and said, "What happened?"

"He's here. Go outside and take him. Here's expense money." I shoved it at him and added, "Settle him, then I'll pick you up."

Hundred dollar bills have a hypnotic effect on a person not used to them. He was thumbing them unbelievingly as I eased him into the hall, locked him out. The next jump was easy, a small shift in era.

*1700-V-10 March 1964-Cleveland-Apex Bldg.:* There was a notice under the door saying that my lease expired next week; otherwise the room looked as it had a moment before. Outside, trees were bare and snow threatened; I hurried, stopping only for contemporary money and a coat, hat and topcoat I had left there when I leased the room. I hired a car, went to the hospital. It took twenty minutes to bore the nursery attendant to the point where I could swipe the baby without being noticed; we went back to the Apex Building. This dial setting was more involved as the building did not yet exist in 1945. But I had precalculated it.

*0100-V-20 Sept 1945-Cleveland-Skyview Motel:* Field kit, baby, and I arrived in a motel outside town. Earlier I had registered as "Gregory Johnson, Warren, Ohio," so we arrived in a room with curtains closed, windows locked, and doors bolted, and the floor cleared to allow for waver as the machine hunts. You can get a nasty bruise from a chair where it shouldn't be—not the chair of course, but backlash from the field.

No trouble. Jane was sleeping soundly; I carried her out, put her in a grocery box on the seat of a car I had provided earlier, drove to the orphanage, put her on the steps, drove two blocks to a "service station" (the petroleum products sort) and phoned the orphanage, drove back in time to see them taking the box inside, kept going and abandoned the car near the motel—walked to it and jumped forward to the Apex Building in 1963.

*2200-V24 April 1963-Cleveland-Apex Bldg.:* I had cut the time rather fine—temporal accuracy depends on span, except on return to zero. If I had it right, Jane was discovering, out in the park this balmy spring night, that she wasn't quite as "nice" a girl as she had thought. I grabbed a taxi to the home of those skinflints, had the hackie wait around a corner while I lurked in shadows.

Presently I spotted them down the street, arms around each other. He took her up on the porch and made a long job of kissing her good-night—longer than I had thought. Then she went in and he came down the walk, turned away. I slid into step and hooked an arm in his. "That's all, son," I announced quietly. "I'm back to pick you up."

"*You!*" He gasped and caught his breath.

"Me. Now you know who *he* is—and after you think it over you'll know who *you* are . . . and if you think hard enough, you'll figure out who the baby is . . . and who *I* am."

He didn't answer, he was badly shaken. It's a shock to have it proved to you that you can't resist seducing yourself. I took him to the Apex Building and we jumped again.

***2300-VII-12 Aug 1985-Sub Rockies Base:*** I woke the duty sergeant, showed my I.D., told the sergeant to bed him down with a happy pill and recruit him in the morning. The sergeant looked sour but rank is rank, regardless of era; he did what I said—thinking, no doubt, that the next time we met he might be the colonel and I the sergeant. Which can happen in our corps. "What name?" he asked.

I wrote it out. He raised his eyebrows. "Like so, eh? Hmm—"

"You just do your job, Sergeant." I turned to my companion. "Son, your troubles are over. You're about to start the best job a man ever held—and you'll do well. I *know.*"

"But—"

"'But' nothing. Get a night's sleep, then look over the proposition. You'll like it."

"That you will!" agreed the sergeant. "Look at me—born in 1917—still around, still young, still enjoying life." I went back to the jump room, set everything on preselected zero.

***2301-V-7 Nov 1970-NYC-"Pop's Place":*** I came out of the storeroom carrying a fifth of Drambuie to account for the minute I had been gone. My assistant was arguing with the customer who had been playing "*I'm My Own Granpaw!*" I said, "Oh, let him play it, then unplug it." I was very tired.

It's rough, but somebody must do it and it's very hard to recruit anyone in the later years, since the Mistake of 1972. Can you think of a better source than to pick people all fouled up where they are and give them well-paid, interesting (even though dangerous) work in a necessary cause? Everybody knows now why the Fizzle War of 1963 fizzled. The bomb with New York's number on it didn't go off, a hundred other things didn't go as planned—all arranged by the likes of me.

But not the Mistake of '72; that one is not our fault—and can't be undone; there's no paradox to resolve. A thing either is, or it isn't, now and forever amen. But there won't be another like it; an order dated "1992" takes precedence any year.

I closed five minutes early, leaving a letter in the cash register telling my day manager that I was accepting his offer, so see my lawyer as I was leaving on a long vacation. The Bureau might or might not pick up his payments, but they want things left tidy. I went to the room back of the storeroom and forward to 1993.

*2200-VII-12 Jan 1993-Sub Rockies Annex-HQ Temporal DOL:* I checked in with the duty officer and went to my quarters, intending to sleep for a week. I had fetched the bottle we bet (after all, I won it) and took a drink before I wrote my report. It tasted foul and I wondered why I had ever liked Old Underwear. But it was better than nothing; I don't like to be cold sober, I think too much. But I don't really hit the bottle either; other people have snakes—*I* have people.

I dictated my report: forty recruitments all okayed by the Psych Bureau—counting my own, which I knew would be okayed. I was here, wasn't I? Then I taped a request for assignment to operations; I was sick of recruiting. I dropped both in the slot and headed for bed.

My eye fell on "The By-Laws of Time," over my bed:

*Never Do Yesterday What Should Be Done Tomorrow.*
*If At Last You Do Succeed, Never Try Again.*
*A Stitch in Time Saves Nine Billion.*
*A Paradox May be Paradoctored.*
*It is Earlier When You Think.*
*Ancestors Are Just People.*
*Even Jove Nods.*

They didn't inspire me the way they had when I was a recruit; thirty subjective-years of time-jumping wears you down. I undressed and when I got down to the hide I looked at my belly. A Caesarian leaves a big scar but I'm so hairy now that I don't notice it unless I look for it.

Then I glanced at the ring on my finger.

The Snake That Eats Its Own Tail, Forever and Ever . . . I *know* where *I* came from—but *where did all you zombies come from?*

I felt a headache coming on, but a headache powder is one thing I do not take. I did once—and you all went away.

So I crawled into bed and whistled out the light.

*You* aren't really there at all. There isn't anybody but me—Jane—here alone in the dark.

I miss you dreadfully!